The Origins of Edith

By C.B. Giesinger

Independently Published. Printed in the United States of America.

Copyright © 2023

First Edition: January 2023

ISBN:(paperback) 9798370548536

Cover Art: Sarah MacDonald

To my grandparents, parents and children, who are responsible for making me who I am.

Acknowledgements

Gianna, you are the missing piece of my creative process. I am incredibly grateful for your ideas, your intuition, hard work and spirit. You pushed me to believe this could be something far more than I imagined. I can't wait to work on the next project with you.

Sarah, another successful collaboration for my cover art. I can't wait for our future projects to take off. In the meantime, we can enjoy your novels and beautiful artwork.

C.B. Giesinger

" You gave me a picture frame,

With a life to place inside

The frame remained empty

And still I'm glued to it, confined

The glass I'm held inside it seems

Is to keep me held to you

I yearned to be upon your wall

But you just shelfed that too

I developed into what you wanted

And I'm left with only blanks

I can't alter the darkness, haunted.

When the light is turned to black

So I'll put away the slides

That I always held of you

And open up my angles wide

To see the real view. "

Chapter 1: Edith 2010

Beep, beep, beep, beep. The sound was irritating. Obviously, a necessary piece of machinery, meant to sustain or prolong the health and life expectancy of its patients. The crisp, wretched wheezing passed through her mother with coarse vibrations leaving no chance for peaceful visits from family. The room gave off an odor, a stench familiar to the residency, which Sam associated with death. As though they had already put the formaldehyde in the patients prior to their eventual departure. This was hospice after all, there was no sugar coating it. In a matter of minutes that machine could let out a long dredged and hollowing sound. The kind of sound that one may expect and fear after a six year stint at a place like this.

Samantha, Sam to her sisters, sat quietly gazing at this strange illusion of her mother with so little life left in her. Edith had been so difficult throughout passages in her life, and yet she had overcome and surpassed the expectations of a woman who had been pushed past the breaking point. It was difficult to not feel a soft tenderness for the woman who brought her into this world.

Sam studied her mother quietly. Humans have origin stories dating back to rust-colored paintings on canvas of stone walls, stained with red berries, blood and soot crayons. Sam would know; she'd excavated artwork in more than one temple or mural; archaeology was her way of making sense of the world, of her own origins in it. But Edith had never been open to digging. Life for Edith had been strange. Hard like stone, sometimes smooth and polished and other times with chipped edges, a composition of different pieces thrown together into one hard-pressed child.

Sam struggled to think of any good memories, anything that might make her more fond of her mother. There was one that stood out, partially because it was so rare and partly because it left Sam with more questions than answers. Her mother had been a slouch in most departments but boy was she a fan of the traditional birthday breakfast. This was something her parents had often done for her before her father's unfortunate accident. Edith would tell Sam and her sisters the story every year. Much like other parents would read "T'was the Night Before Christmas," she would tell the four girls the story of the Traditional Birthday Breakfast.

The story would start off with the same backdrop, a glowing picture of Edith's childhood home. This house she spoke of neither resembled nor represented a life that referred to any other state than bliss. It was so unlike the life she led now with her four daughters that they could scarcely comprehend it. Gathered in a dingy, crowded apartment, the house Edith described to them seemed more likely from *The Waltons*.

Edith's mother and father were both present. The home was warm, clean and filled with fresh cut flowers to accompany the aromas from the kitchen oven. Iris was a gentle woman and affectionate to her family. You could always find her husband, Paul was his name, complimenting her dress or new haircut. He would, without a doubt, be dancing with her in the kitchen.

A portable FM/AM radio would be stuck up high on the shelf crooning a little Cole Porter while the sun poured through the window giving a spotlight to these simple moments between them. Edith would often watch them dance from behind the banister of the staircase, smiling and humming along to the music.

One spring evening her father went out to the grocery store to get some eggs. Iris had planned to make Edith her favorite birthday breakfast and wanted to make sure she had all the ingredients. Monaghan's would not be opened the next day until after morning mass was over. They opened their doors during "their" business hours without much regulation beyond that. So Paul went out Saturday night, and Iris and Edith thought nothing of it when he took a bit longer than normal grabbing only a couple items. Paul and Joe Monaghan had known each other since grade school and liked to catch up on the Red Sox when they saw each other once a week.

Iris became concerned after the patter of rain came down on the window awning to their cape cod style home. Within a matter of minutes the weather turned nasty. What started off as a light drizzle turned into a pouring rain. The winds began to gust, slapping the shutters against the windows.

An hour passed with no sign of Paul. Growing concerned, Iris decided to call around to see if he had perhaps stopped at one of his siblings' homes. Soon enough, she ran out of options, so she donned a rain coat and grabbed a large red umbrella and rushed out the door in the storm. Edith always remembered the red umbrella as a detail in her story. From a distance in the dark of the living room window, illuminated by the street lights and Iris's single flashlight, Edith watched as her mother walked down the road until she vanished into the darkness.

Edith remembered being more worried for her mother out in the rain than for herself, home alone. Pawtucket was full of safe old neighborhoods like theirs. People moved in, but rarely moved out. The yards were always manicured, fences painted. Pies were delivered to the doorsteps of new neighbors, dogs would bark with excitement when someone came to visit. The way Edith described it, she'd grown up in Pleasantville.

The store was scarcely a mile away and it would have taken a colossal accident in the road to block Paul's return to his family. Edith told her daughters that the cake that they were baking that night was for her birthday the following week.

Why the late night outing? Why not wait until morning? Couldn't Iris have made the cake another day? Sam would often lose herself in the story, conjecturing the possible ways that they could have avoided the accident, as if she somehow couldn't wrap her head around the situation.

Nearly an hour later Iris returned, soaked. She closed the door and turned to lean against it with dead weight hard on her forearms. Her hair dripped on the hardwood floors, hanging slightly over her face.

"What's wrong?" Edith spoke quietly. She was frightened after an hour at home alone with no answers of where either her mother or her father had gone. Iris's face contorted into a tight shape of both concern and anger. She turned and leaned back against the door, then flung her head back hard, letting out an agonizing cry. Her clothes were drenched. From the forest green blouse with scattered daisies down to the black pin skirt that continued to drip on the floor. The curls she had pinned up in a new barrette to celebrate Edith's birthday had all but come loose. The mascara and eyeliner dripped down her face, running together down the lines of her face, practically spelling out her grief.

"Mom, what's wrong?" Edith screamed this time. Her mother collapsed to the floor and wept with her knees wrapped tightly in her arms. She couldn't tell Edith what happened, but she wouldn't have to. Outside came a flash of color, then a second flash. Two cars pulled up in front of the house. A couple of officers exited their cars and proceeded to the front door. Edith backed up slowly. She looked at her mother's tears, then back at the two men approaching the door from the front window. There was no reason to question Iris: there were no words left to say.

Iris stood slowly using the door to balance herself. She walked to her bedroom, dragging her feet along the floor, ripping holes in her nude stockings and shut the door with a soft click.

Edith was told to never answer the door for strangers, but these were the men of the law, and so there had to be an expectation of trust in place.

"Hello, is your mom home, honey?" The first gentleman to speak was an older, stocky man with a flat gray mustache and a round, fat face. He was short, barely taller than she was and there was a kindness in his voice that eventually, she would learn, had some purpose to it.

"I, um, she..." The words fell from her lips. How could a child of her age know what to do in a situation like this? Most girls at fifteen were becoming women gradually, not being forced to grow up in one night. Her mother was incapacitated, and the worst cast scenarios running were through Edith's mind about her father. They passed through her eyes like a reel of film, playing out the scenes of carnage. The greatest fear that enveloped her at the present moment was the chance that she may never see him again. The when or how was never a thought that crossed her mind. Instead the words came out with a small sort of mumble, "I will go get her."

The water rolled off the tip of their hats and overcoats, coming down on the porch steps like rain on the Savannas.

Her father had enjoyed watching nature documentaries with her ritually on Saturday mornings. PBS was forever airing educational shows. Her father had dreams to visit these exotic locations one day. He was always ready for an adventure. The memory flashed through Edith's mind unexpectedly, and the word *was* crept into her mind like a soliloquy of stolen promises. She feared that he would never have the chance to see them.

Edith looked at the gentlemen one more time then slowly closed the front door. Opening the door was one thing, but to allow strangers to enter her home without a parent present would not be allowed.

She slowly walked down the perfectly polished floors. Although original to the house and nearly thirty years old, their condition was immaculate. The three of them had never worn shoes in the house and her father and mother would clean and polish them every week. The same floors were now streaked in water from the soaked stockings that clung to her mother's dragging feet.

Edith reached the door to her parent's bedroom and rapped softly with her small, balled up fist. A sound so meek it would be inaudible to almost anyone, anyone but her mother. The sound caused a knee jerk reaction, as though Iris had been alarmed. Edith could hear her mother shift on the mattress, which lay atop a creaky old box spring that her parents had talked frequently about replacing.

"Mom," she spoke in a whisper and then waited a moment for her to respond. "There are some men to see you." Edith breathed in hollow gasps, afraid of how her mother would react to the interruption and more afraid of how her mother could handle the situation presently at the front door.

Another moment passed and there was no answer.

"Mom, I don't know what they are here to say, but they want to speak to you." There was no way around the conversation. No matter what these men came to discuss, it had to be done; it was unavoidable. Iris crawled out of bed, not prepared, but knew she must be the one to address the matter. Edith heard her mother's footsteps as they approached the door and she stepped back to allow her to exit. Her face was solemn. The mascara had run down her swollen eyes and hardened red cheeks to her lips; black streaks that seemed to drip like candle wax. Iris pulled herself down the hall, supported by the wall. She had been a strong woman, but the ability to push herself away from the wall, in order to stand, was a formidable challenge.

Finally, after a few minutes, she walked away from the wall and walked without a stumble to the door where the policeman stood.

Edith heard the soft whoosh of air as her mother opened the door.

"Mrs. Anderson?" the same voice of the stout man that Edith had spoken to just minutes before came through the still-pouring rain. Her mother nodded.

"Ma'am, I have some news about your husband, Paul."

This was the part of the story that Edith didn't tell her girls, because Iris had never told her:

The rain was coming down fast and heavy, unexpected after such a clear starry night. Paul, smartly dressed even for a Saturday night at home, appeared from a shop. He was just turning a corner, and began to cross the street towards his car. Just at that moment, a gentleman in a white Oldsmobile dropped his cigarette onto the floor and reached to grab it. He didn't even know what was happening until *smash*, something large cracked his windshield and thumped over the roof and back down the trunk. The car screeched to a stop and he erratically assessed the situation, bracing himself against the steering wheel. Quickly he reached for the handle and pushed open his driver side door, trying to sidestep the continuous traffic running up and down the road. After a long deep breath, fearful of what has happened, he walks around the back of the car to find a man lying still, dressed for dinner, with white Gerber daisy petals strewn around him like a halo. Iris's favorite. The man looked around him, stunned, and rushed across the street, realizing there was now no traffic to avoid. The cars had stopped, people were rushing from their vehicles to see what had happened. He raced into Whitman's flower shop and told them to call for help. The aged owner rushed to the phone and within minutes the police arrived. The ambulance arrived minutes later and steadfastly began to take Paul's vitals. Cop cars parked around the accident: the body was covered. Paul was too tall for the small blanket, and his shoes were left hanging outside in the rain.

Twenty yards away a woman stood at the corner, rain pelting down, flattening her hair across her face. Her umbrella dangled at her side. Her eyes were fixated on her husband's favorite shoes, black patent leather, with signature red rubber soles. The pair he had received as a birthday present last year. The EMT saw her staring and began to walk over to her, but suddenly she turned and walked in the opposite direction.

This was the end of Sam's knowledge: of the paths her mother's life had taken between that tragedy in her childhood and now, Sam's earliest memories, she knew nothing. Edith never shared what happened next.

Iris took her leave, shutting the door with all her strength, her hand pressed against the solid wood surface. She wasn't sure if had even said thank you to the officers who delivered the information. To be honest, she wasn't sure if it were appropriate for the families to thank the police for delivering such life-altering news. Iris turned from the door and began to step towards Edith. At that moment Edith desired nothing but to feel her mother's embrace. To fall to the ground together and grieve for the loss of her father and the love of her mother's life.

Blindly, her mother brushed past her daughter's face, as wet as the rain that came down on the roof of their Cape Cod home. Within a minute the door was shut behind her once more and her body fell to the bed.

Edith would not see her mother again for three days.

Edith wasn't sure why the coffee cans came to her at that moment, with her mother behind the closed bedroom door and a wet trail across the floor. They were Folgers cans, stacked against the walls in the basement, present for as long as she could remember.

Her father had enjoyed tinkering in the basement and would invite his wife and daughter down to help him put different mechanical pieces together. He was the local handy man in the neighborhood. From lawnmowers, to carburetors, and even bicycles. Paul enjoyed the quietness of tinkering. Iris would sit there for hours watching the gears in his mind work to make these different pieces come back to life.

And he'd enjoyed a hot cup of Folgers on the back porch every morning, like his father and grandfather before him. Like them, he saved every empty can of coffee grounds and stacked them on shelves in the basement, still smelling faintly of coffee.

The can may now have been filled with screws, nuts, bolts and nails, but the faint smell of roasted coffee beans still seeped from the aluminum lining of the Folgers' coffee can.

Edith walked to the door at the top of the basement stairs and pressed her head softly against it. Standing at the top of the dank, musty stairs to the basement, the only smell that could be pin-pointed coming up from the shelves beneath the staircase were the small ground beans still stuck in the seams of the thirty year old cylinders. A piece of her grandfather, a piece of her father, a piece of her family she wasn't sure would ever put back together again.

After that night her mother was never the same. The funeral came and went, relatives that visited during the first few weeks eventually stopped making house calls. Friends who claimed they would be there as they were needed, fell away. Edith was left with a shell of a mother and the responsibility of the house. After two months of feeding her, bathing her and trying to get her out of her catatonic state, Edith decided she needed to get help.

Her neighbor Agatha called the hospital and asked for them to send an ambulance to pick her up. Agatha told Edith that she would stay with her for the time, until they could figure out other arrangements. Agatha was always a tender woman to Edith. Her tight gray curls were often still found in the same foam wrapped curling pins that she had been using since was a little girl. With her mass collection of dolls, Edith wondered if Agatha still missed her childhood, much like Edith did now.

Agatha's husband had died in the first World War and she had never remarried. Living with her elderly neighbor wasn't an ideal situation, but Edith knew that without her, she would have most likely ended up in a foster home.

The day that they turned off the old freezer on the back porch and emptied the fridge of all its food was heartbreaking to Edith. The last semblance of a normal life was fragmented. No more would her father sneak a gallon of ice cream into the back porch freezer as a treat for Edith. No more would he bring Iris white Gerber daisies with a quiet twinkle in his eye.

Gone were the days with just the three of them, happily together. Why her father and mother who had devoted their life and love to one another and had not chosen to have a bigger family never crossed her mind. She had all she wanted in the three of them together, playing board games every night, Dick Van Dyke, and dancing in the kitchen to the Beach Boys while a roast cooked in the oven.

Would she ever laugh and smile again as she used to?

Agatha was kind, but she knew from the beginning that keeping this young girl as her ward was only temporary. What if she were to fall, or even worse, pass away in the home with the girl here alone? She wasn't about to let a small child like Edith be left to take care of such matters. The death of her father and the inability of her mother to care for her forced a certain obligation, but it fell to a woman far too advanced in age to be caring for a child who needed family and a more permanent solution.

After a few very long and dredging weeks at Agatha's, waiting on word of her mother's return to their home, they received a visitor on the elderly woman's doorstep. Edith looked out the window. The visitor was hidden by the rather unkempt boxwood tree that grew beside the front door of Agatha's home. The streets were littered with the fallen seedlings of the summer trees. Branches that were once bare now seemed to come to life.

As the heat of summer intensified the grass had darkened and begun to burn leaving only traces of green left. It seemed at that moment that everything around Edith was dying before its time. Her father's death had taken the color from the trees and all the happiness from her world. Suddenly the suction of the door broke her concentration. The door had opened. A tall man with an elongated face and pinched nose appeared in a very bleak suit, carrying a briefcase. A salesman of sorts, Edith felt sure, but what was he selling?

Agatha held the door ajar only an infinitesimal amount. She was in care of a child, and she was not much of a woman to put up a fight if it came to that. Growing up in a rough neighborhood will force you to put your guard up around people. While Edith's home was situated in a quiet suburban grid, Agatha had grown up in a harder time when desperation got the best of people.

The man smiled at Agatha. Not in a warming way, but in a reassurance that he meant neither of them any harm. Then his face grew somber again.

"I am from the Department of Social Services. May I have a word with you?"

Agatha looked over her shoulder at Edith, who leaned closer to see what they were discussing at the door. But the large solid surface had been barely open enough for Agatha to see the man's face, never mind deciphering the words Edith desperately lent her ear to hear. Agatha had made the call a week ago and had expected the visit, but wasn't sure how she would break the news to her sweet adolescent neighbor, a girl she had long felt was her own kin.

Suddenly Agatha stepped back and the door swung open, allowing Edith to get a full view of the man now towering over Agatha like a totem pole.

"Please, come sit in the kitchen, we can speak there." She lifted her arm, directing him to the kitchen. She then looked at Edith, who had an inquisitive look on her small face about the peculiar stranger. "Edith, please stay here, I will be out shortly and then I'll start making supper." She smiled guardedly at Edith.

Edith had never seen Agatha smile like that before. It was almost a crooked smile, one you hold tight with uncertainty. Agatha was trying to offer this child comfort after suffering so much trauma, but with the presence of this gentleman, it was harder to assure her that everything would remain the same.

The gentlemen put this case on the table and clicked open the locks. The table rocked under the movement. Years of turkey dinners and projects Agatha's husband had brought home to fiddle with her had left the table lopsided and at her age she was not suited to fix it.

"I was contacted by the facility where your ward's mother is being kept presently. We understand that you have had temporary custody of the child, but the court sees fit to place the girl with a next of kin. This has been a difficult situation for the child and for yourself. But we feel now it is in the child's best interest to live with her aunt and uncle in New Hampshire. They are a nice couple and their home is adequate for a child. They have not had children of their own, so it may be an adjustment period for them all. At least while her mother is recovering, the child will be cared for."

Agatha looked back at the closed door to the living room where Edith currently sat. She wondered if she could overhear the conversation between the two of them. Hadn't this child gone through enough? Now she was to be wrenched from her home and all that she knew. Agatha looked back at the gentlemen whose eyes remained relaxed and fixed on her.

"I can't say I have ever met this couple." Her eyebrows pulled together as though she tried to remember all those who had passed over the threshold of the Anderson's home. "I have known these good people for the last fifteen years, sir. I have met their family and friends on several occasions. How come I have never met this brother and sister up in New Hampshire before? I thought that Paul had a few brothers not far from here? What about his brother's that live nearly two blocks away? Why are you taking a child so far from her home and her family here?"

The man let out a sigh. He had come to the home that day to deliver the transfer information and to collect the child. The questioning had become tedious and he knew had to bring it to a halt before it could get carried away.

"Ma'am we approached the families that you speak of. Reluctantly, we were unable to find a suitable candidate to take the child."

"Well that is unbelievable. They are all gainfully employed and own homes, how could they not be qualified to take her for the time being?" She was getting flustered and pushed her metal chair away from the table.

"We went to each home, but could not find anyone willing to take on the burden of raising a child. Many already have children and didn't feel they could house another with the inadequate space that they presently were living in. The other two you spoke of outwardly said that they couldn't take the child due to their livelihoods. Believe me, I have reached out to everyone. This couple is a good couple. They have promised to take good care of the girl in the interim."

Agatha hung her head and slapped her hand down on the cold surface of the table. She stood, flattening out of her rose patterned apron and pushed the door to the living room. She looked down at Edith and then back at the gentlemen.

"This kind man is going to be taking you to live with your aunt and uncle in New Hampshire, while your mother recovers here."

Edith looked from the man to Agatha, then to the floor. Her eyes shifted back and forth. What was she to say? She could not argue with the man and would not dare say no to Agatha. Her parents had brought her up to be a respectful young woman and she was going to make them proud. She placed her hands on her legs and stood up. "I'll go pack my things."

Chapter 2: Samantha, 1994

It wasn't an easy upbringing in the least. Sam was tough, the second daughter and so second in command. Lisa, the oldest, was their de facto mother. Sam functioned as her co-parenting partner, needing a good cop/ bad cop. Lisa was more than willing to play bad cop when she got the chance. She called it "Ode to Mom". Theresa, thirteen years old and moody as she was independent, needed parenting in a hands-off way, but they all sheltered Jessica, only six, as much as they could. And yet with the work of high school and parenting and after school jobs, tenderness was something for cookbooks, not for the living room where they spent most nights huddled in front of the small screen. Even the TV sat upon the poorly crafted, wobbly stand someone down the street had tossed out. Another item neglected, discarded. Sam might as well have been a TV stand.

Edith would come home cigarette in mouth, ash tipping onto the linoleum as she stumbled along the creaking floor before closing her bedroom door behind her. The door was pock-marked with large dings from the countless abusive boyfriends she had let into their lives. Only Sam and Theresa shared a birth father. He was no better than the boyfriends that followed, and had left shortly after Theresa was conceived. The four girls made it work in their little apartment in Pawtucket. They entertained themselves with silly fantasies and local neighborhood kids. They avoided the rough crowds. They were smart girls, not only in school but street smart as well. They knew who to avoid and what not to do without any guidance from a supervising adult.

Mildred, a kind old woman from the first floor of their three story tenement apartment, often knocked on the door to check in on them. She got good at pretending that she just enjoyed baking and delivering goodies. It just so happened that she repeated this action every day. Mildred was a riot, a strange and atypical granny. Her temperament was sweet, true, but she had a side of her no one would notice just looking at her small, meager appearance. She would regale the girls with stories of working as a bartender at a sticky-floored dive bar in her younger years.

Half the time, she discussed her many sexual escapades and late night gambling in her uncle's liquor store in the fifties. Mostly that forced Lisa to cover Jessica's ears.

Theresa, the black sheep of the family, pretended the rest of the family weren't even there. Being the third to arrive in the lineup of children produced by Edith, you would expect a bit of rebellion. Theresa took this task to the next level. The only one who refused to acknowledge the life she was living as reality and couldn't care less what was going on. She instead slid her round glasses up her small turned up nose and pushed her face into a book for most of the day.

She planned to get out of this house as soon as she graduated and head for Yale: she could not be bothered with feeble issues like rent, utilities, or shopping for food and clothing. With two older siblings to watch her, she could stay out of trouble, but she wasn't the maternal type and wasn't about to babysit Jessica. Especially if it were just so her mother could "live her best life." While her personality was polar opposite to her three remaining siblings, her appearance was most like Sam with dark auburn hair, complete with streaks of black highlights cutting through. She put them in by herself one day while the two older girls were at work. When Lisa came through the door, exhausted from a long shift following school, Jessica burst into the living room and grabbed her sister's hand.

"Come Lisa, you have got to see the new girl living with us."

While the two older sisters expected nothing but shocking behavior from their middle sister, they also knew that while experimenting with herself, she was not, at least, lighting fires and vandalizing the neighborhood.

Edith was not perfect, but she was far from unkind. Upon waking in the afternoon, she would thank Mildred for taking the time to bake them sweets. She often forgot to go shopping. This left the girls little choice but to become creative in the culinary department. But they were used to her forgetfulness by now. What surprised Lisa the most was her mother's insistence in closing her bedroom door as soon as she entered the tiny apartment.

Theresa and Sam had the same father, Garret Townsend, someone her mother claims she "lost communication with" when he left town on his bike. A bike that could have been sold to support to raise two daughters that he only genetically provided for. She'd had many boyfriends over the years. Sam thought that the only saving grace was that Garret at least was good enough not to come back and visit from time to time. Granted the other "suitors" only saw their mother for about an hour at a time behind closed doors and snuck out while Edith lay there fake sleeping to avoid conversation. Loneliness can surely drive some to take risks with their emotions and gamble with their prospects. When she had "company" it was completely understandable to have the door shut. Not a single one of them wanted to see what happened,when they could hear it through the paper thin walls. No health class was necessary for these four girls. By the time they were ten or eleven, they had already experienced the unnecessary exultations of a man all over their house.

But what did Edith have that was so important that she couldn't leave the door open when only the girls were around? She had to change? Sam's mother was never a discreet person to say the least. She often walked about the apartment in her undergarments, a regular catalog model.

The one consistent thing that you could count on with their good ole Mom was her tipping herself. She had this coffee jar. A beat up old tin. Every week she would drop a $50 bill into that jar and then tuck it away into her underwear drawer. Sam only knew this because she had decided to poke around one afternoon while Edith was mysteriously out on the town, and she was tired of waiting for her mother to reappear.

Often they wondered if she remembered having kids. Her mother was not a drug addict as far as they knew. They had seen that sort on the streets, camped out in the blue tarp tents. This was not a life that anyone would have chosen to live in, yet so many had come to this decision at some point. With a mess of a mother, Sam wasn't sure how neither she, nor her sisters had not fallen prey to the clutches of drug addiction. But then, between working, school and playing mom, Sam and Lisa had little time to pick up new habits.

This was no different from any other self-sacrificing day. The dishes were piled up in the heavy scum-lined aluminum double sink. It was hard enough on Lisa, working extra hours at the diner to make rent without having to come home and delegate chores. Sam took it upon herself to be the chore hound. She would scrape off the inch tall dust line that swept across the apartment. Removing it caused a wild distress on her nasal passages.

Of all the things to inherit from her mother, dust allergies may have been the one Sam hated the most. If mold were an allergy it was hard to tell over the dust particles from floating through the air on any given sunny day. Most of the time the shades stayed drawn to avoid neighbors peeping in their windows. The last thing they needed was someone calling child protective services on them for being home alone so often. Aside from dust, this place was smeared with grease from bacon fat splattered against the back of 1970s pink tiles. The same kind you were likely to find in dingy motels. *Good luck getting that bacon off,* she always thought, *it would take a pinch of acid to rip that from its cemented position.* The same fat stains as always from "the annual birthday breakfast."

Sam woke that day and laid awake in her bed for a moment. Her room was kept in museum quality as the house outside her and Lisa's room was generally closer to resembling a ship wreckage.

They did their best cleaning the apartment, but with a train wreck like their mother, a thirteen year old sister who left gum on wrappers and Dorito bags shoved in the couch cushion, not to mention a six year old who still picked her nose and did God knows what with it, Sam's room had become her room became her safe space. Luckily, having an older sister guaranteed they were for the most part on the same page. They were half-sisters but only a year apart in age. But still, Lisa was more focused on the boyfriend she lived with a majority of the time, keeping her stuff in their apartment to avoid any awkwardness if the relationship were to end suddenly.

Samantha's father was not what you would call a father. His name was Garrett Townsend. A man of tall stature like Samantha, Garrett was built like he had spent far too many years at the gym. His dusty blonde hair complimented his chestnut brown eyes, and he had a deceiving smile. Edith knew he was the father, having only been with one man at time, even in her days of figuring it out as she went along. Though Sam was confident *that* had never actually ended. Garrett had his own shit to figure out. Afterall, he was too young to have kids when he met Edith. She had fallen in love with him and he had fallen in love with her admiration.

The honeymoon phase of their torrid affair lasted all of two months before Edith discovered the pregnancy with Samantha. She said he stuck around until she was born, already taking up other prospects less complicated than this current situation. As the caretaker he was, he left a few hundred dollars with a note and rode off on his bike. They wouldn't see him again until years later.

The old memory sometimes flashed through Sam's head when she cracked open her bedroom door in the morning, just like she had as a toddler, thirteen years ago.

He came back, drunk as a skunk, one late AugustJuly evening. The air was sticky and the air conditioning had broken down. At three, Sam could remember it. It was so hard to sleep in such thick, swampy air. She and Lisa had decided it would be cooler to sleep on the hard wooden floor, hoping to capture a bit of a chill. The one fan that their mother was able to scrounge up had been put in the living room, being the hottest room in the house. When they asked to sleep in that room though their mother had forbidden it. She said that it would be impossible for them to sleep in a room so close to the television. That night another reason arose.

The apartment was silent. It was about 2am when they heard a knock on the door. The light in the living room came on. Samantha opened the bedroom door a crack to see who was visiting so late in the evening. The living room was adjacent to their bedroom so it was easy to see everything without moving an inch.

Edith stumbled over to the door in her summer nightgown and looked out the peephole. She hung her head down, momentarily questioning whether or not she should open the door. Reluctantly she decided to open it a crack. Outside the threshold leaning slyly against the door was Samantha's father. She had only seen him in pictures her mother had posted of him on the fridge. She wasn't sure it wasn't a constant reminder to her that she can't trust men. Much like other women would tape pictures of obese individuals to ward off temptation of late night snacking. On the other hand, she may have been missing him, avoiding the reality that she may still be in love with him so many years later.

Samantha stood up to go say hi to her daddy, but something in her mother's posture and tone told her to stay put.

Edith stood firmly at the door. Garret pleaded with her sweetly, reaching to touch her cheek gently with his hand. She moved away from his reach and then the fighting began. The neighbors would certainly hear the commotion. She knew that the door would be shut and her mama would go back to bed. Instead her mouth was clasped shut by his hand and he forced his way into the apartment. Her mother was shoved into the wall. She fought back and he slapped her across the face.

Samantha didn't know what to do. So she shut the door and woke her sister Lisa, sleeping peacefully on the hardwoods. She had always slept like a rock. Her mother was screaming, she was struggling. Sam covered her ears. Suddenly there were new sounds, grunting, moaning and crying all in the same breath. Edith groaned loudly. Sam was too afraid to open the door, to help her mother. She was a child, practically a baby, and she cried. Nearly four years old and observing pain and suffering. It had only set her up to never trust men for the rest of her life.

Nine months later her sister Theresa was born. Edith never told her about her father. The pictures were removed from the refrigerator and he never came back to visit. Theresa had the unfortunate gift of receiving her father's looks. A haunting reminder for Edith and Sam that the past can only be buried so deep before it eventually resurfaces.

The cleaning, the memories, the distrust of men and especially her mother all waited for Sam after school, but was able to step outside sometimes when she went out.

After school Sam stopped at the diner where Lisa worked first, hoping to get some studying done.

"Call me crazy, but is Mom starting to get a little fat?" Lisa blurted out leaning over the counter of the diner bar. Sam smiled and breathed deeply from her nose. While she was amused by her sister, she had a trigonometry test the next day and needed to take this time away from home while Mildred watched the girls to get some serious studying in.

Lisa had been a waitress here since she was only fourteen. The owner thought that she was a nice kid who needed a break, and found her to be a hard worker. Thank God for that because the family was not going to get by on their mother's wages. Edith had taken multiple jobs and failed to keep any of them for long.

Sam was the sensible one of the sisters. Her sister Lisa was the more mouthy of the two. While she was the oldest and most of the time the breadwinner, she felt a bitter resentment towards her mother and would only come home most of the time to see her siblings, see the family cat and pick up a few items of clothing while giving Sam some money to spend on the younger sisters. Lisa was not going to stop living or give up her chance to become the girl she wanted to be. At seventeen she was trying to have the life that her mother had failed to provide to them.

Sam slapped her pencil down on the notebook. "Ah, I'm never going to figure this shit out!"

Lisa smiled, looked over at the paper and then shrugged, "Well, there's no way that I am going to be able to help you."

"I am well aware of this fact. I need a tutor, but I doubt I am going to find one at the school. My teacher is a bit of a phony, I doubt they even know how to do this math. They hand out the ditto and then turn around and walk away."

"I guess you can just ask around and see if there is some brainiac out there who can make all your math dreams come true."

"Very funny, Lis, I just don't have time to fool around. If I am going to get straight A's this quarter then I need to ace this test coming up."

"Why do you need straight A's anyway, it seems like you have enough school options to apply to next year?"

"I'm a junior, I'm at a point where I can't wait. I need to know where I am going or else I'm not going to go anywhere. Plus, not all of us have a boyfriend that we can live with, or a volleyball scholarship in the works to escape mom's madness." She rolled her eyes in annoyance. "And yes, she is looking a bit plump." She grunted, "For fuck's sake, I hope she is not pregnant again." She quickly covered her mouth. The swear word had just plopped out there. Lisa stuck her hands on her hips and cocked her head.

"Sam, I am at work. Speaking of which, I need to go help these customers that just came in. Why don't you head to the library to get the rest of that done. Who knows, maybe you'll meet a nice guy who happens to be a whiz in math." She winked at her and then walked down the edge of the counter, grabbing her order pad and pencil on the way. Sam collected her book and notebook, waved to Lisa and headed off to the library.

The library was not going to be a big help. A crowd of people were gathered in the lobby gawking at something or someone. Sam pulled her hair behind her ear and in the corner of her eyes saw someone that made her turn her head. He was like no one she had ever seen before. His eyes caught hers for only a moment and he grinned at her. She reacted with a similar smile, and a rose shade covered her cheekbones. Sam decided to walk the opposite direction of the mass knowing full well she would not be able to give her attention to her work if the hustle and bustle in the lobby continued.

A small cubicle with a desktop computer was tucked in the back section of the library that no one ever seemed to visit anymore. It was one of the only computers they had and it was hardly ever on.

The room was filled with dated magazines for men's fitness and workout videos on VHS tapes. She had seen a number of Jane Fonda videos in her youth. If that was what they were offering, she was not buying it. She was an athletic girl in her own way, walking everywhere she went. Tennis was also something she found relaxing. The tennis courts were right down the street from the YMCA and she had gotten some used rackets from Mildred for a Christmas present a few years back when Edith failed to get them anything.

Sam's eyes remained glued to the gridded paper until the sound of footsteps startled her. She assumed that they would simply walk by but instead a arm became draped over the side of the cubicle and the handsome young man she had caught a glimpse of across the lobby was now staring her in the face.

"Hi." He smiled sweetly at her. "My name's Adam."

She looked back at him for a moment, feeling awkward with the forward approach and little time to plan on a response. It seemed only logical that she be polite and introduce herself.

"Hello. Sam." She extended an arm to shake his hand, hoping this would release the tension from his gaze and offer a distance to keep him away.

"I saw you across the room. I was kinda hoping you would walk over to me so that we could meet, but you didn't. So I searched the whole place and found you back here." He looked around at the men's fitness magazines and turned his head back to her with a twisted expression. "Why *are* you back here?"

"Well, this is the place where you go when you want to avoid people. No one looks at these ridiculous magazines anymore. Granted everyone wants to be Swartzenegger, but they aren't going to watch these videos and read articles, they are going to go to the gym and work out." Her tone exuded a certain crudeness mixed with a bit of sarcasm.

"How very insightful, Sam." He said her name and it moved through her with a sense of warmth. Once again her cheeks reddened. She looked up at him, softening her expression.

"So what brings *you* here Adam…?" implying she didn't know his last name.

"McNamara."

He rolled his eyes with a boyish grin. A smile slowly spread across her face while he said his name, and she felt a bit absurd for her erratic and atypical behavior.

"I am here doing a book reading." He rested his chin on his open palm leaning in his other arm as a brace on the cubicle.

"A reading, what are you an author?" she giggled at the absurdity. He was young, how could he be?

"Yes, though I write under the pen name Charles Stonington." He raised his eyebrows in anticipation of her response. Most of the time when women found out that he was the famous Charles Stonington, the same man who had written such amazing love stories set in the Victorian era era, they would lose all sense of the natural world and fling themselves at him. A reaction he had grown tired of. He introduced himself as Adam mostly, hoping they didn't know his identity by simply looking at him. His books had been flying off the shelves over the last couple of years.

Sam had never been into dramas, never mind chick flicks. She was more excited by history, and archaeology. While he waited for a fan's response, Sam just shrugged. To her, he was nothing more than a kind stranger.

"I don't mean to sound odd, please forgive me if I do." He bit his lower lip turning his glance to the other direction, trying to figure out the right way to say what he wanted to. "I would like to take you out."

"Excuse me?" Samantha dropped her chin and looked up at him in bewilderment. "Why?"

Another first for Adam. Being a teenage heartthrob was one thing, but being completely un-admired was entirely refreshing to him. Some guys his age were in it for the chase. But he enjoyed writing and knew what his target audience wanted to read. So it boggled his mind that this girl would be completely unaltered by his presence and uninterested in his company.

"Because anyone who chooses to be in this fine establishment on a Tuesday night is someone I think is worth getting to know." He smirked and rolled his eyes back "If I weren't here doing this, I'd be here writing or reading a book in a corner over there." He looked again at the men's fitness magazines neatly organized on the shelves directly behind her head. "Ok, perhaps in another area of the library, one with less bulging singlets."

Samantha let out an enormous laugh and then covered her mouth, startled by her own noise, and remembering she was in a library.

"I guess I could grab a bite, I haven't had a chance to eat yet anyway," She smiled and stood up, "but I get to pick the place and I'm driving myself there." She set the grounds while gathering her notebook and pencil, shoving them rapidly into her bag instead of tucking each item into its place. Samantha, ordinarily neat as a pin, but something about this stranger had her frazzled.

Growing up in a household of all women due to lack of paternal stability Sam was neither inclined to accept the invitation to date nor seek the attention of strange men, especially in libraries. She never knew much about she and Theresa's father, not that she ever asked, but Edith never attempted to explain how they ended up breathing on this God forsaken Earth. One thing she was sure of; she was never going to be her mother and so she would date someone that her mother would never go for. A responsible gentleman with a job seemed like a sure winner. Edith's general pick was a scotched up Keno player hoping to bum a pack of Marlboro's and a twenty for odds and ends. Was this guy to be an arms length cautionary tale or would she finally lower the floodgates?

Chapter 3: Edith, Summer 1969

Edith looked out the window of the black chevy impala she had put her belongings into just a few hours earlier. The gentleman driving was not much of a conversationalist to say the least. Once in a while he would ask if she was hungry or needed to stop for a rest. Edith would reply she was ok and continue to stare out the window. Agatha had come into her room that afternoon while Edith packed. She perched herself on the edge of the bed next to Edith, who pondered how this could have all happened.

Just a few short months ago, her mother and father were planning a memorial day weekend together. The beach would be lovely this time of year. Now her father had been dead for two months and her mother was only half alive. The only person she had left was the neighbor she had known her whole life. Agatha wrapped her arms around her tightly.

"Everything is going to be all right. I am sure that this couple, your aunt and uncle, are good people and are going to take very good care of you while you are in their charge." She rubbed Edith's arm gently, reassuring her that she was certain of these strangers she never heard of.

Edith was barely into puberty, how was she to handle this? If things were wrong, how was she to confide in two people just met? Unfortunately, it was out of her control at this point and she must go with the gentlemen who now sat patiently out in the living room waiting for her to pack her belongings.

"Can I call you if I need you?" Edith looked up at the endearing woman whose eyes were as glazed in seeping tears as hers.

"You have my number, you can call me anytime you wish." She hugged her tightly and stroked the back of her head. A knock at the bedroom door startled them and they pulled apart from one another.

"Ms. Anderson, are you ready? The day is fading and we have quite the drive ahead of us."

"Ok, let's get you going." Agatha smiled and stood up to hug Edith once more. She studied her corduroy dress with brown buttons at the pockets and smoothed out a piece of hair that had been caught in her headband. It was as though she felt she would never see her again and was trying to remember her just as she was at this moment. Edith knew this was going to be upsetting for Agatha. She would put on a brave face for her. It was time to face the future.

The highway was a blur of trees. Their bright green leaves blended into one another. It was like a wave, crashing over her. She closed her eyes and rolled the window down to get some fresh air. The car shifted: they were taking an exit, Edith began to become alert to the fact that they may be arriving at her aunt and uncles soon and began mentally preparing herself to speak to them for the first time.

She appreciated the fact that they were willing to take care of her and understood that she may be a burden to them financially. This was a chance for her to grow up, show them that she was there to help in any way she could. After all, they had lost a brother in the mess of all this. She had not met them at the funeral interestingly enough. For someone who cares so much, wouldn't they at least find the compassion to attend that?

The paved road turned to dirt and the car slowed to a crawl. A long driveway up on a hill presented itself. The trees were all pine at this point, ferns and brush rested at their base and filled in the empty space between trees, and Edith suddenly felt a calmness about this place. Perhaps it wouldn't be so bad after all. It would only be temporary and the summer is a beautiful time to visit New Hampshire.

She and her family had come here together one summer to visit the lakes. Lake Winnipesaukee was a massive body of water and they spent a long weekend there boating, eating fresh lobster from Maine and finishing the hot days with generous scoops of ice cream from their favorite shop. The memories dashed across her mind and she was lost in them for a moment. Her chest slowly moved up and down and she began to feel okay about this transition. This was a place to heal with her surroundings. The birds, the fauna, the blue skies with billowing clouds above her. The smell of the fallen trees breaking down to introduce the variety of fungi. It would be okay for a time.

The house came into view up on the right corner of her view. A cabin of sorts. It appeared that they had it built to their own specifications. The driveway abutted the edge of the home meeting a large tool shed and garage. The gentleman driver stepped out of the car and swiftly headed to the trunk, obviously in a hurry to lose his cargo. He pulled out her case and opened the backdoor to ease Edith from the car. She looked at the handle momentarily, feeling the urge to grab it and slam the door shut, insisting that her place was at home with her mother, or Agatha or anyone else who would take her. Instead she stepped out of the car, grabbed the case from his hand and continued to walk up the stone path to the front porch of the house.

The door of the home was old and quaint. There seemed to be a warmth and strength in it. The door was a protector. It kept out the cold wind at night, the animals that strolled across the property, and strangers who may mean to steal or bring harm. This protector seemed empathetic, if a door could be so.

With a click the door opened and a meager woman stepped out. Her hair was gray and a bit disheveled. The kind of woman you would expect to live so far out of the way from the rest of the world. She wore a soft gray, oversized flannel shirt and some black slacks. Edith wasn't sure what to make of her until she extended her hand and smiled at her.

"Hello, my name is Cora. I guess you can call me Aunt Cora." Edith shook her hand politely and took in the accent knowing she was not from nearby.

"Oh, I know what you're thinking, how can I have a Southern accent and be your dad's sister?"

Edith didn't want to appear impertinent in such an awkward yet crucial moment in meeting this woman that she apparently had been related to.

"I, um, don't know much about you. I'm sorry, they just never mentioned you."

"Ah, yes, well that is a whole 'nother story for another day, sweetheart." She took the case from Edith's hands and then looked at the driver. "Could I grab you some sweet tea?"

"No, thank you, I must be going. It will be a long drive back and my family will be missing me." He tipped his hat and then took his leave. Not even a word to Edith. They sat for three hours in the car and did not discuss a single thing of importance. Yet, in this brief moment with her aunt, he strung together more words than he'd spoken to Edith the entire drive. Was Edith that tainted that people were afraid to speak to her?

Cora shut the door behind him and rubbed her hands together, like a chef about to make a pie.

"Now, let me show you your room young lady." She turned and headed up the stairs directly in front of the exterior door. The stairs were soft carpeted that made her socks sink a bit into them. The carpet was a deep green color, much like the cascading trees she had floated by on the highway.

Upstairs were two doors. They turned left heading towards the door on the opposing side of the house. Cora turned the door knob opened and a sweet smell came wafting out Cinnamon mixed with a warm vanilla and it coated her nostrils, reminding her of the pies her mother would prepare for the holidays.

"I saw this candle down at the general store and I thought maybe you would like the smell. It is far more inviting than those dingy carpets that I have been telling your uncle we need to rip and replace for three years now. But oh, Lord, he doesn't listen worth a damn." She looked over at Edith and covered her mouth slightly.

"I apologize, so unlike me to say such a thang."

"It's ok, it happens sometimes." She caught her aunt's look, "don't

worry, it doesn't happen to me." She smiled at her and then turned to look around the room. The ceilings weren't too high and the left side of the room was slightly slanted leaving only a couple of places to put a single bed and a dresser. Under the slanted roof, Edith found a rather large chest with old leather straps. It was like something out of a pirate ship tale.

"Oh, you like that? It has been in my family since the late 18th century if you can believe that. It's made from cedar and though the leather is a bit tattered now, the inside is in pristine condition. I have old blankets in it for now, but I have shown it at multiple antiquities exhibits. It is from a famous ship that sailed in Charlestown, South Carolina, that's where my people came from once. I grew up in Georgia though." She thumbed at herself, "But the chest is from Charlestown, where the British had tried to land to keep control over the naval fort while the colonists were combating to take it back. Now, unbeknownst to them, the French had arrived and took down most of the British naval ships. This trunk in particular had been pulled from the water after the ship sank. My great, great, great, well you get the point, he was great, granddaddy kept the chest as a reminder of their strength and perseverance to keep what they fought so hard to protect."

"Wow, that is one amazing story." Her attention was moved from her aunt and the chest to the bed.

"You must be tired. Your uncle should be back from fishing later on tonight. I suspect we will have dinner in the next few hours. I'll leave him a bite to nibble on, but you and I can take this time to get to know one another, just us girls." She smiled and turned towards the door.

"Just let me know if you need anything darling, I'm here for you."

"Thank you." Edith spoke graciously to her host, feeling calm and comfortable enough to finally sleep. Full clothed and hair tied up tight holding back her dark auburn hair, she closed her eyes and prayed she would sleep at least long enough to face her new reality with a clear mind.

Chapter 4: Samantha, Summer 1994

Curling clouds rolled overhead. It was a warm, yet breezy summer day at Slater Park. The roads were filled with cars zooming by, hoping to get a glimpse of Fanny the Elephant's last day at the zoo. The Slater Park Zoo was famous in Rhode Island and families came from all over to feed the legendary forty year old elephant her favorite snack, roasted peanuts. Samantha laid back on the checkered blanket next to Adam, quiet, reflecting on what this place once meant to her, now that a piece of it was leaving.

She thought back to a day with her mother. One of the best days to date that she could remember. She and Lisa were barely nine and eight years old and her mother gathered them all into the tiny Camry that she currently was driving while she "waited" to get a raise from her boss at the Laundromat.

She watched Theresa climb in and asked that Samantha make sure she buckled her into the car seat. Naturally, Edith couldn't do it herself. It was a blessed miracle that she was even taking the girls out for something other than their semiannual clothes shopping excursions. While the girls tended to outgrow most of their clothing prior to the trip, their mother seemed to not notice that their elderly neighbor Mildred was subsidizing their clothing with sales she got at the Benny's down the street.

For a woman living on a small take-home from social security, she had barely two pennies to rub together even without having to care for then only three young girls. But she thought of them as family and would do what was necessary to keep them protected and safe.

"Are you girls ready for a fun day at the zoo?" Edith smiled. She was clearly excited about something. Usually when Edith was happy about anything, it related to a new guy in her life. He was going to be the end-all cure to their problems, he was somehow going to financially take care of them or was making her feel safe and appreciated at the moment. Most would fizzle out, either from lack of interest or, having gotten what they wanted, they would book it. She had a way of drawing in only the lowest quality of men.

Today her curls were set and she'd even done her makeup. What was the big deal that she would go through so much trouble to look the part of a caring mother? Samantha looked out the car window as they drove through the park. They had never been to the zoo before, so she was excited. It was a rare occasion that they could get their mother in the car, on their way to something that was, just possibly, about *them*.

The trees were filled with bright colored leaves and the picnic tables were filled with families eating their Wonder Bread sandwiches. How much she yearned to have that setting. A loving father, always doting on their mother, grandparents that would come over for Sunday dinners. Her mother would come out in a flowered apron, "putting on the dog" they say. The background would include old music, Sinatra perhaps and the fire would be crackling in the background as they all had their afternoon tea and played board games. The laughter would pierce the walls of the house. Their home would be a single family ranch house, with a big yard and a golden retriever puppy who would come from a room in the back on Christmas. A present from mom and dad for their wonderful children.

Edith pulled the car over, put it in park and then turned in her seat to look at her three kids.

"You guys ready?" she was smiling still. This memory was so vivid, like a snapshot in motion. A video playing on loop for her to remember. They approached the ticket booth and paid to get into the park. Most of the park was free, but the zoo cost a small fee to see the animals. They walked through the different exhibits. Most of the animals were sleeping towards the back of their enclosures. After all this was Rhode Island and the animals on display were used to far warmer climates. When they finally reached the back of the park they came to an oversized fence with benches posted nearly four feet or so away. Samantha wasn't sure why her mother had brought her to see an empty pen.

"Sit down and be patient, any minute now." Edith smiled, looking back and forth between the two girls. Lisa looked at Samantha and shrugged.

"Ugh, mom, what is it that we're supposed to see?" Lisa's eyebrows came together in a serious inquisitive expression. Even at nine years old she wore the pout of a teenager.

"Just wait a second and you'll see."

A second was all it took. Out of the shadows shape came into the sun slowly. As it approached the girls their eyes widened, not with fear but in awe of her sheer size. Theresa, only four, was unaware of the creature before her and chased a nearby floating butterfly. Samantha grew so excited, she almost wanted to pinch herself awake. Perhaps Edith had done this for Lisa and Sam, a special moment to share with them alone.

The elephant extended its trunk down to touch the girls' outstretched hands. The tip of the trunk was pink and wet and the two large holes were creating a sort of suction sound. Lisa reached out first to touch the creature. Sam was in awe of its size at first, unable to grasp how something so large could exist compared to her small stature.

"Here, take these." Edith reached into her purse to grab a bag of peanuts still in their shells and gave each girl a handful. The girls looked at her with interest, not sure what she meant for them to do with it.

"I'm not hungry." Sam said, handing it back to her mother.

"No, silly, feed it to Fanny." She pushed the hand filled with the roasted nuts back in her daughter's direction, "She absolutely loves peanuts."

Edith stood up and gave Fanny a heaping handful of them. Within seconds she had sucked the shells from her hand like a vacuum and proceeded to crush them in her mouth. Her trunk came back over the fence and brushed Edith's face. They seemed like they were old acquaintances.The large gray trunk of the gentle giant was rigid and dense. The hairs were like coarse, hard bristles, not soft like you would expect. So incredibly parallel to Edith that it made

Sam smile a bit thinking back at that moment and the relationship that her mother shared with the elephant. She turned her to see Adam smiling back at her.

"So what are your plans for today, beautiful?" He pulled a piece of her hair away from her face and tucked it behind her ear.

"Well, I had thought that perhaps we could just spend a few hours here and then head back to the house to check on Jessica and Theresa. I know Theresa is old enough to make wise decisions, but not in regards to a small child. Knowing her, she is burning incense and writing dramatic poetry while listening to The Cranberries buried in a corner of her room.

"Hey, I enjoy The Cranberries." He gently tapped her shoulder with his fist.

"Yeah, I do too, not sure why I picked them as a reference." She let out a big sigh "I guess I am just envious of her and her lack of responsibility. I mean granted she is only thirteen years old and the opportunities for a girl her age in the employment aspect is pretty low. I just don't understand how we, Lisa and I, could be stuck working while in school to make ends meet while my mother is doing her half assed routine of being there when she feels it's necessary." She looked down at her watch. "Oh, shit! I'm not free, I gotta go."

"I thought you were free for the rest of the day." Adam leaned up from the blanket spread out over the soft green grass of the park.

"I forgot that today is an extra work day for me. I was supposed to have it off, but Mildred said that she was available to watch Jessica and my mom has been having trouble with the car not starting in the morning so I figured I would get an extra shift in case we need to get another car sometime soon. Without credit or extra cash to pay for it, I will be walking to school and you can add that to the list of things I have no intention of doing."

Adam laughed and touched her cheek. "I could bring you."

Samantha put her hand up. "School is going to be starting up again in a few weeks."

"And." He raised his eyebrows questioning the direction of the conversation.

"And I don't think my life can handle being messy right now. So after the summer is over, I think we should go off into the sunset in separate directions."

"Wait, what?" Adam stood up.

"I mean, it's nothing against you, I really like you. I just think that it's better you get out while you still can." She stood up and crossed her arms. A defense mechanism she had seen her mother use a time or two when she realized that she had to get her way.

"Sam, you know that I am aware of your family life. I get that you are very closed off."

"Closed off!" she pushed him. Grunting as she turned and walked away.

"I didn't mean it in a bad way."

"How can that be interpreted differently?" she put her hands on her hips, extending her neck out, and tilting her head slightly.

She was pissed and he didn't want to anger her further.

"I'm sorry, I didn't mean to hurt you." He let out a sigh of exhaustion. "I have a book tour coming up this month. They gave me a few months off this summer, but I can only make them wait so long. I did this for you, for us. I wanted to get to know this beautiful girl who has captured me in such a way. Everyday you're pulling me in and I don't want you to let go."

"Well, I'm letting you go. Go enjoy your life as a traveling author and I'll return to my place. Maybe one day when I figure out how to get out of here, I'll give you a call and we can pick up where we left off."

"Sam, I want more than this. I want to stay in touch and get together whenever we can. I know you are in your junior year and things are going to be really busy and exciting for you but I don't want you to think that this was a waste. This can be more than just a month, one summer. You could come with me."

"What, come with you?" She laughed to herself, "Great, I can be just like my mother, follow whatever guy is in the picture at the moment." She crossed her arms and hardened her face.

"Oh, I get it, I'm just the guy of the moment, gotcha." He leaned down and grabbed the blanket off the ground. "Well, I guess it's time to go then." He balled up the red plaid squares. "After all, the moment is gone." His shrewd tone lit something under Sam, sparked the old memory of the zoo, but now with a sudden resurgence of detail she had been so carefully leaving out.

Her mother wrapped her arm around the man, practically silhouetted in the sun. She had not seen him before, he smiled down at Sam and Lisa, picking up Theresa in her arms. Samantha could see a shadow of his face as the sun faded behind his eyes. That was the day she met Jessica's father, Dylan and the last time their mother brought them to the zoo to see Fanny the elephant.

Chapter 5: Edith, Summer 1969

It had been a quiet two weeks surrounded by hollow walls and creaky floorboards. Old homes always had an eeriness about them, she felt.

Edith looked strikingly similar to what her mother had as a child. With deep set eyes, creamy white skin and hair down her back, they could have passed as siblings. But while her mother's fair hair had darkened over time into a deep auburn color, Edith's hair had transitioned into a more brilliant strawberry blonde.

In the past, her parents had often taken her to the beach, where they would take long walks along the sands. Her mother had a grace about her; she walked on air around Paul, effortlessly. Her long hair would dance slowly in the quick winds that gusted off the crashing waves, whipping her in the face softly. The color was stunning, like time-hardened amber, brilliant as the orange sky in the evening. Paul often would call it his favorite sunset. Edith would gaze upon her mother sometimes, a beauty to so many. Iris would stand in the fading sun on the docks at the port of Galilee, watching the boats come in after a long day out to sea. The wind would blow her hair into pink and orange waves of color and somehow she would fade slowly into the sunset.

That woman was gone now.

Edith tried to hold onto that image as long as she could, not knowing when Iris would recover enough to come home to their life, their new life without Paul. Edith wished more than anything to walk through the door of their home and see her parents dancing in the kitchen again. But her father was gone and she was sure her mother would never dance again with another.

The atmosphere in Aunt Cora's was very different from the home she so adored and felt misplaced from. Her uncle Ansel kept to himself so much, Edith wondered if he was devoid of personality or empathy to what she was going through presently. He was not a terrible man but she felt disconnected from him and being strangers, avoided being in the room with him outside of dinner. The couple, while affectionate in their own way, did not hug or kiss one another daily.

She would not come into the room to find them nestled on the couch watching Johnny Carson on the television or out for walks holding hands. At night they would sit on separate sides of the room. Ansel would read the paper quietly and then switch to a book. Cora cleaned up the kitchen after serving dinner at 5 p.m. sharp, and then moved to knitting on the rocker. It was a quiet simple life, she had to give them that, but perhaps it was too quiet to keep a teenager settled and calm.

Edith found herself missing all the simple things, being so far removed from what she considered an ordinary life. The casual greeting from a mailman. The exhilaration of opening the mailbox to discover a parcel or letter addressed to her. There wasn't much excitement to be found in the woods. Her aunt would run to town to gather their things for the week and would often ask Edith to travel with her. Sometimes Edith went just to get out of the house. At first the conversation was a bit stale but over time the Edith felt more comfortable and inclined to look out the window pretending to be enthralled in the scenery instead of staring down at her hands.

Saturday morning had become a ritual. Cora would ask her to go to the Farmer's Market in town. Any reason to escape the house was excuse enough for her to go. The first morning she had stayed idly in her room, studying the walls while she waited for her name to be called to head downstairs. Perhaps kids her age would also attend the market. If she did not return to Rhode Island by the Fall, she wanted to have some friends in school.

Despair grew hard like a pit in her stomach when she remembered her original hope; that her mother would be home by this point. But somehow she knew that it may drag out through winter. What would Christmas be like this year? In New Hampshire you can bet on a white Christmas. But what is Christmas without the sound of the radio humming as it plays Nat King Cole. Her father would no longer read them Christmas stories in his favorite armchair while her mother tore strips of delicate newspaper to prepare paper mache for ornaments. Every year they made a new ornament for their tree. Would Cora and Ansel have a tree?

Cora closed the door to the dusty 1945 Ford pick up truck and put it into drive. The clicking and crunching sound of the car as she switched gears made Edith a bit uneasy. Cora saw her face in the corner of her eye and knew immediately what she was thinking and burst into a belly-deep laughter.

"Oh sweety, there is nothing to worry about. Old Jessie is a great gal and she is gonna last me another twenty years I have no doubt." She smiled and returned her gaze back to the winding dusty road.

"You've had this truck for twenty years?" Edith looked around the interior of the vehicle. The seats were worn to the shape of Cora, the leather cracked a bit but held tightly together like it had been well looked after. The dashboard was detailed as though she cleaned it daily.

"Yes, ma'am. See, if you take the time to love something and don't give up on it, it can last you a lifetime." She looked at Edith whose face went solemn for a moment and then turned to look out the window. She saw quite a bit of her father in her aunt: pride of ownership seemed to run in their family. There had always been shoes at the door, clean boots in the car at all times. It was as though he would try to sell his car back as brand new once he was done with it.

Cora wasn't sure if she had said something wrong and began to apologize when Edith spoke.

"I don't mean to sound rude. If I am, I apologize." Edith looked down at her lap.

"Go on." Cora nudged Edith with her elbow, urging her to ask the question held on her tongue.

"How are you my Father's sister when I never knew you existed until now?" her eyes winced a little with regret and eagerness for answers.

"Well see, that is a fair question. Who doesn't want to know about their family and where they come from?" She sighed a moment trying to gather the story before she spoke about it. "My dad was a great and wonderful man, born in Savannah, Georgia, one town over from the woman I call my mama's. Left at only fifteen in pursuit of his dreams. His father was a physician, and well-to-do, but he didn't feel his son should be meddling in an occupation that was outside of duty to his community or his country. It made him angry when our father ran away. No matter how hard Grandpa persisted to change him, my father was indeed a good man, in his own way. He provided for his family and was a devoted father to me and my older brother Kyle.

Unfortunately, my dad was not a perfect man. He would sell milk by day but would play drums at the local club at night. Matter of fact, it was in Rhode Island, a club called The Blue Moon in Providence. The Blue Moon was the best place to catch the really good jazz musicians and he would play with cool cats like Sammie Davis Jr. One night he was playing to a crowd of over a hundred when he saw her sitting in the front row at a table covered in white linens. The room seemed to disappear except her and her maroon dress, and brunette pinned up hair. That was the night he met your grandmother. The affair lasted only a year and I was a result of it.

Shortly after I was born my father decided to stay with his wife. My mother, biologically, decided the best thing to do was to tell her husband the truth about me. Surprisingly enough he said that he would stay with her, but only on the condition that the baby would be raised with its birth father. He wouldn't be able to look at me without thinking of the affair. The idea of losing her child was almost more than she could bear, but she agreed regardless. It was a difficult decision, but the world is not kind to women.

"My father went to his wife, a woman who would reluctantly raise me as her own and made it work. In the end I was raised by two darling people. Papa lost the woman he loved, but stayed with the woman who was willing to raise the child of an affair. Having a child out of wedlock was a serious thing back then. The only rational decision was for them to move back to Georgia and away from strands of gossip. My parents raised me as their daughter. No one questioned it and my parents never spoke about it. I only learned about this on my father's deathbed. He had drunk himself silly over my birth-mother's absence. His liver failed and he died shortly after my 30th birthday.

That is how I came to be in the possession of Jessie. My father had so many wonderful times driving her around. I felt it only suitable that I continue the tradition."

Edith nodded slowly.It all seemed to make sense now. Why she never knew about her aunt all these years. Certainly if her father would have known he had a sister, he would have looked for her.

"I hope you don't mind me asking..."

"Shoot!" Cora winked.

"Is your mama still alive?" Edith felt terrible that she didn't know the name of the brave woman who did such a noble thing.

"She passed away a few years ago now. The house was too quiet I guess. She never married again, not after what happened with my dad. Having one marriage filled with mistrust and a child that is not your own is a lot to deal with. She loved me as her own. I will not say that she was not loving and kind. I only knew her as my mother, nothing else. But she knew that I deserved the truth, should it ever come out.

Anywho, I moved out when it was time to go to college and she did very little outside of working or visiting her sister from time to time. The stroke hit her hard and she was gone in an instant."

Edith gasped, covering her mouth. "I'm so sorry."

"She went the way she wanted, quick and easy." Cora squeezed her lips together tightly. "She always said that if I am to go, don't let me know about it. I don't want to be afraid." She let out a deep breath, "she was not a God-fearing woman, in the least, but she always thought that there was something bigger than God out there, something beyond man's creation."

Cora shrugged, "I guess we will see."

"I guess." Edith smiled at Cora for the first time. Finally they knew a bit about one another. Perhaps this would be a good time to talk about something she needed to get off her chest.

"So my mom," she paused for a moment, "I know after what happened to my dad..." She sucked the air in hard and held it a moment. "Have you heard from the hospital?" she closed her eyes and squeezed them forcibly shut.

"I'm sorry, I haven't heard anything. You have a case worker who is going to call when she hears anything about your mom." She slapped her knee and it startled Edith whose eyes flew open. "All right, this is the deal." She turned her head sideways, pointing her chin out a bit in her direction. "Perhaps life didn't give us exactly what we wanted. Maybe our parents could have done better, maybe not. Maybe life isn't fair and we have to find the joy in it the best we can." She laid her hand flat down on her thigh.

"I will do right by you. If you need anything, you can come to me and we will have a chit chat." She smacked her lips together, "And don't worry about your uncle Ansel, he's harmless, just not much of a conversationalist. He has been a wonderful husband these past thirty-five years, not every marriage is passionate like you see in the films. I'd take tenderness and devotion any day over icky love stuff." She stuck out of her tongue in silly disgust.

Edith laughed and smiled at her aunt's playfulness. They arrived at the market and Cora stepped out, shuffling over to the first stall. The wooden crates were stacked high. Most contained fruits and vegetables of the season, others were meant for jellies and pickling. She pulled her cat eye sunglasses on top of her head as a woman walked up to them, and greeted her with a hug.

"Selma, my girl, how have you been?" They parted: Selma grinned ear to ear.

"Shelby had her baby, a boy, weighing ten pounds."

"Wow, congrats Grandma, a big baby boy, for sure!" She turned to Edith, "This is my niece Edith."

Selma looked at Cora in confusion and then shook Edith's hand gently from her fingertips. Edith wasn't sure how to take the simple hand shake. She saw Selma was interested in her and where she had come from. It was doubtful anyone knew that Cora had a niece, never mind that one was living with her now. In such a small community, secrets told once were bound to be repeated by every needlework group in town.

Cora looked at Edith, "You can look around and feel free to buy something if you see fit." She put a five dollar bill in her hand and then scooted off with Selma to further explain the situation.

Edith poked around the market for an hour, purchasing a variety of her favorite apples to take home and found a small bench to sit on while she waited for Cora to fetch her. This was entirely different from the world she had grown up in. Coming from a city and living in suburbia to this quiet country life where you go once a week to grab your fresh fruits and vegetables, stock your freezer with the farm fresh meat aside from the venison your husband supplies in the fall. It was a culture shock at first, growing up in the city, but over time it might be easier to get used to.

The number of kids in her age bracket at the market were very few. A girl who seemed to be a year or two older was there flirting with a boy who seemed to be an outsider. With his long flowing hair and flimsy blonde mustache, he didn't fit the bill for a country boy. Back home that would have been an average look for a teenage boy, but here the boys were prim and proper, clean cut and shaven. Never would they speak back to their daddy and mama, who expected them to be doing their chores, working down on the family farm. Seemed like everyone she met ran a general store, a farmstand or sold jellies to make a living. They didn't need nice cars or fancy record players. They used the same radio that their grandad had used to listen to the news all those years back.

Cora appeared out of nowhere while Edith dreamed a minute about her new residency.

"All right, you all set sweetheart?" She had big bags of an assortment of vegetables and some smaller bags of fruit. "Oh good, you grabbed the apples."

She gestured for Edith to follow her. They walked back to the truck in silence. After placing the groceries in the back of the truck in a small crate tied tightly for safe keeping, the ladies hopped back into the cab. The ride back home was quiet this time. Edith faced out the window, watching the road swirl around corners of rocks and treelines. Her gaze skimmed the tips of the lakes and rivers, crossing small rickety bridges and took in the sun as it hit her face, dancing down from the leaves of the trees above her.

Chapter 6: Samantha, Fall 1994

Ring! The bell tolled the end to another day. Sam stepped out the back door of the school to face the typical rush of a Friday afternoon. She rolled her eyes at the sight of the cheerleaders decked out in uniforms, with the school mascots painted on their cheeks. Kids pushed and shoved each other to catch their bus or meet up with their friends to walk over to the auditorium together. Pep rallies were anything but exciting to her. She would rather be at a concert or taking in a movie at the theater down the street, even with gum and soda stuck to the floor.

Nothing about the most recent movies interested her, so she spent most of her time putting effort in school, working her part time job at Dairy Queen and visiting with Adam when he came to town. Oh to be on a book tour, traveling the country, met by adoring fans who Sam was sure all wanted to sleep with him! She couldn't blame them, he was a very attractive man. His appearance, while stunning, was nothing next to his charm and intelligence. His characters made you fall in love with reading.

She had admitted to him shortly after they started dating that she had never heard of him prior to that day at the library. The fight that could have ended their brief relationship at the park that day turned into a long distance letter writing love affair. One suitable for his novels. While Samantha was well read, she didn't focus her energy on romantic war time stories from the Victorian Age, rather on the battles on Normandy beach in the 1940's. If anything, love stories didn't appeal to her at all.

She had seen love in her home, or what she thought was love. It was short and to the point. Sex seemed to be the essence of it. Hormones, driving desires that fizzled out with ejaculation, resulting in daughters who are bitter, resentful and full of regret. Except for Jessica, who remained joyful in her fairytale world.

Adam was set to arrive in town on Saturday of Labor day weekend. Sam was counting hours now. Lisa, she was sure, would move out as soon as she graduated, and Sam planned to follow suit the next year. The parking lot was full of cars. Everyone was outside resting their back against the doors though, socializing, almost like they hadn't seen each other all day. *Can't they just find their cars and go on with their simple lives? How hard could it be to live as a jock in a letterman's jacket? Go Tigers!* She rolled her eyes again. She wouldn't be caught dead at a football game. Sam had planned to join a club this year, on the basis that she would not have to act, sing or be on stage in general. The idea was to be more of a behind the scenes girl. If an art director or stage managers or gaffer was needed to manage the lighting design, she was the girl to ask.

Her dream was to become an archaeologist. If that were to happen she would have to add those extracurricular activities to her repertoire. For now, she walked briskly past the jocks and cheerleaders swishing the pompoms in the air in celebration of a victory that would most likely belong to the opposing team Tolman had never won a Homecoming game. Lisa walked up behind Samantha and slid her arm under Sam's right elbow.

"How are you?" Lisa spoke in a high-pitched, spoiled whine. The valley girl routine amused Sam.

"Hey, Lis, conquer anyone today?" Sam smiled at her sister , so full of initiative to get out of the life she was living.

"Yeah, I conquered the University of Rhode Island, in fact." She pulled out a letter and flashed it in front of Sam's face.

"What!" Sam's face lit up, her mouth opened wide with surprise and she quickly embraced her sister. "You got in, oh my god, I'm so proud of you!"

"Yeah, even better, I got a volleyball scholarship. They are paying my tuition, room and board. Guess I can just work for extra cash now."

"God, I'm just, wow, that's amazing." Sam put her hands on her hips and then hung her head. She raised her eyes and stared to the left, avoiding eye contact with Lisa.

"Oh Sam, I won't be that far away." Lisa put her hand on Samantha's shoulder, "I'll be thirty minutes from home. Which means, I can still bring whatever old man I'm dating back to visit you, and drive mom crazy." She cupped Sam's face in her finger tips. "You understand that I love you, right?"

"Yes, I know." The idea of having to handle Theresa's attitude and Jessica's upbringing alone was daunting.

"What if Mildred gets sick and I have to stay home from work? I mean, how is the rent going to get paid?"

"Sis, it's going to be ok. I am not leaving you alone." She put her other hand to Samantha's shoulders and looked deep in her eyes. "I'm not leaving for another year either. I'll just work extra hard to put money away for a rainy day."

"Like if this hunk of shit breaks down again, needs an oil change, new alternator.... I mean this is a twenty year old car, I'm surprised it still runs with only us to look after it."

"Hey, we know how to change the oil, add windshield wiper fluid, check the tires. Plus it's the cleanest car you will ever find on a set of teenagers."

"Oh shit," Lisa bit her lip. "How are we going to share a car next year? I have to have a car to get home from URI."

"It's ok, I'll figure out something. Get a cheap car from the lot down the road from Ernest and Sons Dry cleaning."

"I'm pretty sure every car on the lot is a lemon, Sam."

"I'm pretty sure we were taught enough in life to know that you have to take lemons and make lemonade." Lisa nodded in agreement.

"It's all right, Lisa, I'll find a car for myself. Today is a day of celebration for you. Besides, knowing you, you'll come home with a mechanic or something to look at my car while he's here."

"True." Lisa nodded. "Let's get going, we have to pick up Jessica from school."

The door clicked as the three girls walked into the living room of their apartment. The room felt different. Theresa—usually sprawled out on the couch, headphones covering her ears, messing with bangs that were begging to be cut—was away from her frequent resting place.

"Theresa?" Lisa spoke loudly, trying to reach the entire apartment from the doorway to the hall outside. There was silence.

"Maybe she had drama today?" Sam shrugged her shoulders at Lisa. After a few more attempts to get Theresa's attention, Lisa decided to go into the apartment herself, leaving Sam with Jessica at the door. At her height she felt that she had to be the protector of her family. A minute later she came out to the living room, giving Sam a somber look. The expression on her face left little to the imagination. Sam began to think of every possible scenario to what could have happened, but she said nothing. She was not one to speak of things in front of Jessica.

"Jess, let's go play in my room. I'll get you a snack and you can take out the dittos you have for homework, ok?" She walked her petite younger sister to her bedroom just across the living room. Lisa ran to the pantry and grabbed a pack of animal crackers and a juice box. Sam didn't move from her station. She felt her breath become shallow as her sister pussy footed around the house, almost physically walking on eggshells.

Lisa shut the door to their bedroom with Jessica safe inside and then looked at Sam. As Lisa turned to go into their mother's room, Sambegan to prepare herself for the worst. Would her mother be dead on the bed, drunk to death? She hadn't a clue until she looked into the room and saw Edith curled up on the floor next to the nineteen seventies original water bed.

"Oh my god, is she dead?" Samantha gasped. She covered her mouth, trying to control her breathing. "Oh my god, oh my god." The idea of her and Lisa now being fully responsible, more than they already were, was more than she could handle. The idea of her mother dying was not something she had considered.

"It's ok Sam, she's alive." Lisa was on her knees, listening for breath sounds. She had been CPR certified last year when she decided to become a lifeguard at the YMCA. She turned their mom on her back.

Her face was badly bloodied and was already bruised. This had happened while they were at school, at least several hours ago. Unfortunately, this was not the first time their mother had been roughed up. The night that Theresa was conceived was a doozy for sure. He was kind enough at least to not demolish the apartment. This asshole had beaten their mother and had ransacked her room. He must have been looking for something. Why on earth would she let such a monster in the apartment?

All of a sudden she moved, and the girls jumped back, startled.

"Mom, it's ok, it's Lisa, you're all right." Lisa talked quietly, consoling her. It panged Sam to see her sister comfort her mother in a way she rarely saw Edith console her own daughters. When Jessica would wake from a night terror, it was Lisa or Sam who would run to her, rubbing her back and giving her a glass of water to sip until the monsters returned to their dark cave. Her mother would sleep through everything. Almost certainly due to heavy meds. She wasn't mentally present for anything. Yet, when she was beaten up by a strange man, whom she most likely was dating, the girls again were the ones to clean up the mess.

Sam felt a sudden happiness for Lisa and her ambition to leave this place. Outside of dating idiotic old men, she had figured out how to escape this trap. This endless cycle of giving and not getting.

"I'll go get a washcloth." Sam put her hand on the doorway and Lisa looked up and nodded. She knew that Sam was not ready to assume the position of their mother's caretaker. Perhaps it was time for her to kick her life into gear. Maybe she would take to the open road with Adam. They'd only been together a few months, but they were happy and things just flowed with them. The only thing they ever argued about what whether or not Arnold Schwartzenegger was a sex symbol, which Adam argued for and Sam against.

She returned to the room to find her mother sitting up. Her eyes met Sam. Sam quickly handed the warm washcloth over to her sister and stepped back, away from her mother.

"It's ok Sam, I'm all right." Her mother was practicing today, the right thing to say in whatever situation she was in.

Sam looked at her and her face hardened. Edith saw her reaction and her expression fell as the moment of connection with her daughter vanished. Her auburn hair was knotted and had smears of blood in it from a gash on her forehead. Edith knew she had done this to herself, in a way. She had created her daughter's existence of constant expectation for hardship. This was another Shakespearean sonnet in a life of tragedy.

"I just forgot, I got to go get Theresa today after school." Sam rolled her eyes back trying to play off the moment by inventing chores. "I'll be back." She rushed out of the room; grabbed the keys, slammed the front door. Lisa and her mother looked at one another as she continued to dab the dried blood off her mother's face.

"I didn't invite him in. I didn't know who he was." Edith paused and her mouth fell open in a voluminous way, but no more sound came out. She wanted to cry for what happened, she wanted to apologize for what she had put them through. Lisa could see it in her face, the way she felt the remorse from the many moments that had come before, all the mistakes. She cradled her mother in her arms and gave her the feeling she needed. She was safe, at least for a moment.

Sam rushed down the stairs of the apartment building, her mind rolling through spurts of anger, frustration, empathy and fear. What if this was what her life was to be? What if she was to be her mother's caretaker? Every time a guy came by to get some quick action and left her bloodied up, it would be her position to nurse Edith back to life. Hell maybe she could get a nursing degree, so she'd be better prepared for this wonderous opportunity put before her.

She was never going to let this be Jessica or Theresa's burden. They had lives to fulfill. They couldn't have this hanging over their heads. So she would be the girl to help them to leave, push them to move on and never look back. It would be better for them, than to rot in this sewer she called home. She slammed the front door to the building behind her and grunted loudly, startling Mildred who was sitting on the front porch, her tea cup resting in her hand, listening to the Beatles. Mildred's foot was gently tapped in her cracked leather loafers. She looked over at Samantha, who avoided eye contact. She smiled, sipping her tea and then offered her a sugar free candy.

"Sure would be a waste to buy such a big pack to not share them with someone." She lifted her arm up, gestured for Samantha to take one. Her wrinkled cocoa skin peaked out of the long draped sleeve of the silk robe she wore. Sam took a piece, knowing how much she hated them, knowing she would most likely get sick to her stomach. This was an opportunity that she felt should not be avoided, despite her instinct to run away. Her duty to Mildred was not as to a neighbor, it was out of kindness. Mildred was an example of how people could treat one another. Their neighborhood was rough, it was not beautiful. The landlords failed to keep the buildings up. The paint had long been worn on the shingles, put into place back almost seventy years ago now. The black coating was rubbed off the spiraled surface of the railings from years of folks leaning up against it, holding it for support and using it to guide them home.

This house is very much like Mildred, Sam thought in a flash of insight. Mildred needed as much care as the old crusty building, but she had no children to come and care for her. In turn, she cared for the children in her building and their mother who had lost her way in the world.

"You know that she loves you." Mildred said looking out in the street. Sam turned to say something impertinent to the woman offering solace for a minute. Instead she sealed her lips together and hummed.

"Mhmm."

"Uh, uh child." She wagged her finger at Sam, scolding her for the impertinence.

"Sometimes, you just don't understand and you need to." Sam cocked her head to the side with a matter of fact glance at her friend.

"Your mother and I have had our talks, you know, about you girls." Mildred put the tea cup down and began to unwrap a piece of translucent pink candy. "She tells me about her past, what she wants for your future."

Sam laughed. "What future?"

"Whatever future you make for yourself."

"Lisa got into URI. She's leaving next year. What does that mean for me? Do I get to clean up the puke? Do I get to be Jessica's mom when Edith doesn't feel like doing it that day?"

"Excuse me, I don't care how angry you are with your Mama right now, you will not call her by her first name," Mildred's voice rose sternly, "I thought I taught you better, at least!"

Sam punched the front door to the building. Mildred, caught off guard, fell back in the wooden rocker and rocked back and forth like a pendulum. Mildred had never raised her voice at her before.

"I'm sorry." She breathed out slowly, trying to take in the wisdom of what to say.

"Samantha, she knows she ain't perfect. She knows she hasn't done the best. She doesn't know how to tell you."

"Tell me what exactly?" She was raising her voice now. The warmth rose up in her throat and her cheeks became hot like fire as the tears poured out immediately and uncontrollably., "How she loves us so much that she will leave the world's burdens on us while she has her sexual escapades, drinking, probably doing drugs and all in the comfort of our home!" She ran her fingers ferociously through her hair practically, pulling it out by the root.

"For once I would like to come home from school and not have her be there, to not have to clean up her mess of a life. I would like to be that girl that goes out for the drama club, tries out for cheerleading, dates the jock, has enough of a carefree life that they do not have to come home to find their mother upstairs unconscious and bleeding on the bedroom floor."

Mildred's face went white as a ghost. "What did you say?" She stood up as fast as a woman at her age could handle, bracing against the chipping rail of the porch.

"Is she ok?" She looked back and forth between the irritated child and the front door to their apartment building. The thoughts raced back and forth in her mind whether to run upstairs to access the situation or tear into the child who stood outside casting blame on her mother while she lay seriously maimed in her bedroom.

Sam saw the look in Mildred's eye. The doting old woman had always been like a grandmother to her, but at that moment she saw nothing in her face but shame. Having spent so much time teaching her to be a better person and watching the project fail in front of her eyes was crushing.

"Excuse me." And with that Mildred pushed past Samantha and began the ascension up to the girl's third floor apartment. Their relationship was never the same after that day. Two months later, Sam would knock on her door to have a morning tea with her like they had done prior to the altercation that afternoon. She found Mildred in her bed. The lace quilt covering gently folded under her arms. Her favorite book *Where the Red Fern Grows* lay nestled against her chest.

Her mouth hung open. She had died in her sleep.

Chapter 7 : Edith, December 1969

"Well, that should do it." Cora stepped down from the rickety step-stool, admiring the aluminum star now topping their newly cut spruce. "Don't you just love the smell of it?"

"It's great." Edith tried to smile, hoping to appear cheerful enough. Cora's home had been suitable for a short time, but it was going on five months and no visits to her mother. Edith was in a bit of a funk for her favorite time of year.

It would be her first Christmas without her father coming into the room with a pillow stuffed up his shirt to play Santa, chortling at his own ridiculousness. Her first year with no mother in the kitchen basting the turkey, waiting for family to come over. No chance of Edith begging to grab a piece of crispy skin from the juicy breast still cooking.

Iris was a tremendous cook, even though Paul tried to take credit for every Christmas dinner. It was a tradition of his to announce his accomplishment in cooking when they sat down to dinner, and watch as everyone's eyes rolled at his old joke nineteen years in the running. He would always have a little chuckle about it and then kiss his wife for picking on her again. Just another memory to lock away.

Cora had tried several times to bring Edith to the hospital to see her mother. They had told her three times now that her mother was not in a state of mind suitable for a child. She was not speaking yet. Iris just sat in her wicker chair, staring blankly out of the window into the gardens around the medical center.

Edith wondered if she was waiting for her father to come get her. Longingly gazing out the windows, waiting for him to return from the store. They had told all this to Cora on the phone. Apparently Iris' present version of reality could come and go. Where the latter was more consistent. Eventually, or so they said, she would start responding to therapy and engage in conversation. It was obvious that it takes time for a mind to process trauma. They had assured Cora that she was getting the best possible care and not to worry, just be patient.

Edith, hovering nearby whenever Cora was on the phone with them, could only hear the responses from her Aunt, but as her tone changed, so did Edith's hope of seeing her mother again anytime soon. Edith didn't even wait for an explanation; she left the room.

Her bed was old, but soft. She almost assumed that the mattress was stuffed with goose feathers. Outside now, the snow had fallen and laid a thick blanket atop the dead, decaying leaves of autumn. The colors had been beautiful and they'd distracted Edith from the pain of missing her father, and the fear that her mother would never return to the land of the living. Maybe in her mind, Iris was still with Paul. *They are dancing again to Cole Porter. She looks in the fridge and she has a whole carton of eggs, perfect*

*for making his birthday cake. They go back to
dancing and the music swoons.*

There was something very chilling about
winter in the country. Not just the temperature
outside. Frost stretched out its icy fingers until the
feeling of death surrounded Edith. It was quiet as
the grave, the way the snow blocked the sound;
deafening in its silence. Edith could always hear
her thoughts echoing every time she ventured
outside to fetch wood for the fireplace.

The house with its old wood-burning
stove had belonged to Ansel's father. His mother
had died while Ansel was young. He and his
father had lived a quiet life together for years
before Ansel met Cora. This explained a lot about
Ansel's personality. While he was gentle and kind
to her aunt, there was not much of a
conversationalist with Edith. He would sit in the
corner of the room reading or wood working, or
stay outside working on a project. Edith began to
see the appeal in this type of relationship. He was
supportive, loved spending time with his wife,
and then left her alone to the peace and quiet of
the woods. Cora seemed to enjoy having Edith
around to talk to; she revisited all her old
memories of growing up in a city atmosphere.

"You know, when I was child, I lived at a
convenience store down on Main Street in the
beautiful city of Savannah, Georgia." She nudged
Edith on the couch. The show they were watching
was interesting enough, but Edith was distracted
by the lights and tinsel all over the house. "I hear
that store closed down last year. The owner, Mr.
Grandlen, passed away and his children chose to
sell the business. It's now a flower shop, can you
believe it?"

Edith shrugged. She knew quite a lot about
losing what you love and leaving all your worldly

possessions behind. Flower shops were not her favorite topic either, not after she'd learned of the daisies still in her father's hand as he lay on the street after the accident.. Her aunt never quite knew the whole story, so Edith brushed it off. Cora's intentions at starting a conversation had been kind.

"That's too bad." It was the most she had spoken in the last week.

Cora could see her struggle. "Are you ok living here?" Cora asked, staring at her folded hands. "I mean, are you happy enough?"

"I'm as happy as one can be, I guess." She looked at Cora and then looked down to her lap, reflecting on her words. She had not meant to hurt her aunt with her unresponsiveness. But what child wouldn't rather be at home with their mom and dad? But life has a way of changing its course, and Edith realized she'd have to change with it to make it to the end.

"I heard from the social worker today. I have some news. I'm afraid it's not very good news." Cora bit her lip.

"Please just tell me, what could be worse than I already imagined?" Edith let out a breath of exhaustion.

"The hospital is seeking payment for your mother's extended stay in their facility. Your father left money to her to care for you and the home. But living in a full time care center is a costly thing and the money went fast. Unfortunately, they had to sell the house to pay for the outstanding bill."

"Oh." Somehow the heart wrenching news did not hit Edith as hard. What is a home without a family in it anyway?

"I'm terribly sorry, Edith." Cora wrapped her arms around her niece and held her tight, like a mother would. "This should not have happened."

"Thank you." Edith looked up to her warm red face, still tight in her tangled arms. Then shut her eyes and felt the comfort of her embrace and let it in. She felt it hard, the pain, the loss and the joy of finding family.

"How about I make us some hot cocoa?" Cora let go and sprung off the couch, dead set on making this night a happy time for Edith to remember.

Cora had never known her brother or sister-in-law but she took their daughter in, helping Edith with the hand she had been dealt. Somehow, Cora had taken a shell and turned it into something that resembled a whole person.

Edith sat back, watching her aunt get out a can of cocoa powder and put the kettle on.

What would Agatha do when she found out that they were selling Edith's home? The Andersons had lived there for nearly twenty years. Every Easter they would do an egg hunt in her backyard. Her rose garden was a perfect backdrop for a bunny to lay eggs. Edith always thought it was a little silly to have a rabbit laying eggs in the yard. She knew enough about anatomy to know that rabbits give birth like other mammals. At seven she had told Agatha that she knew that her parents were decorating her yard with colorful eggs every year. She didn't want to spoil it for them, so she and Agatha let them have their fun.

Edith jumped suddenly to her feet. "Wait, what about our stuff?"

"Oh hunny, they aren't taking your belongings." Cora crossed the kitchen to get a single spoon from the drawer. "Your uncles decided to sell the furniture and keep a few family heirlooms at their homes until the time when you or your mother are able to collect them. Your clothes are being sent here with a few particular items they thought you may like. Your father's mementos are of course yours and your mothers, and they wouldn't dream of taking those. They're also being sent up. Mail is slow, so don't worry if it takes a while."

The mail was slow, but a few days later, a gentleman in a blue mail carrier uniform came up the drive in his truck. Usually he would just walk up with the mail in his hand. Edith ran outside to greet the visitor, smiling at the idea of being reunited with her personal possessions. Cora came out to say hello to him. She had known Stan for a great many years. Even Edith was beginning to know members of the community by name.

"Hello Cora, miss Edith." He tipped his hat at her. A bit of snow fell off as he replaced it on his head. "Tough day to drive up this steep hill."

"Sorry for your troubles, Stan," Cora smiled gently at him. "What do y'all have for us today?"

"A few boxes for Miss Edith Anderson, actually." He stepped into the back of the truck and returned with three boxes stacked neatly.

Edith's face dropped and her smile faded. "Is that it?"

"That's all they gave me today." He checked his list of inventory. Cora saw Edith's face and gently fastened an arm around her shoulder. "Now this may just be the first shipment. It is a mighty pricey thing to ship so many boxes. Perhaps they just decided to send 'em in shifts. Maybe next week, there'll be more."

Edith's expression was grim and she stared at the frostbitten porch.

"I don't think there will be." She looked at Stan, who could see the disparaged look on her face.

"Thank you for taking the risk of driving the truck up the drive, Stan. Please be safe on your way back down." She lifted one of the boxes and felt its weight. She decided she could take two of them, leaving one more for Cora to gather. Cora took her cue and acquired the box from the porch, then she turned back into the warmth of the house.

Edith set her boxes in her room, and then went to Uncle Ansel's workshop and grabbed a utility knife from the junk drawer.

Up in her room again, she slid the sharp blade across the taped top and opened it slowly. Inside the first box were her stuffed animals. Her parents were not for buying toys that collected dust, so the three animals in the box were all she had ever possessed. The duck, Mr. Puddles; the giraffe Willy, named after the famous zoo giraffe, and the horse, Ms. Sparkle. Sparkle was the name she was planning to give her own horse one day. She had told her parents on her fifth birthday that she had wished for a horse to ride in the countryside with. She would be black with a diamond on her forehead. Her coat would shine in the sunlight, so she would be named Sparkle. That year for her birthday she received a horse, but instead it was small and stuffed. That horse was just as lovely.

Under the stuffed animals, or "stuffies" as she used to call them, were a few frames that had originally hung in her living room. They were pictures of her with her parents at the beach and the carnival. A picture of her parents when they started dating, years back now, and a picture of her and her mom dolled up for Mother's Day last year.

She couldn't stop staring at the picture of her mother. Her bright bouncy auburn curls were illuminated in the May sunlight. A strange sight to Edith when the memory of her mother's last appearance was hardly bright or shiny. Her face was dirty. She hadn't showered since the funeral. She had ripped her black dress off that night and replaced it with a beautiful cotton nightgown her father had gotten her for a present.

Edith had done everything to care for her after it happened. She brought food to her room, but Iris didn't eat much; she slept most of the time. The few bites of food Edith could get her mother to swallow were spoon fed by her Edith, Edith still processing all that had happened. After the funeral service ended and her father was buried, there were no visitors to check in on the grieving widow and her young daughter: Edith was alone. Agatha came by daily to ask if she needed anything, but Edith was embarrassed by her familial neglect; she would thank Agatha and send her away, saying her fridge was filled with casseroles to feed them for months. Agatha could see that they had few visitors aside from the postman and milkman weekly. So to help out, against Edith's wishes, she would leave chicken pot pies, bowls of pasta and meatballs, and large pots of soup.

Finally after a few weeks, Edith decided to call Agatha over. She was ashamed not to be able to care for her mother as she had been cared for her entire life. But it was time for an adult to take over.

She knocked on Agatha's door. A gentle knock that Agatha heard somehow despite her age. She opened the door.

"Edith, what's wrong dear?" She could see that the tears had been flowing for some time.

"Agatha, I need your help." She escorted Agatha over to the fence line and then stopped. She could not bear to see her mother like that again. Agatha saw her expression and knew what to do..

She looked Edith in the eyes, holding her child gently between her wrinkled soft fingertips "Go over to my house, make yourself a bowl of cereal and read the paper. I put it out on the table on the porch."

She could see that Edith was tired, probably hadn't slept much since her father had died. For the last three weeks she had gotten her mother in the shower, changed her and fed her. Agatha took on the responsibility now and called the hospital to get Iris. Edith had known that Agatha would make the decision that she could not make for herself.

She watched from Agatha's porch as they pulled her mother out of the house on a stretcher, strapped in, her eyes shut. They must have drugged her to get her out of the house. Agatha caught Edith's eyes in the window as she walked back over to the house. She stepped through the front door and watched from across the room as Edith closed the door to the bedroom she would stay in the next few months.

Edith shook her head to release herself from the memory. That shell of a woman was not going to be Edith's final memory of her mother. Gently she put the frames out on the table next to her bookshelf and placed her stuffies gently on the bed next to her pillow. Cora didn't want to enter without direct consent from Edith, so she knocked and slid open the door just enough to slide the remaining box inside. She knew these moments were troubling enough without adding another person to the mix.

The second box contained mostly clothing, shoes and some personal effects of hers. Her toothbrush, hairbrush, her mother's curling iron and her family's classic literature collection. Dickens, Austen, Shakespeare, Twain, Hawthorne were all present. They were stacked neatly on the shelf. While they were the most personal items for her, the third box caught her gaze and she wondered what else could have been sent. She went to lift it and nearly dropped it. The weight of this box was far heavier than the previous two. She decided to open it on the floor and remove its contents one by one. But as she lifted the twin folds she saw something she hadn't expected. A collection of coffee cans.

Edith was confused as to why her uncles would place value on this above other trinkets in her home that she found far more valuable and irreplaceable. These were the cans from the shelf over her father's workbench in the basement. The same ones stacked on the stairs and in the overhead compartments of little nooks on the staircase. She could smell the dampness of the basement right away. The rusted cans and their metal contents. She had remembered they contained mostly screws and nuts, nails and bolts. A cost-effective way of storing your smallest mechanical fasteners to avoid stepping on or losing them in the process. They had been lost and stepped on regardless. The tin covers had all been labeled with their contents written with marker in her father's handwriting. She stroked the letters of the words gently, afraid they would rub off and she would lose yet another small part of her father. Slowly she lifted each lid to examine its occupants. Each can was less exciting than the last. The wrinkled labels, stained by years of storing rusting metal, referenced their age. What was she to find, a note from her father, a message from beyond? The cans, while thoughtful, she supposed, were falling short of what she needed. She needed a family.

Buried under the ten or so coffee cans was a small can, a Folgers, but not the usual silky black variety. The label was not in her father's hand, but her mother's. This intrigued Edith. She lifted the tin lid, but stopped all at once when she examined the contents. Inside the coffee can was a large stack of quarters and an overwhelming amount of folded fifty dollar bills.

Chapter 8: Samantha, December 1994

The draft slipped in through the unsealed cracks in the window by Samantha's bed as before the morning light could pool into the room. She woke up with a brisk chill. She shuttered at the idea that the heating bill hadn't been paid. Sam looked over at Lisa, mouth wide open, a bit of drool dripping down her chin. She had always been a heavy sleeper. A Mack truck could have bombarded their bedroom wall, splitting the room apart and she would jerk slightly and then roll over to continue her slumber.

Sam looked over at the alarm clock. Five a.m. It was far too early to get up during winter vacation. Her mind was racing; there was no way to go back to sleep. Usually her alarm would begin ringing thirty minutes from now, arming her with the energy to get her two younger sisters fed and ready for school. Theresa would stay and hop on the bus to her middle school, but Jessica had to be walked downstairs to Mildred's apartment so that she could wait for her bus to arrive promptly forty minutes after Sam and Lisa's departure. Since Mildred's passing, they had taken Jessica to a before-school program down the street at the local church. The extra money for the morning care was felt hard in the purses of the two girls.

Vacation seemed pointless to Sam at this point in her life. Most kids were out on actual vacations with their families. They visited their extended families out of state, went to Disney World, had friends over for sleepovers, put up their tree, wrapped presents. She knew that it was odd to put Christmas last on her list of thoughts for the impending week of celebrating Christ.

Edith was not a woman who taught or expected religion. She had her own way of describing how things went when people died. This was usually over a tall glass of Merlot, her drink of choice these days. Her mother was not a lush, but when she drank a little, a lot came out. Yes, they would have some normal family time. Every few weeks or so, they would sit down together as a family.

The girls would sit around the six seater oval pine table, chipped with wear and sticky from thousands of pancake breakfasts that Sam had made for Jessica. The amount of Lysol to remove such stickiness had tried Sam's patience. Knowing that the syrup would only be replaced in a day or two made her abandon all hope of ever eating at the table without their forearms sticking to its surface.

It was just as Sam rolled over, trying to regain some warmth, that Adam crossed her mind. Just a few days ago he had called. His tour was ending and he would be returning to Rhode Island before Christmas. The holiday was now only two days away. Only once had he seen her home, when he came to gather her up for a date one afternoon, but most of their time together had been spent outside or visiting museums, cafes, or concerts. Anything that she felt she could afford on her allowance, the hundred dollars that she gave herself once a month.

Lisa had agreed to cover the rent for whatever their mother fell short on and Sam would pay the utilities, cable and food. Edith would go to work. She could often keep a job for six months or so before she would get sick of the management complaining of her tardiness or arriving hung over with the reek of alcohol. It was so severe that they thought she may still be drunk from the night before.

Some months they would have an abundance of food in the fridge, the bills were not piled high on the counter, but were paid off early. It wasn't all bad with Edith. She wasn't a slum, beating her children, she just forgot most of the time that she was the adult, and she shouldn't be the one in need of care all the time.

Sam understood that when your parents get older, you take care of them because they took care of you. The problem with that scenario is Edith has never cared for them. On rare occasions, she'd provide above and beyond: make sure that her fridge was stocked, her clothes were washed and her apartment looked tidy for welcoming "guests" over to the house. What was she doing, shopping for a new "Daddy"?

Sam flung her legs over the side of the bed and put her face in her hands. All of this was far too much to be thinking about at five in the morning. She put her warm feet down on the freezing wood plank floor. The house was silent. A refreshing sound for sure. She could hear the traffic outside, an ambulance racing by to the nursing home down the street. Aside from the general ambience, the rest of the house remained still. She walked lightly, afraid that a creak in the floor would wake up Jessica and the pancake frenzy would begin. Perhaps she would get dressed and slip out of the house before any of the family heard her and have a morning to herself. Lisa didn't have work until later on that night and she was more than capable of preparing breakfast for her little sister. She returned to her bedroom, slipped on pants and grabbed a sweatshirt out of her drawer. Then she crossed the living room and slid out the front door, clicking it shut on her exit.

Caution was over: she raced down the three flights of stairs to step outside and was hit with a massive burst of frozen wind on her face. It had to be twenty degrees outside. The cars were all covered in frost and her breath fogged her view of the buildings for a moment. A sweatshirt may not suffice, but she would find a café and sit down for a cup of coffee to warm up. Dunkin Donuts was just around the corner and she knew they'd been open an hour already at this point.

Sam crossed her arms and walked briskly over to the coffee shop, thinking again about Christmas. Sam and Lisa had sat down a few days prior to go over the budget for the month. Their mother, fortunately, paid most of the rent and a utility bill on occasion. Sam and Lisa were generally tasked with taking on the bulk of the necessities for their sisters when it came to food and clothing. With kids ever growing, that was a frequent endeavor. Sam asked the attendant at the counter for a pen. She slipped back into her seat and grabbed a napkin. After tabulating the expenses for the month she determined that she had a hundred dollars left to spend on Christmas from both them and Santa. Sam and Lisa would often skip Christmas presents for themselves. Their main focus was providing a happy experience of life for their brooding thirteen-year-old bookworm and their rambunctious yet loveable seven-year-old sister.

Often to celebrate the holiday, each of them would give the other a night off to do whatever they wanted with fifty bucks. This was not a wrapped present from under the tree, it was a bit of freedom to be their own person for the day.

They did actually have a tree. A fake one that had been given to them by Mildred on Theresa's third Christmas. She had come over with a pie and saw that they had nothing in the living room under which to put the presents. An hour or so later the doorbell rang. Mildred had brought over a four foot plastic tree. Its branches were already wrapped in lights and its needles, while fake, were green enough to give the spirit of its intentions.

Every year they would pull it out of Lisa's closet and grab the box of ornaments from the bin in Samantha's. Inside the box were pictures framed by popsicle sticks, small painted macaroni art, cut out snowflakes, and pinecones that they collected from Slater Park the Christmas after they received the tree from their considerate old neighbor.

Sam sat there sipping her black coffee. Her home had never had milk when she wanted it and sugar was not allowed in the house after they came home to find Mildred napping and Jessica with her hands in the sugar bowl. She had learned to drink her coffee black and found it actually tasted more like coffee this way. The coffee pot at their house was working, but barely. It was circa 1986 and was on its last leg. Perhaps she could buy a new coffee pot for herself this holiday.

The ideas for the girls were getting harder. Theresa only asked that they get her the latest novel by Diana Gabaldon. She was very much into the historic love story of Jamie and Clare.

Sam had never heard of it, but she didn't find herself with ample amount of time to read as of late. One day soon Theresa would be able to get a job and start contributing to the income of the household; then perhaps she wouldn't read so much either.

Once Lisa was gone it would only get harder to keep going like they were. She had promised to come home regularly, but Sam could not ask Lisa to work full time while in college and commute forty-five minutes home every day to make meals and care for them. She had put in her time and now it was her chance to go free.

Sam ran her fingers through her hair, contemplating what to buy for Jessica. She would need a gift from the family and a gift from Santa. She thought back hard on what Jessica spoke of lately. She always changed her mind on what she felt. Everything was relative in first grade. Though, now that Sam thought about it, Jessica did seem to like stargazing. She'd sit by the grimy front window in the living room when nobody else was paying attention and look out, hoping to see stars through the city lights. And she liked the planets and would talk about the moon at night often if they sat out on the stoop of the house in the hot summer nights. The A/C was often broken and the hot air was stifling in their third floor apartment.

Sam began to relax as the warm coffee settled her, and she drifted from planning ahead to an old memory that layered itself over Jessica's love of the stars.

It was around late last September when they all had the night off somehow. Lisa, Theresa, Sam and Jessica all sat together on the front stairway. The paint was peeling on the rails and the stairs were cement, dirty from foot traffic.

They cared very little for the condition of their pants that night. It was the blackness of the sky. The unseasonable heat seemed to blur the stars. The way the streets create a haze in the summer heat.

Sam turned to her sisters, "Let's take a walk down the road a bit." The girls looked at one another. The streets of their neighborhood were decent during the day, but at night they felt questionable. There were too many dark alleyways. The girls all huddled together as close as possible without actually touching one another in this ninety degree heat with high humidity. Less than a quarter mile down the road they reached a cemetery.

"What do you think we are going to do here?" Lisa looked at Samantha, questioning her motives.

"We are going to take this opportunity to not be surrounded by buildings, lay in a patch of grass that is not already occupied and look up and think of nothing. Just be here, for a moment."

The girls looked at one another. Jessica didn't even blink, she was plopping herself on the ground and Sam followed suit, lying parallel to her sister. Lisa and Theresa eventually shrugged their shoulders and did as their sister had done. The grass was cool and dry. The quietness of the cemetery seemed less eerie and more restful. Sam thought she finally understood why people were "laid to rest." This was when the people would feel most at ease: laying in the grass, permanently gazing up towards the heavens.

Sam thought about her mom. The thought of her being with them hadn't often crossed her mind. She spent time with them of course, but not a normal family way that could categorize them as a unit. Yet at that moment, Sam felt oddly uncomfortable having not asked her to be with them. A strange feeling of detachment, regret and shame fell over her.

Thinking back on hot summer days brought warmth to her cheeks. It was the pit in her stomach, the feeling of shame that brought the redness to her face. She had not spoken to her mother since that day of the attack. The idea that she could have been so delusional to think her mother wanted this to happen was completely ludicrous. Edith may have opened the door, but maybe she hadn't invited him in. She did not ask him to hurt her. What kind of daughter would lack compassion for a mother who was possibly doing her best to be whatever it was that she *could* be.

Sam closed her eyes and asked for forgiveness the only way she knew how, silently and to herself. Fifteen feet across the soft-bladed grass lay a grave slightly overgrown and lacking the traditional tokens of remembrance on its granite sill. The name read Paul Anderson, Beloved Husband and Father April 1st 1928-March 6th 1969.

Chapter 9: Edith, Summer 1971

Silence. Who would have thought silence could be so deafening. Edith looked up slightly, tilting her neck, craning to see the house from the blanket she found herself attached to for the last three hours Just outside the rear of the house, she had discovered a somewhat flat clearing. Her favorite feature of this small space for herself, outside the privacy, was the generous sky granted to her for sunny days and clear starry nights.

Her uncle and aunt had gone to town to visit a friend. The man was willing to sell them a wood planer needed for her uncle to finally build the barn that he had been dreaming about since they acquired the property over two decades ago from his father. Throughout the year he had acquired old beams and shelving from other properties that had sold off a good portion of their lumber prior to raising their barns to the ground.

The clouds were scattered, the rain had held off for a day or two now, giving time for the ground to dry up and for Edith to escape from the house lacking every opulence she had been accustomed to. Her aunt knew she was a teenager and required a bit more liveliness than the escape from civilization she and Ansel had long sought. Edith was growing, and needed connection to the outside world to begin to understand herself and what she had experienced.

The second anniversary of her father's death had come and gone and she found herself numb to the fact. She closed her eyes tightly, trying to think of him. Had she forgotten his laugh? Had she neglected to do her duties as his daughter to visit his grave? Besides the obvious fact that she was hundreds of miles from home, she was months away from her senior year in high school though she still didn't have a driver's license. The idea of leaving the seclusion and returning to society was leaving her shaken.

Her aunt had said that she would bring Edith to visit her mother. Phone calls had been made several times since her arrival at the cabin. The conversations were brief and often ended with a soft click of the receiver. Her aunt would look up to find Edith, but instead would hear the latch catch on her door as she dealt again with the reality that her mother may never return to her. After five attempts, her aunt decided not to call as often, hoping to spare Edith the disappointment. Rejection felt harder with repetition, and often she thought about ceasing the phone calls all together.

Edith didn't question the hospital's excuses for avoiding visits with her mother. She had not been invited to learn more of Iris's condition. She didn't know whether her mother was still catatonic, lucid but not speaking yet, or, perhaps the worst possible answer was staring Edith right in the face: Iris didn't want to see her.

How could a mother wish to be separated from her child? Edith was the last connection she had to her husband. This child was a product of their love for one another. Edith was her daughter.

C.B. Giesinger

Edith slid her fingers through her hair. The color had altered from a dark auburn to a nearly strawberry hazel, a bit of her mother and father. The sun bleached her hair fairly fast. Needing space to collect her thoughts, she found herself outside most days that the sun shone. New Hampshire was a rainforest, and with that came fewer sunny days to retrieve the peace she so desperately desired.

Aunt Cora would catch her anxiety and would persuade Uncle Ansel to leave the house for a bit. It was easier than driving her niece out to town where most of the teenage crowd would spend their weekends. Cora was afraid of the rambunctious teens influencing Edith's behavior. Cora and Ansel were a pious couple. Not in the way that Edith was, being raised inside Catholic-dominated neighborhood that cared little about actual piety. Granted, Edith was raised Catholic, but they attended church mostly on Easter and Christmas. She presumed her parents brought her to appease the overzealous neighbors who would spread gossip if they *hadn't* made an appearance in church from time to time. If you are Irish, you better be attending church when there is mass.

There was a church close to her aunt and uncle's home, within walking distance from their door really. Edith figured that Ansel hadn't chosen the parish, rather inherited it. They were not Catholic, but Protestant.

Edith had been an obedient daughter and had been attending the confirmation classes her parents designated for her. She had sat in the mass, taking the communion and waited for her confirmation to arrive to finally be free of the weekly classes. Now, she would probably never make it to the ceremony. She was also a year short of Catechism to be confirmed. She knew that her aunt and uncle would not be going out of their way to find a Catholic parish to help her finish such accreditation.

Edith was happier for it. She wanted this to be a choice finally that *she* was able to make. She didn't want to believe in anything anymore. She wanted to stare into the sky and know that there was nothing there for her. It was far better than thinking her father was up in the heavens somewhere, looking down at her mother leaving Edith in the dust. No, the emptiness of space would be far more comforting to her father. Far better than the despair he would feel at the failure of Iris to protect their daughter in her greatest time of need.

And how could Edith hold her mother accountable? Iris had suffered a massive loss. The doctor had explained to Cora that her brain had shut off. It was a way to deal with the pain that losing her husband had inflicted on her. Mentally, she was just trying to heal what was broken. Edith listened from Cora's study, the only other phone in the house. Her hand clenched the receiver. Once the doctor had finished, she laid it back down slowly on the base, hoping Cora wouldn't be able to hear her on the line. Cora had looked down the hall shortly after, hoping that Edith would not ask her about the phone call.

That was nearly a year ago now. Surely, Edith would snap out of this. She was going through new things now herself, transitions. Life was coming at her fast and she was stuck out in the woods, living as a hermit with two people who had completely gone off-grid from the world.

Frustration hit Edith, and she sat up and wrapped her arms around her knees. At the same moment the sound of tires on gravel came into ear-shot. Their antique truck came to a halt and they stepped out looking around the side of the house to find a blanket laying on the grass with no occupant. Cora walked into the house and found it quiet and cleaned. Edith was one to sort things when she was overwhelmed. The dishes were washed, the counters wiped down, the windows were sparkling. She walked up the stairs to find Edith laying in her bed reading. Outside she had found that the ambient sounds of the forest had made her restless. The constantly snapping of branches, the chirping of birds, and the hum of the frogs all gave her little peace. Books were the great escape to become who you want to be and be wherever you want. While Cora felt this was an abnormal way for a teenager to spend her Saturday morning, she appreciated her interest in books and saw no purpose to interrupt her steadiness.

"I had an idea, if it would be ok with you." Cora pushed her hand against the doorway, leaning into it. Her voice was sincere, and Edith knew that whatever she had to suggest to her was out of kindness. "I thought maybe tomorrow we would head down to Rhode Island for the day."

Edith perked up and slid her legs over the side of the bed. "Really?"

Cora smiled "Yes," she saw her face and knew the next question was going to come and the answer would not keep the mood in a positive flow.

"My mother?" She stopped herself the moment she looked into Cora's eyes.

"I'm sorry, hunny." She looked to the ceiling as though the roof was going to give her some divine explanation for her to share. As though some words that she could share with Edith might somehow make it easier for her to handle the truth.

"So what are we planning to do?" Edith gripped the side of the bed with her fingers. Cora could see them becoming red as the conversation ensued.

"Well, I know you had some friends there, and your neighbor would love to see you, I'm sure. Perhaps you would like to." She paused and bit her lip. She wasn't sure how to proceed with the next phrase. "Your father." She took a deep breath in. "I never got the chance to meet my brother, but perhaps reuniting you with a piece of him would let him know I am doing my best to do right by him."

"Aunt Cora, you are doing fine." Edith smiled at her sweetly. They had not had a moment of connection in the last two years together. They would speak, but more as distant relatives rather than as a close-knit family. After all, that's what they were. These individuals were kind enough to bring in a stray when her father had died. Her aunt had never met nor known about him until this happened. She was now caring for her niece that, two years ago, she had not known existed. And caring for lonely Edith when her own, well-known aunts and uncles would not take her in.

Cora wrung her dry, cracked hands together, hoping this was the right thing. Edith saw the anxiety in her motions.

"I would like that very much."

Cora smiled, nodded once, and headed downstairs.

The next morning, the two women woke with the morning light and packed sandwiches of peanut butter and jelly from the market. There was a local woman who made the butter and sugary jam spread every year and provided her stock to the local market to share with her neighbors. It was by far the best sandwich of its kind that Edith had ever tasted. They bit into the sandwiches about two hours into the drive. As they passed the sign for Attleborough Massachusetts, she knew that they were approaching her former home shortly.

Edith had driven to her home from Massachusetts frequently with her parents. She had the drive memorized. They had loved to visit Capron Park. Her parents were not adventurous, but they were in love with the trees and the landscapes. They liked to escape the city setting and find peace in the thick grass of the uncut meadows. Her father desperately loved the smell of wildflowers in the summer and the dank smell of rain on decaying leaves in the fall. A love she had never shared with him while he was alive. Now as the smells hit her nostrils, she found her head raised to pull it in. A way to connect to him, the only way she could now.

Cora pulled up to the address that Edith had provided: Agatha's house. Edith looked at the house like a memory from another life. Then she turned her head towards the home that used to be her own. The pain hit her like a ton of bricks. In the front yard of her home was a small child playing with a puppy. The girl looked no older than four, and the puppy resembled a beagle. His long flapping ears flopped up and down as she taunted him with a tiny red ball . In the doorway she could see a woman smiling sweetly at the girl. Behind her was a man, the girl's father, presumably. The woman reached her hand up to touch his hand that rested upon her opposite shoulder. They admired the scene of the girl and her first love. He gently kissed her head; wrapped his arms around her waist. The little girl's glowing auburn hair was held back in a beautiful yellow butterfly pin. She laughed as the puppy licked her face. His force knocked her to the ground, and they played together there.

"Are you ok?" Cora asked. She put her hand on her shoulder. Edith snapped out of it and looked back to her aunt with a sweet reassuring smile.

"Yeah, I'm ok." She turned back to the yard and found the scene had changed. The grass was not cut the way her father would have done. The fence had needed painting and had been left unattended. The shutters were no longer gray but green. The front door was not adorned with the wreath her father made out of a vine that had been creeping up the shed wall. He had a way of taking something destructive and giving it purpose.

The puppy had been named Grover. He was a good dog. His life had been cut tragically short when he escaped from the yard one day. She had been at school when it happened. Her parents struggled to tell her without crying. She thought at the time that there could be nothing worse than losing him. How had she been wrong?

"Thank you. I'll see if Agatha is home."

"Ok hun, I'll be back in an hour if that works for you?" she gripped the steering wheel.

"That's fine, thank you for doing this." Edith stepped out of the car and closed the door gently. Her finger tips touch the window in an affectionate way to say how much she appreciated Aunt Cora's concern and thoughtfulness. The gesture was all that she could manage at the moment.

The door was decorated with a bright forsythia wreath. The same wreath that Agatha had hung on her door for the last ten summers. She had a wreath for every season, but the summer wreath was by far Edith's favorite.

Somehow aware of what she was wearing, she looked down to her outfit. Bell bottom pants and a striped cotton ribbed shirt of purple and cream, and black Mary Janes. She wanted to look her best. The last thing she wanted was for Agatha to be worrying about her. Edith pushed her finger into the button adjacent to the door and stepped back.

From the other side of the house she could hear the heavy metal chair push back and she knew Agatha was making her way over to the front of the house. A song by Etta James crooned in the background, Agatha's favorite. The door opened and an old woman appeared in the doorway. Edith found it almost hard to recognize her. Agatha had aged far more than she expected in the years she had been gone. Her face was sallow. She was thinning and her hair had not been permed recently. There were three things she would always rely on with Agatha. Her nails were always painted a nude color. She felt that nude was the only acceptable color for a lady; anyone bold enough to wear red was most likely a lady of the night and she wasn't about to ruin her reputation. Her kind elderly neighbor would get a perm every month to keep her curls intact, and she would dye it blonde so that she wouldn't appear to be her true age. After you turn eighty, there's no fooling anyone, but Edith wasn't about to tell her that.

"Edith?" Agatha squinted her eyes and then lifted her glasses up on her face. They were still attached to the pearl-beaded string that wrapped around her neck. She was famous for losing her glass.

Edith hunted for words to tell Agatha how glad she was to see her, but none would come. She stood mutely for a moment before she managed to speak.

"Hello Agatha." She smiled, and hugged her dear friend and former neighbor with veracity. A need for connection and affection had long been eating at her. What she desperately wanted was to embrace her mother, but her neighbor, as close to a grandmother she would ever have, was a close second.

Cora was a kind woman, but she had not known Edith before the accident. She had not shared in the many bumps and bruises throughout her childhood. Agatha had mended their fences, their literal fences when she found out about Grover. She had a company come out to secure the fence that they shared. She had felt responsible for his escape, even though no one had known about the weak spot in the fence that sealed his fate.. He was only four years old and he could have lived another ten years. It had hit Agatha as hard as the family she had become so attached to.

Agatha escorted her neighbor, this once little girl who now emanated the beauty of a young woman into the kitchen. Edith had grown a good four inches in the two years she had been away.

"How are you?" Agatha reached across the small round formica table to reach Edith's hands. Her transparent skin had even more spots exposed, and the veins protrude through her soft wrinkles. The nude nail polish was missing and the yellow cracked carotene was left.

Edith felt responsible for the degradation of her sweet elderly neighbor. If she had been living next door, she would have been looking after Agatha all this time. Her parents would stop over with quiche and invite her to dinner on Sunday. Now Agatha stayed in the back of her house, trying to find company in the animals that perched on the many bird feeders and the porcelain bird bath.

The porch was Agatha's favorite place to be during the summer. The back porch had been put on by her husband, ten years after they built the house. They would sit out here for hours in their rocking chairs. After he passed she put his chair in the basement, moved her rocker to the spare room and replaced the set with the table they sat at presently. It was hard for Edith to grasp, replacing items that meant so much to her with things of very little value, based on its current condition. The table was beautiful as the day Agatha's husband made it, still as wobbly too. She put down her hands on the surface. After all he was a serviceman, not a carpenter.

Edith finally looked up at Agatha's face, her warm wrinkles were now drawn with concern. "I'm ok, my aunt has been very kind to me."

"And your uncle..." She looked at Edith to ask his name.

"Ansel, yes, he is also very nice, but quiet most of the time. The whole house is quiet, generally. I miss the music to be honest. I miss the dancing in the kitchen. I miss the Sunday dinners with you." She looked down and away from the conversation.

"I miss them too." Agatha held her hands together. Edith wasn't sure if that was quite honest. The sound of music pouring in through her window from across the yard. Her parents dancing, gazing into each other's eyes, the aroma of stuffed chicken that filled the whole house. Even her father and mother were fighting over who got to try the first piece to "make sure that it's cooked." Perhaps Agatha meant that she missed *them*, Paul and Iris. Both taken from her that day. Two people who were as close to family, a daughter and son, as anyone had ever been.

"I know you do." She reached out and grabbed her hands again. "What shall we do? We have an hour."

"Oh, boy, well, let's go for a drive." Agatha stood up and staggered over to her cane. She caught Edith admiring her stick and snapped back at her.

"Don't give me that look Missy. Just because I require a cane don't mean I can't drive." She grinned and then hobbled over to the hook that held her keys, one for her house and one for her car.

Edith slid into the car.

They crept slowly out of the driveway and turned left, away from the front of the home that Edith dreamed about so desperately at night. She twisted her body around to watch it recede into the distance as they drove out of the street, until she could finally comprehend that it was no longer the place she remembered. It was dark and dreary, lacking the joy that she had felt within its walls. Or perhaps it was just appearing how she felt when she saw it, reflecting her inner heartache for a life lost. Her own life.

She knew where they were heading even before Agatha made the final turn into the gated courtyard. Directly to the right she saw a hearse with a procession parked at the memorial center. The last place that loved ones would share time together before the body was interred.

The car came to a stop and Agatha was the first to get out. She grabbed her cane from the back seat and then stepped around the side of the car and continued to walk onto the freshly cut grass. Edith opened her door and the scent wafted through the air. She knew she was meant to follow her, but she paused for a moment to breathe in the deep fragrant smell. She slowly stepped towards the old woman who had finally stopped. She came around the side of her and held her hand.

Edith held her breath for a long moment before opening her eyes. This was the first time she would lay her eyes on her father's grave and she wanted to remember him the way he had been for just a minute longer. He's there, standing in the doorway in his Sunday best, arms wrapped around her mother's cherry covered cotton dress. He smells her curls and she leans her head into his cheek…

And then Edith opened her eyes.

Chapter 10: Samantha, Spring 1995

A rustling sound came from the living room. Lisa sat at the foot of Samantha's bed. The commotion roused Samantha enough to sit up instead of turning over again. She looked at Lisa, hair tousled.

"What is that racket and why is it waking me up?" she questioned with confusion.

Lisa looked back to her, eyebrows raised "Mom."

"Mom, what do you mean 'Mom'?" Her eyes were squinting still from the light of a sunrise pouring into the room. She grabbed her alarm clock from her bedside table, examining the time "It's 6am. Shouldn't she be passed out from last night right now?"

"Probably, but she's not." Lisa looked back to the door that remained shut. The sound continued on for another five minutes. The girls pressed their back into the wall leaving their feet hanging off the bed, perplexed and frozen in their previous position.

Sam finally spoke "Ok, seriously, what is she doing out there?"

Just as she was about to put her foot down on cold hardwood floors the door flew open. Jessica came in, bright eyed, smiling at her two older sisters, still groggy from the early morning wake up call. "Time to get up, we are packing!"

Lisa looked over at Edith. "Shit, we're moving!"

This wasn't the first time her mother scrambled to pack their things, assuming they were being evicted from their apartment due to late rent. She somehow wasn't aware that her daughters were paying the late rent and the fees that accumulated with it. Eventually, the two girls ended up taking over the bills. Her mother hadn't actually sent over a rent check in a number of years.

The girls would take the checks she'd write a week or two after its due date and would void them. They knew she didn't have the money in the account and they would just add more overage charges against them. The only money that Sam could ever count on her mother having was for that damn coffee can in her bedroom. Every time she caught her mother slipping another fifty into it, it enraged her. They were there scrambling to get the rent, pay the utilities, take care of her daughters and she was tipping herself. Now she was packing again. What had she ever contributed?

"Where are we going now?" Sam asked Jessica. Before Jessica could reply, her mother came walking into the room.

"Get dressed girls, we are heading out in fifteen minutes." She was smiling, alert, and most of all, sober. Both girls' eyes widened in shock. Edith hadn't had a sober moment in months. If she had been, it happened when Sam and Lisa were away. They often would see her slip in and out of the house, early in the morning and late in the evening. The scratched up, pit marked floors were a dead giveaway as she creaked down the hall to her bedroom. They had never known whether she was meeting up with a guy, going to one of her many part-time gigs or if she was joining the circus. After a while, they stopped caring. Why bother wasting your valuable brain power on someone who fails to notice you're alive ninety-five percent of the time?

"Where are we going?" Samantha's face was panicked, disgusted and exhausted all at once.

"We're taking a road trip." Her mother walked over to the girl's dressers and started pulling clothes out of the drawers. "You'll need only a few pairs of pants and shirts, we can make do with that."

Sam turned to see Lisa holding her head in her hands. This was not going to just go away. She leaned over and whispered gently in her ear "Is she having a manic episode?" Lisa shrugged. The girls had always questioned whether their mother was bipolar. Her tendency to switch from sad to happy or angry to spaced out was just expected at this point.

"Wait, where are we going?" she said it a third time with no answer. The fury built up in her throat, her cheeks reddened and she burst out "Edith, look at me!"

Her mother stopped where she stood. Blood rushed to Sam's cheeks in embarrassment. She had called her mother by her first name. Something she had definitely done in front of her sisters, but never directly to her mother. Edith's weakened expression of joy was clearly evidenced by the careless act of her daughter.

"I'm sorry Mom, I didn't mean to."
Apologetic did not begin to describe how
Samantha was feeling now, looking at the joy
leaving her mother's eyes. Edith's smile and
upbeat tempo had left the room. A chill spread
across the bed and her mother looked to the
ground. She took the folded clothes in her hands
and placed them gently atop the bureau.

"We are going to be leaving in fifteen
minutes, please pack your things. I wanted to take
you girls on a trip to somewhere you've never
been. It will be fun."

A certain awkwardness sat between the
two women. Edith looked up and down a
countless number of times, refusing to make eye
contact with Samantha. Finally, and thankfully for
Sam, she left the room, shutting the door quietly
behind her.

"What is the matter with you?" Lisa
whacked her sister's arm with the back of her
hand. "She is trying to do something nice, for the
first time ever, need I remind you, and you just
shit all over her." Her legs slid off the side of the
bed and she walked over briskly to the bureau
where her mother had just laid the pile of clothes
for her to pack. Lisa retrieved a large duffle from
the corner of the room and quickly removed
several library books left inside prior to tucking
her clothes into the bottom. A few essential items
that her mother forgot to gather, most likely for a
sense of privacy were also added to the bag. She
turned to see Sam sitting motionless on the
mattress, having not changed position since her
mother's exit from the room.

"Maybe you could get out of bed and get
ready. I'll see you outside." Lisa clutched her
duffle in her grasp, grabbed the door knob and
exited the room with a bit of force to make a point

As Lisa closed the door, Sam covered her face, dragging her finger-tips down her eyes and continuing over her cheeks in pure exhaustion. She knew she had done something wrong. She had crossed a boundary that no child should ever cross. No matter how much Edith had failed at being a mother, she was making an attempt now to rectify her mistakes and Sam had to try to give her the benefit of the doubt.

She collected the few clothing items set out and added her essential undergarments and hairbrush to the pile. Unable to find a nearby bag to put her clothing into and refusing to once again use a trash bag, she emptied her school bag and placed her belongings inside.

Out in the living room, her mother and three sisters gathered with their packs ready to go. Her mother had also taken a number of items from the refrigerator and stuffed them in the cooler that the girls had purchased for a beach trip the year before. There were even ice cubes in a bag, recently made up for the occasion. Edith was never one to prepare for anything, but it seems she had done something right this time.

"Ok, let's go." Edith waited for all the girls to be in the hallway and then locked up the apartment behind them, like a real mom would. Besides the expected confusion in the moments that had occurred in the last twenty minutes, the girls were slightly intrigued at the prospect of leaving Pawtucket for a few days and spending quality time with their mother.

They got in the car and watched Edith adjust the mirrors, then clasp the steering wheel at two and ten. She seemed to resemble Samantha during her driver's exam the year before. She had been just as nervous as her nearly forty-year-old mom was at this very moment. It had been years since Edith had sat in the driver's seat. She was mainly shoved into the back seat, sprawled out after a bar pick up. It would take the two eldest girls all they had to push her in, and she was not a big woman. Standing at five foot four inches and approximately a hundred and forty pounds, she was generally a petite person. Intoxicated and unable to walk made her a lump for the girls to handle. If the girls failed to answer while calling from the grungy phone booth, she often grabbed a cab or asked for a ride home from whatever stranger was kind enough to oblige her.

This was a welcomed change and a bit nerve wracking for Samantha. She wasn't sure if her mother remembered how to drive. It was, she supposed, like riding a bicycle or having sex, you always remember how to do it again. And Edith, who didn't own a bicycle, was a pro at least at one of those things.

Off they went. They were driving down Newport Avenue and heading for the highway. The windows were opened a bit for some air flow. Sam felt it was refreshing to have the wind blow in her face. The warm air, soft with the fragrance of spring flowers fluttered into her nostrils. A great sense of calm fell over her as she let all the possibility of destination roll away from her mind. They had reached Massachusetts in a matter of minutes, only living a short distance from the border. The girls had each brought a book to read; none of them had ever had any kind of real conversation with their mother. Having the excuse of schoolwork would be far less harsh to explain to her.

Lisa sat in the front with Edith, being the oldest and most prepared to deal with things if they should go awry. Samantha had Jessica sit in the center of her and Theresa. Theresa was without concern and didn't once question where their mother was taking them. She had become a bit awkward in her young age, but neither cared one way or another if she was at home or anywhere else, as long as no one bothered her. She wasn't antisocial in a bad way, she just would rather keep her nose stuck deep into the books that linked her to a better life. In fairness, the books she read and her focus on school made her an exceptional student and artist in her own right. Edith failed to notice the outstanding grades that she earned. Even when they were plastered all over the refrigerator by her two older sisters, she couldn't see what was right in front of her.

The walls to Teresa's room had become a mural. She would spend hours in there, painting every inch of the plaster, the only canvas she had. Jessica would sit on her bed, a notepad in her lap, trying to replicate the images spread out of the wall with a large tin of old, broken crayon stubs. For a seven year old, she was incredibly observant and wished to learn everything she could from her fourteen year old sister.

Theresa didn't mind her little sister tagging along. They had been roommates since Jessica had arrived on this earth. Theresa had changed countless diapers, taught Jessica her ABC's with persistent effort, and even, remarkably, had Jessica tying her shoes by the age of three. For four girls raised in a dysfunctional household, they protected, educated and supported one another as a unit. Edith, this extended and often missing piece that threw itself into the puzzle every so often, was not going to disrupt the well oiled machine that was their quartet.

Theresa caught her little sister studying her every movement, waiting for her to give her what she wanted. Reaching down into her bag, she pulled out a notepad for Jessica. She had packed it knowing full well that Jessica would want to draw like her big sister she admired so dearly. Samantha was proud of her sisters. Learning to figure it out as you went along was not a gift possessed by most children. Lisa had made a phone call to her manager that she would be out today to care for her sick sister. Fortunately, Sam had already scheduled for the day off, so at least missing pay would not be a detriment to their lifestyle for both of them. *Even so,* Sam thought, *this little getaway is sure to be a shit show.*

Spring break was a time for vacationing, it was true, but when had the girls ever had a real vacation? Their vacations were packed with extra shifts or babysitting their siblings. Samantha spent her free moments thinking about Adam. He was due to come back to Rhode Island in the next few days. Sam had become concerned that after their altercation in the park last fall that letter writing was not going to fill in that extensive divide between awkward and enjoyable conversation. He had planned to make his way back to Rhode Island as soon as he was able to, but previous obligations and the success of his novels kept him pursuing his dreams. At least until his girlfriend was out of high school. Only a year and a half to go and she would join him on his travels. He would be graduating by mail. The fascination of homeschooling in the midst of book tours and publicity stunts kept wild-eyed, seventeen-year-old Sam occupied. Thinking of the future was not all joyful though.

Lisa was going to be home until mid-August and then she'd move into the dorms at U.R.I. Perhaps this would be a wake up call for her mom. Edith hadn't been a major part of any of their lives since their infancy. Now her eldest daughter was going off to college and wouldn't be around much anymore. The following year, her *next* eldest daughter would go on to the next phase of *her* life.

Sam sat back in her seat, still looking down at the book she had brought, The Grapes of Wrath. She was a dedicated reader, but her eyes only blankly stared at the words on the page, trying to read them was useless. She had now focused her mind on the idea that her mother had an epiphany and wanted to fix her life, before it was too late. Sam gawked at her mother, driving in silence. The hair, unlike most days, was not as shaggy but generally clean and pulled back neatly. The sun poured in the driver's side window, sliding through the small dark red strands sticking out of the top of her head. Samantha had the same color hair as her mother. Aside from Theresa, she was the only other sister to get her mother's hair and complexion.

Examining her mother's appearance made her turn her glance to Lisa. While they shared the same skin tone, her hair was far thicker. A shade of rich chocolate with thin auburn highlights scattered between them. Lisa never had the chance to meet him. Edith once made up a story about him to satisfy her daughter's curiosity. She stated that the court had decided he would be allowed to negate his responsibilities to his daughter. In other words, he gave up his parental rights and went to Edith directly to deliver the paperwork. She said she'd felt it was a kindness . He was not choosing to abandon, he was doing it because it was the right thing to do. The story was elaborate, dramatic as a Hallmark movie. *She gave him a soft kiss, almost as though she loved him and then slowly shut the door behind him as he walked down the stairs and out of their lives. That would be the only time Edith fell in love.*

Until she got knocked up again a few months later. Edith should have been an actress.

Sam roused herself from the thoughts running through her head. They had been driving for hours at this point. The tree lines were growing thicker and the road narrowed to a single lane. Suddenly they saw a sign that made them all turn their heads. "Welcome to New Hampshire."

Lisa turned to look back at Samantha. The two girls were the only ones who knew anything really about their mother. She spoke to all of them on the anniversary of her fathers death in a drunken slur about the night he died, true, but had only mentioned New Hampshire to Lisa and Samantha, on New Year's Eve a little over two years ago.

They had all been sitting on the couch watching the MTV live countdown, much like they had the last five years. Her mother had arrived around eleven, probably to find a partner to make out with as the lights lit up "1993". The two younger girls had already fallen asleep on the couch. Theresa's party hat tipping off the side of her head, while Jessica slept on the floor, kazoo still sticking to her lower lip. The candy and popcorn had been a great idea to help them pass out. Now if they could only figure out how to get their mother to pass out, hoping to avoid her waking up her younger daughters. Instead, Edith reeking of cheap wine and cigarettes came over to them, stumbling as she went.

"Hey girls." She giggled as she nearly tripped over her own feet again. She sat down on the couch next to Theresa who failed to wake up at the spring of the seat as her mother plopped down gracefully. Lisa who sat in the adjacent chair that she had brought over from the dining room looked across at Samantha. She had taken the other side of the couch, consistently dealing with Theresa's feet kicking her throughout the last hour.

"Hello," they both responded with less enthusiasm than their mother had planned.

Her expression changed from smiling to serious.

"You know,I knew of a place just like this when I was a girl."

Lisa met eyes with Samantha, waiting for the origins of Edith to return to the stage. They already had the tales of her father at Christmas, perhaps they would now get a New Year's story to hear at the dropping of every ball until they moved out.

"I was sent up there to live with my aunt and uncle. It was nothing like it is here, while they had similar furniture, the surroundings were in contrast so different. It's beautiful in New Hampshire. So quiet compared to this place. No ambulances, no cop cars, no drug deals going down outside out the front door. Eaton was something." She then got up and stumbled into her bedroom and shut the door. Within minutes they could hear her snoring loud as a truck.

Now three years later they were driving down backroads with little knowledge of what to expect. The tree leaves had nearly blossomed and the sweet smell of spring flora popping up from the ground caused Edith to inhale deeply. They all put the windows down and listened for the sound of birds.

"A deer!" Jessica screamed, pointing off into a clearing beside the road. She had never seen one. None of the girls had ever seen a live deer. Lisa had seen dead deer on the side of the road from time to time, but never alive and in person.

Their mother didn't stop for the girls to gaze. She had a plan and it wouldn't be altered. Instead they all closed their eyes and took in the smells and sounds to themselves.

Gravel roads quickly ran under their tires and the bumps halted their peaceful mindsets abruptly. After a ten minute ride up a winding road, they came to a driveway. Edith spun the steering wheel and turned up. The driveway was up on a steep hill, where they found a beautiful cabin perched atop. The house was something out of a movie, to the girls, a palace. They had never seen a house like this. They all got out cautiously to explore the yard. Pine trees surrounded the house laced with gray and white birch trees and a dozen or so of maple. In the backyard stood a work shed and a firepit charred from years of use.

Samantha stopped a moment and looked to Lisa again whispering, "Whose house is this?"

Her mother turned her head to her daughter. She had been listening. She seemed alert, and happier than any of the girls had ever seen her.

"This was my aunt and uncle's home. This is where I was raised as a teenager."

"Was? Are we trespassing, could we get shot for this?" Sam looked around panicking.

"No, we are not trespassing." She looked back at the house and closed her eyes. As though she was trying to absorb everything good about the times she had there.

"Okay, then who's house is this now?" Samantha looked at her mother, needing answers.

"It's mine."

Chapter 11: Edith, Fall 1971

Crunch, screech, crunch, screech. Then suddenly a long horn blared as Edith slammed her head down on the steering wheel.

"Oh, come on!"

"I don't care what Ansel tells you, cars are not people and they will not talk back." Cora smiled and pulled the parking brake. "Listen, everyone struggles when they learn to drive for the first time, completely normal, if you ask me."

"I'm not struggling, or at least I wouldn't be struggling, if I wasn't working with a 1930's hunk of junk that Uncle Ansel felt I should start with for my *first* vehicle." She squinted her eyes, glaring over at her Aunt with a snarky expression. "He's at the window inside enjoying this, isn't he?"

She leaned forward and peeked out the windshield to see if her uncle was looking out the living room with a smirk on his face. Fortunately, for his sake, he was nowhere to be seen.

"Your uncle is not punishing you, Edith, I think you know that by now." Cora closed her eyes for a moment and then after a long smooth exhale she opened them up again. Edith could see that her Aunt wasn't feeling well.

"Are you all right?" Edith laid her hand gently on her aunt's shoulder.

"Oh, I'll be right as rain. The weather lately has not been good for my aging bones, you know."

"Well why don't you go and have a lay-down and we can pick this up tomorrow."

"I think I will take you up on that offer, thank you." She smiled sweetly at Edith, touching her cheek with the edge of her fingers, almost like a mother to a daughter. After the moment of adoration she clicked open the door of the old truck and shut it forcefully behind her with a clunking thud. Edith watched her as she walked slowly up the steps. Her Aunt was not an elderly woman, no more than a few years past fifty, but she walked into that house like she was frail and tired. Perhaps she had a virus and it was hitting her harder than she thought. After a few minutes collecting her frustrations in her seventh attempt at driving Ansel's truck, Edith went inside and looked around for her uncle. Just then, the phone rang. She lifted the receiver and put it to her ear.

"Hello?"

"Hey Edith, it's Cindy. You want to catch a flick tonight?" A perky and rather ditzy voice came through the phone like a mouse. The phone was as old as her aunt Edith thought. The service was ancient, probably original to the turn of the century cabin. If she had any more money, she would have helped them get a new one. But no one is in dire want of a new piece of technology in her neck of the woods. A good few gentlemen down at Pete's Pickle Jar would love it if everyone would go back to letter writing.

Cindy was never going to be that kind of girl. She was all about the latest crazes in gadgets. She was one of the first girls to get a new radio in her car, the second person Edith ever met to get an A track installed in her father's Buick. Aside from car radios, she always had the latest model of record player and speaker systems. Her family came from a long line of musicians and were a bit of an outside group to live in New Hampshire. They had relocated to the green hillsides about a year ago from Camden, New Jersey. A place that none of the good folks of Eaton had ever heard of before. They also had never seen a girl like Cindy before. Her long hair, short skirts and tie dye shirts gave them all a run for their money.

Edith was from a city, so it was a little less shocking for her. Even though it had been over two years since she lived in Pawtucket, she still remembered the strong mix of backgrounds, heritages and styles ranging from rock to jock. Her Aunt was not a local from birth, but had lived there long enough to understand that it was difficult for outsiders to fit in; especially when they were so forward-thinking that the rest of the community seemed so backwards.

"That would be nice, let me just go ask Cora really quick, I'll be right back." Edith put the phone down on the end table by the sofa. Slowly she pushed open the heavy oak door of her aunt's bedroom and peeked her head in to look. The room was dark, and it was quiet even though Cora had just come inside so she must have fallen asleep quickly.

Edith closed the door behind her slowly, not wanting to disturb her aunt, and picked up the phone again, "My aunt's asleep, let me just ask my uncle if he will drive me into town. I doubt he feels comfortable with me driving his car at this point. Maybe a few more driving lessons with

'Old Reliable.'" Cindy was closer to the theater than Ansel and Cora's home, so it would be far more feasible for them to meet in town.

"Old Reliable?" Cindy questioned. Even through the phone, Edith could tell that Cindy was confused.

"It's what he calls the beat up old hunk of junk that he gave me to learn driving on," she laughed, "I doubt it would even make it to town without a tire falling off."

"Well, let's hope he will give you a ride. If he says no then give me a call back, otherwise I will meet you for the show at seven."

Luckily for Edith, Ansel enjoyed time to himself and was more than happy to have his niece out of the house for a few hours.

"Thank you Uncle Ansel, I know it's not convenient for you to take me to town. We are going to grab a bite to eat after the flick, so you don't have to worry about picking me up. Cindy rang back right before we left and said her mom would be willing to drop me back off after." Ansel kept his eyes on the road the entirety of the trip into town. It was only a thirty minute ride, but in silence it dragged it out to what felt like hours. He simply nodded his head in acknowledgment.

Edith took the hint and remained silent for the rest of the ride. They pulled up to the mini mall and she hopped out of the truck. Before she shut the door, she looked back to her uncle. "I hope you know, I appreciate everything that you and Aunt Cora have done for me."

He turned his head and nodded at her warmly. Edith guessed that was his way of saying "you're welcome" in his own quiet way.

Cindy rushed over in her pleated red skirt, white knee socks and white button down sweater.

Her hair was tied back in some sort of bow. It was a different look on her for sure. Edith was home-schooled for the first year she had lived with her aunt and uncle. They had assumed that it would be a temporary solution and that the situation would fix itself. But when her mother didn't recover, they decided it would be best to enroll Edith into the local high school. The education was a bit too much for Cora, Ansel and their limited education to keep up with.

Edith kept to herself at first. She wasn't a social butterfly, but also didn't shy away from people when they showed genuine kindness to her. Cindy was the first person to approach her at the school. She had begun at the school only a few weeks prior and somehow was not shy at all. Having someone who could move to a new state and thrust herself into a high school setting with no fear was just the kind of person that Edith needed to make her transition a smooth one. At first it was just the two of them at the lunch table together.

A few weeks later, Cindy added Ronnie and Pennie to the mix. They were cousins and their families had lived near to North Conway for the last two hundred years. They were "old blood" as the townies called them. While they had more money than most of the families in town, they were also the most friendly and humble of the kids at school. They lived in a large historic neighborhood nestled up in the mountains. Their windows looked out on the rolling hills with snow capped peaks in winter, cascading colors in fall and rushing waterfalls in summer. The spring was Ronnie's favorite season. He was a naturalist and loved observing the great thaw, the bloom of wildflowers, and wildlife returning to live in the wooded mountains. While Pennie's father was the head of the railroad commission, her uncle,

Ronnie's father, was the Saco District Ranger for the White Mountain National Forest in Conway.

Having connections that were so important to the culture of New Hampshire gave the newbies an edge, and helped in their assimilation to a more rural environment, now that they were no longer living in the city. Edith took well enough to the changes, but Cindy struggled from time to time as the locals took issue with how she dressed. She was also a bit of a rebel. The great female empowerment movement was running rampant in many parts of the US, and Cindy was ready to hop aboard .

It was more evident than ever that night, as she showed up to the film wearing a white sweater and absolutely no bra. Edith's eyes lit up in extreme surprise at the sight of her erect nipple poking through the cotton knit sweater her friend had decided to wear out that evening. She hoped and prayed that her uncle somehow missed seeing it.

Ronnie on the other hand had no qualms whatsoever with Cindy's radical wardrobe choices. Pennie, while not a prude, was a bit cautious about how Cindy's choice in outfit would affect how people looked at them as a group of friends. Pennie applied her balled up fist to her mouth and began to cough noticeably enough for Cindy to look up at her. Pennie tilted her head down referring to her hard poking nipples standing in attention in the cold brisk air of the fall. Cindy looked down and then back up at Pennie, completely unaware of what might be the issue.

Pennie whispered. "Your top is, I mean your, well you know what I mean."

Cindy looked down at her top again. "Nope, I have no idea. Wait, you don't like my sweater?"

Edith leaned over to whisper into Cindy's ear, "Your nipples are hard and poking out of your *white* sweater."

Cindy looked down at her sweater again. "Oh, I know." She laughed, "I thought you saw a stain or something on it." She rolled her eyes and walked into the theater.

Edith looked at Pennie and they both laughed out loud. "Well, ok then." Edith held the door open for Pennie and then Ronnie held the door open for Edith as they went to find seats for four. Ronnie looked at Edith. "I was going to grab popcorn, did you want something?"

Her face curled into a smile and she nodded appreciatively to him, then she then blushed at the two girls sitting to her right. "What?" Her face dropped the smile.

"What do you mean, what?" Cindy looked at Pennie. "Did you see it?"

"See what?" Edith stroked her fingers through her hair and smoothed out her shirt.

"You like him and he for sure likes you," Cindy said, smiling wryly at Edith.

"That's ridiculous." Edith rolled her eyes and sat back in her seat with her arms folded across her chest.

"I don't know what planet you're on, but on this one, that is called flirting, Edith." Pennie looked from Edith to Cindy and back to Edith.

"Yep, he's sweet on you." Cindy agreed with a massive smirk.

"Definitely not." Edith pulled her eyes brows together making a doubtful expression. "He doesn't look at me like that." She shook her head and then dove into her pocketbook to pull out a tube of lip balm. "I mean, we're just friends."

"Sure you are, and I have a bra on right now."

The three girls erupted in laughter. Ronnie returned to his seat with a big bucket of popcorn. A hush fell over the girls, they snickered trying to keep in the hysterics.

He sat down and gawked at the girls, whose faces were red, barely withholding their urge to lose it.

"What did I miss?" The girls blew up in laughter again.

Edith caught her breath for a moment. "Oh, it's nothing, girl stuff." She smiled at Ronnie. "Thank you for getting the popcorn."

"Anytime." He smiled back and slipped a piece of hot popped corn into his mouth. She never noticed how smooth his lips were before as he licked the kernel saturated in butter. Absent-mindedly, she started putting the pieces into her mouth and chewed each bite delicately, wanting to appear attractive, or better yet, sexy. Ronnie caught her staring at him and turned his head to face her.

"What's wrong?" He grabbed a napkin and wiped his mouth "Do I have something in my teeth?"

Edith released a small, sweet giggle. "No, I just…" She looked at him in a different way than she had ever done previously. Maybe the girls were right and she had been unconsciously flirting with him this entire time. Perhaps they had both been flirting and it was finally time to address it. Edith had never been in a relationship before and was searching for one now either. Her life was up in the air and unpredictable. Even though it had been over two years since she had left home, she knew that one day her mother may recover enough to come and get her. To become too attached to where she lived or the people she spent all her time with seemed foolish.

At the same time, she had been stuck in this cavernous, empty state for far too long and it was becoming stifling, to not have any relationships with people her own age during such a crucial part of growing up. What if it took years more before her mother came out of the time loop in which her father was still to arrive, just having stepped out for milk and eggs? What if she was never able to come back from this? At some point Edith was going to have to return to something that resembled a normal life.

She turned her head back to the screen, the movie was starting, no time to start a crucial conversation. Cindy nudged her with her elbow and Edith turned to see her scraping her to index fingers together implying that Edith and Ronnie were behaving naughty. Edith smiled and rolled her eyes once more before returning them to the screen for the remainder of the film.

The film ended and the lights came on. The four teens got up from their seats and corralled out of the bustling small town theater, stepping across the sticky floor before exiting into the parking lot at the back of the building. They spent their dinner at the small cafe discussing the film and laughing between sips of milkshake and salted crispy French fries. As night fell, they finished up the last overcooked potato stick, paid the tab and hugged goodbye. It was time to go home.

"My mom said she would be here to pick us up at 9, which is about ten minutes from now."

"I brought my car." Ronnie thumbed over to the parking space.

"Oh, well I can give Pen a ride home if you want to drop off Edith?" Cindy nudged Edith to catch her drift.

"I mean, that would be fine with me." Edith spoke up quickly to agree with Cindy's suggestion.

"Yeah, my house is far out of the way from Edith's and it would be inconvenient for Cindy's mom to have to drive two people in the opposite direction." Pennie nodded approvingly.

"Yeah, of course." Ronnie smiled and lifted his arm to escort Edith to his car. The two looked at one another and then back at Cindy and Pennie. The walk to his car was no more than a hundred feet, but the thoughts running through Edith's head made it feel like a full mile. She got into his new Chevy truck and breathed in the fresh leather seats. The pickup was sage green with a long white stripe that wrapped around the exterior. The leather seats were tan and hand stitched. It was beneficial having a wealthy father to fall back on. He never wanted for much, but it didn't stop him from behaving like an absolute gentleman every moment of the day.

The drive at first was quiet. The ceiling wasn't the only thing that hung over her head. The idea that the two girls had planted in Edith's head had her spinning. Was she over-exaggerating? Were they just friends and she was making a mountain out of a molehill? Did he think of her as a friend, or more like a sister? She wondered with panic, did he already have a girlfriend and the whole thing they felt for one another was wrong? The countless scenarios plunged deep into Edith's psyche, making her huff a bit in exhaustion.

"Everything ok?" He turned his head briefly to make eye contact. He seemed serious and concerned about her.

"Yeah, of course, sorry." She screwed up her face to the ceiling fixing her eyes up, rather than shutting them tight. "The girls just said something at the theater that was absolutely preposterous."

"Oh yeah, what was that?" Ronnie was now intrigued, he smiled and nudged her with his elbow.

"Now you're making fun of me." She looked out the window into the blackness. The only thing visible down the long winding dark dirt road was the eyes of the wildlife shining back at their headlight, stunned and as stiff as the trees they lived amongst.

"I am not, seriously, what did they say?"

Edith smiled at him and then returned her eyes to her fingers that played with the tassel on her purse.

"They implied something about you and I," gliding her hand through the air between the two of them.

"Implied? Well now I have to hear it." He laughed and it made Edith look at him before looking once again at the ceiling and delivering the final sentence.

"They said that we, you know." Her hand danced back and forth like it was on a seesaw.

"Nope, can't say I do. Guess you're going to have to tell me."

He was obviously playing hard to get at this point. She had never noticed how much he flirted with her. Edith wasn't even sure she had the experience of flirting before this moment. She had seen it on the television before. In programs her aunt would watch when Ansel went out to work in the shed, but never had the personal experience herself until this moment.

"Well your cousin and Cindy said that we looked like we liked each other." She was now shaking her head again feeling silly for having said it.

"Oh." Ronnie was less humored by the final comment.

Oh crap, now she had done it. He hadn't been flirting and it was all in the two mischievous meddling girl's heads. Who was going to speak next was the real question?

The ride back to Edith's house from that point on was a quiet one for sure. She heard every pebble that ricocheted off the undercarriage of the truck. If only the radio had been on. Should Edith turn on the radio? Was it rude to mess with someone else's radio? What was she supposed to do, ride back to the house in absolute silence? Granted it was only another five minutes before they approached the dirt hill leading up to the cabin. She was going to do it. Her hand reached for the tuner, but then suddenly she changed her mind and put it down. Ronnie saw this and lifted his hand to turn on the radio. The situation was growing beyond uncomfortable and while the conversation had fallen flat, his manners hadn't. Static rolled in and as it cleared the sound of piano keys came through. Within a moment the words *"It's a little bit funny, this feeling inside. I'm not one of those who can easily hide. I don't have much money, but, boy if I did. I'd buy a big house where we both could live."*

Ronnie looked at Edith and then back at the road. "You can change it if you want."

"No, I like Elton John, we can keep it on." She nodded her head approvingly.

"Ok." Ronnie followed suit, also nodding his head. His hands were clammy on the steering wheel, he released it and regripped it several times, hoping that Edith wouldn't notice how he started to perspire, contradictory to the crisp dank weather of a New Hampshire Fall.

The two of them both sat there quietly for the remainder of the ride, listening to the wild artist sing about the passion for his love. Edith's driveway came sooner than expected and they began to climb the hill. After a short distance he pulled over.

"You can pull up a bit further, they won't be going out for the rest of the night." Edith pointed to an open area at the top of the driveway, highlighted by the single outdoor lamppost her uncle had installed at the beginning of spring.

"I know, I just wanted to finish our conversation from earlier." He put the truck in park and turned in his seat to face her.

"I'm sorry, I shouldn't have even mentioned it. I didn't mean to make things awkward between us. I promise I will never mention it again."

"No, it's not that, it's just..." Ronnie looked from her eyes to her mouth and leaned in to kiss her. There was no denying it; Edith was kissing him back. A sweet first kiss, and then more kisses that had them both falling deeply into something only a teen could appreciate: appreciate and then someday forget when life becomes far more complicated than a simple drive home from a movie. Their lips continued, entangled while the words of the radio drifted sweetly in and out of their ears. The two stayed parked there, far enough down the drive to remain unknown to her aunt and uncle. Resting under the autumn moon, lost in their perfect little moment together.

I hope you don't mind, I hope you don't mind, that I put down in words, how wonderful life is now you're in the world.

Chapter 12: Samantha, Spring 1995

Samantha's eyes scrolled across the exterior of the log home. She was transfixed on the words still ringing in her ear. *It's mine.* How long had her mother kept this a secret from her daughters? A secret so big that it took up over fourteen hundred square feet, and acres of land. A secret so big that it could have changed their lives and helped them out of the armpit that she had them living. It's not that Pawtucket wasn't her lifelong home, but it hadn't been all that she dreamed about. How wonderful would it have been to grow up in a place where the sound of ambulances were replaced by the cheerful chirp of a nearby robin? Where the hum of a broken down heater that the landlord often refused to fix over the last five years was replaced by the crackle of a new built fire in a seven foot granite fireplace?

Sure, Samantha thought, *What kid would want to grow up here when they could grow up worrying about dark nights and creepy alley ways, pollution and trash covering the streets? What kind of person would want to live here when they could have the trauma of gang violence and corrupt government officials making it safe for criminals to continue their acts of drug trafficking as long as they got the cut they wanted?*

She may have been a young girl, but she wasn't dumb. *This was a great surprise, Mom*, she thought sarcastically to herself. Samantha felt her anger boiling like a kettle about to blow.

"I'm sorry, but are you kidding me?" Samantha screamed. She threw her hands down in rage, then raised them to pull her fingers hard through her tied back hair.

Her mother turned suddenly, surprised by the reaction. It had not been the one she had expected at all. The other girls stopped where they were. They had all been smiling, looking around the yard, studying the space that their mother had just announced may be their new home. A bit of hope, a tiny scrap of joy had finally come into their life, and then entered their sister who couldn't accept that something good had finally come to fruition. Their smiles turned to frustration and bitterness. For the first time, it was not their mother but their sister who had pulled the rug out from underneath their dream sequence. Theresa and Jessica wandered towards the back of the house.

She hadn't thought for a minute how this would affect them, how they would react. This home was life altering and it would make their lives different, better. The bursting out in rage over something she had not yet fully comprehended was absolutely unacceptable, but the thought of pushing it back down inside was far too difficult a task to do now that Pandora's box had been opened.

"I'm sorry, ok?" She looked at Lisato apologize, avoiding eye contact with her mother who she brushed past hastily to join her sisters in the backyard. Edith stood there a moment. Samantha looked back to see her mother close her eyes and then whisper something. What did she think she was doing? Who was she talking to? Was she praying? Her mother was not a religious woman, and had never raised them to be either. What was she up to? Was this even her house, or was she on something?

Sam turned the corner with the two girls slightly ahead of her and walked up to grab Jessica's hand. She cuddled affectionately against Sam's arm. Forgiveness was always simple with her: she was too young to feel any true resentment towards her mother. Sam gave her five years to catch up to the rest of them.

The grass had been overgrown around the house. It was almost as though the house had been empty for a while. The shed was locked up, but the leaves had piled up in one single bunch. Someone had started a task and never finished it, but who?

The girls circled back to the front of the house, where Edith was waiting, arms crossed, for the interrogation she knew would be coming.

"Mom, who lived here?" Lisa finally asked the question that everyone had been dying to know, but only she was brave enough to ask.

"My Aunt Cora and Uncle Ansel." She looked down at her feet and waited for the next question.

"I have never heard of any such people." Samantha said in a snotty combative manner. The vindication in her voice displayed her fierce feeling for her mother's ability to come up with lie after lie. "When did they come about? Where are they now?"

"Dead." Edith stood there staring at her daughter with a tightly closed mouth.

"Sam." Lisa tried to stop her sister; enough was enough.

"Oh dead, that's convenient." She could feel the burning rising up her neck from her heaving chest.

"Sam!" Lisa walked in front of her.

Sam looked up at her sister, a girl nearly three inches taller than her, then walked away. The conversation was over.

Lisa turned to look at her mother. Tears were in her eyes for the first time in Lisa's life. Her mother was many things, but rarely an emotional person. Her emotions were only expressed in drunken stories. Never once though did she share a story about this couple that she apparently had a history with. Why not share it before now?

Edith turned and walked back to the front door where she pulled out a key chain. It was faded bronze and had a tiny carved wooden bear on it. She pushed the key into the lock and with a click turned it to open.

The rush of stale air as she pushed open the front door for the first time in eighteen years was enough to take her breath away. The smells of her former life hit her. Burnt oak logs sparked the smell of bacon crisping in their cast iron pan on the stove. Hickory and cinnamon brought her mind to the days she spent cutting red berry bushes to make wreaths for Christmas. It was all so easy to slip back into.

Sam and Lisa followed her in first, making sure it was safe for their younger sisters to enter this place they had never set eyes on before, then Jessica and Theresa were allowed to enter. Both of their mouths fell open. They had never seen a place so big and exquisite. Living in the city had given them a false sense of reality. They had only known life the way it had been presented to them.

Now they could truly start to dream about what their lives could be, here in this place.

Her mother turned to Sam and spoke quietly, "I would like us to move here."

Sam didn't know what to say. She didn't make eye contact. for a long moment she studied the interior of this architectural marvel. The banisters were all smooth and hand-carved. The countertops were thick butcher block surfaces and every fixture was coated in seasoned copper. It was as though the entire home had been built from scratch.

"Someone made this by hand, didn't they?" Sam finally returned her eyes to her mother for a brief moment and then back to the fireplace that had her entranced.

"Yes, my uncle Ansel, *your* uncle Ansel." The words made Sam snap her eyes back.

"He wasn't *my* uncle." Her own shrillness made Sam shudder. "I never met the man, you made sure we never met him or our aunt. We had no one."

"Sam, I—"

Sam cut her off "No, I'm good without this fantasy. You can move up here and raise your daughters on your own. Lisa is going to college in a few months and I will figure out somewhere to go until I graduate next year. This is not my home and it won't be."

"I felt the same way once." Edith looked at her daughter with begging eyes and gently raised her hands to place them on her enraged daughter's arms, hoping that her sincerity would bring Sam down to see her mother was willing to try to do what she couldn't before. Unfortunately, it was far too late for Sam.

She brushed her hand away and stormed out the door, letting the screen door slam behind her.

Lisa said gently, "Mom, it's a great house. She is right about one thing, though, I won't be here next year. I will be gone after graduation next month. I got into a dorm on campus and picked up a summer job at the clam shack. I think you are doing the right thing for Theresa and Jess though. I'm happy for you and for them. I just don't think Sam will come around, not at least for a while."

Her mother looked to her feet slowly kicking the mud-ridden thatched rug at the door and nodded in understanding.

"Theresa, what do you think?" her mother asked her, praying she would have a response that she could live with.

"As long as I have a place for my books, I couldn't care less where we live."

Her mother smiled and released a small controlled laugh. The thought of Sam never coming back to her was a tough pill to swallow.

"Why don't you go upstairs and check out the bedrooms. My room was the one all the way down the hall to the right."

Theresa and Jessica began up the stairs. Jessica stopped and said, "Where will we sleep?"

"My room is down here next to the fireplace and you and Jessica can pick from one of the three rooms up there."

"Wait, we get a room to ourselves?" This was an idea that the girls had never expected to hear.

"Yes, you do. I think you waited long enough." The girls looked at one another and scrambled up the stairs to pick out their new bedrooms. A space where they could start to plan out their new life, in their new home, with apparently their new mother.

Lisa studied her mother. She appeared a far different person than Lisa had ever known her to be. A smile spread across Edith's face. She was happy.

"So, what happened, exactly?"

Her mother looked at Lisa with questioning eyes. "What do you mean?"

"How come we never knew of this place, or your aunt, or your uncle. If this was such a wonderful place to grow up, how come you never mentioned it to us, not even once?"

Edith looked at her eldest daughter. A girl who had become a woman right in front of her eyes at that moment. With poise and control over her mind and emotions. Who had raised her to be such a marvelous person? She knew that she had not taken part in that process, and she felt only shame for it. The truth was more than she could summon the words to tell. The absolutely god-awful reason she had not come back was worse than that. There was a lot to be ashamed of; there was a lot to be thankful for.

Edith knew all this and still looked at her beautiful daughter who desperately sought the answers that her mother had failed to provide these many years. The years that Lisa and her sister were left to struggle and figure out life, raise their sisters and navigate a world that they genuinely were not prepared for and feared would only disappoint them. Their mother had given them *that* for sure. She was the epitome of disappointment, but she needed redemption now more than ever as the ghosts surrounded her, beating down on her heavy heart.

C.B. Giesinger

Edith didn't answer Lisa. Walking across the room she stopped at the bookshelf. Bins full of needlepoint kits, drawing pads, and picture frames bursting with contented people. A large oak frame, handmade, was leaning up against the shelf. The picture was old enough to tell a bit of its history. A man and woman smiling at one another, in front of the very house that her children stood in now. The couple's hands clasped together, their smiles uniting their hearts for a lifetime of happiness.

On the next shelf sat another frame. A picture of a young girl. A girl with long auburn hair in a violet blouse during her senior year of high school. Lisa caught her mother's eyes and followed them to the picture. The girl in the photograph was so close to resembling her daughter Samantha that Lisa almost mistook her for her own sister. Lisa had a strong resemblance of her father or so she assumed, having never met him, and barely little characteristic to her mother and her strong features. Sam, on the other hand, had always been in her mothers shadow, both in her eyes and how she lived so fiercely. For a girl who wished to be nothing like her mother, she fell into her footsteps. Instead of lashing out in a drunken daze, she raised her voice and screamed to the heavens.

"Mom, it's you, isn't it?" Lisa stepped over to the shelf and picked up the small cherry wood frame, using her fingertips to gently smooth off the dust caked on the surface.

"Yes." She smiled and took the frame "It was my senior picture."

"Mom, what happened?" Lisa put her hand on her mother's arm and smoothed it down, rubbing it gently in comfort.

Her mother took the frame from her daughter's hands and slid it close to her chest. "I promise I will tell you, just not today." She smiled and kissed the back of Lisa's hands held tightly on her own. Small tears gathered again in the corner of her eyes. "Okay?"

"Okay, mom." Lisa nodded, understanding.

While her mother wished to move them in and start a new chapter, she knew that it would take time to adjust to the confusion and what they may have felt was deception. Reluctantly she changed her plans.

"I think we should wait to stay here when we finally can move in as a family. Let's head home for now." She gave a warm smile with a half truth to her statement. While she wished for this place to become a home, she knew that they would never live together again as a family, like they once had. That blame would inevitably fall on her.

The girls piled back into the car where Sam waited patiently for them to return to her previous life. Their vehicle was silent the entire way home. The two youngest girls read their books while Lisa listened to the radio, tapping her fingers on the passenger door. Sam stared out the window, following the tree lines that blurred as they passed them. The world was spinning out of control and she wasn't sure how she would get off without it all crumbling down upon her.

Chapter 13: Edith, Summer 1972

"Damnit, another one bit me." Edith slapped her forearm. Her eyes moved up from the small red mound on her arm to meet a pair of gorgeous blue eyes and a crooked smirk, "Don't laugh at me!"

"I'm not laughing at you, I just think you're adorable when you react to mosquitos like you're not expecting them to bite you, at dusk, in the middle of summer, in New Hampshire." Ronnie lowered his head, keeping his eyes on her. He wore a matter-of-fact expression.

"Fair enough," she rolled her eyes, "Well whose hair-raised plan was this to lay a blanket out under the stars, trying to be romantic or something?"

He rolled over on top of her, gently brushing the bangs off her eyes. "It was all mine and it is terribly romantic."

"Okay, fine, it is. Now get off of me before Ansel comes out with the shotgun. I mean, he's ok with you coming over, but if you think he would be ok with you mounting me in their yard, you've got another thing coming."

Ronnie rolled over her with his hands raised up "I'm sorry Mr. Becker, I promise to leave your niece's virtue intact. No matter how much she may want to undress me and does so frequently with her eyes." He flung his silky hair off his face. He was a stud in school and could have any girl he desired. He was definitely boastful, but Edith certainly did undress him with her eyes, and in her dreams, practically every night since they kissed.

"Oh shut up." Edith grabbed him by the shirt and pulled him into her. After dating for nine months, kissing had become a regular thing and patting on the surface of clothes was never far behind. She had no intention of sex before marriage. Her parents and aunt had made that a staple in raising her. She could get ears pierced and do all the "far out" hippie things she wanted, but drugs and sex were a sure-fire way of becoming a homeless teenager.

Their lips parted and he stroked the side of her face with the back of his index finger. "So your birthday passed a few weeks ago. I thought you might bring it up."

"Yes, and…" She hadn't quite expected to do something ceremonial for her annual special, she-was-born-that-day event.

"I know, I know, you don't celebrate birthdays. I mean you're not Mormon. You are allowed to, right?"

"No, I'm not Mormon. I just..." She paused and thought about that night. A night she dreamt of often. It had happened so long ago now, but yet it haunted her. "I just stopped finding joy in birthdays."

"When did this happen?" He sat back and wrapped his arms around his corduroy pants. "Or have you always been such a strange girl."

She put her hands on her hips.

"Ok, in all fairness, I love that about you. Seriously though, why don't you celebrate birthdays?"

Edith thought about it long and hard. The silence seemed to drag on for hours, even though she was only lost in her subconscious for a moment.

"So you know I used to live in Rhode Island?"

"Yes, you moved here about three years ago." He slapped a mosquito that landed on his cheek and Edith giggled at the blood stain it left.

"I don't really talk about it, I mean, I don't talk about it at all. What is there to say?"

He leaned over and rubbed her arm gently. "I'm here to listen, if you're ready to share."

"I was fifteen and my father's birthday was coming up in a couple of days. My dad was big into birthdays and my mom would always make it super special for him. I mean, banners across the living room, homemade cake, party hats, kazoos and once even a hired a circus performer to come and entertain our guests. His parties would have nearly a hundred people at them and they would go to the wee hours of the night. The whole neighborhood loved him and would come out to the annual block party to celebrate another year with my dad. That night, my dad went out to get a few ingredients for his cake and he eyed the flower shop across the street from the convenient store. He wanted to get a bouquet of daisies, my mother's favorite flower. A rainstorm hit the streets hard. The visibility was terrible and while crossing the street with flowers in hand he was struck by a car and was." She stopped.

Ronnie pulled her into him and tightly wrapped his arms around her. She didn't cry, she wouldn't cry anymore. "I'm so sorry." He pulled away and cupping her face in his hands, he kissed her. "I wish none of that had ever happened to you."

"Hey, I never would have met you." Edith stroked his chin, wanting to pull him in for a kiss again.

"I love you," he said it without caution or understanding of what it would mean to her, "But I would give this all up for you to have your father and family together again."

Edith's cheeks reddened. "Thank you, I love you too." Curling tightly into his chest, he put his arms around her and listened to the crickets chirp a moment.

"What happened to your mom? She must have been devastated." He pulled the hair off her shoulder.

"She's dead." Her eyes stared off into the distance blankly.

"Edith." His voice dropped off into a grieving tone.

"I don't want to talk about it." Instead, her face lit up again, "I would so much rather kiss you instead.

"I can live with that." He pulled into her a deep kiss. Within an instant, the screen door creaked open and a shadow blocked the only lantern that provided light to the stargazing platform. Aside from the fireflies it was the only way of drawing the plethora of bugs from their blanket.

"I think it's time for Ronald to go home." Cora spoke in a tone, much like a mother, but with a bit of sass to distinguish that she was still the fun Aunt in her own way.

"Yes, Mrs. Becker." He went to kiss Edith goodnight and stopped himself. Instead he stood up, gathered the blanket and folded it neatly before handing it to Edith.

"Miss Anderson, always a pleasure." He waved to her aunt whose face hid in the shadow of the porch light covered with flickering bugs, "Thank you, good night."

Edith watched him walk down the drive to his truck and then turned to head towards the porch. Her aunt was still there, unwavering from her position.

"He's a nice boy." She smiled at Edith.

"Yes, he is." Edith smirked back at her inquisitive aunt. "Do you have a follow up comment to that or do you honestly just think he is a nice boy?"

"I think that you could have a nice and comfortable future with him. I mean he comes from a very nice respectable family. He plans to go to college for business management, or so the town says. You could do worse."

"Aunt Cora, I'm not even seventeen yet and you're already picking out a husband for me." She gave her aunt a cockeyed look.

"Well when a boy and girl lay on a blanket together for hours, you have to wonder if there will be a wedding there sooner or later."

"We were just stargazing, not doing anything sacrilegious."

"Let's hope so." And she did the sign of the cross.

Cora wasn't an overly Christian woman. She attended church, but more as a way to socialize. There wasn't much for entertainment up here in the trees. Her greatest fear was that Edith would get pregnant and that boy would ruin her life. She never said the words, but Edith knew every time she walked out on that porch that she meant it. Cora was an understanding woman, but she wasn't about to bring a baby into the house with a barely 18 year old mother. The scandal would be all they talked about in church for the next decade. She had avoided being the talk of the town for the last twenty three years and wasn't about to start up some gossip for the local rumor mill to splurge about. She left the south for a reason, after all.

They walked back into the house and found Uncle Ansel asleep on the sofa with his newspaper open on his chest. His head was tilted back and his mouth partially open. He gently snored with an occasional snort or two. Cora laughed at it and left him there until he decided to join her in their room.

They truly had a great understanding of one another. He would do his part to care for the home, having his own love and interests when the daily grind was done. Likewise, Cora would do the same. It was a marriage of mutual affection and enough shared interest to stay together while having a balance of their own ideals, dreams and lifestyles.

"Aunt Cora." Edith spoke softly not to wake him. Her aunt turned her head.

"Is my mother dead?"

Cora's face sank and her eyebrows drew in together. She walked over to Edith and placed her hands on her niece's shoulders. "Oh, dear, dear girl." She pulled her hard into a hug. "I don't know what to tell you, as I have no answers for the questions of life's struggles. But, no, your mother is not dead."

"She apparently just doesn't want to live anymore."

"When one goes through something so..." She licked her lips while she looked for the right words. No word could properly execute or justify the way she wished to say. "Your mom went through something terrible, and she's recovering from not only losing someone but *seeing* it. To witness death is nothing I would wish upon anyone."

Edith looked up at her aunt. "Did you lose someone?"

Cora looked off into the distance again and breathed out a deep sigh "We did." She looked up into the ceiling as though it would give her an answer, "Our daughter."

The word caught Edith off guard.

"You had a daughter?" She covered her mouth, wondering if Cora had watched her own daughter die.

"Yes, her name was Susan. She was so beautiful." Her eyes trailed off around the room. It was as though Cora could see her there at the living room table coloring, or eating with her and Ansel in the dining room. Had her room been the room that Edith lived in now? Had she died as a baby, or a child? These were all questions Edith wished to ask her aunt, but much like she refused to talk about her own grief, she could barely ask her aunt to talk about something so deeply personal. An event still so harrowing is a difficult tale to tell.

But Cora looked at Edith and surprisingly responded. "She was nine, she and Ansel were out in the woods," she squinted, searching her mind for the memory, "It was dusk and the woods were getting dark. Ansel had his flashlight and they were heading back to the house. He walked ahead so that she could follow the flashlight. He heard a branch snap on the soggy leaf floor. He said that part so many times, I know it by heart." Tears began flowing from her eyes.

"We had a well on the property, an old well that someone had covered up a good amount of years back. She fell in, it was quick." She wiped the stray tear as it drifted down her cheek, "Ansel was beside himself. He felt he was to blame. It was no one's fault. It was just unfair."

Cora looked at Edith again. Tears just seeped from her eyes. Edith embraced her aunt and wept for her. Their pain collided in a flash of rage and sorrow.

Behind them, Ansel snored loudly. The two women pulled apart. Edith smiled slightly at the idea that he could finally sleep soundly. This had explained so much about Edith's uncle. He was never a warm and fuzzy man. He had given her a home. Being polite and engaged in simple talk at the table, but was unable to give her the love that was still wrapped up in the daughter he lost. How could he bear to love another little girl who would just leave him one day? And with Edith going to college in just two years, time was slipping away from them.

Edith headed up to her room and shut the door. Her bed was welcoming and she closed her eyes. After that interlude with her aunt, she would need to suffer in silence. She pulled the elastic from her hair and smoothed out the strands as she rolled over to face the ceiling. It was inevitable that she would toss and turn. Her thoughts were endless. Dreamless evenings followed by zombie-like mornings had become a regular event. At some point she would need to learn to sleep, and better yet, dream again. She flipped on her side again. Being a slanted roof, her bedroom ceiling grew closer to her bed as she rolled to the right. There she saw something inscribed on the wooden post, where the wall meets the roof. It was carved, not written, as though someone had been chipping away at it with a butterfly knife. She couldn't see what it said in the dark and so she switched on the lamp that sat on the desk near her bed. The letters were visible now. She studied them with her eyes, then her finger tips, tracing the edge of the imperfect letters. Her eyes closed tight and her lungs released the air locked inside. Inside a space where we all keep our secrets. This was *her* room. This is where her cousin slept the nine years she was alive. This was where her mother would read bedtime stories. The same place her father would tell her before bed that he would be taking her fishing over the weekend. It's where she would have dreamt of kissing a boy one day, where she would have hoped and dreamed. It's where she had her whole life ahead of her.

The name was there, carved in wood. It wasn't going anywhere. Immortalized in the thick beam that held up the weight of the roof and the weight on their hearts. *Susan.*

Chapter 14: Samantha, June 1995

"Well that's the last box." Samantha closed the lid to the empty trunk and trudged with Lisa up the two flights of stairs and down the hallway reeking of young adults who had failed to shower. Lisa laid the final box of her belongings on the floor of her dorm room. It had finally come, the day Sam would start off on her new role as sister-in-charge.

"Thanks Sis. I know it's not going to be easy with everything changing. I'm here if you want to talk, literally at any time." Lisa wrapped her arms around her little sister.

"Nah, I want you to actually enjoy college." Sam smiled and gently punched her sister in the shoulder. "You don't need our family drama getting in the way of all this," she raised her hands to highlight all that surrounded Lisa. While the room was dingy and smelled of mildew, this was a brilliant change for her, and a chance to have a new beginning.

"You know, you will be out of the drama next year too." She wagged her finger at Sam as though she was giving her the final lesson of childhood.

"I will be out far sooner than that. Mom has decided to move this weekend as well." She leaned into the door frame, resting her head on the hard wooden surface.

"So what does that mean for you?" Lisa opened the box and then paused, waiting for her sister to answer.

"What do you mean?" Sam raised her head off the molding.

"Are you going with them?" Lisa ran her fingers through her hair, still slightly panting from the walk up the stairs. The room was stifling in the early summer heat. The stains on her white tank top were really starting to show through. Sam wished there was a way that she could help Lisa start off her new life in better circumstances, but at least she had somewhere to live. Sam would be homeless, unless she found a place to stay in the next five days. There was no way that her mother would get her way and have Sam move out to the hills of New Hampshire.

"I have a plan, don't worry," she slid her bag on her shoulder, "Hey, I got to get going. Hopefully this new clunker I picked up cheap from Tommy's will actually get me back to the apartment."

Lisa laughed and wrapped her arms around her sister tightly, "I am only a phone call away. You have my number." She pulled back and looked down at Sam.

"I know, now let go of me, it's absolutely nasty in here and I don't need your sticky sweaty body all over me." Sam smiled and turned to leave.

Something made her stop and turn around.

"Hey Lis."

Lisa looked up at her sister, "Yeah, Sam."

"Give 'em hell." She slapped the door frame and walked away.

The student parking for the dorms was nearby, but visitor parking was damn near a mile away. Sam had followed her sister down in her new "junker" to make sure they could move all of her college equipment in one trip. URI was only forty-five minutes away from their house, but it wasn't a trip that either one of them wanted to do twice. Her sister was lucky to be getting a full ride scholarship. That was the only way she was able to afford attending the school.

Her mom had wanted to move her in, but at the last minute she was asked to visit with the lawyer to settle her uncle's will. With everything going on with their move to NH, needing a moving truck, having to find another job to care for her two younger children and pretending like she had a clue as to what she was doing, Edith had her hands full. Lisa hadn't had her mother there for most things in life, so this wasn't a surprise nor disappointment to her whatsoever. Having Sam there meant she had someone reliable by her side. One day, Theresa and Jessica would follow suit and be able to laugh with them about all the crazy stuff they put up with in their mother. Until then, they had each other.

"Sam?" Sam stopped in her tracks. She knew that voice from anywhere. She turned and saw Adam coming down the path from the library.

"Hey stranger, what are you doing here? Did you just get in today?" She smiled and pulled him in closely, running her fingers through his hair. They hadn't seen each other in a few weeks. He had been caught up in meetings as of late. A big opportunity had been presented to him a couple of months ago. Amblin Productions had contacted his agent and were planning to buy options to make his books into a movie. Better yet, he had been asked to write the screenplay for it. Why he was at the University of Rhode Island was beyond Samantha's knowledge.

"Was today Lisa's moving-in day?" He looked at the surrounding dorms.

"Yeah, I just finished loading the last box into her room."

"Nice." He paused and then realized she had asked him something.

"Sorry, yeah, um, I just arrived this morning, my first flight into Rhode Island. I had an early morning meeting with the producer, director and the President of URI about using the campus as a filming location for my movie. I'm sorry I didn't call you, I just haven't stopped since I arrived and I wasn't given much notice."

"Wait, what?" she screeched, "That's amazing, don't worry about calling me. I know you're crazy busy right now." She was confused and excited all at once.

"Yeah, it's completely crazy, right?" He put his hands on his hips and then wiped the sweat dripping off the tip of his nose. "God, it's hot out." He looked at Sam, also red faced and sweating through her top. "What are your plans for the rest of the day?"

She looked up at him with keen eyes, "Whatever you want to do."

He put his hand out and she gladly accepted it.

"So, where are we off to?" she asked. He draped his arm around her neck as they walked down the street, and he leaned down and kissed her forehead.

"You'll see." He opened his car door and allowed her inside, shutting the door behind her. The air conditioning blasted on her face and she laid her head back into the headrest as the cool breeze hit her face.

"God, you're beautiful." She looked over at him before leaning in to kiss his lips gently.

The drive was peaceful. It was nice to ride in a car for once that didn't click and clunk when you took turns. He was a successful guy, barely even old enough to drive, but had his life working out exactly how he wanted it. Sam envied his dreams coming true and his freedom to pursue them. He looked over at her, and he could see the questions rolling through her mind.

"So are we going to talk about it?" He looked from her to the road and back.

"Talk about what?" She shrugged as though her innocent expression would be bait enough for him to take it.

"I'm not buying it, something happened and you won't tell me for some strange reason."

"Nothing happened and I'm not hiding anything."

He laughed, "Wow and now you're lying to me about it," he lightly elbowed her, "Spill it."

Sam let out a grunt and then crossed her arms in rebellion. She saw his face and knew that Adam was not one to give up easily.

"My mom inherited a house in New Hampshire and is moving my sisters up there this weekend.

"Wow, that's great!" he said. And then he looked at Samantha's reaction, "Or not?"

"How is that great?" Sam ran her fingers through her hair again, but this time in frustration.

"Well, haven't you always wanted your mom to get her act together and take care of your sisters? You know, so that you could go on and live your own life?" He talked slowly so as not to have to repeat himself. His eyebrows couldn't have been raised any higher. Sam took the hint.

"Yeah, but why now?" A whine came out. The bitter, resentful cry of a small child who had been denied a childhood rang out and she heard it in her own voice.

"Why should your sisters have to endure the same hardships? Didn't you do all this so that they wouldn't have to worry about doing anything but being kids? Isn't that why you and Lisa sacrificed your weekends and stayed up late to do laundry and did the cooking for years?"

She knew he was right. The itch in her throat was turning into a wad of something, a bitter pill she knew she had to swallow.

"I should be happy for her, for them. I should be elated and join them in celebrating."

"But you're not, are you?" He pulled over on the side of the road. The weeds were high on this side of the highway. Large bugs pelted themselves against the windshield trying to gain shelter from the hot summer heat. Sam wasn't sure how she was supposed to respond to him. She knew he was right about everything he said. She just couldn't let it go.

"I told my mom that I'm not going. My little sisters are so excited and have already picked out their rooms. Lisa is off at college now and I have one more year of high school. I am not picking up my stuff and my entire life and leaving my home to follow my half-wit mother to New Hampshire, so she can ruin our lives there too."

"If you really thought your mother was going to ruin your life in New Hampshire, why would you let her go up there alone with your little sisters?"

He had a point. He always had a point. Aside from being desperately attractive, he was brilliant to a fold.

"You turn eighteen next week, right?" she asked

"Yes, you turned eighteen, what, eight weeks ago?"

"Seven."

He looked at her, eyes squinted, asking for more information, "Why?"

"Well, we're almost adults, I could just stay with you."

He nearly dropped his jaw on the floor "What?" He clutched his chest

"Who are you and what have you done with my girlfriend Sam?"

"She's still here, she's just all grown up."

"Well, it's funny you mentioned that." He bit his lower lip. A deep pink color appeared next to his stubble. He ran his fingers through his dirty blonde hair, his biceps bulged from his sleeve. It was her turn to bite her own lip.

"Go on."

"See, I was going to see a place today." He pointed across the street. The sign said "For Rent."

"I was hoping that I could interest you in moving in with me. I know you don't want to leave your home and your friends, but I would love to have you, if you would consider it."

"I can totally switch schools, and what friends, exactly?" She laughed and leaned in to kiss him. They looked at the sign together and then got out of the car to walk around their possible new home.

Edith walked through the door and found bits of paper, miscellaneous socks strewn all over the floor, empty dressers and stains on the rugs where the furniture once was. Her daughters were no longer there. The place that she walked by at night, silently examining was now bare. On the counter was a note. The words were brief, the handwriting familiar, the meaning clear:

"It's your turn now

-Sam"

Chapter 15: Edith, February 1973

"Do you think I have a shot though," Edith eyed her aunt's expression, "to get in for next semester?"

Cora exhaled slowly, picking up another clean sweater from the laundry basket. She looked at Edith and then back at the white, knit garment. She folded it neatly and set it on a stack of Edith's sweaters. "Out with the old, in with the new. This spring is going to be warm, I can just feel it."

Edith had pounced on Cora to boost her morale the first moment she was available. Cora hadn't been home often lately. Her friend Muriel was a florist and. Cora insisted on helping her prepare for the regional flower show every year. It was a task and a half for her to cut, trim and arrange twenty-five bouquets, wreaths and string garlands around the entrance to the show. The event was not a competition, but it sure brought attention to Muriel's sensational flowers. Not to mention, it drummed up enough business to last the rest of the year.

After three weeks of inventory, they put the show together and it was a hit to say the least. The last day of the flower show was just two days ago and while Edith wasn't involved in the planning or design, she knew the amount of work that Cora had put into it to help out her friend.

Edith's eyebrows narrowed and her eyes became slits in frustration.

"Are you seriously just going to ignore me?" Edith's hands were on her hips faster than a cricket leaps, and Cora noticed how much she was getting under Edith's skin. Cora and Edith had developed something of a sense of humor together, over the last few years. Cora may not have been the mother Edith hoped for, but she was more than enough mother to make life meaningful.

Cora raised her head, her expression widened. It was her turn for her eyebrows to come together, not in fury, but in curiosity. Her mouth formed an "O" shape. She seemed to recall something that she wanted to share explicitly with Edith.

"Oh yeah, something came for you the other day."

"The other day?" Edith's face lit up like the sky on the Fourth of July. "Do you mean…?" She looked around the room, her eyes darting into every single corner until she spotted it on the small bookshelf next to the China cabinet. She ran over, dodging the small box of light, "spring" clothes placed in her path and quickly retrieved it. Her hands were shaking. The emblem on the envelope had her squealing with excitement and anxious about its contents. What if she had gotten what she wished for? What if this was her chance to go home?

Of course, she wouldn't be going home. The house was gone and in all senses of the word, her family was as well. Her closest relatives had all but abandoned her in her greatest time of need, her father was dead and her mother's mind might as well be. She looked up at Cora for encouragement.

"Well," she urged, "go ahead and open it. You know it won't change a thing about the contents dilly dallying now. Rip the Band-Aid darling."

Edith had become the daughter she never had the chance to raise. After that one conversation about Susan, the two women had grown closer. Edith knew now that she had someone to confide in, who would confide in her. Something about the connection between them supplied a small part of what Edith had lost in her mother. A bridge of trust existed between her and Cora now, and Edith had blossomed with it. A small part of her adopted Cora's history as her own, and it gave her a solid place on which to set her feet.

Edith's father's accident was nothing in her or her mother's control. It was a terrible thing that neither would ever recover from but could learn to live with. Cora was this proud example of where a new kind of mother could come from.

Edith stood there in her aunt's living room holding a letter of either acceptance or rejection from the University of Rhode Island for the upcoming fall. The idea of her life changing again was welcome, while unnerving. She had grown fond of Cora, and even her uncle for that matter. He was a hardened man, but Ansel was not a cruel one. He would say good night to her every evening and then kiss Cora on the forehead before taking his leave to their room. All this would be changing again and it was going to be a wild ride if her aunt had anything to do with it. Edith slit open the envelope with her index finger, ripping the edges of the formally licked paper erratically. She hastily opened the letter and read it out loud.

"Dear Ms. Anderson, we would like to welcome you to the University of Rhode Island." She looked at Cora and jumped into her arms.

Her aunt embraced her tightly, then leaned her head into Edith's and whispered "I knew you could do it. I am so proud of you." They squeezed one another in excitement and adoration.

"Thank you for helping me with my application and all my exams. I was really concerned that they would look at me and skip to the next application without even looking at it." She gazed down at the letter again, re reading the first line over and over again. Her face beamed with excitement, "Now what?"

"Well, now we have to figure out where you are going to stay while living there. I will call the school and let them know that you are going to be enrolling and that you will need housing in the fall. It's ok," Cora rested her hand on Edith's shoulder once more, "you will be fine."

Edith watched her aunt walk away and her smile faded a moment. Her aunt seemed a bit saddened by the news. She might be over the moon for her niece to continue her education, but she was once again losing a daughter. Edith walked briskly over to the woman whom she had come to love and once more wrapped her arms tightly around Cora.

"You will be too."

They pulled apart and Edith could see that Cora was crying.

"I am so very proud of you, as proud as any mother could be of a daughter." Edith cleaned the tear away with the back of her index finger.

"What do you say we call up Ronnie, Pennie and Cindy and see if they want to go out and celebrate. I have some money saved up from the booth last week, it's my treat. It's the least I can do to say thank you to you and Ansel for everything."

"Oh, that would be nice dear. I'll go tell Ansel and you go call your friends. Who knows, maybe one of the other kids got their letters in."

Ronnie and Cindy were the only two that had planned to attend college that Edith was aware of. Pennie had settled on the notion that she would stick around closer to home and pursue a career with close ties to the family tradition.

Ronnie was planning on attending school in New Hampshire so that he would be close to his family. His long lineage here and stamp on development had him stuck here for the long run. While Edith and Ronnie had a great thing going, they both knew that this was the beginning of their lives and they had to go for it.

The idea of studying nature and its biology was another thing altogether. She had developed a keen interest in fungi and medicinal plants while helping Cora and her friend Adeline in their community greenhouse. Adeline was a provider of holistic medicine and while that wasn't a very welcomed specialty to traditional medicine, it was starting to make waves. While Uncle Ansel thought that meant she was a pot-smoking hippie, Adeline actually was a board certified physician who sought to treat ailments the way they had done before the creation of modern medicine. Perhaps that would be a route for Edith to take in school. She could study pharmaceuticals, plant biology or perhaps medicine. Wouldn't that have made her father proud, having a doctor in the family?

But Edith's strongest hope was to be home, close to her mother again. She had been to visit her two years ago, and it had hurt her horribly.

Cora had driven her to the hospital. The room was quiet as she stepped in. What was she to expect, seeing this woman for the first time in two years? The woman was her mother in theory, but currently off-planet. The smell of the air was stale and sour. Edith kept moving into the room slowly, shuffling her feet, until she saw Iris behind a group of individuals playing a game of cards. The women all looked up at her, having never seen her in this facility before. Iris sat there in her rocker, pushing it gently back and forth with her left foot. Her hair matted down, stringy and graying. The bright red curls had long faded and her face appeared tired.

"Mom," Edith whispered and reached to touch her mother's left arm. Why was Edith so afraid? What was Iris going to do, bite her? Cora stood back to let her niece have this moment with her mother. She never had the privilege of meeting Iris before Paul had passed. Somehow meeting her now felt a bit untoward. This was a visit for Edith. She needed her mother and with Agatha's health in decline, Cora knew that soon Edith would have very few people in the world on whom she could rely.

Edith rubbed her mother's arm, slowly and soothingly, whispering something to her for several minutes. After that time she stood up, kissed her mothers forehead and turned back to Cora, "We can go now."

The idea that her mother was ever going to come out of that state now was unfathomable. Still, one day she would return to see her and try again, she just wasn't sure when she would have strength.

Perhaps another year older, stronger, living on her own and going to college, she would finally be able to really help her mother.

"Ronnie and Cindy are in. Pennie had a prior engagement, but sent her many congratulations with a promise to meet up soon to celebrate," Edith looked at her aunt, who seemed a bit flushed, "Are you ok?"

"Oh yeah, I just feel a bit dizzy. Most likely something I ate."

"Well, if you aren't up for it, we can cancel."

"No dear, you go with your friends. Ansel and I will have dinner with you tomorrow to celebrate." She smiled sweetly at her and then gripped the doorway to her bedroom. She stopped for a moment, steading herself and then shut the door behind her.

Edith beamed at the idea of getting into her college of choice. Aside from the University of Rhode Island, she had also applied to University of Massachusetts, Dartmouth and Rhode Island College. But she'd known she wanted to go to URI since she was a child.

Her father had taken her to the school one summer to eat lunch on the quad. They were on their way home from the beach and he wanted to have a talk about the future. She was only a small child, but she had a great appreciation for the beautiful buildings and their natural surroundings. While Pawtucket was her home, she dreamed of somewhere quieter, with wildlife surrounding her. Somewhere like Slater Park, where she could walk between her classroom feeling the soft breeze on her face and admiring the trees as they changed from lush green to golden orange, blanketed in snow and then bloomed into cascading flowers. In a way, she was able to hold on to a part of her father there, too. A piece of them would live on that quad, and she would have a picnic with him as often as she could.

She grabbed her bag and spoke loud enough for her aunt to hear. "Ok, I'll be back in a few hours."

There was no response. Ansel was outside chopping wood. Cora must be fast asleep. She had been tired lately. The stress of her niece getting into school, helping her get all the applications in, and preparing for the annual flower show down in the center of town had her busy.

Before closing the door she saw something across the room. A beautiful rose colored vase containing a dozen yellow roses was placed on the dining room table. A thank you from Muriel to Cora for always being there for her. Yellow roses were her favorite and every year there they rested there, a reminder of her kindness and servitude.

Edith smiled, closed the door behind her and set out of the diner. Ronnie and Cindy were already there talking to Bill, the head cook, when Edith arrived. She walked in and was greeted with a boom of applause. This was a shock: she had not yet told them that she was accepted.

"I don't understand." Edith's facial expression said everything she could not fit into words.

Ronnie came over and kissed her on the check. "Cora told us."

"When?" Edith looked puzzled. "I just opened the letter in front of her."

"She put it up to the light and found it a few hours ago." Cindy smiled and ran over to hug her best friend. "You must be so excited."

"Wait, what about you two?" She looked back and forth between her best friend and her boyfriend.

Cindy smiled and looked at Ronnie "I got into UCLA and Ronnie got into Plymouth State."

"UCLA?" Edith didn't understand. "When did you apply?"

"I have always wanted to travel and California is about as far away as you can get from New Hampshire."

"Well then I guess congrats are in order!" She hugged her and then looked at Ronnie. She pulled away from her friend and then walked slowly over to him. Her fingertips stroked his cheek and she kissed him, as though she were kissing him goodbye. As much as Plymouth State and URI were only a car ride away, the two of them were practical for their age and knew that while they did not plan to break up, living apart for most of the year surely would do that naturally.

One night about a week prior, Ronnie had asked her a serious question. He turned off the engine of the car and shifted in his seat to face her.

"Do you think that you will end up going to URI or UMass Dartmouth?"

"Depends on where I get in. I, of course, would prefer to go to URI, but I can find happiness anywhere," her mouth twisted, "why?"

"I just didn't know if you would consider going to a place closer to here," he rubbed her hand with his thumb, "closer to me."

She leaned in and kissed him gently. "You know I love you and I don't want this to end."

"But," he said.

"But, we are eighteen, whatever we want, we can still get. I have to go for it now and so do you."

"I get it, as much as I don't want to."

"I don't want anything to change either. I don't want to leave Pennie or Cindy or Cora and even Ansel." She looked out the passenger side window.

"Hey, it's going to be ok." He turned her so that he could embrace her.

Now, a week later, he looked at her in the diner: their dreams were coming true and everything seemed to be on track again. Bill provided milk shakes and burgers for the group as congratulations. After eating the last fry on her plate, Edith walked to the car and blew a kiss to Ronnie from across the parking lot.

The sun was setting on the lake across the street. The mountains dipped and peaked behind her. She would miss all of this, but she knew it was time to go back. Maybe being closer to her mom would change things.

The car pulled up the driveway like it had so many times in the last three years. The fallen acorns from the previous autumn still rested between the crushed stone, and broken pieces of branches were strewn across the yard. Edith closed the door to the car and stopped to admire the exterior of Cora's home, of her home. She knew that she would come back to visit this place on break. This would be where she would spend her Christmases, and one day bring her own children to for Thanksgiving. The moment was fleeting but long enough to anchor the smell of the pines deep in her memory, so that she could return to it when the smell was accompanied by the salt air of the ocean.

"I'm home." She looked around the house. She heard some sort of banging coming from Ansel's workshop and she knew he was up to his old habits of playing with his tools. As Ansel often said, "there's always something to do."

She looked around the house for Cora and then decided she must still be napping. Just like a mother always checking on her daughters when they are unwell, Edith had grown accustomed to nurturing her aunt and uncle when need be. It felt good to take care of someone else again. She opened the door gently and peaked in. There she was on her bed, laying on her side. It was seven pm now. Uncle Ansel had not yet eaten, that was evident and it didn't seem that Cora was in any state to be cooking. "Cora, do you want me to make some dinner?"

The room stayed silent. "Cora, sorry to wake you," Edith rested her hand on her aunt's arm. The moment felt surreal. She stepped back quickly, covering her mouth with her hand. Then she edged closer to her aunt once more. Cora lay there, still, cold, breathless. She was dead.

Chapter 16: Samantha, Christmas 1995

The lights twinkled brilliantly against the prickly needles of the tree before her. Sam felt warm arms wrap tightly around her waist, and she closed her eyes as they enveloped her body in a warm safety net. A net she had become accustomed to.

"What are you thinking about?" Adam whispered in her ear, just louder than the whirling of the wind outside against the old shingles of the beach house.

She shook her head, "Nothing, I promise."

He spun her around. "Ah, breaking promises already, are we?" Adam cocked his eyebrow at her. She could see he wasn't going to back down and leave her alone about this.

"Fine," she rolled her eyes. "I just..." She sat down on the couch and collected her face into her hands and then stood up abruptly. "I just hate that it's Christmas time and I am here without my family!"

"You're not alone," Adam pointed outside, "Lisa is literally ten minutes away from us. We can visit her at any time."

"And what about Jessica and Theresa?" She put her fists on her hips and pouted a bit like a small child failing to get her way.

"And your mom." Adam came over and rested his hands on her arms, stroking them gently, "Don't you think that this has a little bit to do with her too?"

"Oh great, here he comes, Dr. Adam."

"Hey, that's not fair. I'm only trying to help you." His lips were tight in anger. She could see the flare of pink in his cheeks and she knew she had been unjust.

"I'm sorry," she let out a sigh, shaking her head slowly, a constant battle raged inside of her, "Do you have any idea how hard it is when your family is torn apart?"

"Ugh, yes," Adam gave a matter of fact look, "in fact, you know this about me."

"Adam, it's not the same thing."

"What's not the same thing? My parents are divorced, I have no siblings, therefore I have my family separated at Christmas and news flash, I used to feel alone on most holidays." He walked over to the wall in the kitchen and picked up the phone. The pale beige receiver blended slightly in with the original yellow wallpaper, now barely clinging to the walls of the house. Adam had gotten a good deal on the rental with the notion that he would be fixing it up while they lived there.

Bit by bit, they redid the floors, painted the bathroom and bed rooms. Sam had purchased curtains for the rooms and brightened up the mantel and dining room table with small vases of flowers.

"Having a woman's touch is everything," Alfred, their kindly landlord, had said in his last conversation with Adam. Alfred was an aged man, but still had his wits about him to give sound advice to two young lovers. *Listen to one another*, he'd said, shaking his finger at them in a mild manner.

Sam knew that Alfred was right again in this situation. She walked over and lifted the phone from Adam's hand. She keyed in the number for her sister Lisa and then let it ring. After five rings the answer machine picked up. *"Hey guys, it's Lisa, I am out of the room right now. Please leave a message if you need to talk. Thank you."*

"Lisa's not home?"

Sam shook her head. Her eyes wandered about the room, avoiding Adam's gaze. She knew what he would say next. *Call them.* She hung up the receiver slowly. Adam was still looking at her when she turned around.

"I just don't know what I would say."

"Say you miss them, ask them how their new school is, what they think of the house."

"I just feel terrible that I haven't gone to visit them since they moved up there."

"So go and visit them then." Adam reached into his pocket to retrieve his wallet, "Here's some gas money, go visit your sisters for Christmas. Obviously Lisa is busy with school or a boyfriend. I'm sure that Theresa and Jessica would be over the moon to see their big sister."

She planted a big kiss on his cheek and then hugged him.

"I love you, you know that, right?'

"Yes, I do. And I love you too and know you need your family right now."

"How about you come with me?" Sam laid the palm of her hands on his chest. He pulled her fingers into a soft grip.

"I guess, I could make that work." He gently rubbed his nose against hers and pressed their foreheads together.

"Really, you'll go?" her voice lifted in excitement.

"Shouldn't you call to let them know we are coming?" he gestured towards the phone, "What if they aren't home or decided to come here for the holidays, then what?"

"My mother has no family here that I know of, and I'm assuming she thinks we have no interest in seeing her this holiday season, given it's so close to Christmas and she's had no word from us at all. So it will be the perfect surprise." Her mouth went crooked in the corner displaying her doubts in the plan, then shifted remembering something else, "I have a couple of things that I got for my sisters that I can pack and just a couple of items of clothing to pack and then we can go."

"What about school? It's only Thursday and you have midterms tomorrow."

She placed her fingers on his face and kissed him gently, "It's only one day, I'll be just fine. Besides, I've already been accepted into URI and a few bad grades won't change that."

"Well that's not the Sam I used know. How about we make sure you get your tests done, hand in your projects and leave first thing after school?"

That pout resurfaced: she hated not getting her way, but also couldn't refuse a man who looked out for her as Adam did.

"Fine."

She left the kitchen to pack her clothes and heard a sound coming from the corner of the living room. Slowly she crept out of the bedroom and stopped for a moment to see if she had been right. Adam was indeed placing something under the tree. Why he had chosen to put it under the tree without her watching confused her. It wasn't as though she was blind. It was sitting there, wrapped up neatly in a tiny red box, desperate to be opened. *I see what you're doing Mr. McNamara.*

Then Sam's doubt kicked in. Perhaps the box was a present for someone else. But his parents were divorced and he had no siblings. Perhaps he had gotten something for his girlfriend's little sisters. A little trinket or something. Yes, perhaps a charm for a bracelet. Charm bracelets had become all the rage. Maybe it was a gift for his editor, Clarice. She was a sweet older woman with sagging skin and wiry gray hair. The ideas spun through her head like thread on a spindle.

"Can I help you?" Adam peaked around the corner, completely catching Samantha off guard.

"Sorry, but what is that?" she pointed to the box under the tree, then proceeded to bite her nails frantically.

"Oh that. I figured you would be frantically wondering about that from the moment I stuck it under the tree, which is why I waited for you to leave the room."

"So, who's it for?" She smiled, hoping he would say it was for her.

Her wish was granted almost immediately, "Who else? You, silly."

"What is it?" Her wry smile slid farther sideways by the minute as she contemplated the many possible contents of a box that small, "Earrings?"

"Can you ever wait for anything?" he laughed at her eagerness, and seemed to taunt her, but she responded by tickling him to the ground. The fingers went from poking to gliding and they began to kiss one another passionately on the living room rug. She slid her hands underneath his shirt and he stopped her for a moment, pulling back. "Sam."

"What?" She looked back and forth between his eyes.

"Are you sure you want to do this?" he spoke softly, sincerely. His parents may have been divorced, but they'd raised him right. Samantha had very few role models in her life so that department was mainly pushed on her by Lisa.

The conversation went as such, *"First you need to make sure you buy condoms. Actually, first, don't have sex at all, ever, you'll just end up with four kids like mom. Just kidding. But seriously Sam, you need to bring the rubbers because guys don't think about anything and it's up to us to make sure we don't end up with children to feed and no father to help out. Which takes me back to my original statement. If nothing ever goes in, nothing can ever come out. Right?"*

Lisa always had a way of making difficult situations a little less serious, while still being terrifying. But this was not the same. This was

Adam, this was a man she'd been in love with for over a year now. This was a guy who put her needs before his own. A guy who took her in when she had nowhere to go. And even now in this moment of passion, he refused to push her into a situation she might not be ready for.

"Adam, I want to," she pulled him in to kiss her, "besides, I got on the pill the moment I turned eighteen, I'm not my mother."

Adam laughed and leaned down to kiss her. His hair was getting long and dangled slightly against her cheek. It tickled a bit and she tucked it behind his ear.

"You're going to need a headband pretty soon, or a boyband," she laughed and he rolled his eyes at her this time.

"Shut up and kiss me then."

As they kissed his arm pulled his shirt over his head and she shimmied out of her pants. The fire was blazing and the room was glowing. The brief release of pressure from their relationship was enough to make the room spin. They laid there tangled up in one another and fell asleep as the snow began to fall outside.

Morning broke and Sam opened her eyes to find herself in bed. She sat up and looked around, but found that Adam was gone. Stepping onto the cold hardwood floor she walked into the kitchen to find a breakfast made for her, consisting of eggs and toast. The whole house was still, minus the sound of bells ringing jubilantly. Adam had put out an antique Santa toy that once belonged to his grandmother Maria. The wind-up figurine was nearly a foot high in tattered red clothing and held a small bell in its hand. Every three steps, it would stop and ring the bell. It would have freaked out anyone else to see a toy Santa walking along the floor by itself first thing in the morning, but to Sam it was like a kiss good morning from someone who knew she needed a little Christmas magic to start this holiday week.

She dressed warmly, grabbed her books and headed to school just in time for first period. Narragansett High School was only a five minute drive from their house, but figuring in the snow removal from her car and giving the engine time to heat up, she had lost a good fifteen minutes from her doorway to the school entrance.

Adam had decided to finish high school in a brick and mortar fashion. While going to school on paper was fine for a traveling author, he wanted to finish off his teens with somewhat of a resemblance of normal life. His girlfriend had grounded him in that way. They had helped one another grow in the short time they had been together, trying to leave behind the past and grow in a combined future. His first period was on the other side of the building, so she wouldn't have the opportunity to see him until later on in the day.

Sam's class line-up included tests in biology, ancient civilization and trigonometry, and then an easy ride for the rest of the day. Perhaps she could come up with a stomach cramp to get her out of the remaining time sitting in a class where they'd be watching the 1979 classic rendition of Romeo and Juliet. The idea of heading north right about now was sounding far more desirable by the minute. The traffic would be horrendous if they waited, with Christmas Eve being Sunday; who wouldn't want to spend the snowiest holiday up in the mountains with their loved ones?

Fifth period finally came around and her classes were done aside from health class. The idea of sitting through another boring lecture with

Mr. Cumberlong was exhausting. Adam was in study hall this period, so there was only one logical thing to do. Samantha raised her hand and her teacher bent his long nose down, looking over his spectacles at her.

"Yes, Ms. Anderson." The irritation for the disruption of his class on the benefits of running to improve respiratory distress was only further exaggerated by her question.

"Could I go to the nurse, I'm not feeling well." Her voice sounded tired and she groaned a bit to pull off the illusion as she finished her sentence.

"Go ahead." He muttered to himself, then proceeded to turn his back to the classroom and continue on with the lesson. Every kid in class looked at Samantha with envy.

"Excuse me," Samantha tried to get the attention of the secretary behind the desk in the corner, "I need to see the school nurse."

"Do you have a pass dear?" the batty old woman looked at Sam. The secretary was just as ready for a vacation as everyone else. Her cheeks were flush and her lips cracked. She had probably been suffering from a cold for the last week, but didn't want to give up her vacation time when they were so close to holiday break.

Samantha handed the pass over then glided behind her to Nurse Gilbert's office. She was a plump and pleasant woman with curly white hair. Standing just over four feet eleven inches, she was the cutest thing that Samantha had ever seen. There was no way that she was less than seventy years old. Her skin was dry and patchy, practically a loose band elastic. Her nails were hard, but brittle and had that rather yellow tinge that all older woman's nail beds tend to have. She was a heavy smoker, and reeked of Menthol Lights all day long.

"I have been having some serious menstrual cramps all day today. I didn't want to miss school though because I had midterms. Luckily I have finished all of them now, so I would like to go home early to rest."

"Well, I don't see why you can't do that." Nurse Gilbert placed the back of her hand on Samantha's forehead and the smell of nicotine filled Sam's nostrils, almost making her nauseous. She ripped a slip of paper from the pad on her desk and Samantha was excused. The note was to be given to the secretary at the front desk. Sam then waddled out of the office as though the pain was unbearable. As soon as she cleared the stairway she was running out the door and to her car.

The car wouldn't go fast enough. She pushed through the door and yelled for Adam,

"I'm home, are you ready?" She looked around and couldn't believe her eyes. Suddenly her face was actually flushed, she was no longer faking the pain in her stomach, the knots tightened. Her eyes were darting back and forth, and she couldn't breath. It was too much, too much to believe.

Adam walked out of the bedroom dressed in a button-down white shirt and khaki slacks. The room was filled with lit candles and warm red rose petals were scattered across the floor. The box she had seen the night before was no longer under the tree but in his hand.

"I thought if you saw it last night it would get the initial worry off your chest and you wouldn't feel so ambushed."

"What do you mean?" She pulled her eyebrows together, tightening her mouth, "what is all this?"

"I love you, Samantha Anderson. I have since the moment I met you. The first time you spoke to me, I heard them, the bells. That's why I took my good friend Nick out of storage. I wanted to hear the bells again. You're like waking up on Christmas morning, every day that I am with you. I just never want to be apart again like we were for so long. Having you every night for the last four months have been the best times in my life and I want that forever. I spoke to Alfred last week about buying the house off of him. He said that he planned to leave it to us in his will. He has no living family members. And so I got this…"

Sam's eyes glistened,and tears slowly trickled down her face.

"Adam."

"So Sam," he knelt down on one knee, "would you make me the happiest man in the world and be my wife?"

Sam knew the words were coming, but couldn't fathom why they were coming out. She could argue that they were young. Everyone would say they were not capable of taking of themselves, yet they both had done it most of their lives. He'd become a successful author and she had raised her siblings without parents to guide her. What couldn't they do on their own that they couldn't thrive doing together?

"Yes." And she pulled him up. He wrapped his arms around her tightly and then they kissed passionately. His hands pulled in closer to him and she ran her fingers slowly through his hair. Adam opened the small red box that had been on Sam's mind since last evening. Inside was a beautiful art-deco designed ring. The diamond was almost unimportant; the meaning behind the ring was everything. Sam slid the ring on her finger and kissed Adam again. The passion in the kiss grew until they parted laughing in excitement. Who would they tell first?

"Could we tell my sisters first?" she pleaded.

"Lisa?"

"Yes, of course, she will be my maid of honor," she bit her lip, "but really I want to tell my little sisters and my mom."

"Wow, never thought I'd hear that." He was taken aback by the words. "Of course, we can call my parents on Christmas to give them the news, we have plenty of time for that conversation.

Sam picked up the phone and dialed Lisa. It rang a few times and then the phone picked up.

"Lisa," Sam tried to contain the excitement "It's me."

"Hey Sam, what's happening?"

"First off, are you going to New Hampshire for Christmas?"

"Yes, why?"

"Never mind, I'll come pick you up in twenty. Adam and I decided to surprise everyone by going up for Christmas."

"Oh, Ok. I will see you in twenty." She was about to hang up when she stopped herself, "Sam, you know that it's not just mom and the girls right?"

Sam froze, "What do you mean?"

"I mean, mom is seeing someone. He has been staying at the house quite a bit, the girls said," her voice sounded less than excited by the prospect of her mother dating someone.

"Is he a good guy or another cretin?"

"I don't know, it's hard to get anything out of Theresa, and Jessica is no help."

"Well I guess we'll just have to approach Christmas with a five foot pole."

"Ok, well I'll see you shortly."

Sam hung up the phone and thought about the holidays in a different light. She wanted to take this time to share the news with her siblings and had even pondered the idea of making this a moment to bring her mother into the picture. With a new guy in the house it would be less likely that they could have that warm, fuzzy moment.

Lisa got into the car with a shudder.

"God, it's freezing out," she patted Adam on the shoulder, "Hey man, how's it going?"

Adam turned his head, "Lisa, how have you been?"

Sam looked at Adam and then at Lisa. They were acting incredibly odd.

"What is it?"

"Well?" Lisa looked at Adam and then Sam, and then grabbed Sam's left hand. The ring rested on her ring finger, sparkling in the light of the sun filtering in through the window.

"Ah!" she screamed in Sam's ear, "You said yes!"

"Wait," Sam once again darted glances between her fiancé and her sister, "you knew?"

"Of course, I knew." She laughed and leaned forward hugging her sister from the backseat. "Why do you think I didn't answer yesterday when you called. Yes, Adam told me. I was out looking for all those frickin' roses. Do you have any idea how hard it is to find roses of that quality in December? Even harder to find said roses and then have to rip them apart for you to walk in on. I'm just saying, you're lucky I like this guy, Sam."

"Thank you?" Adam said awkwardly and then smiled as Lisa whacked him in the arm.

"Oh shut up. There is no one in the world I would want for my sister more than you." She sat back in the seat with a look of accomplishment across her face, "How are you planning to tell Mom?"

The joy was short-lived. Sam had not thought that part through. Luckily, she still had another few hours of driving to get to the house to figure it out.

Her mother did not have a track record with men and could hardly be angry with Samantha's choice to get engaged at eighteen. She was, after all, a mother to four children with three fathers. After three botched attempts at claiming a father for a daughter, she decided finally to start taking birth control last year. Theresa had called Sam to ask her about a new medication her mother was taking. As soon as she described its package, Sam felt a sigh of relief. While she knew nothing about the jabroni that her mother had living with them in New Hampshire, at least there was the luxury of knowing she would not be adding any more siblings to the roster.

While Edith wasn't a model parent, she did on occasion have a special moment or two with the girls. She was never violent or coarse with them. The problem with Edith was that she had never figured out how to leave her old life behind to start over.

Sam thought this through, questioning whether this was the reason her mother had decided to take the house her uncle had left her. Maybe she was trying to redeem herself and this was her chance to prove she could be worthy of the name "Mom."

They pulled up the long driveway and parked next to a tall snow bank. They had already gotten a good deal of snow this year in Rhode Island, but never like New Hampshire. Jessica and Theresa came stumbling across the yard desperately avoiding black ice and jumped all over Lisa and Sam. As soon as they saw Adam though, the two older sisters were tossed aside to make room to jump onto their favorite. He had always made an effort to be part of their family. The girls considered him a brother. The tie breaker in every argument they had with Sam. The guy who gave Jessica piggy back rides. It was as though the family was all back together now.

"Adam!" the girls hugged him tightly, "You came!"

Even Theresa was over-the-moon about seeing Adam. She rarely had this reaction to anyone. Her face was brighter and less severe. She wasn't donning dark makeup anymore. Her clothing was no longer dark gray hoodies and baggy jeans but more fitted sweaters and evergreen corduroy pants. Theresa had found a bond with Adam through literature, being just as obsessed with the written word as he was. She often said she would become a writer like he did, and he encouraged her to go for it.

"You look great, Theresa." Sam smiled at her sister who was nearly as tall as she is now.

"You can call me Terry now."

"Ok, Terry." Her little sister smiled and then turned to run back in the house.

"Mom!" she yelled into the house, "Sam and Adam are here, and Lisa!"

Sam pushed the door open and felt the warmth of the fireplace brush her face like a warm wind. The whole house was inviting and cozy. The furniture was new and the place was spotless. She had never lived in a place like this until she moved in with Adam. It had been a struggle to make ends meet while living with her mother. The place had never sparkled.

Her mother walked out in a soft white sweater holding the hand of a taller gentleman. She stepped over and embraced her daughter without pausing to assess the situation. This was nothing Sam had ever experienced before with her mother.

Her mother stepped back a moment, releasing herself from Sam.

"I'm so glad you came, Sam. This is Arnold," she smiled sweetly at him. Sam studied her mother's face. She was wearing makeup. Her clothes were washed and smelled of fresh cotton. Her hair was curled and pinned back and her nails were filed neatly and painted a deep red.

"Pleased to meet you Sam," he said politely.

Sam shook his hand then patted Adam on the chest.

"This is Adam. Mom, you have met each other before."

"I know that, Sam," she nodded, smiling. Sam felt the tension eerily building.

"How do you know each other?" She looked at Arnold and then to her mother.

"I work in town, I'm a carpenter. Your mom was looking to fix some shelving up in the bedroom and I came up to check it out. After a while we started talking and realized that we had graduated two years apart from each other. Your mom was homeschooled when I graduated. It was just too coincidental."

"Wow, that's interesting," Sam looked at her mom, nodding her head slowly up and down, biting her lower lip, trying to tread carefully, "You look good, Mom. I hope it's ok we didn't call ahead."

"Thanks Sam. It's been a rough few months getting this place back to its former glory, but I think we figured it out. Uncle Ansel was a very meticulous individual, but at the end of his life he just didn't have the energy to keep it going. I am so very thankful to him for giving this home to us."

Sam looked around the room wanting the conversation to pause.

Her mother recognized the awkwardness and changed the subject.

"Why don't you put your stuff upstairs in your room. You can bunk in Jess's room and Lisa can take the room next door. Terry and Jess will bunk together for the night in Terry's room. Is that alright girls?" she addressed Terry and Jessica for a moment, then turned back to Sam, "We are having dinner in ten if you want to freshen up."

Sam and Adam walked up the stairs and headed down the hall to her room for the night. The hallways were dark, faintly lit by a few perfectly placed sconces to give the look of a nineteenth century cabin lit by candlelight. It was hollow. The hall was empty, ghostly, yet peaceful. Between the lights were frames softly glowing of Edith and a woman she did not recognize. Her soft gray hair and warm smile gave the appearance of a proud mother posing with her daughter.

There was so much Sam had failed to inquire about in her mother's life prior to children. The girls had only known one side of her. Questions raced through her mind. Who was the woman in the photo? When had Edith transformed from the girl in the picture to a negligent mother? Why did she only now feel she could change once again?

She closed the door behind her and found Adam sitting on the bed. "That went well," he said.

"Uh-huh."

"I think that Arnold is a pretty normal guy. He seems to be providing some stability to your mom and she seems to be pulling it together for your sisters. This is a great situation here, don't you think?"

"I don't know." Her elongated pause said far more than the few words spoken.

"About what?" Adam's face twisted in concern.

"Should we tell them now? Can't I just write them a letter or something. Take a picture of my hand with a ring on it? Say, ta da!"

"No, I'm sorry, but you can't get out of this one. We are here, it's going to be fine. Your mom and sisters are happy. Lisa is happy. This is going to be a great night." He put out his hand to collect hers. It was time to tell them the great news.

The two of them walked down the stairs holding each other's hands. Sam began to squeeze, so tightly Adam began to lose feeling and whispered out the side of his mouth,

"Woah, bear hands."

Sam shook it loose, "Sorry, I just..."

"Deep breath." He said it low and slowly.

They sat down at the foot of the table to make sure that they were facing the group. Lisa was a sure giveaway. Her face was red and she looked like a bottle rocket about to explode.

Adam looked at Sam and then down to the lasagna on the table. He put a slice of it on his plate and then another on Sam's and passed the spatula. He knew he would have to be the one to speak first.

"Sam and I have some news," he spoke up, forcing everyone at the table to stop instantly.

"We are getting married," Sam said, lifting her left hand up.

The girls all shrieked in excitement at the prospect of having Adam as a brother. Arnold shared his congratulations. Adam looked at Sam, put his arm around her and kissed her forehead gently.

"Are you serious?" Edith spoke sternly over the uplifting tones of glasses clinking in celebration.

"Mom," Sam spoke before she was interrupted.

"Are you pregnant?" Edith's tone was serious.

"What?" Sam stood up and threw her napkin down, "You think the only way a man would marry me was if I was pregnant?" Sam pointed aggressively at her mother, "That's rich coming from a woman like you."

"And why do you think I would be elated at the notion of my eighteen year old daughter getting married when she was still in high school?"

"I don't know, maybe because you have never been happy for me in my entire life. Maybe because you have *missed* my entire life."

Her face went from her mother's to Arnolds, "I hope you know what you got yourself into. You are dating the most selfish woman in the world. I don't know why I thought this would turn out differently. Why is it that we are not allowed to feel loved?" her eyes began to well, "Why is it that we were never good enough for you to love us?"

"Sam, I—," Her mother's facial expression softened, she realized she had made a mistake. This time, it would cost her everything.

"I guess I thought you'd change, I thought things would get better. I'm glad all that money you've been putting away these past nineteen years have gone to helping absolutely none us of except yourself, Mom."

Adam took her hand and walked out of the room. Upstairs, Sam unpacked the gifts she had brought for her sisters and laid them on the bed. The whole house was quiet. The dinner was over before it began.

The next morning, Jessica and Terry woke to find their sisters had left them presents and had left before the rest of the house had woken. They left two letters. One apologizing to the girls and inviting them to come stay at their beach house over winter break. Sam would wire bus fare if she had to. The second was to Edith. The words were simple and absolute.

"Fool me once, shame on you, fool me twice, shame on me."

Chapter 17: Edith, November 1973

"Well, I guess it's that time," Edith looked down to the golden leaf in her hand, "we always knew this day would come." The leaves were dried and cracked, save a few who still clung to their color, praying for just one more chance to change how the world sees it. Edith had come to the same realization. How could she hold on for another day when the sky was always falling down upon her?

"I know how much you love fall." She twirled the leaf in her fingers like a dancing ballerina. The paper-thin leaf allowed the last bit of warm light to seep through its veiny structure.

"Ansel is ok." Her eyes shut tight, "He misses you, of course, we both do." She laughed slightly before feeling it was wrong to crack a smile.

"We still don't have riveting conversations, but we are getting on ok. I know you said that I could do anything I set my mind to. Trouble is, I have my mind set on you right now," her breath cracked as she inhaled, holding back the tears, "I deferred going to school for a semester. I didn't want to leave Ansel all alone here. He still hasn't cleared out your closet. I think he figures, eventually you will just come home to us. Yes, I call this home. This is, after all, my home with you. I know you're still here. I promise I am not putting any glasses on the table without coasters and I make sure Uncle Ansel's greasy hands don't touch your dish towels. I know how much you hate that," she paused, "hated."

Edith reached out and slid her fingers down the smooth surface. The letters were hand chiseled. Gently, Edith traced the inlay of each curve. Her aunt had chosen to be cremated but had some of her ashes spread at the site of her headstone. Ansel had told her at the funeral parlor that her aunt had wanted a head stone for the irony of it all, being that there was no head there. She always had a way of making the heavy situations a tad bit lighter. As if death could be a light topic.

Her body had been on display for her loved ones to share their grief and give their goodbyes. The whole town came to console Ansel and Edith. A great show of adoration for the woman and friend that they had lost.

"Ronnie is doing well. He called me last week, just to check up on me. Everyone is crazy concerned that I am not going to go to college and will waste my life away. Well not everyone, but Cindy is. She is good, working hard at school. Her family is going out to visit her for Thanksgiving this year. Most likely we will just stay in and watch the parade on television. I have been working on getting Ansel to go out to a show on the weekend. He won't even budge a bit. He can't for a minute understand why a grown man would spend his hard earned money on a film. He bought a new saw the other day. It's the one he has been saving up for the last three years. I guess he figures life is too short to wait on some things."

Edith bit her lip and looked around at the fog settling on the lake. It truly was a picture perfect place to rest forever. "I wish there was something I could have done," her voice was shaky, getting out the words, "I'm sorry I didn't get to say goodbye. I'm sorry I didn't get to tell you that I love you."

She wiped the tear from her eye. Ansel had given her Cora's hand sewn handkerchief. Her initials were sewn into the corner with a dark red thread. Edith used it to dab her eyes, not wanting her makeup to run again.

"The doctors who examined you said that it was an aneurysm. It would have been so fast, you wouldn't have felt it coming. I guess that's the best case scenario for dying right. Total surprise, while sleeping in your own bed. We just wanted more time is all. And time is all you have now."

She looked up at the sky, pondering the existence of everything beyond what she knew. Something in the rustling leaves behind her make her jerk around.

"Hey beautiful." Ansel tipped his hat down at the stone before him. "I just thought I'd come out and say hi. Seems I wasn't the only one thinking about you today," he patted Edith on the shoulder and she thanked him by placing her hand on top of his. His hand was cold and leathery and the veins began to bulge through the thinning layer of skin, the way they do when time pushes on and our bodies tire from having to heal over again.

"I know you probably want some time alone with her. I'll go," she stood up and brushed the leaves and dirt off her corduroy pants.

"No, you stay. After all, there's only two people that your aunt would want to spend her birthday with."

"Paul McCartney and John Lennon." She smiled.

He chuckled, "Other than those two." Her uncle was a quiet man, but had never been a cold and withdrawn man with her. The last six months had been hard on him, but with Edith there it had been bearable. "You know, your aunt wanted you to go to school more than anything."

"Get me out of the house." She cracked the same smile again.

"Nah, she was just dreaming big for you. Boy was she proud."

Edith looked up again, this time to keep the tears from falling, "I want to go, but I want to make sure you're ok."

"Well that is mighty nice of you, but I can't keep you forever. I have to learn to live without Cora and you need to go out and conquer the world, my sweet girl."

She knelt again and embraced her uncle. His six foot stance made him tower over her, but the sheer size of him made her feel safe and comforted. He was the closest thing to family now, he was all she had left.

"How about we head home and make Aunt Cora's favorite meal to celebrate her birthday and then watch Casablanca?" she looped her arm in his and leaned her head against him, bracing herself on his strength.

"Casablanca again?" He rolled his eyes and groaned, "do you have any idea how many times that woman made me watch that God-forsaken movie?"

"Yes, but let's be honest here, how many times were you actually watching it?"

He patted the hand latched to his arm.

"True," he looked up to see the fading light coming through the trees illuminating her aunt's truck, "I don't suppose you want to take her to college."

"What?" Edith pulled away from him, her face beaming with excitement, "No way! Far out!"

"Down girl." He calmed her as she jumped up and down in the damp leaves. Her bell bottom pants were soaked up to the knee now. It had rained the night before.

"I think this is exactly how she would have spent her birthday this year."

"Oh yeah, how's that?" Ansel fluffed his newly groomed mustache a bit with his forefinger.

"Giving me her truck, of course."

A belly laugh like she had never heard before came from somewhere deep inside her uncle. "Oh, you do make me laugh, I thank you for it."

"To be honest, I didn't even know you laughed before."

"I guess I just find it easier to focus on my work," he opened the door to his truck and stepped up into it.

Edith placed her hand on the outside of the door, "What changed then, from then to now?"

"Well, Cora always said that laughing is the easiest way to send our love out into the world. Laughter heals us and heals others without a single word spoken."

"I guess she was right."

"Oh, your aunt was generally right." He grabbed the door handle on the interior of the truck, "But I can only say that now, since she isn't here to hear it."

A warmth rose in Edith's cheeks against the cold wind that rustled her hair. She had seen a different man, a man that had loved this woman, a woman she had admired and wanted to be like someday when she finally figured everything out.

"Hey, um, I have to stop somewhere on the way home," she ran her fingers through her auburn hair, "do you need anything at the store while I'm gone?"

"No, thank you for asking though." He shut the door and then cranked the window down, "Hey Edith."

Edith, who had turned to walk away, spun her head around, "Yes?"

"She always thought of you as a daughter. She knew you had a mom and you were not our little girl that we lost so many years ago. But she loved you fiercely and I promise you that I will continue to look after you as long as you need, while I have breath in me."

Edith's eyes brimmed with tears from the first words. Towards the end of the sentence she was already leaping up through the window into his arms.

"Love you." Edith said, eyes shut tight.

"I love you too, Darling," he let go of her and shifted the gear to reverse, "And hurry with whatever you are up to, I'm hungry." He smiled and backed out onto the road and turned toward their house and out of sight.

Edith got into her aunt's truck, a picture of her aunt clipped to the visor from their first Christmas together a few years back now. Behind it was a stamped envelope. She pulled out and grinned at its insignia. The roads were dry and the sky was cotton candy pink against a fading orange landscape of trees. She drove down the road about two miles before coming to an old building circa the late eighteenth century.

The door slid open, knocking the bell on its reversed door knob. A tall skinny man came out from the backroom. His white hair lay flat, nearly plastered to his head. He pulled his glasses up onto his face with the chain attached still dangling beside his ears.

"How can I help you Edith?"

"Hello, I need to send this out with the express mail. It has a deadline for next week."

He pulled his glasses a little further down on his nose and examined the label. Everyone in a sleepy town like Eaton was a bit on the nosey side.

"University of Rhode Island?" He pulled the spectacles off his face and studied Edith's face for a response.

Her closed-mouth smile stretched from ear to ear as she thought back to the picture clipped to the visor of Cora's truck. The picture represented all of Edith's hopes and dreams, and in turn Cora's dreams for her. Every time she looked at that photo she would be reminded of her. *"All beginnings have ends and all ends have beginnings, It's just what keeps time going,"* she'd say. She was right. As Ansel said, she was always right. And for Edith, the right time had finally come.

"I'm leaving for college."

Chapter 18: Samantha, Spring 1996

Samantha studied herself in the full length mirror screwed to the back of their bedroom door. The woman in the reflection was not the same person she had seen just before Christmas. This woman stood makeup done, lips painted red, wearing a long, thin-strapped red gown and heels to match. Her hair curled and pinned neatly up away from her face. The light came in through the window on the opposite side of the room tracing her like spot light. As she moved to open the door, the room sparkled like a chandelier. Her ring had made this moment far more magical than she could have possibly imagined.

"Wow, you look—" Adam was standing in the doorway in his rental tux looking like a scene from a movie. His hair long enough to gelled back, acting cool and collected as he always did. He leaned ever so slightly in the door with his arms crossed. So handsome that she fantasized for a moment, biting her lip. Then she caught herself dreaming and snapped out of it.

"You don't look so bad yourself there, Dylan McKay." She walked over to straighten out his bow tie.

"I was going more for James Bond, but I guess I can take Luke Perry." He leaned down and kissed her. A shade of red lipstick stuck to his lips and Samantha laughed for a moment before reaching for a tissue next to her bed to wipe it off.

"You are handsome, but I don't think you should go with that shade of red, sorry 'bout that." She wiped it gently off his lips and went to kiss him again. He pulled away.

"I'm going to be covered in red lipstick by the end of the night, aren't I?" he pulled her away, barely a few inches, giving a look of concern.

"If you're lucky." She scrunched her nose up, like she always did when she flirted.

"Oh really," Adam stretched his face in a pondering frown, "well I guess it makes sense, with it being prom night and all."

"Stop it, it's not what I meant." Sam gently knocked him in the arm with her fist. "I just mean, I'm glad that you're able to come with me."

"Where would I be otherwise?" He twisted his jaw awaiting the answer and then spun her about to wrap his arms around her waist.

She nuzzled into him lightly, "Well a year ago, you were on a book tour and we spent weeks, sometimes months apart. I wasn't sure if that was going to start up again and you'd leave."

He turned her around once more, cupping her face in his hands, "I am not going anywhere. Besides, even if I did, you'd be coming too."

"What?" Her tone was more of surprise than anger at his assumption.

"You think that they would make my fiancé stay at home while I run around the country signing my name to books and giving lectures?"

"Well, I…" she meant to say more, but at the risk of getting more lipstick on himself he placed his finger just before her lips.

"I love you too. Now what do you say we get this show on the road so we can come home and celebrate prom the right way." He put out his arm for her to take and they headed off to the school gymnasium.

The drive was short, but just long enough for Samantha to think about all the girls in her school taking pictures out in front of their parent's homes. Five of their friends and all their matching boy-toy dates would be lined up in the yard for a photo shoot. She was happier than she had ever been. If someone had asked her if she would attend her senior prom as a kid, she would have laughed. The idea that she would have had money for a dress, or that she'd even know a guy who would want to put up with her family drama was unimaginable.

Adam had been the exception to everything. He knew her family, loved her sisters, respected her mother regardless of her opinion of their marriage. He gave Sam the life she had wanted all along. She knew he had been correct, if there was a book signing, she would have been sitting in the front row, watching him at the podium while he spoke, beating off all the girls with a stick.

His eyes had only ever been for her. From the moment she met him, she was aware that he was not like any man she had ever known or would ever know. That was the reason that she agreed to marry him at the mere age of eighteen. Neither of them wanted to get married right away, it was more the promise that they would when the time was right. Something they had failed to explain to Edith when they visited at Christmas.

Often she wondered if Lisa had called her mom the next day to explain the situation or if she had let sleeping dogs lay. It wasn't Lisa's place to argue for Samantha's future or her marriage. Samantha was just not ready to forgive her mother for the way she behaved. It doesn't go without saying that if she had a daughter, and said daughter ambushed her at Christmas at the age of eighteen with talks of getting married, she wouldn't laugh her out the door. It was quite possible her mother was level-headed in her reaction.

Most eighteen-year-olds could barely do laundry, cook, pay bills, hold a job or be responsible for anything. Samantha, however, was no ordinary girl. She had lived an accelerated life where she played the role of mother even as a child. Instead of playing with dolls, she mixed up a bottle of formula for her sister Jessica. She was always more of an adult than a child. More a mother than a sister. For years she and Lisa prepared school lunches and did the grocery shopping, cooking, laundry, bills. How much more adult did she have to be before she was old enough to marry someone, before she knew what it meant to trust someone?

She had not seen her sisters since Christmas break. Lisa had gone back to NH, stayed overnight and then brought the girls back to visit for a few days. They opted to stay at Sam's house rather than the dorms with Lisa. The dormitory was already cramped and the smell of body odor was enough to deter anyone.

Adam was more than ok with them coming to stay with them. He had made the two days memorable with Christmas movies, baking cookies and a number of board games. He even coaxed Terry to play. This was a task that had become easier to accomplish. So many girls at her age hid out mostly in their rooms, avoiding the world and filling the air with snarky, sarcastic remarks. Terry, on the other hand, had been hiding out since she was only ten years old. At fourteen, she was coming out of it slowly and engaging in conversation as a young adult.

Terry and Jessica had talked about Arnold for a good hour or so. For the first time ever, the girls seem to have a rounded family experience. He had only recently started staying at the house. Knowing that Edith had come in a package with children, children who were impressionable, made him evaluate his decisions more closely before engaging in a relationship. He spent his nights watching movies, playing cards with the girls, painting murals by the pond and even helping them with homework. He was great with them, from everything Sam could observe. But while Sam was thrilled for some normalcy, she was only tentatively excited; her mother always found a way to ruin relationships.

One of the nights Lisa had come by. The girls were on their way to bed and Lisa had asked to talk to Sam outside for a minute about something to do with school. Adam saw her face and knew it would not be about school at all. Adam decided to draw the younger sisters' attention away.

"Hey girls, I just recently found this new book at the library, I didn't know if you wanted to read a bit of it." Terry couldn't resist a good book, and Jess was following more and more in her sister's footsteps.

The two older sisters stepped outside. The air was cold and Sam buttoned her fleece coat up and pulled the hood over her head. She bounced up and down to keep her legs warm, feeling the tingle hit her toes as she stood in the snow of the front steps. Lisa looked anxious, and she hesitated. Her long pause made Sam a bit uneasy. Was something wrong?

"Sam, I know you don't want to hear this, but mom is really sorry about everything."

"Oh really, did she say that to you?" she pulled her arms tightly together, hugging herself. The wind from the ocean blew harshly onto their front porch, whipping up their hair into a vortex.

"Yes, she said that she didn't mean for it to come out as it did and that she wished you would just slow down and not rush things."

"Rush things!" Samantha practically snorted, "I'm not rushing things, I had someone who rushed things. I had someone who forced me to rush growing up and rushed me to make adult decisions. But this man, in the house over there with our sisters, is not rushing me to do anything. We're not getting married next week, you know that."

"I know, I told her that. Once I explained that you were just making a promise to each other, she calmed down a bit."

"A promise, yes, we are *getting married.* This is not a promise ring, Lis, it's an engagement ring." Sam stopped for a moment and then looked her sister in the eye and began pointing her index finger at her severely.

"You don't take this seriously either, do you?"

"No, I mean, well, you're a bit young. You don't even really know each other," she saw the look in Sam's eyes and knew she had said something wrong.

"I think you should go," sam looked away from her sister and pushed the hair behind her ears.

"Sam," Lisa sighed apologetically, "I didn't mean that I don't support you."

"Seriously Lisa, anything you have ever needed, wanted, I have supported you. I fought for you to have a normal life. I watched the girls, so that you could go out with your boyfriend at the end of the week. I let you go to the library to study when you had finals. You want to know why you are doing so well in college? Because I let you have the time you needed to get your work done in high school. All I ever asked was that you be there, be on my side, for this. You are on hers!"

"I am not hers!" Lisa was shouting back and the conversation grew loud enough that Adam came to intervene.

"Girls, you are getting a little bit loud and your sisters can hear you." He looked back at the girls who were holding a thick, leatherbound book together on the couch, illuminated by the sofa lamp. They both had their eyes fixed on their elder sisters.

Sam closed her eyes and breathed in deeply through her nose, "I will talk about this later, but for now, let's go back inside and have a pretend Christmas with our *real* family."

The girls walked back in the house, shaking a bit from the cold that they had somehow ceased to notice. Adam came around behind Sam and massaged her arms to warm her up.

He whispered in her ear, "You ok?"

She looked over at her sister Lisa, emotionless. Lisa had been her confidant her entire life and the closest thing outside Mildred that she had to a mother. They had never fought before, at least not like that.

"I'm fine." Her first lie to him.

She didn't realize that they had arrived at the school until Adam opened the door to his black 1998 Chevy Charger. He helped her step out, handing her the red roses that he had bought to match her dress. The slit in the front of her dress was flashy, but she had seen Jamie Lee Curtis in True Lies and wanted to look like a knock out for him. Adam had been homeschooled for the last few years and missed out on so many of the general rite-of-passage moments in his life. This was one that he had hoped not to miss, and having the moment with his beautiful bride-to-be on his arm made him so proud he was damn near ready to burst in tears.

Sam saw the glow in his cheeks and knew it was not the late spring air, but love and adoration for his forever date.

"Hey Sam." A blonde girl with long straight hair looked up at her from the table where they checked the tickets, "Here are your tickets, pictures are being taken around towards the back of the room under the giant moon sculpture. You and Adam have fun tonight." She winked.

Tracy was her lab partner their last semester of school, and even so, Sam barely recognized her, with only a year of school together.

"Thanks Tracy, you too." Sam looked at Adam, who saw her lost somewhere in her mind at the moment.

"Smile!" the photographer said enthusiastically, with a less believable leer, as though he was photographing a toddler's birthday party for too little money. *Flash!*

They were slightly blinded but managed to make their way into the gym, where garland had been hung around the walls accompanied by hundreds of paper stars. They managed to find a table where they could drop off her flowers and Sam's clutch bag for the evening. The music blasted making it now impossible to hear anyone talking.

They had only known their classmates for eight months, which couldn't compete with friendships that had been built over the last six to ten years, and few people stopped to talk with them. Sam and Adam both managed to find a friend or two to greet every morning, but mostly they simply blended into the crowd, with the knowledge that no matter what, they always had one another to come home to at the end of the day.

Half of the room was set up with tables while the other was open for dancing. With half the seniors drinking prior to the prom, most were already dancing, poorly in fact. The girls wore floor length dresses of every color. Some were satin, others taffeta and one or two were wearing a plumed out tulle skirt. It was the first chance for girls to feel like princesses. The next would be when they were married.

Sam looked at her fiancé, his eyes were taken in by the disco ball spinning around the room creating the starry sky above. It had been a great idea by Carina, a well known artist of her highschool, to incorporate the starry night theme with something that generated a twinkle in everyone's eyes. This was the moment she needed to remember. Her hand extended to clasp his and she led him out onto the dance floor. He wrapped her arms around his neck as "Iris" by the Goo Goo Dolls began to play in the background. Her eyes dizzily drifted off into his. Who needed beer when she felt drunk, drowning in his eyes?

"So how many?" Adam slightly shouted to get over the music.

"How many?"

"Kids."

Sam's eyebrows raised, "What?"

He saw her expression and laughed, "Not *now*, Sam."

"Oh." A sigh of relief came out of her mouth and he saw it and excused it.

"I don't want kids now either," he looked around, "I was just wondering how many of these we were going to have to look forward to."

"Oh, I see," she closed her eyes and nodded a tightly sealed smile, "You want to know how many dresses, tuxes, bouquets and boutonnieres you will have to buy before they leave for college. For our hypothetical children," she laughed this time, "Hell, I may be sterile and you just won the lottery."

"That was something else, I'll have to start saving now. I was just thinking more along the lines of how many times I'd have guys come to my door to ask my daughter to go out to the movies. I'd politely shake his hand, measuring the intensity of the shake, you know, to see what kind of man he is."

A smile spread across Sam's face and giggled at his make believe future.

"Then I'd ask him what he intended for her, what dreams he has, if he would support her dreams."

"God, I really hope we have sons then, cause you're going to scare the crap out of those guys. Our daughters will never have dates."

He laughed, "I have my ways." He leaned in to kiss her neck and then whispered in her ear.

"I just want to have you in my arms as we wave them off to start their own lives, that they have parents that love one another as much as you and I do, that they will know what to look for, what they deserve and why it's worth the wait."

"I love you, you know," Sam placed her hand on his cheek. She was desperate to kiss him, but had learned her lesson from the previous time she marked him with lipstick.

"I know you do, I love you too. And just so you know, everything with your mom will figure itself out. You just need to forgive her."

Sam wanted to be enraged, but she knew that Adam would never side with her mother and her previous behavior for one minute. She pulled him into her and they danced until the song played its last note.

The lights came on a couple of hours later. The teenagers had swollen red, sweaty faces. The once neat-as-a-pin hair styles were drawn-out, sagging mops of knots and hairspray. The mascara had run, the lipstick smeared and body odor stunk to the high heavens.

Sam grabbed her flowers from the table, still dolled up as ever, and Adam escorted her to the car. The drive was quiet. It had been a great evening and a beautiful night, everything they imagined.

"What do you say we go to the beach?"

"Right now?" Sam looked down at the satin dress she was wearing.

"Well, yeah," He gave a sad puppy dog face, "You up for it, Anderson?"

"Fine." She was always ready to give in to him.

They pulled down the narrow opening to Sand Hill Cove, a beach not too far from their house in Narragansett. The air was warm and soft as it flung her tendrils of curly hair into her face.

"Wow, you are amazing, you know that?" He kissed her.

"Wait, my lipstick."

She pulled back, but he caught her and pulled her into another kiss before saying softly, "This red is *so* my color."

The sun had gone down long before, but she felt like this was a moment for a sunset. Something slow and soothing, a fleck of passion before the night sky enveloped them.

The beach was empty and the waves rolled in to crash on the shore. He put his coat around her shoulders and they watched as the clouds danced around the light of the stars.

The wind began to pick up and Adam rubbed her arms. "You ready to go?"

Sam nodded and they drove back to the house. As she pulled up, something felt different. They walked into the house and heard nothing, but still the air was different. Smoke.

"Oh my god, is it a fire? Adam!" She ran into every room until she saw the light coming from their bedroom. Then she stopped, the fear that was always lingering there, in her mind. She saw the same red pedals poured on the bed, the candles lit around the room, creating a glow perfect for the mood while Boyz to Men played in the background.

"The beach, huh?"

"Well Lisa needed time to set it up. She wanted you to have the perfect prom. I guess she still feels bad about Christmas."

"I'll call her tomorrow and thank her."

"And?" He looked down at her with questioning eyes.

"and apologize."

"That's my girl." He kissed her and then slid the door shut.

Chapter 19: Edith July 1974

Lisa was the first person to smile and say hello to Edith when she set foot on campus. Consequently, she was the only person Edith recognized at lunch that day in the cafeteria. Neither girl really knew anyone, so they latched onto one another and quickly found out how much they had in common. Having Lisa in her life made things easy to adjust to.

She was born in California. Lisa's mother had left when Lisa was only two; her father raised her himself until he remarried. While Lisa wasn't sure why her mother had left, there was no doubt that drugs were involved in her decision-making, and her father wanted his daughter to grow up away from that.

Lisa ended up calling her father's new wife "Mom," and she was the person that Lisa had needed. When she was ten years old, her birth mother had shown up looking to reconnect with her daughter, but without giving up the substances that had forced her to leave. Lisa's father, Ben, wasn't having it and went to court to get full custody of his daughter. His wife, Lynn, begged Lisa's mother to give up her rights so that she could adopt Lisa. It took two months to locate her while she was on a bender and two grand for her mother to relinquish her rights as her parent, but eventually she did. After three months they won the case, and they packed up their family and moved to Rhode Island to start over.

While they were reluctant to share much about Lisa's mother with Lisa, they knew that she had been privy to most of it and she was far more observant and mature for her age than most girls. While Edith's story had not been the same line for line, they both had lost parents and had gained surrogates in their place. They were both able to find happiness and light in darkness. Most importantly, they had found one another and in this they found something that was unmatchable, friendship in its purest form.

Lisa was a short, thin gangly girl with a wide nose bridge, often found with large green plastic spectacles nestled on top. Her short, red, bobbed hair was a fad of the times, and as much as Edith had considered the idea of cutting her hair, it seemed too radical to adjust to in the long run. She had been blessed with long auburn hair, smooth and straight since childhood and she wanted to keep as much of that memory, for as long as possible.

Her father had taken a job not far from the university so they thought it ideal for her to attend, even without a clear major in mind. She loved the arts like Edith, but the idea of trying to make a career with her lack of focus seemed a little out of reach. With almost three semesters completed and very little direction, her father urged Lisa to consider going into clerical work. His company could always use more reliable staff and he was keen on his daughter getting a practical education.

Harlem had lived next door to Lisa's family for several years. He and Edith had been introduced over the summer while she visited Lisa for a Fourth of July cookout.

Edith was taken by him immediately. While Ronnie was a handsome man, she was smitten with Harlem within minutes of looking at him. It had played out like a scene from a play. Boy glances across the room, finds a girl, plating her second course of dinner, a single hot dog not sufficing for the inner hunger. She looks up to see him following her every move. He smiles and pushes his long black hair behind his ear, waving silently and mouthing the word, "Hello."

In fact, the moment was a little less exciting than a stage performance, but Edith was taken in by it regardless. Edith blushed and picked up another piece of corn, not realizing her entire plate was now consisting of macaroni salad and corn on the cob. Harlem took the opportunity of her confusion and walked briskly in her direction to introduce himself. Edith saw him coming and again looked down at her plate and the ridiculous selections before her.

"Hi," he extended a hand to her. "I'm Harlem, Lisa's neighbor." Edith accepted his hand and shook it gently to avoid knocking her food over.

"So you're loading up on carbohydrates, I see."

Edith looked down at her plate, embarrassed. "My goodness, I'm an idiot, I swear it."

He laughed a bit before changing the subject "What are you studying at URI?"

Across the room Edith gave her friend a death stare, realizing Lisa had been talking her up the last month with her neighbor, probably with intentions of them connecting on a higher level.

Edith studied Harlem's mouth and watched as he licked his lips. This guy was hot and available, groovy. So entangled was she in the attraction with his mouth she failed to notice what he was saying to her.

"It's there, right in the corner of your mouth."

A blot of mustard had been stuck in the corner of her lips for some time now and he had probably seen it from across the room and came over to relieve her from her misery.

"Oh God." She quickly grabbed a napkin off the yellow checkered tablecloth and wiped it.

"It's ok, it happens. In fact, I got a massive spot of ketchup on my shirt about an hour ago and I am far too lazy right now to go wash it off." He pointed to the stain, instantly making Edith feel far more comfortable with her slobbery. His eyes were green like leaves and in the sun they shimmered brightly. She knew she was daydreaming again, but she didn't care.

"Sorry, you asked about what I'm studying," she tapped her head gently to imply she had lost it a moment, "I'm really interested in nursing."

"Nursing, really?" He stroked his chin with a tight grin.

"What, you think I am too stupid to become a nurse?" she put her free hand on her hip, "I'll have you know, I did very well in highschool."

"I'm sure you did. All I was going to say was I pegged you more for a doctor."

Edith immediately relaxed, surprised again by his reply to her utter chaos.

"Oh, well, thank you." Her face tightened in confusion, "How do you know I am capable of something like that when you barely know me, outside a few details that your nosey and intrusive neighbor may have led you to believe?"

"I know that you are standing here, looking beautiful and not knowing it. I know that you are friendly, and you smile at every person that walks by, whether you know them or not. And I also know that you have been sitting on the grass all afternoon playing with the three kids and adorable little puppy instead of drinking with a few of the other questionable invites to this event."

She put her hand up, "Whoa, wait there a minute, I am not a boring girl like you are implying. So you are saying I must be a dork because I play with kids instead of drinking, so naturally I would make a great doctor?"

"No," he laughed again, this time smiling wider, "I thought that you were endearing to all those around you, a real caregiver. Plus Lisa told me that you had amazing grades in school."

"Wow, must be nice to know so much about someone." She put her plate down realizing she wasn't going to get much eating done. "What do I get to know about you?"

He tilted his head back and forth, looking sheepishly from side to side. "Well, you could have dinner with me."

"I mean, I could, but what if you are a serial killer and you abduct me?" She grinned wildly, waiting for a sarcastic answer to her reply.

"Then I guess you will be dead and won't have to worry about next quarter."

They both erupted into laughter.

"Seriously though, when you want to go out sometime," Edith pulled a pen out of her purse and began to write her number on the palm of his hand, "this is my number. I am renting a cottage out for the summer. This fall Lisa and I are rooming together at Thornsbury dormitory."

"Well, you take your life into your own hands when it comes to her," he laughed a bit, "but seriously, I'm glad she introduced us. Especially since in a week I'm going back to Massachusetts."

The floor dropped out from underneath Edith, "What?"

"I'm visiting my parents' home in Sharon."

A sigh of relief spread over Edith, "Oh! I hail from Eaton, New Hampshire, not too far from there."

"Rad! Dad started his publishing business there, and there's a large commercial section booming right now."

"That's exciting." She watched him close his hand tightly, hoping his sweat didn't wash away her number. At that moment she wished she had paper to write her number on, but would seem too eager if she asked to give him her number again. After all, if he wanted to call, he would.

The party ended a good five hours later as the sun went down behind the hills. Lisa and Edith had made their way down to the beach to feed the gulls the remaining hot dog buns. Edith parked herself next to Lisa and took a deep breath in, slowing her heart rate. The rush had been ongoing since she said goodbye to Harlem.

The wind was cutting into their faces and her long hair whipped her back. Lisa pulled the blanket around them and they snuggled as the light faded around them. It was funny how the sun was gone but an echo still remained for several minutes after.

Edith leaned her head up and looked at Lisa. Her cheeks were burnt red from the summer party. With her pale, Irish freckled skin, she was prone to burn rather than tan and avidly scolded Edith for having auburn hair and color to her complexion outside the average rouge of redheads.

"So you think this guy is ok?" She looked out into the ocean. The tide was coming in and the gulls floated along the wind.

"If I didn't think he was ok, do you think I would have set you up with him?"

Edith cocked her head to the side. "True, but I just needed to be sure." She buried her head into the fold of her arm.

Lisa smoothed her flying hair down and whispered in Edith's ear. "It's ok to be happy."

Edith sat up and looked at her friend, "I know it is, but I just wait for the day I am unhappy again."

"Then stop waiting," Lisa smiled gently at her best friend.

The girls stood up and walked back to the house wrapped together in the blanket, saying nothing at all. Back at the house the party was over and the mess was ready to be cleaned up. Red cups were lined along the table. Cigarettes were in the ashtrays around the pool and the bowls of chips were left with nothing but crumbs.

Lisa dumped the ashtray into the garbage bag, "So disgusting."

"This is why we are friends," Edith turned her nose up at the smell, "I can not for the life of me stand cigarettes or their nasty smell. I would rather never date than date a smoker."

"Well then you know that you are good on that end, Harlem won't touch the stuff."

"His breath was great, smelled of fresh peppermint." The girls laughed . Just then the phone rang.

"Probably my parents. They will be back tomorrow and I don't want them to know about the party."

"Don't worry, we'll have the place cleaned up in no time. Hand me that broom while you get the phone."

Edith watched as she pulled the phone off the receiver

"Hello," she looked outside.

Were her parents calling and angry? Did they find out that she had a party and there was a huge mess?

The tone changed when Lisa began to smile at Edith. She hung up the phone and walked through the slider to get outside.

"Well, what was that about?" Edith held the trash bag in one hand and the broom in the other.

"Oh nothing. Harlem said he would be picking you up tomorrow night at seven for your date and he wanted you to know he meant it."

"Wait, I gave him my phone number and he called you?"

"Well, he said you were going to mention that. See he tried calling you when he got home, but you didn't answer and he was too impatient to wait, so he called here, figuring we were hanging out a little late tonight. He even offered to come and clean up with us. Most likely just an excuse to hang out with you."

"And?" she was on the edge of her seat, "What did you say?"

"I said if you want to see Edith then you will have to do it the right way, and not by watching her pick up other people's trash."

The air filled with laughter as the two girls giggled at his expense.

The next day Edith stood in front of the mirror gleefully examining herself. An antique ivory comb slid through her long hair, a length that now had needed further attention than the previous months. Cora had given it to her about a year after she'd come to stay with them. Edith studied it for a moment, thinking about how Cora may have wanted to pass something down, almost generationally.

Perhaps she had used it before to comb her daughter's damp hair after a bath. When Susan would have come of age, Cora would pack it away in her daughter's boxes to move on with her to the next chapter in her life. Just hoping, perhaps, one day she may come across it and think of those times with her mom. Edith had lost a parent and Cora a daughter, and in turn they had found one another. Six months ago the thought of such things would have extinguished her happiness. Now, it brought a slight crook to her smile.

Edith looked back to the mirror. Her hair was neat, but something was missing. She slid her hand into the narrow drawer just below the vanity top, looking for a hair piece. It was generally used for jewelry, but she was not one for such lavished items. Instead she placed momentums. Tucked in the back of the drawer was a small sleek plastic barrette, perfect for the occasion. A barrette that had been taken with her from Pawtucket, her previous home. A way to tie in the old and the new. She placed it in the top corner of her hair, near her grown-out bangs. From her purse she withdrew a light shade of rosy lipstick which she applied over her lip gloss. She didn't wish to seem overly interested, but absolutely wanted to look her best.

Like clockwork, Harlem showed up at seven to pick her up. Lisa, who loved to meddle, had called him back after Edith left to give him her address, knowing full well that Edith wasn't brazen enough to do it herself. He was dressed in slacks with a button down shirt, and his long hair was combed back and styled for the evening. She was glad that he had hair that was a manageable length compared to ruffians she knew from school. Most wore thick mustaches that covered their mouths, and hair down all the way down their backs. How was this such a trend?

Harlem's hair went just below his ears and he was clean shaven. Never having been a fan of mustaches and all that gets stuck in them, she hoped that he would omit growing one.

"So what's your plan, Cassenova?"

"Who said I had a plan for tonight?" he cocked his left eyebrow, which heightened her excitement. Who was this guy? Someone she had only met a day ago: a man who had suddenly waltzed into her life carrying a burst of joy that she only could have hoped for these past few years.

"Ok, you got me." He shrugged. "Just stop acting like I am so predictable, like you can tell exactly what I am dressed for."

"Well, if you must know, I can." She said it in such a matter of fact way that his expression turned offended within seconds. They walked out to the car. He opened the door and put out a hand to help her inside. It was not the type of car that she'd found in New Hampshire. Edith's hand-me-down truck from Cora had looked like a garbage truck compared to this marvel. It was a 1973 Stingray.

The idea that perhaps Harlem had come from money was now set in stone. He had not only come from money, but quite a lot of it. Coming from humble means, she was not about the almighty buck. She was rich in personality and intelligence; something far more valuable than a wallet stretched to fit hundred dollar bills.

But nowadays, her wallet was far from being filled, having lived on her own for only a few months. The idea of a gentleman treating her to an expensive dinner in the city may be just exactly what she needed. Instead of turning left out on Route 1 though, they took a right, heading back to his neighborhood and the beach. Perhaps she was wrong. Then again, a good amount of fine dining was in Narragansett and many were along the water's edge.

She could still be right about the trajectory of the evening. Then they passed the street with all the high class dining. Where was he taking her? The streets continued to whizz by along with any prospects of dining in Narragansett. Most of the restaurants were located along a long strip of shore line. Tourism in the summer is how they made their money for the year. Come October, the restaurants either closed until spring or went down to part time for the locals. Most of the area was residential.

As she passed through the different sectors of Narragansett, she began to understand the diverse and eclectic grouping of homes. Some were from the past century, while others were thrown up quickly after the second world war to accommodate the baby boom. Then came the vacation home for every day folks, people who would come down and rent a cottage for a week in the summer. A local getaway or a beach vacation for those coming in from out of state. With the nice restaurants behind them, Edith had run out of ideas of where Harlem could be bringing her. *I guess tonight the menu would consist of clam cakes and chowder at Aunt Carrie's,* she thought wryly.

Finally he made a turn she recognized, yet her confusion had reached an all time high. They were heading for Lisa's street. Did Lisa have something to do with this? Was she hosting a dinner at her house and Edith had just thought that this was a private date for some reason? Was this romance all in her head? And there went Lisa's street.

Edith couldn't take it any longer, so she turned to look at him. She had avoided it until now, knowing full well the second she looked at him, he would get the satisfaction of being right, that she had absolutely no idea where they were going tonight. That he had planned a completely sporadic evening that she could not figure out. For a guy she had just met, she was really starting to like him a lot.

The car suddenly turned to the right and they were driving into the beach parking lot at Sand Hill Cove, a state beach near Galilee.

Edith threw her hands up into the air, "Ok, I give up, you were right!"

Harlem threw the car into park and turned in his seat, his left arm still resting on the steering wheel.

"I know." He turned in his seat and without another word he got out of the car. Edith looked back and forth, dumbfounded by the events that were occurring. Then her door swung open and his hand was again there to help her out.

"Did you pack sandwiches?" She sounded snooty, but she couldn't help feeling a bit presumptuous. Just because he drove around in a beautiful, expensive car, didn't mean he automatically had to be taking her out for a night of luxurious expenditures. Instead perhaps he was trying to just win her with personality, that and being overall the most attractive man she had ever met.

Honestly, he didn't have to be a nice guy, he had enough looks to outweigh the benefits of anything else. The fact that he had let her out of the car by offering his hand was putting him into a whole other bracket of potentials. Edith suddenly had no idea what to imagine for the evening.

They slowly ascended the sand dunes. The wind, held back slightly by the broken dune fences, whipped the sea grass into their legs. The sun was setting and the scene was spectacular. Edith had spent many a night down at the water with Lisa, but this was like nothing she could have ever imagined. Not only was the sky painted in a smears of pink and lavender, bright yellow and fading oranges, but amidst the bold and brazen colors was a blanket, held down by four big rocks, a wicker basket with two folding tops, a bucket of ice with two bottles of champagne and multiples plates covered with sterling silver platter tops.

A gentleman stood there in white coattails decorated with a thin trim of gold. He was an older man, perhaps in his sixties and he seemed delighted to be there. To say she felt astonishment was the understatement of the century.

Edith realized that her mouth was hanging open and closed it abruptly. "I just…" She looked around at the blanket again before looking out into the fading glow of the falling rays.

"So I did good?" He was smiling from ear to ear.

"Good? Are you kidding me?" She was practically laughing as a reaction to the shock she was experiencing. "I have never seen anything like this before, so why?"

"Why what?" His eyebrows came together forcing a rather muddled expression. Of course he didn't understand how someone like her would be overly impressed by such a romantic gesture.

"Why me? I mean, you don't know me at all." She put her hands over her face realizing that he had gone out of his way to make this an incredible night and she was ruining it by overthinking it entirely.

"Well, I may have just met you, but you see, any other girl would have just taken in this moment of joy and splendor. They'd assume from the beginning that they had a shot with the guy who did it. You were different. I've known that for a while. Lisa is always talking about you, telling all the groovy things you two do together. I had to listen to her go on about you for months until we were introduced.

"Then I saw you and though I didn't know who you were, I thought you were the most beautiful woman I'd ever seen. You seemed to look like you were having trouble fitting in, you were just like me. I am terribly awkward in social gatherings. Then when you ate the hot dog and got mustard all over your face, I knew I had to walk over and meet you.

"Lisa came over later and said, 'Didn't I tell you that Edith was amazing?' I wasn't even sure it was actually you and you had stolen my mind. So I knew I had to do something wild for you, a massive gesture that would knock your socks off."

"Well you certainly accomplished that." She looked over at the gentlemen still standing by the blanket, beginning to now feel awkward that they were never introduced. "Hello, I'm Edith."

"Oh, I'm so sorry. This is Edward, he works for my family. When he heard I was going to try and pull this off with only a day's notice, he was more than happy to help out. Edward has been in my family's employment since I was eight."

Edward bowed his head at Edith "Pleasure to make your acquaintance." He then turned his gaze to Harlem, "I think I will take my leave and let you two enjoy your evening. When you are done, just let me know and I will come by to collect the dishes."

"Thank you, Edward." Harlem shook his hand and clasped his arm with the other. A sign of respect for the long serving member of his family's staff.

As soon as Edward was over the dunes, they took their seats on the blanket.

"Harlem, this is way too much."

Harlem stopped her and put his finger to her lips.

"It's nothing, I'm happy to see you smile so much."

The first lid came over revealing chilled oysters with horseradish cocktail sauce and a light pink mignonette. They each made up an oyster and tipped the shell, allowing the mollusks to slide off into their mouths. While the sauce was tangy and spicy, the salty treat was smooth going down. They finished the oysters off in minutes.

The second dish contained a variety of soft and hard cheeses, salted meats and decadent ripened fruits. Some she had never seen or heard of. Edith followed Harlem's mouth as he told her about each kind, tearing off a piece for her to try. The brie and prosciutto were by far her favorite. She placed a piece of the brie and a plump blackberry between two salty slivers of meat and gulped it up. After the second course she had no idea what to expect next.

Then the third and final dish was lifted to parade a tray of chocolate covered strawberries. It was a beautiful presentation but Edith, no longer starving, could resist the delicacies before her. She was not about to be the first person to eat a chocolate. She had already gorged on the first two courses. Instead she waited for her host to make his plate, giving her the excuse to go to town.

The food was delicious, salty and well balanced. Harlem popped the champagne and the cork flew clear across the blanket. The two strangers, more acquaintanced now, laughed as the head foamed hastily from the narrow-necked bottle. It was an easy moment of joy. The meal was the easy part, before the date would begin to get complicated.

What would they talk about once the food was gone? Edith sipped the drink slowly. It was incredibly refreshing going down, glass by glass. She realized that while it was sweet like soda pop, it was alcohol and she would have to take it easy in order to not *get* easy. She was a virgin after all and wasn't about to give away the milk to the first guy that took her out to pasture. The idea of it was so utterly ridiculous it made her laugh and spit out a bit of the champagne. Immediately embarrassed, she covered her mouth, searching the blanket for a clean napkin to wipe up her mess.

Harlem burst out laughing "What was so funny?"

"Oh nothing, just me coming up with jokes in my head that only I would laugh at."

"Oh my god, you do that too?" He was overjoyed. Edith realized with a shock that this guy who drove a fancy car, and had a butler serving exquisite meals on the beach was just an average kind of guy after all. One who made silly jokes and acted foolish like the rest of the mere mortals, no matter how God-like his appearance was.

"So if you don't mind me asking, how did your family get to where your family is today?" Edith thought about it for a second and then realized the question may have seemed impertinent to a man she had only met a day ago. "Sorry, you do not have to answer that."

"I can absolutely see why you would ask me, so I, of course, will answer you." He leaned back on his elbows, "Well, my grandfather had a shipping business and his father ran it before him. This went back generations, back to when things were transferred only by sea. My father's inheritance made him wealthy when my grandfather passed away. Business became a massive responsibility for my father to undertake. At the end of the day, he had never wanted to be in shipping, regardless of his father's wishes. He had plans to go to school to start a printing company.

"So my father sold the business and brought his new-found wealth into the modern world. In Cumberland, he bought up a commercial building where he could print his favorite thing in the world, books. This may surprise you, we may look like Astors, but we are more like Chaplins. He started small, marketing his company through local business. Bookstores, supply chains for office products, libraries even. Once he had a foothold in the publishing world, he decided he was going to go big or go home. Home just happened to be in Massachusetts."

"Wow, that's amazing, how brave to forge your way through so many obstacles."

"Yeah, but enough about me. Tell me something about you." He leaned on his side handing her a chocolate covered strawberry. She waved him off, not wanting to talk and chew at the same time.

"Well, what do you want to know?" She folded her knees, wrapping her arms around them tightly, like a security blanket, protecting her from the words that would inevitably leave her lips.

"I don't know, tell me about your parents."

And there it was, the moment she had been waiting for. What would she tell him? Should she ruin such a fine evening telling him the tale of a dead dad, a comatose mother and a dead aunt who practically was like a mother to her? How would that go over? How could he look at her the same way after that? He would, in turn, look at her the same way that everyone does the moment they learn the truth about poor little Edith's sad and pathetic life. The pity would be so absurd she would exit the dinner like Cinderella leaving only a sandal behind.

Edith felt suddenly weary from the weight of so much loss, and the pity of everyone she'd known in Eaton. She may have lost her parents, but she was a college-attending nursing student, not some pathetic orphan. Edith bit her tongue quietly when she realized she was releasing her parents and embracing Cora and Ansel as her truest family.

"Well, I was raised by my Aunt Cora and Uncle Asnel," she began.

Chapter 20: Samantha, Late Spring 1996

Atop the kitchen table sat a small card stock with small printed letters accompanied by a name in bold black ink. Samantha lifted it closed to her face and read it aloud.

"Samantha Anderson, class of 1996, Narragansett High School." She let out a huff with the last word.

"Oh come on, it's not going to be all that bad." Adam came around behind her, wrapping his arms securely around her chest. His lips grazed her neck gently, and she jerked away.

"You know that tickles. I swear you do that on purpose." She grinned and backed away slowly.

"I do what? No way, no chance." He edged towards her, his fingers reaching out ready to grab her, and then the chase ensued.

Sam darted around the sofa, putting space in between her and Adam. They both laughed hysterically. Across the room, the phone rang. The chime stopped them both dead in their tracks and they turned to face the distraction.

"To be continued," Adam said before sliding into the bedroom.

Sam rolled her eyes and picked up the receiver, "Hello?"

"Sam." A single word had caused her mood to shift drastically.

"Hello, Mom." Her tone deflected any sincerity that had been in Edith's voice.

"I know I am probably the last person you want to talk to right now. My behavior over the holidays..." she paused, reflecting on her words. The thoughts of that night had scrolled through her mind time and again, leaving her restless, knowing she was consistently falling short as a mother. This had to be a turning point.

"I have somewhere to go, sorry, I don't have much time to talk." Sam's eyes darted around the room, wishing to avoid small talk. The fire rushed up her throat, but she pushed it down, trying to restrain the anger she was still repenting of after all these months apart.

She had never had a family, aside from her sisters. Mildred had played a major role as caretaker, but she was not necessarily family. Now, Sam had a man that she planned to spend her life with. What was her mother's intention for this phone call out of the blue? Was she finally now offering to fix what had been long since broken?

"That's actually what I called to talk to you about," Edith's voice was begging for a moment of reprieve.

"What's that?"

"I heard from Lisa that you're graduating today." Her voice choked up for a moment and Sam stopped breathing, a silent gasp. While she resented her mother, she was still incapable of not feeling guilt when her mother was falling apart. Afterall, she had years of practice.

"I knew I would not receive an invitation, I understand that." She coughed to cover the sniffle. "I just wanted to tell you, that you and you alone got yourself to this moment and that aside the fact that you do not wish for me to be part of it, I'm so very proud of you, Samantha."

Tears rolled down Samantha's cheeks and she wiped them quickly. As though her mother was expecting a reaction and she wished to not disclose the candor of the moment.

"Well, I just,—" Sam paused to choke up a little and then cleared her throat again, "I just figured you wouldn't be able to make it. New Hampshire isn't right around the corner, you know."

"Sam, I wanted to be there. I should be there, and I should have been there, all along." Sincerity rang through the phone and Sam looked over to see Adam leaning against the doorway of the kitchen. His chin dropped and his eyes looked up at her longingly. He knew that she needed to finish this moment with her mom before he embraced her, but he was ready to catch her the second she was finished.

"Ok," she breathed out loud and said slowly, "Well, I gotta go now."

"Oh, of course you do." A silence took over the phone and Edith waited for her daughter to say the words. The single most important words that she needed so desperately to hear. The words she would do anything for. *I love you.*

"OK, bye Mom."

"Bye." The phone clicked and Samantha fell into Adam's arms. The tears poured from her eyes, reddening her cheeks in anger, resentment, hostility and pain. Edith had been given endless chances to become a mother. Naturally, just in the moment that Sam had given up on ever having what so many possessed and failed to appreciate, her mother threw a Hail Mary.

"Are you ok?" Adam stroked her arm with his thumb and kissed her forehead, trying to ease her pain.

"I don't know." She looked up at him. Her skin was blotchy and her makeup ran down her puffy cheeks. She nestled deeply into his chest, as his hands stroked her arms.

"Hey, I have an idea." He kissed her head again, and his cheery voice helped her snap out of the moment. "Why don't we go to the ceremony and then we can figure this whole thing out when we get home?"

Sam nodded her head in agreement. This day *was* a celebration and she knew that she had everything that she needed for it. Lisa had planned to show up for the ceremony, coming straight from her finals. She would be her surrogate mother for the evening.

Adam opened the closet and pulled his robe out of the plastic liner they had picked it up in from the dry cleaner. His hat barely fit his head of hair, having grown it out to celebrate actually graduating from a school. Having the chance to join his future wife at prom and now their graduation brought his immense satisfaction. Sam studied his face. A bright aura of yellow fluttered around him, a halo of sorts. A sign of true contentment.

Her thumb smoothed the edge of his cheek and she wrapped her arms around his neck, kissing just below the chin.

She whispered, "I love you so much."

"What do you say you put on this cap and gown and we go start the rest of our lives?"

She rolled her eyes at him for the millionth time and took the cellophane wrapped garment from his hand.

"Let's go."

They stepped out of the car and closed the doors. Slowly they took in the hundreds of families gathered with their special graduate. Most were taking pictures together with friends and neighbors; many whom they had known their entire lives. Having only moved to Narragansett at the beginning of the school year, Adam and Samantha had not fully formed any emotional ties to the community. They recognized a few classmates, including a stoner kid named Chris Henshaw whom they had met at the beach one night.

Adam saw him across the parking lot. While Adam usually tried to avoid detection, he knew at that moment Chris had seen them, and he smiled. Chris was completely harmless and quite entertaining, so Sam and Adam greeted him with open arms. Practically their only friend in common at the school, they were happy to be welcomed by anyone in the desperate moment. A moment when they were in need of acceptance.

"Dude, today is the day." Naturally he was still stoned. They were never quite sure if his mind was actually ever clear.

"*Today* is the *day*." Adam said emphatically enunciating the first and last words of the sentence to match Chris's laid-back enthusiasm. Adam turned his gaze over at Sam to find her barely able to control herself. She was snickering desperately in his shoulder.

"Do you want to meet my folks?" Chris's arms stretched out across the parking lot to indicate his family was just over the line of bushes, where he had apparently descended from.

"Sure, why not?" Adam grabbed Samantha's hand and whispered, "Here we go," as Chris led them through several families dressed in their best attire.

"Mom, Dad, this is Adam and Samantha."

Sam was suddenly stretching her arm out to shake the hand of Chris' mother. She was a shrill woman with a tiny frame. Her hair was wiry and she looked a bit on the outside of society, based on her mannerisms. She was continually glancing over her shoulders, mindlessly pulling at the cotton sleeve of her dress, or fixing a loose curl that repeatedly sprung out from the bobby pin she had fastened tightly around it. This would be interesting.

"Hello, I'm Samantha."

"Hi Samantha, I'm Christopher's mother." Her dainty hand briefly touched Sam's fingertips before slipping back to her side.

"Shep, Chris's father." A tall, burly man stepped forward and gave an engaged handshake, almost crushing Sam's hand in the process. The handshake was released a moment later. She looked to Adam, who was too busy shaking his hand to meet Sam's gaze. While Shep was not a laid back surfer like his son, it was obvious that he knew how to let loose, and also probably manage situations when his son decided to get into more mischief than he could swallow.

"Dad's a state trooper." Chris smiled from ear to ear at the words. His pride in his father was outward and heartfelt. "Served now for twenty years."

"Sir," she felt it only right to address him in proper fashion knowing his authority.

"Don't be silly, you can call me Shep." He waved her off chuckling. He was not going to take his position too seriously on a day like this.

The brief laugh brought ease to the conversation for Sam for a short while. Adam could see the color coming back to her face. She was never one to take men of authority lightly. Every time she passed them on the highway she would scratch her nose. It was almost a tick. Something she would do to tell them that she didn't notice them and had been behaving like an admirable citizen all along.

The other families seemed to be heading in the direction of the auditorium now.

"Should we follow them?" Chris's mom, while quiet, was persistent in them moving along toward the event and away from any awkward moments with strangers.

The students were all lined up in the front of the auditorium according to their last name. Sam was in the first row as usual with all the A's and B's. Oh how she had wished that she and Adam were married already and she could have had his last name. At least that would have guaranteed someone to smile at while she threw her hat in the air. Instead she was placed next to a brunette with stick-straight hair named Melissa Allen, a punk fresh chick with several non-traditional piercings, and some carefully chosen overly colorful tattoos to boot. She barely knew her outside of their mutual History of War class last semester. To the right of her was the star jock of her high school, Jason Andrews. He was the captain of the football team, the wrestling team and the baseball team. He was good looking, of course, but his smug attitude turned his dimpled chin into a place that Sam would have liked to rest her fist once in a while.

The letter of acceptance from University of Rhode Island had come in just before Christmas. She had always had a knack for science, but her recent studies in history had her heading down an alternate path. Sam had decided to combine both science and history and study human origin. Something she felt a deep desire to understand about herself.

The day the letter came was like no other. Lisa was standing there, giddy as a school girl, the day Sam had received it. After they read the letter aloud, Lisa had blown a kazoo. She couldn't wait to have her sister around more often than she already was. Perhaps being the only family that Lisa had made her hold fast to her little sister's company more than ever. While living with her sisters and mom, Lisa had spent so much time trying to find a way out that she failed to see what she was leaving behind. Her visits to see her mom and youngest sisters were infrequent. With work and school in play, the opportunity for R&R became less frequent.

Sam spun her head around, taking in the stands surrounding the students. Families packed like sardines on the bleachers, hoping to get a shot of their little graduate crossing the stage. There in the back of the auditorium she saw Lisa. While she was nearly ten rows back from her, the tears in her eyes were visible. The flush in her cheeks were irrefutable. She was the mother that Sam never had, the best friend she always needed and the sister that everyone wanted. If Jessica and Theresa had been there, it would have been perfect. While they loved their big sister, they also didn't yet understand the importance of this day. Besides, Edith had not put any effort into ensuring that her sisters would be present. She blew a kiss at her big sister, only thirteen months older than she and wiped a tear as it fell from her eye.

"Today is the day you start a new chapter in your life. Today is the beginning of so many tomorrows. Remember that only *you* can predict where *you* are going to go. You are your own wings, only you can fly to where you belong in this world, my little sparrows. And so, I would like to read something to you that changed my life when I was just your age."

Principal McIntire reached into her suit jacket pocket and pulled out a folded piece of paper. Her tightly curled, bleach blonde hair was perfect as usual. She pulled her glasses up from her chest and perched them on the tip of her pointy, shriveled nose. At her age she was most likely going to be sharing a quote by Walt Whitman.

"And now a quote from my favorite author, Walt Whitman."

Sam heard the words and her head tilted back in laughter with a little snort. She quickly corrected herself. Everyone around her gave her a crude look. She mouthed *sorry* and then shifted her eyes back to the old woman on the podium.

"There was a child that went forth every day..."

The passage from Walt Whitman was sweet and kind, but formed a drowsy spell over the ceremony. Most of the classmates at this point were getting fidgety in their seats and began talking before the poem even concluded.

"...And these become of him or her that pursues them now."

The crowd applauded as she finished the poem and she nodded in gratitude. Then leaned into the microphone and said, 'Students, please rise."

Sam was used to being called up among the first. Having a last name starting with A you were sure to be close to the beginning for everything. She stood up and gazed around the room as she approached the stairs to the stage. The auditorium had to have been filled with at least two thousand people. Flashes were scattered throughout the crowd, temporarily impairing her vision. After a moment she caught Lisa waving at her eagerly. She turned her eyes to see Adam smiling at her. Her name was next. She got on stage and shook Ms. McIntire's hand and accepted her diploma.

The rows of students went through like sand through an hourglass. Parents sat watching as their little Timothys and Sarahs walked across the stage to grab their small certificate. Grandparents stood up and took photos with their disposable cameras. Sam wondered if the pictures would come out clear at all. Most students stopped and would smile for a photo while others hooted and hollered. Finally Adam got to the stage. He turned and blew a kiss through the air to Sam. She lifted her hand swiftly to grab it.

At that moment she looked out again into the crowd. Her eyes shifted, searching the outer rim of the room, she looked down the rows and aisles rapidly, expecting to be wrong, hoping she had been a fool all this time. In the crowd she would see her. Then the fleeting moment was gone and she closed her eyes tightly, fighting back the tears. That was the first time she missed her mother.

Chapter 21: Edith, June 1975

The neighborhood was built high up into
the hills, perched among the lavish homes erected
for the business elite away from the rush of city
life. Gated communities built in the last few years
met turn of the century single family homes,
grandfathered into the neighborhood. Some were
left to flake paint in the early summer sunlight
while others were getting a facelift, their owners
hopeful that they could sell and move to Florida
come the end of summer.

It was not the usual type of neighborhood
that Edith had experienced. Her first home had
been in Pawtucket. Tight knit families all
squeezed together in grid lock communities.
They'd drop by the chain link gate every day to
say hello. Neighbors would stroll by with their
small lap dogs, who drained themselves on the
grass that was mostly a nuisance to cut. This often
infuriated her father. The grass was never the
same shade of green. Every other patch of grass
would return, but that one spot was damaged
beyond regrowth.

Edith smiled, thinking for a moment about
her mother and father and realizing it didn't cause
her pain. Perhaps there would be many more days

like that to come. Her father was at peace after all, and while her mother was unaware of the fate of her father, she might be spared from ever knowing the true burden that comes with feeling everything at once.

A thumb slowly slid across the top of her hand and Edith came out her daze to meet Harlem's eyes. He smiled and then kissed the back of her hand before returning his own to the stick shift. The engine was loud, but his car seemed to sail down the smoothly paved streets of his family's neighborhood.

"So, your parents live *here*?" She craned her neck to look out the window up at the towering homes with sculpted lions and dragons balanced on the posts of the columns, framing the entrances to the elongated driveways. He could see the fear in her eyes.

"Yes and don't worry, they will love you." His voice seemed sincere enough that Edith relaxed for a moment. That was until the car shifted its gears slightly, pushing the engine harder as they began to ascend to his parents' castle on the hill.

"I'm not sure I agree with you on that, but I am willing to give them the benefit of the doubt. What did you say your surname was again, Kennedy?"

"Ha ha, very funny." The car came to a stop at the peak of the driveway. The driveway circled next to the garage and they parked there to avoid detection for a moment. He stepped out of the car and watched her as she leaned forward to look up at the front door.

"They won't bite, I promise."

She got out and quietly shut the door to the car, as though stealth would keep his parents from hearing their approach and she could scuttle her way back into the vehicle to hide.

"That's what everyone says about their parents."

"And how many people's parents have you met?" His eyebrow raised in an inquisitive fashion.

"This *would* be my first." Ronnie didn't count after all, having known his parents longer than they ever dated each other. Harlem had gone to see Ansel with Edith in March, and shook his hand in a way that Ansel winked and smiled at Edith. He observed the boy's mannerism and prompt respect for him as her father figure with gratitude. Ansel was becoming more than a father figure every day. And so he was introduced to Harlem as only he could have appeared. Edith had described him as her dad after all in general conversation. He knew nothing different. While her own father could never be replaced, Ansel had grown into an ever-necessary role that a young girl would need in trying to navigate life.

Now it was her turn to impress Harlem's family. But looking at the gorgeous brick exterior and lavish gardens, never mind the gold plated door knocker and glamorous name plate on the house wall, she was intimidated.

Before Harlem could ring the bell, the door swung open to reveal a very beautiful, bouncy woman. Her hair was as blonde and curled as Farah Fawcett, her gleaming white teeth were accented by the long strand of pearls clasped tightly around her neck. She screamed in exultation and ran to hug her son. Within a moment she turned to Edith and without a thought, wrapped her arms tightly around her too.

"Hello, I'm Edith." Edith looked at Harlem, her eyes wide, speaking through a griddy smile, not quite sure what else to say. Her arms struck straight down on her sides.

"Edith, it is such a pleasure to meet you," her southern accent came out thickly. Edith was not expecting it at all. She looked to Harlem once again, indicating her shock. The accent, while unexpected, was slightly comforting. Cora had always had a southern drawl and she had come to miss its twang these past years.

As soon as his mother made room for them to walk inside, he leaned over to whisper in Edith's ear, "Yeah, she was the runner-up for Miss Georgia, 1950."

Edith's mouth hung open. His mother caught it and jokingly commented,

"If you leave that open too long, you'll catch flies." And then responded to her own joke with an ingenuine laugh. Edith's face must have flushed because his mother immediately rubbed her arm.

"Oh sweetheart, I'm just joking with you. Y'all come in and join us for a brandy."

Harlem had a brief moment of pause. Edith, ill prepared for their southern hospitality, swiftly kicked Harlem in the shin, while his mother began to raid the liquor cabinet.

"Um, Mama, we don't really drink."

She had already picked up the decanter, "Oh," a pout spread over her glistening skin, "well then, how about some sweet tea?"

"Sweet tea will be great, thank you Ma'am." Edith said practically sweating through her shirt. She pulled Harlem down far enough to whisper in his ear, "We do drink, you know that, right?"

He smiled and then whispered back, "Not like they do." Edith readjusted her stance.

"Oh." She looked to see his father in the corner of the other room with a cigar in his mouth.

"Bill." His mother said forcefully.

"Yes, Judith?"

The paper folded down as Harlem's father realized that his guests had arrived. He stubbed out his cigar and picked up his hard blown glass of what she could only assume was whiskey by its coloring. Ansel wasn't much of a drinker, but he often would have a drink to warm up after shoveling in the dead of winter.

He stood and began walking steadily over to the two of them. Harlem reached out his hand to shake his father's. Edith was a little taken back by the gesture. Wouldn't he hug his father? Ansel hadn't been the most heartfelt man, but by the time she had left, they had enough of a rapport to warrant a hug. Perhaps in their family, they didn't have the same familial responses. She hadn't been from a traditional family, so she was in no place to be judging others on their public displays of affection.

"Hello, Sir," Harlem greeted his father with a tight smile.

"Harlem, who is this beautiful young lady?" He reached over to hold her hand in his two.

"Edith," she curtsied, not sure what to do.

"It's nice to meet you, Sir."

"Sir, what? You can call me Bill." *So I can call him Bill, but his son had to shake his hand and call him Sir?* This was a head scratcher for sure. It seemed that if she was going to survive this meeting, that she would just have to pretend like this was just your average family meal. For a day, she could pretend that she belonged in a neighborhood like this and that Harlem wasn't out of step bringing her home to meet his affluent parents.

"Well if y'all are done chit chatting, dinner is about ready." Judith turned to Edith with a toothy grin, "Are you familiar with gumbo?

Edith wasn't sure what to say: she had never tried it before. "No, I'm sorry, I'm not."

"Don't be sorry, dear. Besides, I haven't made that, I made chicken parm." She snickered again, "Well, actually Bettina did. She is a great cook," she whispered behind the back side of her hand, "from El Salvadore." She saw Edith's expression and explained further.

"No dear, I know what you're thinking," she cocked her head to the side, "is she making it the same way I am used to, or is she making it all spicy like they do where Bettina is from?"

"No, ma'am, I was actually wondering where the restroom was." Edith's neck was sweating profusely, she was sure she could feel the beads of sweat pelting down her forehead. It was early summer in Massachusetts, not notable for excessive heat waves, but standing in that hallway at that moment, it could have been a hundred degrees. She was afraid that they were about to roast her over dinner.

"Sure thing, it's the third door on the left." Judith pointed down the hall and returned to the dining room. Bill looked at Harlem and shook his head before sipping from his glass.

Edith took the chance and booked it down the hall. She didn't really need to use the restroom, just to wipe the glaze from her forehead and wash her hands. Minutes later, after fixing her bleeding mascara, she returned to the dining room where a beautiful set of china had been put out for the special occasion.

Edward had put out the food in a large spread. Edith was delighted to see him standing back by the sideboard, a familiar friendly face in this elegant house. He smiled quietly and said nothing, so she followed suit.

A small bowl of rolls was set on one end of the table. A pot of fresh pasta and chafing dish consisting of pounded chicken breast smothered in marinara and provolone cheese sat before her. The food was delightfully aromatic. To her surprise, Judith stood up and leaned her head towards the kitchen and began speaking Spanish. Judith saw Edith's expression of surprise before Edith noticed it herself.

"I know, right? I have been taking courses to learn Spanish. Bettina is a student at the culinary school and we are her international placement. I figured I could at least learn her language to make her feel a bit more comfortable in our home. To be honest, she speaks English very well, far better than some Americans I know in Massachusetts."

Bettina appeared in the room carrying a bowl of salad, which Edward brought to the table. She had been wearing a proper chef smock with her name embroidered into the coat just below the collar.

"You must be Bettina, thank you for cooking for us this evening." Edith smiled.

"You're very welcome, enjoy!" Bettina bowed slightly and left the room to go clean up.

"Look at you going and getting the most polite young lady we have ever seen, and a beauty no less."

"Mom, don't embarrass her." Harlem put his arm around Edith and rubbed her back slightly.

"What did I say? I just feel that my son deserves the best and I am *glad* that he has found her."

Edith appreciated the compliment, disregarding the fact that Judith had known her a whole twenty minutes, "Thank you, it's very kind of you to say so."

"See? No harm, no foul." She picked up the spatula and looked around the table. "Who wants the first piece?"

After dinner Edith grabbed the folded napkin that had been placed in her lap during dinner and wiped her mouth, "Thank you so much for having us over for dinner, it was lovely."

"You're very welcome." Judith motioned to the dishes "Don't worry about the dishes, Edward will clean them up. Why don't you two go for a walk and digest and we will meet back here in about an hour for a nightcap."

"Sure thing, thanks." Harlem held the door open to let her walk out. His hand immediately went to clasp hers, a natural sensation she had quite gotten used to over the past ten months.

"So when did your folks move to Sharon?" Edith looked around at the tall oaks that hung over the estates, winding down the road ahead of her.

"Shortly before I left high school. The house I live in currently was the home I grew up in, just down the street from Lisa. Though she's only resided there for the last nine years. My parents met in college and have been together ever since. They just love to have a good time, hosting guests is their favorite. They often find themselves entertaining men in the publishing business two or three days a week, with hopes of making healthy financial relationships."

"Well they have been doing well for themselves, that is obvious." Edith huffed a bit of air from her nose in a matter-of-fact expression.

"They sure have." He stopped and leaned down to kiss Edith. She was lost for a moment in the kiss. Another thing that had become so natural to the two of them, that it almost seemed that she missed it when they weren't kissing. Not being a girl of sentimentalities, she never expected herself to fall in love with someone like this. Ronnie had been a great guy and she thought she had loved him. Now she was sure she hadn't been aware that you need to be totally vulnerable to another person to truly feel love. She opened her eyes and a curl spread across her lips, lifting slowly at the edges.

Behind him she heard a little girl giggle and she shifted her position around him to see a small child with auburn hair in a sweet buttoned overall outfit. Her stockings had frilly lace tops and her hair was tied back in little pigtails and red ribbons. She couldn't have been more than two years old. Edith's smile went from endearing to a smoothed expression. There was something about the little girl that she felt was familiar. She couldn't tell what it was, but it made her feel a sense of unease. Then she heard a voice calling out the door. The little girl turned to hear her mother's voice.

Edith stopped in her tracks. Her heart raced, it was nearly ready to burst as its beat intensified.

"No, no, no."

"Edith, what's wrong?" Harlem put his hands on her shoulders, "Honey, what's wrong?"

He turned to see her looking up at the house. A woman with auburn hair was walking down the lawn and gingerly scooped up the girl into her arms. She began to sway the child back and forth, as though she was an airplane soaring in the air. The woman didn't stop this motion until she caught Edith's stare from fifty feet away. Iris hadn't seen her daughter in six years.

"Edith?" Her voice cracked.

Edith didn't speak, she just ran. She didn't know where she was running to, but she was running. The tears flowed, ran down her cheeks, like they were on fire, and the tears might extinguish the agony. She wanted to scream, but she was running, the breath escaped her. And besides, there was nothing left to say.

A mile down the road she came to a stop when a red Chevy pulled up in front her, forcing her to stop running from her past.

Her mother got out of the car. Her hair was curled and pinned back. Similar to the night her father died. Thin lines of gray streaked her temples, a testament to her age. She wrapped her sweater tightly around herself. As the night approached, the air was cooling down. Edith could once again feel the burning heat of her cheeks, this time from running and latent exhaustion.

"I know, I mean I don't know what you must be thinking." Her mother put her hands out, placing distance between herself and her estranged daughter.

"How about, what the *fuck* are you doing here?" Edith screamed at her mother, not caring to have respectable language or proper behavior. The anger built up in her stomach. She thought she may vomit.

"I live here."

She squinted her eyes in disbelief. Her mother had said it so cool and calmly. Like small talk between neighbors.

"What?" Edith shook her head, "Since when?"

"Since I left the facility nearly four years ago." She waited for Edith to blow. The inevitability of it was her only solid footing.

"I went there four years ago and you were *there*, out of it." Edith's temper intensified.

"No, I wasn't," she looked at the car, "Can we sit down and talk?"

The two women got in the car. The awkward silence was enough to clear a room at a bar, a storm was brewing.

"Your aunt came to visit me four years ago. She said that you wanted to see me. I was just getting back to normal and I wasn't ready to see you yet. She brought you to see me knowing that I would play it off like I wasn't better. It was just easier for her than having you wondering from afar. You would have seen me and thought I was all better to go just because I was no longer lost in my own thoughts. My dear Edith, I wasn't ready yet."

"Well, you sure look fine now." The resentment in her tone made her mother cringe a moment, but she continued.

"I met Ted when I was at the facility. His wife Anita had passed away delivering his daughter Anna. They were both lost so quickly that day. With their death, he found he was lost too. It was a traumatic thing that we both seemed to understand and share. We both had each other to lean on. A short while later, I felt that I was ready to go see you. So I drove up to New Hampshire. It was snowing, probably just a few weeks before Christmas." Her eyebrows pinched together as she recounted the evening.

"I parked the car at the end of the driveway, not sure if I would reach the top of the hill in Agatha's car. I saw you there, having dinner with your new family. You looked happy and healthy. That was when I realized that drawing up the old pain would not be better for you. That if you could leave it behind, leave me behind, that you would live a fulfilled life. So in turn, I moved into this house with Ted, we got married a year later and had your sister Shauna a year after."

Tears rolled down Edith's face. She wasn't sure if her mother loved her deeply or if she was eager for a chance to get off the hook.

"I guess then you have everything you wanted before. Dad and I are gone and you get to start from scratch."

"It's nothing that I wanted, none of it, it's just what happened. You understand, right? You are doing well for yourself. I want you to have that wonderful life you deserve."

"You mean with Cora and Ansel?" Edith wiped a tear from her cheek, the softness was gone, "Cora, my new mom, she's dead." She opened the door.

"Just like you. Goodbye mother." And she shut the door behind her.

Chapter 22: Samantha, Fall 1997

The chair legs screeched on the ceramic floors as the student stood up and scuffled awkwardly between their desks to the door.

"Now don't forget, your papers on naturalism in Classical sculpture are due Thursday promptly at the beginning of the class. This will go towards your final grade, so please make sure to put your best foot forward."

The short, balding man at the front of the classroom craned his neck as the students began to shuffle out. While this had not been a major requirement for Samantha's degree as a historian, she was eager to travel and thought that the Italian Renaissance sounded far more interesting than twentieth century American politics.

"Do you think he could have yelled any louder?" a girl about Samantha's age spoke to her.

Sam turned and saw that she had a very freckled face with bright, strawberry blonde hair tied neatly in a bun. Her outfit screamed grunge, yet she seemed to be creating her own vibe by carrying around a CD player blasting Boys 2 Men. The paradox was enough to make Samantha giggle a moment. Then she noticed that her sudden outburst must have made her seem either ridiculous or insane, possibly a little of both, and she straightened up.

"Yes, he can. I had Mr. Sherman last semester for History of the French Revolution. Sorry…" she placed her hand out between them, "Hi, I'm Samantha Anderson, Sam."

The young girl returned the gesture, "Hi, I'm Audrey Anderson."　　　　As they shook hands Sam studied her face. The likeness of her classmate and herself were oddly very similar. She had only hoped that she was not just now meeting one of her siblings, lost in the shuffle during one of her mother's many forgotten evenings.

Interested in learning more about her new friend, Samantha decided to investigate further. "So where are you off to? Are you free right now?"

"Yeah, I don't have class until three, so I'm around for the next two hours, why?"

"I just wanted to grab a coffee and I figured I would ask if you wanted to join me. I could definitely use a study partner for the course. Mr. Sherman is a nice man, but he's a tough grader and I could see him putting red lines all over my paper."

"Sure, I could grab a coffee. Lead the way." Audrey put her arm out suggesting that Samantha should show her which café she had in mind. There was only really one café on campus, unless you count the dining hall, and there wasn't a single soul brave enough to drink the coffee there. One cup of sludge was enough to make Samantha eat at home for the rest of time.

"So, Audrey, where are you from?" Sam wanted to know something right off the bat and not give her time to think about it. She felt as though this girl must know that Samantha suspected something strange.

"Pawtucket." Audrey pulled a wisp of hair away from her eyes as a few maple leaves fell from a tree and caught in her hair. It momentarily distracted Samantha before she processed it. The word *shit* came to mind. This could have been her sister. They were nearly a year apart. Perhaps she *was* Sam's younger sister. She definitely could not have been older than she; Lisa was only born thirteen months before Sam, but Edith definitely could have squeezed out another one after Sam and before Terry. Maybe she just wore big clothes or wasn't home or Samantha was too young to know her mother had been pregnant. She would have been an infant if that were the case. It was totally possible.

Samantha realized while her cogs were turning away that a blank stare had sprawled across her face, giving her the look of a deer in the headlights. She quickly came back to the conversation to cover her tracks.

"Oh, wow, Pawtucket. My family is from there." She studied Audrey's facial expression with the confession.

"Really, what part?"

"Darlington." Samantha's eyes perked up, trying to sound peppy and not so obvious that she was digging deeper into this stranger's past.

"Funny, my father's from Darlington. I lived there only a short while before we moved to Cumberland with my dad's new job."

"Really? That is too funny, small state." Sam was nodding and smiling with narrowed eyes.

"Are you ok?"

Samantha realized now that she had been acting a bit strange. It was probably not the best decision she ever made, but she might as well tell Audrey what she was thinking before it burst out of her.

"What's your mother's name?"

"Wow, um, Sharon?" Audrey's tone implied confusion and wonderment.

"As in, you don't know."

"As in, why are you asking?" Why was a girl she had just met interrogating her?

"Oh my god, I'm so sorry." She placed her hand on her forehead. "I just, ok, this is going to sound crazy."

"More than it already does, you mean?" Audrey's face immediately lit with a smile.

"Well at least you find this funny." A whine in her voice had implied that she was struggling to articulate what she was trying to say.

"How about you just tell me and I won't judge?" she nodded, "Fair?"

Before the chance came around for her to burst into a million pieces, she decided, *just come out with it already,* "I thought you may be my sister."

"Oh, well I wasn't expecting that, but ok, you got me, why would you think that?"

"I um, well, first of all, you have the same coloring as many members of my family and your last name is the same as my mother. You were born in the same city as me, plus my mother does have four children, so what's one more?"

"Well, I am very sorry to disappoint you, but my mother and father are Sharon and Doug Anderson. I am their only child and I have the exact same freckles across my nose as my mom and the same blue eyes as my father."

A mix of relief and sadness spilled over her in a moment. While Sam was happy that her mother had not abandoned a child, she was eager for more family. Especially with Lisa being the only sibling that lived nearby nowadays.

"What is your mother's name, Samantha?" Audrey asked, holding open the door to the café, "Maybe we have a common ancestry."

"Edith. Edith never married, and so she kept her father's name. I never knew my grandfather, he died when my mother was only fifteen."

That was when the conversation turned. Audrey stopped suddenly while walking through the door.

Samantha turned to see Audrey looking at her and realized that she knew something. "Does that mean something to you?"

"My father lost his uncle when he was only sixteen. His uncle's name was Paul Anderson. I believe we're cousins."

Audrey moved fully into the building, and Sam slowly sat in the chair closest to the door. The eeriness of the situation had completely caught her off guard. If she had learned that her mother had birthed another child, it would have been far less unusual to the situation. Instead there was a girl, a member of her extended family, sitting in front of her. A girl her mother had never made an attempt to introduce to them. To finally meet her cousin this way was breathtaking.

While the state that they lived in was small, the likelihood that she would find her family easily gave her hope that one day she would learn more about where she came from.

A wide grin spread across her face at the idea of learning more and without a pause began diving into more questions.

"So did you know my mom at all?" she leaned deeply into her arm that rested on the table, softly cupping her chin as she listened to the story of her mother's unknown past.

"No, honestly, I know of her, but I have never *actually* met her. It all changed so quickly when my dad was younger. He had shown me pictures of his dad and uncle, your grandfather, in their hey-day. Pictures of Paul and Edith down at the beach with Paul's other siblings, Tommy and Gertie."

"How many uncles and aunts does my mom have?" Sam leaned into her elbow, enthralled by the conversation.

"Well, aside from her dad, Paul, there's also Bobby and Gertie, and *my* grandpa, Tommy. My dad has a sister Shelby. Her husband is Ted. His parents were Irene and Tommy—a different Tommy. And Doug, my Dad, his grandparents were Henry and Estelle. So they are your paternal great grandparents. They died before I was born. I honestly don't know a ton about them." She caught Sam's awestruck face, "Sorry, just threw a bit too much at you all at once, huh?"

"God, no!" she shrieked, "Anything you know is far more than I have ever been told, so please feel free to share with me as much as you want."

The two girls sat nestled into the seats, eager to continue with their family tree. A few minutes later, a waitress came over with a folded pad of paper, "What can I get you girls?"

"Two cups of coffee. How do you take yours?" Samantha inquired of Audrey.

"Black, please."

Sam smiled, "Same." Another thing in common. They were both smiling now. A redness moved across Audrey's face, knowing how special this moment was.

"Ok, what about my grandfather? Honestly, I don't know much about him. My mom has a day every year that she drinks too much and talks about a rainstorm. A lot of it is lost to us. We don't know what she means. We always assumed he died suddenly, maybe from a car accident. She never mentions her mother really, outside her parents dancing in the kitchen to Cole Porter."

"Well, it was a car accident. Your grandfather was struck by a car one night, a couple of days shy of his forty-sixth birthday. It really hit the family hard. Your grandmother was a mess. She had asked him to go out for eggs, I guess. It was hard to get information out of the cops and your mom was just trying to hold it together for your grandmother, Iris. I guess it started to rain shortly after he left the house, he crossed the street without looking, and was hit by a distracted driver. Your grandmother went out looking for him and saw him dead in the road. She lost it, and went catatonic. After a while they placed your mom with a neighbor. She—the neighbor—was too old though, and after a number of weeks, they tried to put her with another member of the family."

"Why didn't she stay with your family, if my grandpa had so many siblings?" Samantha had heard the story, and while it was terribly sad, this was the part that always struck her the hardest.

"My father says that Grandpa Tommy had been struggling to take care of his own family. After my aunt was born, they had too many mouths to feed and it just didn't seem feasible.

Grandpa Tommy also had a drinking problem for a while, so no one thought that living with him would be best. Gertie was in a wheelchair and Bobby was her roommate and caregiver, being her twin brother. It just happened so fast and no one was expecting to take in a fifteen year old girl."

"So what happened to my mom?"

"I don't know," Audrey paused, "wait, *you* don't know?" Audrey sounded puzzled.

"My mom is not one for disclosing matters of the heart to her children. The only time she really talks about her past is when she is intoxicated and we would rather steer clear when she's like that. We have enough responsibility without having to take care of her emotional messes."

"Wow. All I know is that your mom moved away and her mother was institutionalized for years. I... Honestly, I don't know if she ever recovered or if she died in that place. *My* family was never the same after that. My father, Doug, moved to Cumberland with his folks a few years later. On his deathbed, my great grandfather, Henry, told my granddad Tommy that he was so ashamed of Tommy for letting Paul down. Great-Grandpa Henry hoped that when he reached heaven, his son was there and that he could forgive his siblings for not being there for Iris and Edith when they needed them most. Everyone makes mistakes, but he couldn't let it go, most of them couldn't."

"I honestly didn't know any of this. My family dynamic was pretty small before now. I kinda wish my mom would have been more open about her family with us. Although by the same token I understand how it must have been incredibly painful for her to talk about it."

"Maybe you can call and ask her?" Audrey shrugged.

"I guess, but so much has transpired recently between my mother and I. To be honest, we are not on speaking terms and it's partly my fault. I guess now knowing why she was moved to New Hampshire explains more about her excitement to return. She's home now."

"So she is in New Hampshire now? My dad would love to see her again. Maybe we could re-introduce them. I mean, maybe she remembers him."

"Maybe, granted, they weren't little kids when it happened, so there's a good chance she *will* know him."

"I have a family game night coming up this weekend. Why don't you join us?" Audrey's voice, suddenly high pitched, showed an eruption of excitement.

"Could I bring my fiancé?" Sam's face twinged, just remembering Edith's reaction to their engagement..

"Of course, what's his name?" Audrey was excited for her. "I didn't know you were engaged, have you been engaged a long time?"

"About a year now." Sam saw the look on Audrey's face. " I know what you're thinking, we are very young."

"Nah, there's no such thing as a right age for anything," Audrey waved her off, "bring him, yes."

Adam and Sam showed up to the address that Audrey had written down in Sam's notebook at the cafe. When she entered the house, a flood of people gathered around Samantha. To say she was overwhelmed was a slight understatement. Two older men and a handicapped woman approached her along with a couple whose arms were braided around each other. They seemed to all want a hug from this stranger who had just entered their home and their lives simultaneously.

"It is so nice to meet you, I'm your Great-Uncle Tommy." A tall skinny man with bright blue eyes framed in oversized tortoise shell rimmed glasses interjected.

"You look just like him. Paul, I mean. I'm Gertie," said the older woman with wiry cat eye glasses and softly curly gray hair in the wheelchair.

"She has Iris' smile for sure," said the other tall gentlemen towards the back. He wore an oversized shirt and had long sandalwood hair. "Sorry, I'm your Great-Uncle Bobby." He shook her hand.

Samantha wasn't smiling, at least she didn't think she was. Judging by their expressions, she must have appeared happy. Better than looking scared out of her wits. She looked back at Adam to find him shaking hands with the men and hugging the women hello. He was acclimating to the situation without a problem at all. If only she had the same social skills he did. After a while on a book tour you must get used to introductions with total strangers.

Just in the center of the crowd Samantha saw her cousin, Audrey. She seemed eager to show Samantha something in the back of the room. She grabbed a hold of Sam's hand and led her from the crowd. Resting along the back wall next to the opening of the kitchen sat a sofa table. A long oak pedestal, honoring all those whom they loved. It was a table boasting pictures of their family. Black and white still shots, slightly damaged from years of storage in humid attics. Edges torn, color faded in the natural light. Smiling faces throughout decades.

In the corner of the table stood a large black walnut frame with a tall light-skinned, freckle-faced man, a woman with obvious auburn hair and a little girl who could be Samantha's sister: it was her mother Edith.

She turned around and looked at her family, once distant and now closer together than ever before. The words came out quickly and she realized later that it may be too much to ask, but when would she have this opportunity again?

"I know this will be a lot, but I need to know about my mom, about my grandfather *and* about my grandmother. I need to know everything you know."

The siblings looked at one another and the oldest of the two pushed his glasses up his nose with his wrinkled hand. He had to have been in his sixties.

"I think we had better start with the night your grandfather died."

Chapter 23: Edith, Late Summer 1976

The red light on the phone indicated yet another message for Edith. She failed to notice. Her eyes were transfixed, staring blankly across the room. Her hair was wildly tossed, no comb pulled through it for weeks. An occasional shower was all that held her above the level of the rats that ran across the grounds of her apartment complex after it rained in the summer. She knew who had called her. It was the only person who called her continuously. There was nothing left for her to say or to do. There was no way she was ever going to be the girl he fell in love with again, no matter what he said.

That night his parents had been gracious enough and casually excused them for the evening. She hadn't even said goodbye, a simple, "Thank you for dinner, it was nice meeting you," was all she could muster. The saunter to the car resembled a drunken walk from a bar. She hadn't cried until she got home.

Harlem had pulled into the driveway slowly. Edith was grateful he didn't say anything. What was the right thing to say? He had thought her mother was in a facility, lost to her mind somewhere. How should one react when they find out their mother has chosen to abandon them and start a new family? While she appreciated his caring nature and the way he rejected her mother's decisions, the last thing she needed was someone who might push their own opinions of how to handle the matter.

The car had come to a stop and she pulled the handle and opened the door. Never once did Edith look at him. She looked half-dead as she pulled her body out of the car and dragged herself into the apartment. Her roommate was inside: Lisa would know what to say. The door stood ajar, but the apartment was empty, silent as the grave. Eventually she would tell Lisa how it all happened, what transpired that evening. For the time being the only thing she wished to do was sleep. If dreaming was an escape from reality, she would dream forever.

That was eight weeks ago and she had not yet called him. When he had showed up with food or flowers, she ignored the knocking. Lisa would tell him, "It's not a good time," like she had for the last several weeks.

Perhaps this had been Edith's moment to understand what Iris had gone through; what it's like when the air is knocked out of your chest, your heart is broken and you have no legs left to stand on.

"Edith," Lisa leaned into the other side of the bedroom door, she dared not enter without permission, "Edith, Harlem is here. He came to see you, since you won't answer his calls." She looked up at the ceiling searching for the words that would tell Edith what she needed to hear.

"If you don't want to be with him any longer, if you don't love him, maybe it's time that you let him go." This was the one thing that Lisa thought would get Edith to snap out of it. He was the only guy Edith had ever met that really made her light up inside. The thought that the light could burn out *had* to be enough to make her come back to life.

The room remained silent on the opposite side of the bedroom door for several minutes. Lisa turned away from the door, now face to face with Harlem. At her invitation, he had come inside to help Edith out of her trance. Lisa had hoped that if Edith wasn't willing to talk to him on the phone, that she might be accepting of his presence in her apartment after so many weeks apart.

"I just can't." Harlem shrugged, his hands dug deeper into his pockets "I can't just let her go, she needs me and I need her, Lisa."

"Right now, there's nothing that any of us has that she needs. Something in her mind is broken and only she can fix it. I guess that will take more time than what she's had over the last couple of months. Imagine thinking your mother was practically dead to you, that she would never return, only to find out this. She's despicable; how can she call herself a mother?"

Harlem pulled his hand out of his pocket. A small black box came out in the palm of his hand.

"I wanted to do it." He stopped a moment to close his eyes tight, "I wanted to do it after she met my parents." He looked up in an effort to hide the tears filling his eyes.

"I guess that will never happen."

"This isn't over, she loves you, she just..." Lisa's eyes found her feet.

"She just may never be the same again." He pursed his lips and looked around the room, avoiding eye contact.

"I'm sorry, if I thought she would, I'd give you hope." Lisa walked over and wrapped her arms around him. Edith opened the door a crack, the light pouring slightly onto her face. She saw Lisa, her best friend, and her boyfriend embracing. Her feeling was nothing of malice or resentment. She neither took it as love or betrayal. If someone was to find happiness in all this, it should be the two people she loved most in the world. The door creaked and the two of them parted.

Harlem looked up and saw Edith standing there. Her bathrobe was tied tightly around her waist and her auburn hair had been put up in a bun to control the nest that had formed. Her face was sallow and blotchy, from weeks inside lamenting over the life that was.

"Edith, hi." He looked at Lisa and then at Edith. "I hope you don't..."

Edith lifted her hand up to stop him before he said something foolish. "Hey Lis, can you give us a minute?" She wrapped her arms around herself and looked down at her shuffling feet.

"Sure, no problem," she grabbed her keys, "I have to go to the store to get some milk anyway, I'll be back." The door clicked behind her.

"Can you sit down?" She motioned to the couch and took a seat beside him, "Harlem."

"Before you say anything, I'm sorry if I'm pushing in too fast. I know you said you needed time, I am just so worried about you. Lisa said you're not eating and you haven't left the house in weeks. Luckily, your professors have given you a chance to make up your course work due to the circumstances, but you only have a small reprieve to get the work completed, Edith."

"I have decided not to go back." She looked coldly into his eyes. Not shrill, but matter of fact, without regret or notion of uncertainty.

"But why? That's not necessary, you'll be fine." His hand reached up to stroke her cheek "we will be fine."

She gingerly grabbed his hand and pulled it down to her lap, "I think Lisa is right."

"What? About what?" His face expressed concern and then fell, "No, no Edith."

"We've been kidding ourselves, Harlem." Her face hung, desperation pulling down the sides of her cheeks. "You know I'm never going to be a girl who could fit in with your family. I grew up in Pawtucket, I hail from New Hampshire for goodness sake."

"Why does that matter?" He bit his lower lip, then let his eyes roam the room for answers, to find once again, the right thing to say. "My parents love you. You're smart and beautiful and you love me."

She looked into his eyes and tears welled.

"I mean, you love me, right?" He let go of her hands and stood up. "Edith."

"I think it would be better off, if we stopped this before it got beyond what we could end. I'd like to stay friends."

"Friends!" The anger in his voice rose high. "Edith, I'm in love with you." And he pulled the ring out of his pocket.

She just looked at it and didn't say a word. Her mouth hung open, pain clung to her face like a hook wretched in her skin, pulling her apart. She succumbed to the finalization of her decision.

"Oh, Harlem."

His eyes grew hard.

"See, I had this with me." He walked over to her, shaking the box in his hand "This was with me that night." All he could do was study it as he moved it around single-handedly. "I wanted to give this to you after we left my parents. There's this park that I played at as a kid and I was going to bring you there. In the spring at night there are a million stars that you can see from that park." He choked up a bit, "I thought it would be the best night of our lives." A tear fell down his face as he lifted his head to look at her, "I guess, I was wrong."

He put the ring in her hand and kissed her forehead. "Goodbye, Edith." His movements were quick and he was out the door, which closed behind him with a soft click.

Edith wailed in pain. She thought she was doing him a favor, that he had loved her less somehow now. Finally finding her footing, she stood up swiftly, grabbing her coat and rushing for the door. She could run after him, tell him she was sorry and she did love him, she was just scared and screwed up. If he was willing to love her no matter what she had been through, then maybe he was worth it after all.

Her hand grasped the door knob and began to turn it. Something stopped her and she released it. A sinking feeling in her gut, a sudden urge to throw up where she stood. She dashed away from the door and ran to the bathroom. Before she knew it, she was vomiting heavily into the toilet. The pain in her stomach was unbearable. The taste of bile clung to her lips and tongue. She could feel it rising up in her throat again and again. Her bare red knuckles clung tightly to the toilet and she thanked god that Lisa had cleaned it that morning. The fresh lemon scent still rested on the rim of the seat.

Edith leaned her back against the wall, touching her head back into the tile. The sudden nausea was confusing. She scrolled through a calendar in her mind. She covered her eyes when she realized that it had been ten weeks since her last period. What was she going to do now? She couldn't just go to Harlem. To deny his marriage proposal and then trap him with a pregnancy seemed cruel and unusual punishment. He would, of course, think that she was lying about it. How perfectly convenient that at the moment he walks away, she finds out that she needs his financial support. Harlem would just be another man who married a woman out of obligation.

No, this had to be dealt with differently. How could she pull this off without anyone being the wiser? *Well*, she thought sarcastically, *I have everything going for me.* The list was hefty. Aside from being broken, Edith had no prospects in life, two dead mothers, a dead father and a boyfriend who should probably be dating her best friend. After all, both came from affluent families and had all the right connections. Lisa was the kind of girl Harlem belonged with. Yes, she was doing it for him.

Edith stood up and wiped her mouth. The smell was too much for her, and she almost gagged even while she gargled with mouthwash and cleaned up the mess she had made in the toilet. Lisa wouldn't be home for a little bit. Edith had just enough time to sneak out. Hopefully Lisa would assume that Edith was with Harlem and be none the wiser.

As she stepped out the door, a rush of uncertainty hit her. How did she go from having everything to this travesty of a life?

Down the street there was a small pub, one that generally catered to the college crowd. Edith had an idea of what she had to do; what would give Harlem the humiliating ending that he needed in order to move on.

As the door to the pub pushed open a small bell rang, announcing her arrival. It was a Saturday night and the bar was lively. It had given way to disco and heavy clouds of smoke that choked her lungs. She saw an open seat at the bar and sat down immediately to get the bartender's attention. He saw her hand up and walked over. His hairy hand was deep up a pint glass. As he dried it, he studied her up and down, predicting the drink of choice for his new customer.

"What can I get you?" he shouted over the music.

Edith leaned towards the barkeep "Glass of merlot, please." She sat back and began looking around the room for someone who would recognize her. The purpose was not necessarily to get them to come over and talk to her, but rather to get them to notice her presence at the bar. If she was going to force Harlem to move on, then she would need someone to have seen her at the bar that night. This was a small college town after all and nothing seemed to stay quiet for long.

The bartender grabbed a sleek bottle with a cream label. A bit of French was written on it. Edith could care less what kind of wine it was, she wasn't there for pleasure. She wasn't even there to drink really. The glass was put in front of her.

"Two dollars," he said, raising his eyebrow. She forgot that her overall appearance was not for the faint of heart and touched her hair. He must have assumed she was homeless and wasn't going to pay for her drink. Naturally, when she pulled out the money and extra for a tip, he curled his lip and walked back to put her cash in the till with the extra in the tip jar labeled "Bahamas."

Edith grabbed her glass of wine and slid into the bathroom. She placed the glass on top of the single laminated countertop. Looking in the mirror, she studied the dark shadows under her eyes: her pale complexion left very little to the imagination. To any onlooker she would appear suicidal, not seductive. This was never going to work. She pulled her hair down and began to smooth it out. Her shirt was wrinkled but there was very little she could fix about that now. She pinched her cheeks a bit to offer a rouge color, lacking make up beyond a light pink lipstick she had in her purse. The lip stain was applied liberally, hiding the fact that she had been living under a comforter for the last two months.

"I guess this is as good as you're going to get," She said in her reflection and gently pulled her bra down to make her boobs pop out a bit on the top. The round curves bulged out of the v neck yellow striped shirt she had thrown on two days ago when she last showered.

The door to the bathroom swung open, and she lost her balance, practically falling into Mary-Louise Percket, whom everyone called Mary.

"Edith?"

Edith smoothed her shirt again and stood up straight.

"Hello Mary." Mary was still stuck in her former cheerleader phase. She spent most of her free time stopping in at her old high school to check on her cheer squad.

"I haven't seen you around, did you miss finals for biology?" She cocked her head to the side as she maliciously chewed her bubblegum.

This was the opportunity to let the lie begin. Mary was the perfect person to help pull this off.

"No, I ended up taking them a week out, I was on vacation with my family and I got an excuse to make them up."

"Wow," Mary seemed reluctant to believe her. "So you just get special privileges? Why?" She surely was enjoying giving Edith the third degree in front of her crude, brainless entourage. How or why she was in biology was beyond Edith. The classes she was taking reflected a desire to become a nurse, not a brainless twit. Who would give a girl like Mary a job as a healthcare professional?

"Well, at least I didn't have to *sleep* with my professor to get my grades up. I guess he was just sending his appreciation for me doing the work myself."

Mary's mouth flew open, and her hand flew high and across Edith's face. The rouge was far more observable now. Edith touched her lip with her forefinger, the blood wasn't much, but still had a strong taste of iron in her mouth. The lip must have been pierced by one of her incisors. She raised her glass, smiled at Mary and gave a silent toast to her friends as she turned and walked away. Her former seat had been taken, but further down the bar another seat was open. A young and quite attractive man sat eating peanuts in between sips from his sweating bottle of beer. Perfect.

"Is this seat taken?" Edith gestured at the bar stool to the left of him.

"No, it's wide open for you." He smiled at her before noticing her cut lip and his face turned serious quite suddenly. "Oh my god, are you ok?"

He put his hand on her arm and looked around the room.

"Yeah, I'm fine, I mean I guess so. I'm sorry, could you ask me a different question?" She smiled at him, her lip swelling to a deep cherry red.

"You look like you could use a drink." He closed his mouth, smiled slightly and cocked his head; he seemed quite serious. His hand shot up in the air as he motioned to the same bartender down the counter to take their order.

Edith threw her glass of wine back in a gulp. The throbbing in her head was enough to make her think it may come right off. She felt her eyes rolling to the back of her head.

"Ok, so do you want another one of those?" His voice held a lack of surety. Edith was clearly a hot mess.

He looked at the barkeep, "Sorry, could you give us a minute?"

The heavy-set, hairy man walked back over to his stool to his still burning cigarette and waited impatiently for their order.

"I'm not quite sure you need another drink." He rested his arm on the bar.

"And why is that?" Edith gave a snarky, knee jerk reaction to his presumption.

"I happen to be a psychology major and I don't think you are drinking for fun."

Edith turned her eyes from the empty glass in her hand to her new bar friend, "I just need one night where everything in the world isn't falling apart."

"Well, I happen to be a very good listener, hence the career choice." He put his hands in his lap. "Tell me what's bothering you."

"I can't just open my soul to you, you're a complete stranger."

"That means that you can bare your soul to me and then never see me again." His left eyebrow lifted and Edith's face brightened up.

"I broke up with my boyfriend tonight. Something happened a couple of months ago and I have just been, well, not dealing with it very well. He has been wonderful and supportive, while I have been ignorant and selfish." Her fingers played with the stem of her empty glass.

"So why did you break up with him?" He was pulling off the role of shrink quite well and Edith was enjoying this encounter of mere strangers. Perhaps this would work for her.

"He was too good for me. I'm damaged goods, I have no family, no money, no future. He deserves those things."

"So what I just heard was that you feel that he deserves everything good and you don't." He stopped a moment, looking intently at Edith.

Edith went to respond and stopped herself. He was right. She was so busy thinking about what he deserved, that she failed to see that he wasn't the only one who deserved to be happy and successful in life. Everything up to this point just made her look at herself in such a way that she couldn't see past it and assumed no one else could either.

"I'm Edith." She put her hand out.

"Mitchell." His hand met hers and he shook firmly.

She grabbed a handful of nuts and began breaking them apart. " You know, I probably should have spoken to someone a long time ago." She blew a deep sigh out and stared blankly at the counter.

"I just figured, I had put everyone else in such a predicament as it was, they didn't need a crazy girl making it that much harder."

"Woah, wait, talking to someone doesn't make you crazy."

"Doesn't it?" her head tilted longingly to the side.

Mitchel leaned over and tapped his forefinger on top of her hand, "No, it doesn't." He spun around to face the mass of drinking college students.

"See this room?"

Edith turned to join his gaze. "This room is full of people just like you. Maybe from different backgrounds, perhaps some come from money, others have financial struggles, some have parents, some have grandparents, some come from parents who are happily married with a dog named Rufus." Edith giggled at this.

"Others are divorced and forced to deal with their neighbors looking at them like Hester Prynne, rather than a couple who just would rather live their lives no longer married," he shrugged, "My parents are divorced, and I find that they are happier now. Both are remarried and I have a stepsister from my dad and a stepbrother from my mom. I mean, we all deal with something different, but we are all dealing with something."

Edith turned to him, a thought crossed her mind, one she knew she would regret. She could take him in the bathroom and have sex right then and there. She would have eyes on her, taking him here, inside. Anyone who knew Harlem would tell him the goings-on of the evening and he would move on from her. The truth was, he was in love with her and would stick by her side through everything with this pregnancy. Her question was, why should he have to? Edith instead leaned over and kissed Mitchell on the cheek.

"What was that for?" he smiled at her and touched his cheek, as though he wasn't expecting the gesture.

"You were exactly what I needed, even though you weren't what I expected." She placed her hand on his and softly rubbed it, "Thank you, Mitchell."

She walked out of the bar, with no regret for letting her plans fall through. This would have to be something she handled on her own. To be with a man that wasn't Harlem would have only caused her more pain. To find out that she had betrayed him, it would have crushed him. Instead, the problem that she was presented with fell down to the baby and how she would pull off a pregnancy without him knowing about it. Edith knew that Lisa would help her. If there was one person that Edith trusted to get her through this, it was Lisa.

Edith opened the front door and glanced around. She'd found a home pregnancy test at the convenience store, and she covertly slid into the bathroom, hoping to evade Lisa for the time being, and pulled down her underwear. The box said to wait three minutes before examining the results. The wait was terrible. Maybe she was just sick with regret and she wasn't pregnant. She suddenly heard Lisa come in the door.

"Edith, it's just me." Edith could hear Lisa's voice getting closer to the bathroom, "I stopped and got us some chow mein and chicken wings." Edith could tell that Lisa was looking for her around the apartments as the sound of voice grew closer.

The bathroom door slid open and Lisa looked down at the counter to see the two pink lines on the stick. Edith saw her expression and turned her head to see the indicator with two bright pink lines.

"Oh my god."

"Oh, Edith." Lisa's face said it all. "Does he know?"

Edith threw the test into the trash, "No, I ended it before. Before the test, before the ring came out; he left and isn't coming back." She was wiping the tears from her face.

"Tell him, he will forget the whole thing. I mean, he loves you."

Edith slid past Lisa, "And do what, leave school, get married to the baby mama, waste his life away rather than chasing his dreams. I don't want that for me, why would I want that for him?"

"Because he already knows he wants to spend the rest of his life with you and having a baby is inevitable in marriage anyway, right?"

"Lisa, I'm twenty-two years old, I can't be a mom." The words came out angry, but she was afraid. Afraid of turning into her own mom, afraid of failing her child the way she had been let down.

Lisa came over and wrapped her arms tightly around her friend. Edith finally allowed herself to sob into Lisa's shoulder.

"It's going to be ok. I will help you with this. Don't you think he should know though? I mean he's the father. He should pay to help raise the baby, even if it doesn't work out."

"No, I will do this on my own."

"No, you won't." Lisa collected Edith's hands in her own and kissed them gently. I will help you. If you decide to tell him in the future, I will be there with you. You will never be alone."

"I appreciate that. One day though, in the short future, you will meet a man and you will fall in love. That man will want you to be his wife and ask you to raise his children. I will have to do this on my own, eventually."

"Maybe, but until that day, you have me, Auntie Lisa, and we will figure this out together."

Chapter 24: Samantha, Spring 1998

"Hot dogs?"

"Check." Adam marked off the listed item on a lined piece of paper.

"Burgers?"

"Check." He looked at Sam in a way that stopped her in her tracks. There wasn't much that he did that didn't make her want to stop what she was doing and fall on the couch with him. Life was a bit simpler with Adam. He eased her mind and warmed every frigid part of who she was. At this moment, his glance told her that he saw that she was overwhelmed and that she needed to relax a bit.

"I know, I know." She ran her fingers through her hair.

"Everything is going to be ok." He came over and tucked a strand of her hair still hanging in front of her eyes behind her ear. A calmness fell over her.

"How on earth can you say that?" She still had an overwhelming gut feeling that something bad was going to happen. Something that she had been mentally preparing to meet for weeks now.

"It's just a cookout with your family." He draped her arms over his shoulders as though he was preparing to dance with her.

"Oh yeah, just a normal cookout with my new cousins and aunts and, oh yeah, mother!" Her eyebrows furrowed and her nostrils flared at the thought of it.

"Nothing is going to happen. Your mom knows most of these people anyway. I mean they are *her* aunts, uncles and cousins. The only people she doesn't know are her cousin's children. She should be able to pull this off without a hitch."

"You definitely don't know my mother." She put her hands on her hips, then instantly shoved them through her hair, pulling it hard.

"Let's not pull our hair out before the cookout. If you want to shave your head afterwards, I've got a nice razor to help you along."

"Yeah and if it goes bad, I can use the razor for something else." She bit her lip.

"I see we are going dark now, great, my fiancé is suicidal over a cookout." He rolled his eyes. "Should I warn my family that you are not good with crowds?"

"It's not crowds or my family, it's her." Her voice was whining.

"Now, now, let's not jump to conclusions. Since we last saw your mother she has established a safe home for your sisters. She has a job in town in Eaton running the small general store and she has sent several letters conveying her apologies for that Christmas, which was almost three years ago."

Her foot was tapping absentmindedly, "Fine."

"Fine, what?"

"Fine, I will be civil and give her the benefit of the doubt." She huffed a bit of air, "I mean, Theresa said that she has been very different and they do a lot more activities together. Far better than cleaning up the apartment like they used to. She has them horseback riding up at Black Mountain, can you believe it?"

Adam looked at her like he had no idea what she was talking about.

"Sorry, it's a ski resort that they use for horse trails in the off-season.

Apparently, she has taken them several times and Jessica has a knack for it. Theresa is happy because my mom bought her a ton of new books to read and there happens to be a series of bookshelves that were left in the house."

"See? Progress. You have nothing to worry about." His arms wrapped tightly around her and he whispered in her ear, "And besides, if you feel at any point in time that you need to leave, you only need to say the word."

"What's the word?" she asked immediately, as though she was certain she would be using it. His chin dipped down, causing her to change her tone, "I mean is it a special word?"

"How about pickles?" He raised his eyebrows.

"Nah, I love pickles too much, plus it's a cook out and there's no way that I am not going to say, *Where are the pickles, do you have any more pickles?*"

"True, how about bananas?"

"Perfect, no one ever has bananas at a cookout." Her index finger and thumb stroked her chin "Unless they have a banana cream pie."

He rolled his eyes, "Ok, let's go, smart aleck."

They got into the car and headed toward the address that her cousin Audrey had given her the week before. It was the home of her Great Uncle Bobby and Great Aunt Gertie, whom she had only met one time previously. Bobby was the uncle of Audrey's dad, Doug. Despite being so closely related, their personalities were entirely different. Upon meeting them both last fall, she found Doug to be very laid back and soft-spoken, and his uncle Bobby to be the wild one of the family. He was the first to crack jokes and make an inappropriate comment causing his brother Tommy to smack him in the back of the head. While Audrey's grandfather was an older man, he still had some snap in his bones to discipline his siblings.

The house was large and stately. Not much like anything she was expecting for a family that hailed from Pawtucket. When Uncle Bobby and Gertie had moved them from Pawtucket to Cumberland in the 1970's it was obvious that they had grown wealthier.

The driveway felt like it stretched for miles. The line of cars that filled it was nothing compared to the long stretch of cars that went up and down the paved entryway. Beyond Edith's aunts and uncles and cousins, it seemed that second cousins and in-laws had come to the family gathering as well. As Samantha walked past each one, she looked for her mother's vehicle. While she had acquired her uncle's old pickup truck recently, making her new motif as a woodswoman all the more accurate, her old Camry was more conducive with the drive down to Rhode Island. Samantha was sure that she would be driving that rather than a truck that was at least fifty years of age.

C.B. Giesinger

Audrey saw her coming up the driveway and ran down to meet her two new guests.

"Oh I am so happy that you two came." She hugged them both and then grabbed Sam by the hand and dragged her into the house where a mass of people stood around a table of chips and dip. A large commotion outside drew her eyes to the backyard where several chairs lined an inground pool. A professional grill on the large patio was cooking some sort of meat that hit Samantha's nostrils enticingly.

Audrey caught Samantha's glance over at the grill, and she gestured in that direction, "It's incredible." She pointed to another area set for meal prep,, "Wait until you taste Aunt Gertie's famous smoked brisket. It's over there." "Wait, as in Aunt Gertie, our sixty-something year old handicap aunt?"

Audrey laughed, "Yeah, she's old and handicapped, she's not dead Sam."

"Sorry, yes, of course. I'm just really not used to this at all." Her eyes wandered around and Audrey could feel a sense of uneasiness in Sam about the whole thing. She looked over to Adam with a questionable expression.

"She has been like this all day, well more like all week, if we're being honest."

"Oh, shut up Adam." Sam's eyes were still scanning the room for her mother.

"Dad, you remember Sam." Audrey used her arms to present Sam to her father, Doug.

He smiled and hugged her without a second thought.

"Samantha, my dear, how are you?" His face was beet red and sweating. The house was warm from the open windows and doors, and most of the women in the family were in the room also. They were frantically gathered together in order to sample the meat and cheese platter put out by Audrey's mom, Sharon.

"Thank you so much for inviting us." Sam's eyes, still wandering, prompted her uncle to look around the room.

"Honey, who are you looking for?" he chuckled, "Or are you just completely overwhelmed by the amount of people you have in your family?"

He was right. Aside from the cousins she knew, there were other cousins, cousins once removed, great aunts, and great uncles. Growing up with three sisters and an elderly neighbor as her only consistent family, this was culture shock. A sea of smiles across the spacious backyard kept her enamored a moment until she snapped out of it to answer the question.

"Yes, I am absolutely surprised, that's true. I was expecting to see my mom here." She looked at Adam. "She said she was coming in a message she left for us the other day."

"Well, I haven't seen her yet, but there are so many people around," he laughed, "there's a good chance I could have missed her. Granted I haven't seen your mom in over twenty-five years."

Samantha hadn't thought of that. "Of course, that was silly of me. She wouldn't look the same as she did when she was fifteen."

"I hate to break it to you," he grabbed his round belly, "None of us look like we did when we were teenagers, that's a fact." That same belly laugh came out, "After forty, it's all down-hill."

C.B. Giesinger

The four of them laughed now. The commotion caused his wife to turn and see what the fuss was about.

"Samantha, I'm so glad you could come, and you Adam." She pointed around the kitchen, "We have plenty of food, please dig in and don't be shy, you're with family."

"Thank you, um..." She wasn't sure what to call her. Should she call her Sharon, Aunt Sharon even though she wasn't technically an aunt, or Mrs. Anderson? What was the proper etiquette for this situation?

"You can call me Aunt Sharon, if you'd like." Her smile eased Sam. The corners of her mouth pulled up, returning the expression.

"Thank you, Aunt Sharon."

"You're very welcome, Samantha," she rubbed Sam's arm lightly before walking away. As her aunt passed by her, the faint scent of lilac filled her nose. Her aunt's smell was as peaceful as her demeanor. Audrey was so lucky to have been brought up by such even tempered and *normal* parents.

In the corner of her eye she saw someone walk in the screen door on the porch and even with only hearing a few words spoken, she knew her mother had arrived.

"Hello, Uncle Tommy." Tommy turned to face his niece Edith. A girl who had grown into a woman the last twenty-five years. While not perfect as a mother, she was stunning for her age. The last year in New Hampshire had brought out a sparkle in her complexion. Her hair was neatly done and she even wore a slight pink nail polish to compliment her summer dress. In comparison, Tommy had aged considerably to her last meeting. With wrinkled skin and thinning hair, her uncle was nearly unrecognizable.

"Edith?" he studied her up and down a moment before wrapping his arms around her. Samantha watched his movements almost as closely as she scrutinized her mother, waiting for an underlying facial expression to come through. To her surprise her mother remained smiling jubilantly.

"Yes, how are you, Uncle Tommy? It's been quite a while."

"Edith?" Doug turned to see his cousin standing at the door. Her soft appearance made her easy to approach. She had aged far more gracefully than he. While her hair was graying as time went on, it was still brilliantly red. Soon the room was filled with people who wished to lay eyes on their missing family member. Edith accepted them all and hugged them for several minutes, taking in the family she had missed all these years. The backyard grew quiet as the house grew louder. The back door slipped open and Bobby walked in to see his niece, a girl who held her father's stature and her mother's looks. He didn't say anything for a moment, causing the room to grow quiet. The circle spread open between the two of them and Samantha waited for an outburst.

Instead, Bobby walked across the narrow passage of space and embraced his long misplaced niece. The crowd all clapped at the reunion. Gertie was pushed closer and Edith leaned over to hug her, as the rest of the family approached to give their introductions. It had to have been at least thirty minutes until Edith actually entered the kitchen where Sam, Audrey and Adam were standing. Audrey was one of the only family members who had not rushed to meet her cousin. It was a tender moment. Audrey felt that Samantha, with her mother being so distant, would need another ally at this time.

Edith wasn't sure what to do. Having just hugged and received kisses from a large number of people her cheeks were rosy and her hair tousled a bit in her scrunchie.

"Samantha," Edith said without moving from her spot on the floor.

"Hello, Mom." She was holding Adam's hand and felt him gripping tighter as the conversation ensued. "I wasn't sure that you were going to come."

"I said I would, didn't I?" Edith's breath was uneasy, far more shaky at greeting her daughter after two years apart, than the family she hadn't seen for decades.

This would have been the normal occasion for Samantha to make a sassy remark at her mother. *Yeah, don't you say things that you usually never actually keep? You love to keep promises, don't you? Award winning mother, Edith Anderson.* Instead she kept her calm, and squeezed hard enough to cut off the circulation in her fiance's hand, knowing that he would figure out how she felt after the conversation had concluded.

"Adam, you look well." Edith said, smiling and nodding. Her voice was sincere and she meant her kindness. Nothing that had happened between her and her daughter had ever been her future son-in-law's problem. What they discussed was long overdue and far more complicated than a marriage of young adults.

"Thank you, Ms. Anderson, you do as well." He looked around the room, causing Edith to follow suit. Outside of having Sam in common, they didn't know each other at all, nor have anything to discuss. Their family cookout with estranged relatives was an awkward moment for them to generate a relationship from thin air.

Sam nodded at her mother in a civilized way, a way that an adult would in a conversation with a stranger and then turned to her fiancé.

"Adam, I am starving, want to grab something to eat outside?" Sam took his opposite hand, trying to give the hand she'd squeezed a break. They walked past her mother and outside to the patio where the smell of ribeye, chicken breast and pulled pork filled her nostrils and dissuaded her from walking back in the house to have it out with her mother.

Though Edith had done nothing to provoke her to lash out, it had been building up in her. To be neglected through her whole childhood and then watch her mother blossom into a kind, caring, and put-together woman was too much. It was only a matter of time before the powder keg would light and obliterate everything within ten square miles of her.

They made up their plates and sat on two of the available lawn chairs. Sam had seen so many unfamiliar faces that she didn't even approach many of them. It was overwhelming and illogical to think she could meet and greet everyone in one cookout. The only rational thing to do was return for another cookout at some point. Sam could introduce herself and Adam to the rest of her estranged relatives the next time.

Her cousin Sebastian, whose parents she couldn't quite place, walked over with a beer in his hand. He'd only met Samantha once before. He had stopped by Audrey's dorm one evening, while Sam and Audrey studied for midterms.

"I'd offer you my advice, but I'm not sure you'd take it."

"On what?" Sam asked in confusion.

"Whatever it is you're racking your brain over."

He laughed and turned to Adam. "Sebastian," he introduced himself and shook his hand. "It's nice to meet you, Adam."

A puzzled expression fell over Adam's face. He wasn't sure how Sebastian had known his identity without being introduced.

"Oh, don't worry, I know all about you, the rumor mill is spinning wool again."

"Oh for God's sake 'Bastian, leave them alone. They have enough to deal with just having relatives like you to get used to." Audrey scolded.

"I was just saying," He put his hands up, "Sorry."

His laid back California way of talking stemmed from his time at South California University where he went to study film. Instead of acting, he ended up a tattoo artist for "*The stars*" to help pay off his rather extensive student loan.

"You know what I always found interesting about you, 'Bastian?" Audrey crossed her arms.

"What's that Cuz?" Sam realized he sounded stoned

"How you are a tattoo artist and yet you do not have a single tattoo on your body." The group all snickered, except for Sebastian.

"Well, I just don't want to influence my clients into getting something they see on me, I want them to be individual spirits, learning to balance their chi in this vast field of unknowns."

"Or maybe you just can't afford to get inked because you spend all your money on something else." Audrey's hand made a gesture toward some bad habits her cousin had become fond of. Her attitude suddenly made sense to Sam as the truth finally came out. Sebastian took his cold can of cheap beer and his braided hemp necklace and scurried out of the conversation before Adam and Sam could even say goodbye.

The three of them had a good laugh over the next few minutes until they heard shouting coming from the house across the yard. It had only been an hour since Edith had arrived, yet Sam was confident she would know her mother's voice from anywhere, especially when it was not in a sober condition.

They ran into the house and as Sam expected, her mother had a glass of wine clutched in her left hand.

"You know, if you wanted to be my family, perhaps you should have thought about that before you left me to figure it out at fifteen years old." Sam's great aunt and uncle were there as bystanders as Edith and Bobby fought it out in the kitchen.

"All I said was that I wish we hadn't lost so many years together." His voice remained calm, and genuine as one could be under the circumstances.

"And all I am saying is if you wanted to find me, it wasn't too hard. I wasn't in another country, I was three hours away." She pointed in the general direction of New Hampshire,, "The difference between you and I, is I am here trying to make amends and you are making excuses."

"I wanted to be there. I wanted to help your mom, we all did."

"Well, that's just rich, isn't it? Sounds just like a fucking Hallmark card."

The hush fell over the crowded kitchen and the BBQ outside seemed to fall silent as they all hung on the next words.

"Mom." Samantha's eyes were tearing up. The family who had given her and her mother a chance to be part of them, the same who had opened their doors and hearts to second chances were all now looking at them as outsiders to their annual family event. A family they haven't even begun to know, and she was already tearing away from them. Edith turned to face her daughter. Her face was blotchy and red, both from the heated argument and the scorching temperatures of the summer. Tears were forming in the corner of her eyes.

"I'm sorry, Samantha." She wiped the tears from her eyes and collected her now empty bowl once containing her box-made macaroni salad. "I'm sorry, everyone. I guess it's easy to forget that you haven't had a family since you were a child, when you're surrounded by people who make you feel whole."

Samantha walked a step towards her mom and then stepped back.

"Mom, I think it's time to go." She led her out the door and stopped a moment to turn to Adam. "I need to talk to her. I'll be back inside in a moment."

Sam hurried after her mother down the driveway. The tall cedar trees lining the driveway were shaking their needles loose in the summer breeze like a surreal snow storm. Their sap made them stick to her as they landed. She brushed them off hastily as she went.

Edith turned to face her daughter. She was sobering up quickly. "I had no intentions..." she put her hands on her hips, "this was not what I had planned."

"I know." Samantha knew her mother had not arrived planning to bring scandal and strife to a family event. She herself had been just as uncomfortable with the idea of being around strangers. While they may have considered Edith and Sam family, the group watching from inside the house had never been part of their lives until recently. For the first time in a long time, Sam began to understand her mother just a little bit. While she half expected her mother to be drinking at the party, she also slightly hoped that they would be able to evade a scene that would lead to her mother exposing their entire past.

"Mom, I..." the thought of her mother leaving at the present moment brought a grief down on Samantha. The thought of inviting her over to their house, having a meal together crossed her mind. The idea was gone just as quickly as it had surfaced.

"I hope that Jessica and Theresa are doing well. I was kind of wishing you had brought them, but I understand why you didn't. This was enough to deal with alone, without adding more children to the mix. Not to mention having to explain everything about their dads." She realized she had hit a soft spot, her nervous rambling had created a hole in the conversation. Edith nodded her head. Sam was implying her life was a mess and it was just enough to have her show up, never mind add the multitude of mistakes she had committed since she last set eyes on her perfect aunt and uncles.

"I'm really sorry that I didn't turn out to be the kind of mother you could be proud of. I wanted everything for you. I had the best of intentions when it came to you and your sisters, Samantha."

She meant every word, and that's what hurt the most. Not that she had lost so many opportunities to have a relationship with Sam. Even knowing Edith was honest in her notion of caring for her, Sam still couldn't believe it really meant anything beyond words. The fact that she and Lisa had to support their family through times when money was tight had left a bitter taste in her mouth. Then at times like this, that damn coffee can with all its wadded up fifties would resurface into her memory, and that fire in her belly would rise up in her throat, burning the words that would follow.

Edith waited for the next words to come from her daughter's lips, the words of forgiveness. The tender moment when daughter embraces mother and the world is right. Lisa had forgiven her and moved on with her life. Her two younger daughters had found room in their hearts to give their mother the benefit of the doubt and be happy. Yet, her second eldest Samantha held such a grudge that the weight was crushing her.

Edith could see that the moment would not happen.

"Well, I have to head back to Eaton. Theresa is at work until nine. She got a job at the Dairy Barn to save up for a car. Jessica is with a sitter, but she won't be able to sleep if I'm not back by bedtime. I will tell them you love them. Maybe you could come visit sometime or they could come down and spend a week with you and Adam." The smile cracked across her face, unable to tell whether or not the response from Sam would be what she had hoped for.

"Yeah, that would be great. We would love to have them." That had not been what she wanted to say, but it was all she had to give at the present moment. "Drive safe." She looked around the yard and then smiled tightly, and turned around to walk back up the driveway. She turned once more to see her mother get into her Camry and drive away up the road. At the top of the driveway she saw Adam waiting for her patiently. He knew full well that she would need him. She nestled her head deeply into his shoulder and cried. He wrapped his arms around her, wondering how many times Edith would leave without knowing just how much her daughter truly missed her.

C.B. Giesinger

Chapter 25: Edith, February1976

"Well, that's the end of that thread." Lisa began to gather her sewing supplies, putting each piece back into the box. She was in no way a seamstress, but she did have a knack for fixing things in a pinch and was getting better by the day at letting out Edith's clothes to accommodate her ever-growing stomach. "You know you can just get maternity clothing."

"And where's the fun in that, what would you do with your free time?" Edith smirked at her, causing Lisa to throw a pillow in her direction. "Besides, maternity clothing is too frumpy for a person my age and would definitely draw attention from people who know *other* people."

Harlem was still on her mind, even after so many months had passed since he graced her doorway requesting to speak to her. It got to a point where he would call and Lisa would just say that she was out of the state and eventually that she was dating someone else.

That night at the bar, thanks to Cindy, word had gotten back to Harlem as Edith had predicted and hoped for, but instead of him giving up on her, he only chased her harder. Aside from the fact that most rumors were purely just that, he knew that they had something real building between them and he trusted her enough to know that she would never throw her life with him away over an indiscretion in a pub bathroom with a stranger.

Now approaching her eighth month of pregnancy, the obviousness of her situation was sure to get out, so she kept a low profile around town. Lisa did most of the shopping and if Edith did go out, it was only to work and most of her shifts were at night at the university library, returning books and adding new collections to be cataloged in the Dewey decimal system. It was quiet work that allowed her the time to think without much strenuous activity. Those days were over. She did not long for stocking shelves, waitressing, bartending or working as a cashier even. The size of her ankles were reflected in the sheer mass of her belly. At times she would ask her ob-gyn if he had been wrong in determining the number of babies she was carrying. There was no doubt that he had miscounted. There had to be at least three in there for her to be this rotund. Her weight gain was not extraordinary, but the baby was large regardless.

Her doctor would simply say, "Some people just have big babies. Counting your blessings that the baby is healthy."

He had one thing right there. The baby *could* have been sick or had other, more pressing complications than chubbiness. The one downside to her working at the library was the endless volumes of books on birthing children. She had read books on teething, potty training, breast feeding, safety in the nursery and even how to co-parent. Though why she might need the last of those was unknown to her. At the end of the day, perhaps she had hoped that she could resign

C.B. Giesinger

herself to the idea of Harlem being in the baby's life and raising the child together.

She hadn't even requested the doctor to determine the sex. If she were to find out, she would want to do it with him. But at this point, the odds of her telling him were less likely than her having twins.

At night she would have dreams about the baby emerging from beneath the blanket, its face moist and red. The cry radiating across the room. A little boy sometimes, a little girl in others. The only constant was his face next to her with tears in his eyes, the mask he wore to keep her and their child safe, only pulled down to kiss her forehead and tell her that she did an amazing job. The dream was vivid, and every time left her waking up screaming, sweating and panting.

Lisa often came in to comfort her. She'd get into bed with Edith, placing her hand on Edith's moving belly. And through her calmness, Edith would finally get back to sleep.

"So what are your plans today?" Lisa said, biting into a piece of toast. Crumbs began to gather on the round table that they sat at for breakfast every morning. Edith would generally wait for Lisa to leave in order to clean up after her mess. If the worst thing she had to complain about in her roommate was a few crumbs, she could handle the burden.

Edith shrugged her shoulders as she rubbed the center of her belly. "At this point, there is not much I can do. I won't be able to work at the library after another three weeks. They don't necessarily want a woman dropping a baby on the new rug they just installed last month."

"I'd suppose not." Lisa bit into the toast once more, "Well I have a class 'til ten and then a break between then and two, so I was probably going to go to the library to study a bit. Probably with David," Lisa blushed, and looked at Edith to see her reaction, "Midterms are coming up after all and we will have a screaming baby in the apartment, before we know it." She snickered, knowing full well how serious it was. Edith seemed caught up in her own thoughts, and said nothing about David.

The girls had learned to just go with it. The situation would not improve by them moping around about it. Yes, the baby would cry and poop on them. They would endure years of sass from a toddler and want to rip their hair out. Lisa signed up to be Edith's support system though, so she wasn't about to back down at the idea of a little throw up and a few sleepless nights, though she was beginning to wonder whether there was room for David in this life she'd planned with Edith

As much as she had promised to be there for Edith and act as an aunt to the baby, Lisa knew would not be able to hold a candle to the actual role of another parent, or more importantly a father figure.

Lisa looked down at her empty plate and then up at Edith. Edith knew the face all too well.

"Just say it." Edith said with an attitude.

"Say what?" Lisa shrugged in a comparable moodiness.

"Whatever it is that you are wanting to say and think that it will upset me."

Lisa rolled her eyes. Her facial expression went from moody to anxious in a matter of moments. "Edith, I saw Harlem the other day."

Edith knew where this was going. It was only the most talked about topic in their house.

Call Harlem, forgive Harlem, raise the baby with Harlem. Had Lisa not realized that if Edith wanted Harlem back, she would have called him during the last seven months? Regardless of her desire to speak to him, the prospect of hearing the details of their conversation was far too great to pass up in this rather boring time in her life.

"Okay, so what did you talk about?"

Lisa was intrigued that Edith actually wanted to hear about what they discussed. This would be a great opportunity to remind her that Edith was the baby's mother, but that Harlem was the father and had a right to know about its existence.

"He asked after you, said that he hopes you are well."

The conversation needed to get a bit more exciting if it were to keep Edith's attention. The baby was enjoying a nice trip into her ribcage and it was far more distracting than the simple banter of Lisa's idle conversation.

"Okay," she winced, "and."

"Well, he said he hopes to see us around sometime." Lisa stood up and took her plate away. The dishes were done last night, leaving her space in the sink to put the dish. She spun around waiting for Edith to respond. She sat there, sunk in her seat, her head slightly turned down so that her chin was practically on her enlarged breasts and her eyes were upward facing Lisa.

"That's it?" Edith's tone was yearning; her voice cracked a little as she spoke the words.

"That's it." Lisa said in a matter-of-fact fashion. She picked up a coffee mug and proceeded to pour herself a fresh cup.

"But." Edith's face scrunched in disbelief.

"But what?" Lisa saw that she was bothered by the message and felt that this may be the push that she needed to finally call Harlem.

"But that is what you say to a friend, a mere acquaintance. You say I'll see you around, but you have no expectation of that ever happening. Are you sure that's what he said to you?" her eyes welled in tears.

Lisa's face grew longer, "Yes."

Edith stood up balancing herself on the chair. She took her coat off the hook and turned the door knob.

"I'm going to go out for a bit. I'll be back by lunch, okay?" With that, she shut the door behind her and with the assistance of the rail, walked slowly down the front stairs to the driveway.

Her car was parked just fifteen feet away. She knew where she was heading but wasn't sure what she was going to do once she arrived. The only thing she could hope for was that the address had not changed in the last seven months.

She pulled up to Harlem's, nearly fifteen minutes later. Maybe Lisa was right, maybe it was time to tell him, get back together, let go of her mother and have her own life with her new family. Uncle Ansel was the only parent she needed in her life in spite of everything. Her belly moved about as she slid her hand across the bulge.

"I want to talk to your daddy. I know you deserve to have both of us in your life. Your dad is going to love you, just like he loves me." The kick was immediate, it was as though the baby could hear her plea for approval. This was as good a sign as she needed to get out of the car. She pulled on the handle and pushed hard on the heavy metal door, using all her might to pull herself to a standing position.

A few deep breaths was all that stood in between her and the rest of her life. Did she have the strength to walk forward?

"Come on, let's do this."

She coaxed herself into heading for his front door. This was the house he had rented shortly before their breakup. Edith looked at the bright shiny windows, red shutters and pristine wooden shingles. The door was graced with a wreath of forsythias. It would have been perfect for a baby. It had slightly more room than the last place that he lived in, almost adjacent to Lisa's, and it offered more amenities, such as a golf course for his family to use in the summer months. Lisa's had a pool and plenty of privacy, but not the glitz and glamor that Judith and Bill were accustomed to. She looked back to her beat up car. It was the only thing she could afford at this point.

The truck was getting to be more than she could handle, so Ansel had taken it back to Eaton and replaced it with a car that would be cheaper to fix in a pinch and on a budget. He had been gracious with the knowledge that he was to be an uncle again, more like a grandfather. Over the years he had not so much replaced the value that she held for her father, but rather created a new role all to himself that gave her peace of mind in this particularly crazy time.

When the events surrounding her mother happened, Edith had left Harlem's house and immediately drove back to Eaton.

The night she arrived was hot and muggy. The bugs had smacked into the windshield of the truck, creating a glaze of oozy insides. So much so, that the wiper fluid was all but gone by the time she reached the hill that ascended to their home. While it wasn't a splendid estate like Harlem's family home, it was like a castle to her. A place that harbored those who loved her and would hide her from everything else that crashed down. She'd called ahead, and he expected her arrival. He had waited patiently on the front stairs for her to arrive, and she gathered from their conversation that he'd been sitting there since she called from Rhode Island. She stepped from the car slowly, her face hardened and saturated with dried tears. Her skin held streaks of redness from the trails of tears. How had she lost her mother all over again? She was an orphan now.

Ansel said nothing, but wrapped her arms around his daughter. His hand slowly slid up and down her back and he shushed her like a mother would a baby, soothing her.

"It's going to be ok." She looked up at him, tears once again smeared across her face.

"How could she leave me?"

"Well the trouble with parents is that they are humans. I mean, you're never going to get a perfect one. Darling, she thought she was doing right by you." He side-stepped and put one arm around her, "Now, I made some beef stew. You and I are going to share a bowl and talk as long as you want." Edith nodded and placed her head on his shoulder to follow him inside.

Months later, Edith sat in front of Ansel, having just told him about the baby. Just across the table from one another, feeling miles apart, the words had not yet surfaced.

"So what does Harlem have to say about all this?" Ansel tried to break the ice and reintroduce a major component to the conversation.

"Harlem has no say in any of this." She pushed her spoon in the tomato soup he prepared for her arrival.

"No say? I *see.*" Ansel looked down at her his soup, his mouth closed tightly forming a frown, less discouraged and more bitter.

"No, *I am* the mother, *I* can determine what to do with *my* child." She put the spoon down and crossed her arms.

"Well that is spoken like a true adult there, Edith." He threw his spoon down on the table.

"Why are you on his side with all this?" she shouted back, standing up.

"Side? He doesn't even know about the baby." Ansel stood up and slammed his fist on the table.

Edith had never heard Ansel raise his voice before, never mind getting aggressive. He caught her reaction and saw a tear form in her eye. The idea of trying to figure out this situation in this manner was ludicrous.

"Even if he knew, he wouldn't want to settle down with someone like me. I mean it's all fun and stuff until it gets serious. His parents want better for him, a girl like Lisa, for instance. Good solid background, two parents, job prospects."

"Yeah, every man's dream is to marry a girl's parents." He huffed and put his hands on his hips.

"Well, it's even worse than that with me because I don't have any." She covered her mouth as the words came out. She had only meant that her father was dead and her mother had all but abandoned her. The look in his eyes was too much for her to bear. He had lost his daughter at a young age and Edith had been a gift to him and

Cora. Against all odds, he had the opportunity to love another child again.

"I'm sorry." Edith shook her head nervously at her mistaken words.

He put his hand up to stop her. "No, don't. You don't need to apologize to me. I know you didn't mean it."

"I just don't know if I can do it, Dad."

At first the words struck him hard. Though she had implied their relationship in her how she spoke to him and hugged him, until now she'd only called him Ansel. He took in a deep breath, closed his eyes a moment and then reopened them slowly as he exhaled.

"Do what?" His face urged for an answer.

"Believe that someone is going to stick by me long enough to raise this baby with me." Her hands found her face and she sobbed. He walked over to her and squeezed her tightly in his arms.

"I may not have given you life Edith, but I *am* your father for all intents and purposes. I will be here for you and that baby for the rest of my life, which I plan on being a very long time."

She pulled away from him. "Oh, Dad." Again she used the word and hugged him.

Edith paused on Harlem's front step, glanced down at her stomach and closed her eyes once more to picture that moment with her father just five months ago. If he could learn to be a dad to her, why couldn't Harlem forgive her and raise their child together, get married, buy a house and do the whole living a normal life together thing? The same plans that they dreamed about so many times together. He had intentions to propose to her, why wouldn't he still want that? Had too much time passed?

She opened her eyes and began to climb the last few steps to the door. The house had many windows, wide and new, that gleamed in the sunlight. It was no more than a few years old, probably a gift from his parents. At that moment she saw him in the window. He was smiling, joyous even. He sported that tweed jacket that she loved so much, but could never get him to wear for her. He faced the opposite angle of the room, living room, she assumed. He must have company.

Glancing to the right of her, Edith saw a white Cadillac in the driveway. It wasn't a car she had seen in his parents driveway. Maybe they had traded it in, maybe it was a cousin or a friend from school she had yet to meet. Perhaps he had met them in the last seven months she was gone. Within seconds she stopped walking. A tall brunette crossed the room. Her perfect shoulder length hair swung softly just over her cardigan. She looked up at him, her bright blue eyes glistening at him in such adoration. A look of love, one that Edith recognized so easily. It was the same look she herself had given him. Harlem looked down at the woman and kissed her gently, smoothing her hair behind her ear.

Edith doubled over and then turned to run back to the car as fast as her legs would take her. She couldn't let him see her, it was enough to stand there and see he'd moved on, was in love with someone else, completely over her. But to have him witness her shame was more than she could bear. To tell him the truth and then be rejected by yet another person she loved would finish her.

She threw the car into drive and drove past the house as though she hadn't just stood on the lawn with her ridiculous swollen belly protruding out of her coat. The car sped down the street and in fifteen minutes she was back to her own house. Lisa was still home, Edith was back so quickly. She had hoped to avoid seeing Lisa. And yet, it was inevitable that she would find out that she was stuck with Edith for good.

The door opened and she pushed herself into the house, collapsing against the door behind her. Lisa, stunned by the abrupt entrance, turned her head to Edith. Edith's face said everything she needed to know. They never spoke of Harlem again.

Chapter 26: Samantha, Spring 2001

"Happy birthday, little Jessica, happy birthday to you."

The little girl seated behind the pink frosted cake promptly blew out her fourteen candles while her sisters clapped. Lisa entered the room with a large knife to cut the cake. The rectangular dessert was presented in the shape of a makeup box. Jessica had gone from princesses and dress up to makeup and boys.

"Do you want a corner piece, Jess?" Lisa leaned over, placing the knife slightly in the frosting.

"Yes, thanks Lis."

"So what did you wish for?" Sam smiled down at her little sister, not so little anymore.

"Well I was going to ask for tickets to the Britney Spears concert, but I know it's expensive." She shrugged her shoulders, reluctantly accepting the fact that birthdays were never a big thing in their family. Jessica had attended a number of birthday parties over the last few years. In New Hampshire she had met quite a few acquaintances. Enough so that Sam could relax, knowing her sister was getting out into the world.

The kids from New Hampshire had elaborate parties that included several extravagant gifts from all different kinds of family members. Jess had only ever had her sisters and her mom. Having a family gathering that may include a grandmother, aunt, cousin or step-dad threw her for a loop. She did her best to acclimate to her surroundings, living with her mom. Compared to the apartment in Pawtucket, she found the house quiet and peaceful. Having friends was a bonus.

"Theresa." Lisa called over to her sister who's headphones were blaring music that she could not decipher at such high decibels. "Theresa!"

The headphones were pulled down momentarily

"What Lisa?" The attitude of a teenager was more than Sam or Lisa felt like dealing with at the moment, but it was their job to keep her in line as it always had been. Her nose piercing accompanied the several on her ear. The black eyeliner reflected not only her music, but her overall mood. While she looked like she could be in a punk band, she was getting straight A's at University of New Hampshire. That was all they had wanted for her.

"I believe you had something you wanted to give Jess for her birthday." Lisa's eyebrows arched to imply that Theresa was forgetting something.

"Oh yeah." Her tone held no great emotion, but there was a kindness in it for her youngest sister. Having lived alone with her once their old siblings moved out, she and Jess had become closer than ever. She brought something over to the table, but instead of sitting down there, she returned to the corner of the room where she slumped over on the couch, replaced the headphones on her ears and closed her eyes. An envelope sat on the table addressed to Jessica.

"Thanks, Theresa, amazing job." Lisa rolled her eyes and gave a look of disgust at her laziness and then handed the envelope to Jessica.

"Okay, Jess, open it up." Her face lit her, her eyes twinkled a little bit at the thought of the envelope's contents. Sam watched her big sister eagerly anticipating Jessica's reaction. Lisa was only thirteen months older, but she'd always been far more anxious to grow up, be mature, be the caretaker.

"Britney Spears tickets!" Jessica jumped up and down, stopping only momentarily to hug her sisters before making her way over to Theresa who seemed interrupted by her sister's squirming, attempting to hug her.

"How did you guys do this?" she looked in the envelope, "Wait there are two tickets." She looked between Sam and Lisa. "Who is this for?"

"Whomever you want to bring." Sam said, smiling ear to ear, "Happy birthday, we all chipped in."

"Some more than others," Lisa said grumbling under her breath in reference to Theresa's lack of effort. Sam elbowed her into a fake smile to appease the moment.

"Well I mean, this is so great, I, um, I might bring..." She looked at her two sisters. To any other bystanders, they'd look more like mothers than older siblings.

The choice would be too hard. There was only one thing to do. "I think I might bring mom."

Both girls stopped smiling for a moment. The pause was noticeable and it caused Jessica to react. "No, I don't mean, I wouldn't *want* to take either of you. I just can't choose."

"It's fine Jess, you can take whomever you want. It's your present after all. I think mom would like it a lot. You may just have to remind her who Britney Spears is." Lisa giggled to herself. To be completely honest, she had never listened to a single song of hers either. Jess had been talking longingly about having missed Britney Spears' last concert in Boston for the last several months and Lisa knew she had to do something special for her last year before high school.

"I have some news too, I wanted to share." Lisa cleared her throat. The two girls went silent. Even Theresa noticed the lack of chatter and removed her headset.

"I got a job in Sacramento."

Sam's facial expression seemed to drop immediately, "What do you mean? When did you apply for this?"

Lisa's feet shuffled awkwardly, her eyes avoiding her sister's gaze.

"I applied for it a few months ago, but they just returned the call last week. They want me to start right away. They are paying for housing and moving expenses. Jared is so excited and has a lot of job prospects too. Even better—" Her hand swung out to reveal a big emerald-cut diamond ring on a gold band, "he asked me to marry him."

The girls surrounded her with hugs within moments. Even Theresa gave a plucky "Congrats," and granted Lisa a smile for the occasion, "That's wonderful Lisa. I'm happy for you both."

"Thanks Theresa." She was slightly caught off guard by her sister's emotional response to the situation.

"That is *so* wonderful, oh, congratulations." Jessica smashed her face into Lisa's shoulder.

"So when do you leave?" Sam crossed her arms. The excitement for her sister was diminished by the idea that she was now to lose her best friend.

"Six weeks from Tuesday, we are so excited. The wedding will have to wait until we are settled and have enough time at our jobs to come back and have it here. Maybe next fall."

Sam nodded her head gently at Lisa, dropping her eyes to her feet "Yeah, I think that would be a great time of year to have it. You always loved fall."

Theresa returned to the couch to listen to music and Jessica was on the phone calling her girlfriends about the concert tickets within a minute of the news. Sam stood there blankly looking at the wall adjacent to her.

"Are you ok, Sam?" Lisa put her hand on her shoulder.

She turned with a fake grin, "Yeah, of course."

"Your big day is coming up soon too." Lisa nudged her a bit "Well, two of 'em."

"Yeah, graduation is only a month away and the wedding is the week after that." She bit her bottom lip, "I guess you'll attend and then ride off into the sunset. I always thought the bride and groom were supposed to have that moment." Her laughter eased the friction in the air. "Seriously though, I'm happy for you, Lis. Thanks for always being there for me. I'll miss you."

"I'm not dying, just moving to California. With your Master's done now, you'll be onto bigger, shinier things anyway. And you and Adam better come and visit us," with a gentle punch to her arm, "okay?"

"Of course, we will." Sam's mouth pulled to the right as though she had something more to say, but she withheld it.

Lisa turned and walked over to her purse that sat on the chair.

"Well I hate to run, but I told Jared we would grab some dinner, to start sorting out our stuff. We can't bring it all. The amount of junk you collect in three years is absolutely ridiculous." She hugged Sam and then blew a kiss before closing the door behind her.

Sam watched her walk to her car through the picture window of her living room. She had seen Lisa leave their house a number of times, but this time felt different. Everything was changing again. They had reached another milestone in their lives and they were going to keep moving farther apart, while Sam desperately tried to hold them together.

Theresa suddenly realized that Lisa had left and knew it was her cue to collect Jessica's birthday gift, her bag and head back up to New Hampshire. The three hour drive was going to be a long haul and in the spring you never knew how the weather was going to cooperate.

"Thanks sis, it was nice to see you, please say hello to Adam. We'll be back in four weeks for graduation and your bachelorette party." She winked. This was the only part of the wedding she had been looking forward to.

"You wanted strippers, right?"

Sarcasm was part of her vernacular and Sam expected a bout of it every time they spoke.

"Let's hold off on the naked men, your twelve year old sister will be joining us for part of the evening."

"What, the shower?" she grunted, "that's boring anyway."

"Well boring or not, Adam's mom decided we should have one, so we are to graciously accept her gift. After that we will drop Jess off at her friend Beth's house and head out to whatever you have planned."

The smile returned to Theresa's face. "Oh, don't you worry about *that*, Lisa and I have it all covered. Audrey has been giving us slight hints as well. She won't be back in time for the shower, as you know, but she is incredibly excited for the night out."

"I'm really happy that she can come. Since she transferred to UConn, I haven't been able to get the time off of work to see her very often. Her mother is always calling me to check in. I think she figures I'm a surrogate daughter now, who knows."

"Well, after the last time they saw our mother, can you blame her?"

"No, I guess not. Although I figured by now Mom would have called her to bury the hatchet. After all they are family."

"You're one to talk. You haven't talked to mom either." Theresa pulled her backpack on her shoulder and picked up the envelope that had been addressed to the birthday girl.

"When are you going to forgive her?"

"It's not about forgiveness." The fading sunlight drew Sam's eyes to the window, "I just can't seem to wrap my head around her."

"Well, she misses you."

"I know, I mean, we invited her to the wedding."

"Yeah, but did you mean it? I think she feels ashamed."

Sam jerked her head to the right, "Well, I guess she should a little bit."

"Then I guess you won't be surprised if she makes her excuses." She put her hand on Sam's shoulder.

"After all, she wouldn't want to ruin the happiest day of your life. All right, let's go Jess." Jessica quickly said her goodbyes to her girlfriends and put the phone back on the receiver.

"Thank you, Sam," Jessica hugged her tightly, "I love you."

"I love you too, Jess." She pointed at Theresa "You too, dark angel."

Her eyes rolled at her sister's attempt at being funny.

"Bye."

The couch looked inviting and the dishes would have to wait. Sam covered her eyes for a minute when suddenly the front door opened. Adam walked in.

"I just saw the girls leaving, how was the party? Sorry I missed it." He walked over and kissed Sam sweetly on the forehead.

"Work was slammed."

"Do you still *love* your job?" Poking fun at his first adult job. Sam turned onto her stomach folding her legs into an x, leaning her chin in her hands while Adam fixed himself a plate of leftover hot dogs and macaroni salad. It wasn't the most glamorous birthday food, but it was what Jessica had requested.

"Well Jeff is great, don't get me wrong, but I have a degree and years of writing experience: I think I am more than qualified enough to edit a book without him looking over my shoulder every other minute."

"Yeah, but you were an intern up until last month. It will take time for the seniority to kick in." She stood up and walked over behind him, wrapping her arms around his waist, "Before you know it, you'll be bossing someone *else* around."

"God willing." He smiled and kissed his soon-to-be bride.

"How is the training going at the lab?" He sat down at the round metal table, shoveling food into his mouth after every other word.

"Well it's not so much training, it's a bunch of tedious bickering between professors on a grant proposal for upcoming dig opportunities. A lot of red tap to cut through. I am lucky enough to be their errand girl. I get to make sure their travel papers and work visas are in order. Maybe one day I will actually be treated like one of the adults in the room. Better even, to get invited to the dig site too." She pulled the chair out across from him, "I have a good amount of research to do to get my thesis done before our trip."

"You know, the idea of us spending our honeymoon in England for you to work is spectacular."

"I doubt anyone wants to spend their honeymoon working." She raised an eyebrow at him.

"To be honest, it sounds amazing, you get your practical experience at the dig sites and I can edit manuscripts from anywhere. It's a win-win."

He could see there was something else bothering her, "What is it?"

She realized he could see her face changing and tried to brush it off to something else. "What?"

"There's something bothering you, don't bother to try and hide it now."

"My sister just said something to me, that's all." She looked at the floor.

"Are you fighting about something?" he spooned another bite of macaroni into his mouth.

"No, it was about my Mom." She shook her head. "It's not that I haven't forgiven her, it's just hard to believe that she's different now. I mean we invited her to the wedding, but Theresa thinks she will make her excuses, so as to not ruin our day. As though we invited her, but didn't mean it."

"That's absurd, I don't have anything against your mom."

"Neither do I!" Her hands slammed, tight-fisted, on the table and she quickly slipped them into her lap in embarrassment.

"You sure about that?" Adam's face read like a Maury Povich paternity test, *She is, in fact, a liar.*

"Fine, let's settle this now." She got up and briskly walked over to the wall where the phone hung. Sam hastily grabbed the phone up off the charger. She purposefully avoided eye contact with Adam while she dialed the number, reading the digits from the laminated sheet attached to the phone charger.

Sam looked at Adam, the phone pushed hard up to her ear. It rang, and rang some more. Suddenly the answer machine picked up.

"Hello, you've reached the Anderson household, we are not in at this time. Please leave a message after the tone." Beep. The room was silent. Sam didn't know what to say. She had been so ready to shove it in his face. Previously all calm and collected, now clammy and anxious at the next words out of her mouth. She had barely spoken five sentences to her mother since that day at her aunt and uncle's house. The words hadn't come then and didn't seem to want to come now. She had to make a decision, hang up or speak.

"Hey mom, just wanted to make sure you got the invitation to the wedding. Um, the girls are on their way back home. You should expect them around seven." She looked at Adam, he waited for her to say something beyond small talk, some idle chatter you speak of with strangers. What he didn't understand was the strangeness between mother and daughter. Perhaps the space had become too great to reach one another. "Ok, well, goodbye."

She pushed the off button and replaced the phone on the charger. "Well that wasn't awkward." Adam said with a bland expression.

"Shut up." She sat down on his lap and kissed him. Her chin rested on his shoulder and she purposefully wrapped her arms around him tightly. It was harder than she thought it would be to call her mother and Adam felt it in the tightness of her embrace.

Edith sat on the couch looking intently at the answering machine: The tension still remained in her daughter's voice and she didn't have the strength to tell Sam the truth.

Chapter 27: Edith, April 1976

"Edith, she looks just like you." Lisa cradled the one month old wrapped up tightly in swaddling. "I love the name you gave her too, I mean it just fits," she added cheekily.

"Well, I thought she should be named after the person who helped me get her here."

"Hello Little Lisa, I'm your Aunty Lisa, I don't know if you know this, but one day you're going to grow up big and strong like your mom."

"Strong, that's hilarious. I have a newborn and I can't bring myself to tell her father that he has a daughter."

"I mean, it's not too late, it's never too late." Lisa turned her head back to the kitchen where Edith was leaning against the counter, arms crossed, looking exhausted as only a new mother can.

"Actually it can be too late," she leaned forward, "Besides, we have everything we need, right here, with me and you."

Lisa's expression changed, her mouth dropped the smile. A difficult act when presented with such a beautiful baby girl.

"Actually, I need to talk to you."

"What?" Edith froze. She had enough surprises in her life to know when some new challenge was coming, or some new heartbreak.

"I know I had said when you were pregnant with Lisa that I would be here forever. I just never expected this to happen." Lisa placed her hand out in front of her long-term roommate. A dazzling circle hung on her ring finger.

"David asked me to marry him." Her face was glowing, illuminating the room while the darkness of the situation fell over Edith.

"But you said you weren't interested in marriage! You said you were just dating for the fun of it and that we were going to raise Lisa together."

"I'm so sorry." Lisa laid the baby in the bassinet and walked slowly over to her frazzled friend.

"I just never thought that I would fall in love with him the way that I did over the last few months. You see the way he and I are together. The way he holds my hand. It was so hard to not fall in love with him. I felt so terrible about what I had said to you, the promises I made. I actually refused him at first. But in the end, I had to tell him yes. I love him, Edith."

Edith's face hardened as a tear trickled down her cheek, "Well, I guess you're moving out then?" she was absentmindedly nodding, "That's what you're trying to tell me?"

"David is coming over to help me pack next Saturday, and I'll move out two weeks after that."

"Wow, that's wonderful, thanks for the heads up Lis." She slammed her fists down on the counter causing a crack in the Formica. Her face reddened and blotchy, she turned away into her room and slammed the door.

Over the next few hours when she heard the baby cry, Lisa heated up a bottle and fed the baby. She waited for Edith to emerge, to forgive her for the rush of it all. While she knew it was her own life to live, she knew she had betrayed her friend and the end cost would be devastating.

The silence persisted between Edith and Lisa. This kept on for the next few weeks. Then the inevitable day finally came. David arrived, and Edith heard them sorting out Lisa's belongings from her own. Tape was wrapped tightly over the seams of the boxes and the door eventually shut again, behind David and Lisa, the baby crying once again in the living room. This time without the help of her Aunty Lisa.

Edith lay gazing up at the popcorn ceiling, much like she had for the last several hours. The moment to go and pick up the baby had come. The blood curdling cries could only last for so long. She knew she had become Lisa's sole parent now, and it would be her job to take care of her. She approached the bassinet slowly. Edith had never felt fear of her daughter, but the idea of raising a child alone at twenty-two was daunting.

The only thing she could think of was to call Ansel. He had planned to come and visit her over the next couple of weeks. Why not see if he could come down a bit earlier to visit? Especially with a bedroom wide open and cleaned out for him to stay in.

She picked up the phone and slid the dial around nine times to get his number connected. It rang several times. Edith thought he may not be home and was ready to hang up when she heard his voice on the other end.

"Hello?" A voice that she had yearned to hear. A bit more crackly than when she had last left him in New Hampshire a few months ago, it was still unmistakable.

"Ansel, I was wondering if I could convince you to come and visit tomorrow. I'm assuming it's far too late to come out today. Maybe first thing in the morning." Edith's tone was light-hearted and cheerful. She was not about to appear desperate for her father, nor disclose the fact that her roommate and assistant mother had moved out just a few hours previously.

"Sure thing," he stopped for a moment, "is everything ok, sweetheart?"

"Of course, why wouldn't it be? Lisa is just dying to meet her grandpa."

Those were the only words that Ansel needed to hear to get him to agree. He would leave around five am to arrive as early as possible..

When he knocked on the door the next morning, Edith practically jumped out of her skin in excitement. She opened the door quickly and wrapped her arms around his neck.

"Whoa, what's all the excitement for?" he pulled back from her for a second, concerned slightly for her erratic behavior.

"Oh, you know, a first-time mother with a newborn gets no sleep at all."

He stepped over to Lisa's cradle, and stroked her cheek with the back of his index finger. Lisa cooed at the gentle touch.

"Why don't you take a nap and I'll give Miss Lisa a bottle." Ansel's baby voice emerged so fast that Edith wasn't sure how to process it. She had somehow been the only person who was incapable of making funny faces or high pitched tones when talking to her own daughter.

"Okay, I could really use it, thanks." She pushed open the door to her bedroom and turned around to watch him pick her up. Her legs dangled, slightly kicking about until he pulled them closer to his chest with his remaining hand. She shut the door and laid her head on the pillow. She fell asleep immediately.

When Edith opened her eyes the room was no longer filled with gray filtered light but was dim with small light specks on the wall from the streetlights outside her window.

She stepped out of her room and found them cuddling on the couch watching the evening news.

"Oh look who it is, Lisa, it's Mommy."

Things seemed to be on the up and up. Ansel would come and live here, help her pay the rent and raise Lisa. Or perhaps she would give up the lease and move back to NH. It didn't really matter, she was to have family there to help her through this.

"I'm really glad you're here." Her face lit with a soft glow. He was the dad she never got to have, the dad who would finally get to be a grandfather. Ansel was not blood, but he fit the mold quite easily.

"Where's Lisa?" his face twisted, looking around the room at the missing furniture and space on the walls where frames once hung, "She's your roommate right?"

"Oh, well, that's what I wanted to talk to you about." She started rubbing her fingers. The sweat made them clammy. "She got engaged." Her tone was less of happiness and far more of uneasiness.

"Edith, what happened?" His smile faded.

"She moved out, I'm raising this baby on my own now."

"Well, what about the father, you said that you were going to have him be involved in the raising of his daughter. It's a man's responsibility to do so."

"That will be pretty tough if he doesn't know about it," she joked. Ansel's facial expression changed quickly.

"What do you mean he doesn't know?" He put the baby down and stood up.

Edith saw he was upset and slowly backed up into the wall for support.

"I went to tell him a couple of months ago. I finally had the guts to say something and he was with another girl. It was too late."

"Too late for what?"

"To be together as a family." Her eyebrows came together and her voice cracked.

"How is he supposed to make a decision on being together if he thinks you don't love him and doesn't even know he has a daughter, Edith?" His head swung back and forth between her and Lisa like a pendulum. It was as if he was winding up to deliver an ultimatum.

"Well, I thought maybe Lisa and I could go live with you." Edith attempted to smile in a plea of hope.

"Edith, you can't just run away from this. You need to tell him. It's his child and his responsibility. I love you darling, I brought you into my home and made you my daughter. But now, you have a daughter, it's your job to be there for her." He grabbed his coat.

"Wait, what are you doing?" Her voice was panicked, "You can't leave, I need you!"

"You need to figure out how to be a mom and being here is only going to inhibit that. Tell Harlem the truth. I love you." He walked over and kissed her forehead. The door shut softly behind him. His decision was final.

Edith sat down on the couch and held her head in her hands. She wasn't sure how she was supposed to know how to be a mother, when her experience with mothers was all but nonsense. Between a dead mother and a mother who abandoned her, she had no track record set before her to indicate that she could do this alone. Harlem was a wonderful man, but was he going to forgive her for not only hiding the pregnancy, but also not allowing him to be at the birth? As much as Ansel felt that all families needed to have a male role model, she was not sure that Harlem was going to be willing to have a girlfriend, and still raise a child with another woman who broke his heart.

Somehow she made it through the night, leaving the television all night in an attempt to feel less alone. The next evening, Edith called a neighbor, who had said she would be willing to babysit for two dollars an hour. A thirteen year old girl who wanted to save for a new bike was just the ticket to getting out of the house and away from all of this for a while. Half an hour later when she heard the knock on the door, it startled Edith, who was herself half asleep on the couch.

She stood up and answered the door. Marley Jacobson stood there in long braids and a red sundress with white polka dots, seeming eager to start earning her way.

"Hello, Marley." Edith moved out of the door frame to allow her to come in. "Lisa has been fed and changed, so you should be good for a little while. Emergency numbers are on the fridge next to the grocery list if you should come into any issues. I will be back in a couple of hours."

"Okay Ms. Anderson, don't worry about a thing, Lisa and I will have a great time together. I'll put on cartoons for her to listen to."

Edith was only half listening at this point and pulled on a coat.

"Okay, sounds great, thanks." She stepped out the door and headed for the beach. With Harlem now in a different neighborhood and her body having returned to somewhat a normal shape, she was less afraid of running into him and having to explain herself. Now she would just appear to have put on a bit of weight and the awkwardness would be purely because she had nothing further to say to him.

The water was rough and salty. The air brushed her face coarsely with traces of sand. Although the sand beneath her was cold and dank she felt compelled to fall to it and rest. The briskness of the evening left Edith shaking. Too many times she had come into another day with uncertainty of her future. How many times was she to pick up the pieces and force them back together with some superficial glue? It was getting too heavy, the bonds that pulled her down. Like the vast ocean ahead of her, her grief was desperately deep and filled with a darkness that she could no longer run from.

The choice had been made. The action would be swift and the repercussions would not fall on her own ears. She would never hear another cry, another farewell. She would never have to endure another mother leaving. She would never have to bury someone she loved. Her daughter would find happiness with a family who could give her what she needed, something that had been stripped away from Edith again and again.

She stood up and walked slowly toward the crashing waters. The foamy edges stuck to the sand before receding back into the depths. It would be quick, it would be painful, but then it would be over. The tide was going out and it would take her with it. She closed her eyes and the tears slid down her cheeks once more. The last time she would have to cry. Her toes felt the icy water and she braced herself. Every pore closed up tightly and her feet began to feel numb.

"Just a few more steps Edith, you can do it," she whispered to herself. The moon hung low above the water and its reflection sailed on the rows of parallel flowing waves, drawing her closer. Its face gave her comfort. She would not have to die alone.

Out of the corner of her eye, she saw a shadow. She would have to run for it. The water would take her and hide her in its waves. There would be no screams to lend to her discovery. Should she have left a note? The thought crossed her mind now, it hadn't been premeditated after all. If she were never seen again, they would search for her. There was no way to turn back now. They would figure it out, she had made enough mistakes to allow for the notion that she'd run away. Let them believe she was just as bad a mother as they expected, let them think she had flown the coop. They'd be so happy in their correct assessment. She would soon be forgotten.

The shadow was coming closer to her down the beach. The moon hit the figure just enough to tell it was a man. A larger stature than a woman and with short hair. This had to be done now. Another hesitation: She thought of Cora and Paul. Perhaps Cora had found her brother in heaven, they had properly met now and were friends. She wasn't quite sure why she thought of the afterlife now. What if it didn't exist? What if it did and she found herself even more alone than ever? What if they weren't there waiting for her?

She shook her head and wiped the flowing tears from her cheeks. The dampness left her face cold as the wind whipped her hair back and forth abrasively. Edith took another step forward. Her lips came together to blow out a long winded exhale and she felt the first surge of water knock into her shins. The pain was quickly being replaced by numbness, and she felt a sense of calmness wash over her like the salt water on the tumbled rocks ahead of her.

She lost sense of time. The waves became a blur in her vision, grew sharper against her shins. A voice spoke out to her and she opened her eyes to see a handsome gentleman smiling at her. She blinked rapidly, trying to focus. It took him a minute of looking at Edith's face in the moonlight before seeing the tear trails trickling down.

"Are you all right?" He said for a second time.

Edith wiped them quickly. "Oh, I'm fine, the wind just makes my eyes water." Her solemn gaze once set upon the vastness was washed away like the beach. Across her mouth spread a smile.

"Oh, well that's good. I thought there may be something wrong." He extended a hand. "It's nice to meet you; Garret, Garret Townsend." Edith smiled at the stranger and shook his hand reluctantly. His gentle features put her mind at ease and gave her the strength to answer back.

"Hi, I'm Edith Anderson."

Chapter 28: Samantha, Summer 2001

Long layers of white taffeta traipsed down, stitched together with silk thread into the satin gown staring back at Samantha in the mirror. Her gold ring glowed in the streak of the sunlight coming in through the window of the bridal suite.

Lisa came up behind her and fluffed out the bustle of her gown.

"You look just like a freakin' princess Sam."

Samantha spun around slowly, her long auburn curls flipping from side to side exposing a blue stone amulet that hung around her neck.

"I love this by the way," placing her hand on the stone. "something blue, right?"

"Well, every bride deserves to have it done right, at least once." Lisa smiled with thick tears on her lower lids. "Oh dear, seems to be an allergy issue in this room. I mean, I am really allergic to dust."

Sam wiped the tears from her sister's eyes, "It's ok to cry Lis."

"I know that. I'm just so happy for you two. Adam is such a wonderful guy and you both did the right thing, waiting until you got your life sorted out."

"Speaking of which…" Sam bit her lower lip.

Lisa stopped, "What?" She jumped on Sam's every word, clasping her hands, "Wait, are you pregnant?"

Sam rolled her eyes. Her sister was always asking if she was going to be an aunt soon. Sam would gently remind her that if Lisa wanted to have children, she could pop them out herself at any time.

"No, I'm not pregnant, for the fortieth time. Actually it's a work thing."

"Work thing?" A small whine emerged from Lisa; she had hoped for more exciting news.

"Hey, don't trample on my happy news. I'm not having a baby, but I'm moving to England." She smiled an enormous toothy smile.

"You got the grant?" Lisa's face tightened up with a burst of joy.

"Yep, we will be leaving in the next few weeks, hence the honeymoon shortage."

"I just figured you were both just out of college and broke and that had something to do with it."

Sam threw her hands on her hips.

"Ha ha, very funny. I'll have you know that Adam is releasing a brand new novel."

"Wow, that's great news. Is he still taking the publishing job?"

"Yes, he will be working out of the London office. This way he will have the time to edit and write his own works simultaneously."

Lisa walked over to the table to grab the large bouquet of white roses gathered together in a similar satin coloring to her sister's gown.

"What about kids?"

"Lisa, there is plenty of time for kids. Don't worry, the moment he impregnates me, I will inform you."

"Oh Sam, please not the moment. At least take a second to clean up."

"Now that is disgusting." Laughter filled the room.

They both turned when a knock rang on the door. Lisa walked over and opened it slightly, afraid that Adam was there to grab a peak of his bride. Instead Edith stood there in a maroon, ankle length dress. Her hair was curled and half pinned back. Lisa never noticed before just how similar she and Sam looked to one another, especially with the long flowing auburn hair. Lisa turned to look at Sam and opened the door a bit more.

"I'll give you a minute." She nodded and left Sam and her mom to speak.

Edith's face was soft and filled with pride at the view of her daughter dressed all in white. A girl who had grown into a woman. If only she had been there to see it for herself. She had missed so much.

"Hey mom." Sam walked over and kissed her mom on the cheek. It was strange for her to react this way. She had never kissed her mother before. Somehow this just seemed like the right thing to do at that moment.

"Hello, Sam. You look…" Her words trailed off into a cough to cover up the fact that she meant to cry.

"I wasn't sure if you would come." Sam looked to the ground, not sure how to react.

"I wasn't sure you would want me." The quietness following the few shared words between mother and daughter with far too many absent memories left the two of them at a loss.

"Well, you sure make a beautiful bride."

"Thank you."

"I know you don't think I am happy for you and Adam because of what happened so many years ago."

Sam threw her hands up. "It's fine, it was a long time ago, it's over now."

The end to the conversation was less of forgiveness and more to focus on the day at hand. Edith reached into the small purse that hung on her shoulder.

"I brought you something," she pulled out a small velvet box, "now, you don't have to wear these." She opened it up to reveal a lovely set of pearl earrings. They were not new; judging by the box they had been sitting inside its container for some years now.

"Whose earrings were these?" Sam touched the small white orbs. Her fingertips studying the imperfections of the true pearls.

"They were Cora's." She saw Sam's face and realized that there was so much that Sam just didn't know about her. Was there a reason she never told Sam about Cora and her life growing up in New Hampshire? Sam had wondered where the house came from. Had Edith told her before and Sam had failed to listen?

There were so many gaps in the origins of Edith that it was hard for Sam to piece together who her mother truly was, and essentially where she had come from herself.

"Who's Cora?" Sam looked up at Edith "Was Cora your grandmother?" She had known Edith's mother to be Iris, though she didn't know much more than her name and that her husband, Edith's father, had died many years ago. Audrey's family had keyed her in on some major events, but having been removed from Edith's life for so long, they lacked major moments of her development as a child, her young adult years and procession into womanhood.

"Cora was my aunt. She was the half sister of my father. No one ever knew she existed. Sometimes we find out that the people around us have more secrets and depth to them then we give them credit for. And sometimes it explains why they are who they are."

Sam looked at the woman before her. Resentment faded and she began to listen for the first time in her life to the woman she had written out of her story a long time ago. This felt like a good time to change her narrative.

"So I have some good news." Sam's face lit up once more. "I have been accepted for a dig in England, it's about an hour outside of London. You know how I have always loved history."

"Since the days when we went to the natural history museum." Her mom grinned sweetly.

"What museum?" Sam's eyebrows gathered in thought.

"You were about four, I'd say. Lisa was just starting kindergarten and we went to New York City for a little trip. The bus ride was long with two little kids, but we got there. I sat you on my lap and you played with my necklace for three hours straight. Lisa was more interested in looking out the window than anything to do with me. She is still like that. Always looking ahead. You though, always focused, steady and strong. We walked through that museum for what felt like hours. You weren't able to read, but you connected with the stuffed creatures and tall figures. You loved to touch everything and anything that brought you closer to what fascinated you. I knew you were special. Even when you grew to hate me eventually. I knew you were special."

Tears fell down Sam's eyes. "Mom, I—"

"I'm so proud of you. You are going to do wonderful things. I'm glad that you will get your happy ending at last. Just know that I am here cheering you on." She hugged her daughter tightly, wiped the tear from her eye, kissed her cheek and then turned and walked to the door.

"Mom."

Edith turned around slowly to see her daughter looking at her as though she may actually miss her when she was gone. "I'm..."

"I know." And she left the room, shutting the door slowly.

Ten years later

The phone rang causing Sam to jump off her seat. She had been up all night long, documenting her findings from the dig the day previously. After four years as assistant supervisor, she had yet to receive the privilege of controlling her own project. Adam was working part-time at the New York MacMillian office nowadays. They were trying to make better connections between their two major branches. His success had helped him climb up the ladder and he couldn't refuse the opportunity. He would come back to England and stay for a month or two before he had to return to New York for several weeks. It was a job that he had grown to hate.

While he started off writing his own novels and became an editor with intentions to still create, his passions had taken a backseat to the demands of the publishing house. It was far too much stress to have an inch of creative process left in him at the end of the day. Worse than that, his wife had become resentful of his consistent absence.

They had two daughters now, Paige and Holly. At the tender age of four and six they were enough to drive anyone crazy. Add an absentee husband, a full time job and zero family nearby to alleviate the stress of motherhood, and Sam was falling apart.

"Hello," Sam answered eagerly.

"Sam." Adam was on the other line, sounding off. Less than enthralled at the idea of calling his distant wife.

"What's wrong?" She could feel it in her throat, the need to throw up. She had felt something strange going on. She hoped it was all in her head, but she knew eventually it would be said. There was probably no better time than the present for her to hear it.

"Why don't you just say it?"

"I slept with someone else." There it was, the blow, hitting her like a brick in the gut. She had known he was busy in New York and while he loved her, the pang of loneliness was becoming ever-controlling over his mind. "I'm so sorry, I just don't know why I did it. I promise it was only once and it meant nothing and will never happen again."

Sam was silent on the other end of the phone. Words had failed her.

"I'm going to come home and fix this. Please, I need you to forgive me. I wanted to tell you in person, but I couldn't wait. I feel so terrible and I can only imagine the pain that I'm causing you.'

"I'll see you when you get home tomorrow and we can talk then."

She hung up the phone and closed her eyes tight.

"I'm not going to cry." As though coaxing herself into feeling less would actually work. Then the phone rang again.

"Adam, I just can't." She stopped talking when a woman on the other end of the phone's voice came through with a faint static sound, muffling her voice a bit.

"Mrs. McNamara?"

"Yes, this is she." Sam didn't recognize the phone number. She had hoped it was not the dirty mistress calling to scuff things up, but this woman rather professional.

"Hello Mrs. McNamara, my name is Dr. Tromwell, I'm your mother's doctor here at Memorial Hospital in North Conway. I'm calling to inform you that we are almost at that point. If you want to make arrangements for your siblings to join you, I would contact them. I'm not sure how much time she has."

"I'm sorry, what?" Thousands of words came to mind, but none of them were the right response. "Who are you calling about?"

"Your mother, Edith Anderson... You *did know* about your mother's condition, didn't you?" Helen took a deep breath in. "I'm so sorry, I thought you knew."

"Knew what?" she could feel the bile rising up in her throat.

"Your mother has early onset dementia. She has been suffering from it for years now. At first it wasn't consistent. Often, at times, she would become forgetful. Then she would find herself at the grocery store, and not be sure how she got there. Eventually she started noticing symptoms; close to ten years ago now.

"After a few years, she ended up moving herself in a facility, concerned she may fall or hurt herself, or worse hurt others—,"

"Yes, I know she was in a facility," Sam interjected, "she had a breakdown six years ago."

"Well," the hesitation in the nurse's voice was evident, "that's mostly true, but it was certainly dementia and not a breakdown. Though whenever we discussed medical disclosures, that's what she asked us to say. She always said you all thought she'd have a breakdown eventually, you know!" Here she chuckled a little.

"Your sisters Terry and Jessica have been maintaining her care and monitoring her for some time now. Your other sister comes to visit on occasion but, while she knows her mother is in a facility, as I said, Edith requested that we not disclose the reason for her move. She said she put you and your sisters through enough. But since Edith is declining rapidly now, we wanted to give you the full situation as Edith's designated next of kin."

Sam's face contorted. How dare she laugh? She had not been there for the shit-show that was growing up with Edith as a mother. She didn't have to raise her siblings and watch her mother pay herself for the work they did. Every once in a while, when the accounts got low, Sam would think back to those cans, rusted and filled to the brim. Must be how Edith paid for all this end-of-life care. She knew that Terry and Jessica had done well for themselves in school and obtained jobs to pay their own way, but not enough for a full time care facility. Sam wasn't sure anyone would have the income to handle such a burden. Had this woman called to collect a bill upon her mother's death? Why not? Just add another layer to the onion that was Edith Anderson.

"I can be there tomorrow. I just have to get things in order over here." Sam's jittery reaction to the news left the woman at a temporary loss for words.

"Well then, we will see you when you arrive," she stopped Sam before she could hang up, "I hope you know, first, that I did not mean to cause you any further pain. Secondly, I don't think she did either. I have been your mother's doctor now for over thirty years: I consider her a friend. She was a bright young woman when we first met back in college. Life just doesn't always give you the choice to change your fate."

"Okay, well thank you, I will see you when I land. Goodbye." Sam abruptly hung up and slammed her fist into the wall several times. She caught a shadow in the corner of her eye and found her two daughters emerging from their bedroom in pajamas, dragging a stained and worn teddy bear and a blanket that they slept with each night. Their strawberry blonde hair was tossed about, reminding Sam that they had been sleeping prior to her assault on the wall. It was far more to process than she could handle. Her husband cheating on her was a side note at this point. He would have to wait to apologize. For now she had to pack and book a flight.

She was finally going back home after all these years.

Chapter 29 Edith, Spring 2010

Her eyes were cloudy as she opened them to the sun beaming in through the window, hitting her face. It seemed to know it was pestering her, the way that woodpecker had every morning for two years out across the yard. She sat up and looked around the room. Everything seemed a bit funny, out of place. The bureau had moved from next to the bedroom door to the far side of the room, closest to the window. Where was her bedside table? And Cora's picture frame next to her bed. Nothing seemed familiar, everything was out of place. There was a feeling, an unease spreading around the room, making her feel closed in. Suddenly the door pushed open and a woman in scrubs came in with folded linens in her hands.

"Good morning, Edith," she spoke in a cheerful, yet increasingly overbearing pitch that made Edith squirm in her bed. Who was this woman? A housemaid for the cabin? Had she become such a lazy leech? Were her daughters so incapable of helping out that she had to hire a housekeeper?

She nodded thoughtfully at the guest, not wishing to appear rude, then got up and grabbed her housecoat off the chaise lounge in the corner of the room and draped it over herself, tying it tightly. There, that would make her feel more comfortable. She had never been much for guests, but this woman was probably just doing her job. At this point, she had just wished the girls would tell her that their mother was still asleep and should not be disturbed.

She searched for her slippers. Usually on the side of the bed, they were missing. Edith bent over to browse for them under the bed. Even the bed was different. It wasn't the same bed she had slept in the last several years. The oak frame made by Ansel, the same bed where he and Cora's had carved their initials was not there. In its place was a hard metal-framed striker bed.

"Where's my bed?" Her tone indicated not only fear but mistrust. The housekeeper stopped for a minute to put down the linens and turned to move slowly toward Edith. Her arms were outstretched low to her waist. The way a dog catcher would attempt to collect a runaway with calm, soft-toned behavior.

"Edith, it's ok, it's Mable, I know this must be very confusing for you."

Edith began to back up slowly, eventually hitting the bedside with her calves. The bump stung, but she was caught up in another bit of a crisis.

"Who are you? I don't know you. How do you know me?"

"Edith, I have been working with you for some years now, it's ok, we are friends and I will do my best to explain this to you. But first, please sit down so that we can go over this calmly."

"Calmly?" Edith moved forward quickly to the other side of the bed. Her palms were sweating, she could feel the dizziness taking over.

"Edith, please sit down." She moved slowly not to startle, then saw Edith's eyes roll back and lunged forward to catch her. "Edith, Edith," She looked up to the door and hit the button behind her bed. "She's coding!"

Edith woke to a large plastic mechanism blocking her vision. The beep was getting to her now. It had only just become distinct to her, but she realized she had actually been hearing a ring in her ear for quite some time now. Her eyes tried to focus on the room, but it slipped in and out, that same feeling of being half asleep, still dreaming, but knowing that none of it is real. On her left hand she could feel an IV taped tightly, snaking down from a bag of fluid hanging above her. To her left she saw a face. The face was blurry, Edith was tired from trying to focus from the crisis before and the mask distorting her perceptions. She pulled it down slowly, breathing heavily.

"No, mom, don't." Sam grabbed the mask and gently replaced it on her mother's mouth.

"Sam?" Her voice was weak and cracking. "Sam, is that really you?"

The sound of the once strong and wild woman her mother used to be, now withered down to the frail, tired creature left Sam feeling uneasy about everything that had once been stable in her life.

"Hey Mom, yeah, it's me. I'm here." She held Edith's hand steadfastly. "I brought the kids with me; they're with Jessica today. They wanted to meet their grandmother."

"You have kids?"

The words hit Sam like a thousand daggers. "Yeah, Mom. They are right here." She lifted a picture of herself with her two daughters at the London marketplace last fall. "Remember, their names are Paige and Holly?"

Edith looked away; the confusion was disheartening and she felt it easier not to listen than to try to understand what was impossible to comprehend. Sam sighed: she felt she was to blame for her mother never getting to know her grandchildren.

Even as Sam sat there, wondering how they'd come to this, Edith's mood suddenly shifted, and she smiled brightly.

"You're too young to have children. My dear Sam, you're only fourteen years old. You have all the time in the world to have kids." Her smile was radiant. Sam had never seen her mother so happy before. Lost in the moment, thinking of her children still growing, with every part of life still ahead of them.

"I need to tell you something. I know that Lisa is going to go off to college in the next few years and you will feel unprepared to let her go. She is my first-born, she is strong, she is feisty and I know she will do great things in her life. But Samantha Cora Anderson, you may be my second born, but not second strongest." Sam's eyes teared. "You are beautiful, smart, loving and you have made me work harder to be a good mom than any of my other daughters. My failures as a mother hit me the hardest when I know how that affects the way *you* see me. I don't know if I ever told about my mom.

"My mother was my entire world. Every Saturday, she would make pancakes and then we'd eat them at the kitchen table. There was nothing in the world she would rather do on a Saturday than spend it with my dad and I. When my dad died, that woman that I loved so desperately just disappeared. It was as though, when he left, she joined him. I spent years wondering when she would come back to me, love me again, for us to be a whole family. Even if my dad couldn't be there, we still had each other. Ansel and Cora raised me and loved me as they would have their own daughter, Susan, who passed away too young. Cora was my mother for all intents and purposes until she was taken away one evening too. Yes, I named you after her. Well, time moved on and I grew up and stopped believing that things could work out the way I always used to think they would."

She stopped a moment, pressing her lips together and binding her eyes shut, as though wincing in pain.

"It's ok, Mom, you don't have to tell me any more."

"I should have told you sooner, but when your mother abandons you to start a new family, you're so ashamed of yourself, it's hard to put it into words. Maybe if my mother could give me up as a daughter, I wasn't worthy to be your mother either." Edith opened her eyes to see Sam's mouth hanging open, tears streaking down her face.

Edith's head swiveled over to the alarm clock on the bedside table next to a picture of her four daughters down at the beach, "I need some rest now, but perhaps the five of us could go to the beach later."

Sam nodded, wiping the tears from the bottom of her chin. "Yeah, Mom, I would really like that."

Edith turned over and closed her eyes.

A slight knock on the door came from behind Sam and she turned to see Lisa come in. Before she could think, she was on her feet embracing her sister. Sam grabbed her by the wrist and dragged her into the hallways, closing her mother's door behind her.

"Oh Lis." She cried deeply into her shoulder. "Why didn't you tell me?"

Lisa wiped the tears from Sam's eyes one at a time.

"When mom got sick, she didn't tell any of us. It was in her directive with her lawyers to not burden us with any of it until the end. I guess she thought that she had done that enough already."

Sam rubbed her face in her hands, trying to make sense of it all.

"How long?" She closed her eyes, wanting to say the words, but not wanting the answer to the question, though she needed to hear it. "How long does she have?"

"They don't know, but they assume with the deterioration of her mind, it most likely won't be very long." Sam hugged Lisa again and squeezed tighter, having needed her sister for far too long. Lisa pulled back a moment.

"Where's Adam?"

"He's in New York. Or maybe London by now. Oh Lisa, I don't know how we got here. Everything is so messed up now." She laughed in irony, "And oh yeah, before the hospital called I found out my husband had an affair."

"He didn't, the fucking bastard!" Lisa went straight into her normal, protective sisterly role, "I will knock him out, where is he, in New York?"

"It's not all his fault. We have been very distant for a few years now and I have not given him much cause to think I still love him. He said it happened once and it just needed to come clean about it so that we could fix things."

"So that's it?" Lisa's face reddened, "You're just going to forgive him?" her hands landed on her hips, "I swear, if my husband ever did that, he would not live to see another day."

"Sorry, how is Jared?" Sam rubbed her sister's arm in an attempt to calm her down.

Her face perked up quickly. "Oh he's good. And we have some other news." She dug into her pocketbook that swung around her hip. After a moment she pulled out a small photograph, "This is our baby." The photo was of a small baby, nearly six months old with golden brown skin and sparkling brown eyes.

"Oh my god, you're getting a baby?" Sam grabbed her sister and hugged her again tightly. Her face tilted down at the picture once more.

"Oh Lis, you and Jared have been waiting for so long to have a baby, and now you are able to give this beautiful darling a home of her own with adoring parents to care for her, and aunts to spoil her rotten. What did you decide to name her?"

"Mildred, but we'll call her Millie." Lisa smiled at her sister, knowing she would love Lisa's commemoration of the closest person they ever had to a grandmother.

"She would have loved that, Lis." Sam nodded at the smiling baby in the photo, "she really would have."

"Well, I have to get home, the adoption agency is going to be bringing her here in the next few weeks and we still have some serious shopping to do still. The last four months have been a little hectic and I'm a bit lost to be honest. I'm so glad you're here."

"I will bring the girls to see Mom soon, I promise. I have been thinking about coming home for a while, I think it's time."

"I thought you loved your job?" Lisa cocked her head, waiting for an answer. Her sister was always so predictable and never seemed capable of change.

"I did, but when I had the girls, they became the priority and the digs started going to others who were willing to travel and be away for months at a time. So now I'm more or less a stay at home mom, while Adam travels with the publishing company and tours with his books. To be perfectly frank, we have been underwater for some time. Spending more than what we earn and it's so costly living in London. Book sales haven't been great and..."

"Sam, it's going to be ok. In fact, we have a guest house above the garage. You and the girls can stay there for as long as you like while you sort everything out."

"Really?" Sam's voice cracked.

"Like you even have to ask. Besides Theresa and Jessica have been missing their sister, they will want to visit with you more than the few occasions that bring them to Europe." They both smiled.

"Ok, well, I'm off. I'll stop by Jessica's for you to see the girls and ask if she needs any help with Paige and Holly. She's still recovering from that first-trimester morning sickness, you know." Lisa smiled and walked away down the corridor.

C.B. Giesinger

Sam returned to her mother's room and sank back into the big armchair next to the bed. She grabbed ahold of her mothers warm, motionless hand. Edith's skin was cracked, so Sam squeezed a small amount of lotion into her palm and smoothed it over her mother's, rubbing it in deeply. A sense of ease fell over her. She was caring for her mother, the way her mother should have cared for her as a child. Being a mother now for some years, she had learned a great deal about what goes into raising children. Having only two, it gave her a deep appreciation for her mother's role of caring for four girls on her own, alone besides Mildred.

Her head fell back into the chair's headrest as she thought about moving from England finally, an inevitability. She knew that it would be good for her daughters to be close to family and have cousins to spend time with.

For her mother to grow up and raise kids without any family to support her, it was truly an incredible thing. How had she done it with a handful of ill paying jobs and no fathers there lending hand with the cost? Somehow she had figured out a way. Sam closed her eyes and let her mind drift off. She could think about it more tomorrow.

The days seemed to drag on for her. The light shifted in the window outside the bedroom. Edith woke up occasionally. She would make eye contact with her daughter but then close them again to resume her rest. Her mind must have been working tirelessly, trying to heal, trying to come to terms with her prognosis. Sam wasn't sure Edith even understood what that meant.

Ten days had passed. Edith was coming in and out of consciousness. Eating sparingly, smiling in between naps. The doctors had given her a catheter and IV to deliver her medication, and supplemental vitamins to keep her going. Sam had brought the girls twice, and once Edith recognized them briefly.

Edith opened her eyes, her lips were dry and cracked. The chair next to her bed was empty and she looked around the room confused again. Sam opened the door and came in.

"Mom, I didn't know if you were going to wake up. I went and grabbed something to eat." She came over and put the pillow behind Edith's back to help her sit up.

"Can I get you anything, are you hungry?"

"Sam, I don't understand, where am I?" She looked around the room again, "Also when did you get here, are the girls with you?" She was lucid.

"You know about them?" Sam smiled at her mother, who gave her a look of twisted perplexity.

"I think I would know about my own granddaughters, granted I haven't seen them in person in some time now." She looked behind Sam, "Is Adam here? I am not sure that this place is a good one for babies to be in, but I have to admit, but I would really like to see them. Kids grow up so fast."

"Mom, can I show you something?" The caution in her voice led Edith to feel unnerved.

"Yes." Edith looked at her daughter, waiting for some sort of bad news, some shock. Sam reached over to the bedside table and picked up the photo of her daughters. Her hand shook as she gave it to her mother.

"Oh, my dear, how long have I been gone?" The small girls with curly strawberry blonde hair smiled, the taller one through gapped teeth. They each held a small pumpkin from a booth in the London marketplace.

"This was taken less than a year ago, but they are six and four now. I'm sorry it took me so long to get here." Sam sniffled a bit.

"Oh now, let's not cry. After all, I was the one who didn't tell anyone about my dementia for years. That's on me, not on you or your sisters." Her hand rested on her daughter's, and she noticed the IV in her vein.

"I'm really sick, aren't I?"

Sam cried and nodded simultaneously, "Oh mom, I don't want to lose you."

"Sam," she held her daughter's face in her hands, "I need something from you."

"What is it, Mom? I'll do anything you need." She sat up and studied her mother, looking for a reason she would need her now.

"No, it's not something I need you to do for me, I think you've done enough. I need you to never lose the relationship you have with your sisters and your daughters. It is the greatest relationship you will ever have."

Sam wept, "Oh, I love you Mom." She leaned forward and squeezed her mother. Her mother's hair still smelled of flowers. The same shampoo she had been using since they were children. It was as though she stepped back in time. Her mother was standing behind her while she stood with her feet high up on the fence reaching to feed Fanny the elephant roasted peanuts with her tiny fingers. *Do you see that Sam? She loves you just as much as I do.* The long repetitive beeps came to a draw and the long tone rang across the room as her mother's body became limp in her arms. Sam's head pushed deep into her mother's neck and she sobbed, "I love you, Mom."

Chapter 30: Samantha, Summer 2011

"Well that should be the last of them." Lisa plunged a large cardboard box to the floor.

"Well let's be thankful that box wasn't listed as 'fragile,'" Sam displayed with finger quotes.

"I looked first. Actually I think Jessica may have a few small items to bring in, otherwise, the truck is empty." She looked around the new home. The walls were perfectly white, the floors had a fresh coat of urethane and the windows sparkled. She breathed deeply in through her nostrils and stretched her fingers up to the ceiling. "Feels good to have you back, sis."

"I do have a few things being shipped separately. I knew that the moving company would do an adequate job, but I had some artifacts from my digs that I felt were too valuable to trust to movers who no doubt just got out of college."

"Fair enough." Lisa shrugged her shoulders. The conversation was interrupted by two small children pulling small wheeled suitcases behind them.

"So what do you girls think?" Sam crouched down close to her daughter's faces to see their reaction to their new home.

"I love it." said Holly. Her polka dot yellow sundress and bright flowing hair gleamed in the rays of sunlight coming through the picture window of their new home.

"Me too." Paige's eyes scanned the open space, cluttered with boxes and disarrayed furniture. "Which room is ours?"

"Well actually, you two get your own rooms in this house." Sam's face lit up waiting for their cheers.

"What!" The two girls ran to the back of the house in search of the space they would have to themselves.

"You didn't tell them that they had their own rooms?" Lisa brow creased. "How did you hold that secret for so long?"

"I needed leverage in case things went awry on the plane."

"Duly noted. See these are all the things that Jared and I will have to learn when Millie gets to that age." The two women scanned the room. "Now I have to unpack these." Sam's lips curled into a frown.

Jessica laughed, "My kids will never know everything. Moms need to have their own special secret ways of manipulating their children." She rubbed her belly, "Little mister Benjamin will learn that."

Lisa and Sam just rolled their eyes at their sassy youngest sister. At twenty-four Jesswas married and pregnant. Early motherhood was surely a trend of their family. While she was young, she had set herself up in a home-based job working on computer software. She and her husband bought a house in Cumberland and she struck up quite the relationship with her extended family after introductions were made at the wedding. The sisters gawked for a minute how far she had come from princesses and unicorns. Somehow she had escaped the trials of growing up as they had, but they were happier for it, knowing she was ignorant to the hardships.

"So when does Adam arrive?" Lisa turned around as someone came through the front door.

"Yeah, why isn't he moving his own furniture into the house?" Theresa asked in her normal crude fashion. A new piercing had arrived, this time in her nostril, a small stone in the crease.

"He had to finish up a couple of projects, he will be here next week, but the sellers were adamant that we close on time." She breathed out deeply from her lips and closed her eyes for a moment.

"It's ok, we don't have to talk about it." Lisa laid her hand on Sam's shoulders.

"Oh, he and I are fine. We are working with someone to figure out how things went wrong. In the end, I think we both stopped trying to make it work. But we love each other, so it will be ok." Sam closed her lips tightly forcing a smile. It would not be an easy road to get through a spurt of infidelity, but she knew that they were stronger than one mistake. Her eyes grew heavier as the moment sank in.

"So what's wrong then? This is a great day, you're finally home with your family. We have so many holidays and barbecues to look forward to." Lisa squeezed the edges of her sister's shoulders in her hands. Their eyes met and she knew instantly what was troubling her sister.

"I know, I miss her too."

"Can I ever say that though?" Sam's eyes creased, questioning herself. "I had a mother for thirty-four years and I got so little out of it," she licked her bottom lip, "cause I gave so little into it." Sam studied the floor, noticing every dent and crack as she dwelled on the past.

"Mom was complicated, she was hard to be around, sometimes. She did her best though." Lisa tilted her head, finding the right words, "You were dealing with all of it at once and you did your best too."

"Mom left the Eaton house to the four of us." Sam looked to Lisa for a response.

"Yeah, I know. I'm surprised that she didn't just give it to Jess and Terry."

Sam laughed, "I know, if I were them, I'd be pissed off to find out that we got a chunk of the house that we never lived in."

"Yeah, but Sam, she wanted us to spend time together and have a place to do it. That was a place she called home, so we have a part of her there too."

"I guess, but Mom never had much to herself. She never kept trinkets or collected the normal tchotchkes that most parents do. That house has remained the same since she was a kid, she kept it all as it was. As though she was still expecting her aunt and uncle to walk back in the door." Jessica slid into the conversation.

"I didn't know that. There's so much I didn't know." Sam looked desperately at her sister Jess. Lisa saw the day getting glum and decided to whisk the conversation in a different direction.

"How's the job hunt going?" Lisa pulled one the box lids open and began unwrapping the pieces of a small lamp, entangled in the paper.

"It's going. There isn't much for someone with my qualifications right now. Adam's book isn't going so well and the publishing company has been laying people off left and right. He had a meeting today to find out if he was able to keep his editing job. If it weren't for our savings and the low market, we would never have been able to buy this house."

Jess deemed the mood light enough that she could step outside and make a quick call. The back door closed with a muted bang.

Sam sat on the couch a moment, thinking about her mother and all the uncertainty she must have felt caring for four girls on her own. They were good kids, but they were children. Messy, loud, unruly and an assortment of ages and temperaments. That would have driven any parent to drink. She laughed to herself.

Outside they saw a truck pull up. The tires came to a screeching halt.

"I guess we're not done, I thought there were only two moving trucks, Sam?"

Sam peeked her eyes over the window sill.

"I don't think that is a moving truck. I honestly don't know. Maybe Adam had some last minute things added to the shipment. It's coming from England so anything is possible." She slumped, exhausted. The last three months had been a whirlwind of emotions. After the funeral she and her sisters spent most of a week together. While Sam could feel bitterness towards them for alienating her from the truth, she understood that her mother meant it as a kindness and honoring her wishes to save her from yet another burden was virtuous and selfless.

Adam came and cared for the girls at his mom's house, giving his wife time to get her head together before seeing them again. While he and his parents were not what you would describe as close, they had become good grandparents to the children and wanted to be more involved now that Sam and Adam were going to live closer.

Sam enjoyed the space and solitude with her sisters. They had not spent this much time together since Lisa left for five years in San Francisco and she departed for England. When the week was up, Sam was ready to go back home to England with her family to organize their move back to the states. She called Adam and told him that it was time to come home. He agreed that it was overdue and they began house shopping. Three months later, life was starting to piece itself back together, but the exhaustion had finally sunk in.

Lisa could see the struggle of her sister. "Sam, it's fine, I'll grab it."

A man came up the door with a clipboard. "Hi, Sam McNamara?"

Lisa smiled, "Yes," the high pitch voice was a little overkill and it made Sam laugh out of loud. She found the energy to stand up and approached the delivery man.

"Hi, I'm Sam."

He handed her a large clipboard. "Can you please sign for the items?"

She hesitantly took the clipboard and signed the document.

"I guess I should have asked before I signed it, but what did I just sign for?"

"We have a number of parcels that were shipped to the post office, but there were too many for the mail trucks to handle. So they were outsourced to our firm."

"Oh, okay, sure." She looked at Lisa, not sure what response she should give.

The gentleman returned to the truck and slid open the back door. He was inside the cavity of the vehicle for a minute before returning with a big box. The weight of the box was evident by his struggle. "Where can I put it?" he said with a strained voice

"Um, over there." She pointed to the available space in the living room.

"It's only one box and they couldn't put it in the mail truck?" She rolled her eyes.

"That's not the only one," he interjected, not sure if he should correct her.

He returned to the truck and pulled out a similar size box and placed it next to the other. This continued for ten more boxes. Sam found herself just leaning against the storm door of her new home as each box passed her by view. Lisa looked from her to the gentlemen.

"What is going on?"

Theresa appeared from down the hall.

"Well, the girls picked out their rooms." She saw the twelve large boxes. They did not match the boxes Sam had unpacked so far.

"Are you planning on someone else moving in?"

"No, they were just shipped here. I'm honestly not sure *what* they are." Sam lifted her hands in confusion.

The man finally drove away leaving the treasure trove of mysterious boxes and three sisters staring at them, afraid to know what had been brought before them. The doorbell rang, startling them, Jessica walked in.

"Sorry, someone locked the back door on me. I had to call James to check on Isla and Isabel." Her two Scottish terriers were quite the handful working from home, but she enjoyed the busyness. She had told Lisa that they better prepared for her having kids. The incessant whining and needing her attention constantly.

"What this little boy and his father are going to do with those two nutters is beyond me." She rubbed her belly and walked into the living room. Her short curly hair bounced about with each waddle of her rotund frame.

"Wow, so we have a lot of unpacking to do." She looked at her three sisters on the floor, entirely overwhelmed.

"Ugh, so those are Sam's boxes." Lisa said, pointing to the medium sized Lions head moving company emblem, "While these are unknowns."

"Unknowns, you have no idea what's inside of them?" her eyebrows furrowed. "Okay, so who has a blade?"

The three older sisters saw the twinkle in Jessica's eyes. Once the baby of the family and now a beautiful woman..

"Nothing? Ok, I'll use my scissors." She knelt down next to Samantha.

The three girls watched as Jessica sliced through the seal and opened the first box.

Inside the girls found ten coffee cans filled to the brim with folded fifty dollar bills and beneath them, a thick layer of quarters. "Are you thinking what I'm thinking?" Lisa smiled from ear to ear. The girls began tearing through the boxes, each revealing the same contents. Piles of cash collected in coffee cans, with labels ranging from the 1970s to the present day. The last box was finally opened. This was different. On the top of the cans lay a letter. The words read, "To my beautiful daughters."

Their eyes teared up. The wound was still fresh. The moment had finally come when they would get to hear the final words of their mother.

Sam picked up the letter and began to read it slowly.

My dear daughters,

When I was only fifteen years old, my father was killed in an accident. This changed my whole life. Upon his death, I not only lost my father, but my mother, my home and all my possessions, save a box or two. When it came time to divvy up my father's possessions, my uncles took what they wished and tossed the rest of our belongings in the trash or donated it to the shelters. One day while living with my aunt and uncle, a set of packages arrived. Inside the box lay multiple coffee cans with folded fifty dollar bills stuffed inside. My father's only wish was for me to want for nothing when he was gone. This money remained in my care until it came time to free my children of burden.

Unbeknownst to him at the time, his generosity would pay my years of medical bills. After all the burdens I laid on my children, I could not let my illness and eventual death be one of them. I'm so incredibly proud of the women you turned out to be, so reliant on one another. While I tried to be the mother you deserved, I often fell short. I know this. Since my aunt and uncle took me in as a child I have started my own collection. I hoped that one day I would be fortunate enough to have children of my own to pass on my love to and perhaps a bit of tradition.

Throughout your youth, I saw you persevere and grow into fine adults. The luxury that you experienced in the lives of your friends seemed futile against the time you spent together. Money didn't seem to have a factor in your happiness at all. I figured as you grew into adults the ease of your life would change and perhaps so would your needs. The contents of these cans is for the four of you to share. Do what you wish with them. All I ask is that you continue to look out for one another, as you always have. I will be watching over you from afar. Against all odds, the best thing I ever did was become your mom.

I love you,

Mom.

Printed in Great Britain
by Amazon

25863048R00209